Kelly Elliott is a *New York Times* and *USA Today* bestselling contemporary romance author. Since finishing her bestselling Wanted series, Kelly continues to spread her wings while remaining true to her roots and giving readers stories rich with hot protective men, strong women and beautiful surroundings.

Kelly has been passionate about writing since she was fifteen. After years of filling journals with stories, she finally followed her dream and published her first novel, *Wanted*, in November of 2012.

Kelly lives in central Texas with her husband, daughter, and two pups. When she's not writing, Kelly enjoys reading and spending time with her family. She is down to earth and very in touch with her readers, both on social media and at signings.

Visit Kelly Elliott online:

www.kellyelliottauthor.com
@author_kelly
www.facebook.com/KellyElliottAuthor/

Also by Kelly Elliott (published by Piatkus)

COWBOYS & ANGELS
Book 3

Tempting Love

KELLY ELLIOTT

piatkus

PIATKUS

First published in Great Britain in 2018 by Piatkus

1 3 5 7 9 10 8 6 4 2

Copyright © Kelly Elliott 2017

The moral right of the author has been asserted.

A CIP catalogue record for this book
is available from the British Library.

ISBN 978-0-349-41844-5

Printed and bound in Great Britain by
Clays Ltd, St Ives plc

Cover photo and design: Sara Eirew Photography
Editor: Cori McCarthy, Yellowbird Editing
Proofer: Amy Rose Capetta, Yellowbird Editing
Developmental: Elaine York Allusion Graphics
Interior Designer: JT Formatting

Papers used by Piatkus are from well-managed forests
and other responsible sources.

A Note to Readers

Tempting Love is book three in the Cowboys and Angels series. The books in this series are not stand-alone books. Stories intertwine between books and continued to grow within each book. If you have picked up this book and have not read *Lost Love* or *Love Profound,* I strongly suggest that you read them in order.

For a list of characters in the series as well as other fun extras, please visit the series website: www.cowboysandangelsseries.com

PROLOGUE

Mitchell

Dragging my hands down my face, I dropped my head back against my truck seat.

What in the hell did she do to me?

I lifted my head and glanced over to Corina's house. The last twelve hours had been the most amazing of my life. The feel of her lips on mine, moving in and out of her body… Fuck. It would forever replay in my mind.

"What in the hell did you do, Mitch?" I whispered as I stared at her door.

It was pretty fucking clear what I did. I spent the night with Corina like a greedy bastard. Took everything I could get from her and seared it into my brain…and now I was going to walk away, too damn afraid to admit I had feelings for her.

With a shake of my head, I started my truck and headed home. The sound of her sweet moans was still vivid, and the feel of her hands moving over my skin had left a burning trail in its wake.

"Fucking hell," I yelled, slamming my hand against the steering wheel.

I made a U-turn and headed to Cord's. He lived above his bar, and I knew he would be home. It was too early for his ass to be up and gone.

After parking, I made my way around back and hit the intercom. It didn't take long for him to answer.

"This better be good!"

"It's me…Mitch. Can I come up?"

"Jesus. You slept with her, didn't you?"

"Can I come up or not, asshole?"

The door buzzed, and I took the steps two at a time. Cord had remodeled the historic building. The bar took up the first two floors, the third and fourth housed Cord's bachelor pad—except I was pretty sure he'd never actually brought a girl up here.

The door to his place was open slightly, so I walked in. I could smell coffee brewing as I met Cord in the kitchen.

"Coffee?" he asked, holding up a mug. "Or something stronger?"

"Coffee *and* something stronger," I mumbled, sitting at the countertop island.

He poured some whiskey into my mug and set it in front of me. "You know Tripp called dibs."

I blew out a long sigh, and I took a drink.

"Fuck Tripp and his damn dibs. He knew I liked her and that was the only reason he *called* dibs. Don't make me feel any guiltier. Just remembering her face this morning as I left is killing me."

"What do you mean?"

I shrugged. "I mean she had that look, like she hoped for more."

"Did you give her the impression that it was more than a one-night stand and wait a fucking second, did you say *this morning*?" His eyes widened. "Dude, you didn't. Please tell me you didn't stay the night with her."

"I was only going to walk her to her door and one thing led to another and…yeah, I stayed all night."

Cord's head dropped. "Aw, hell. Mitchell, Paxton's gonna kick your ass. Dude, you can't be playing around with a girl like Corina. She's not like the ones who are happy with a quick piece of you. She's the long-term, want-to-settle-down-with-a-nice-guy kind of girl."

I groaned. "Fucking hell. The worse part about all of this is I *wanted* to stay with her. I stood at her door this morning and stared into those blue eyes and had to force myself to leave."

Pushing off the counter, Cord walked closer. "What do you mean, you wanted to stay?"

I dragged my hands down my face. I felt like shit. "I mean I didn't want it to be a one-night stand. I wanted to spend the whole fucking day with her. Find out every single thing I could about her. Go to breakfast and all that stupid ass shit a guy does when he's attracted to a girl. Take her somewhere fun and devour her again later when we got back to her place."

His brows pinched together. "Then why didn't you? You can't say it was Tripp because we both know he would have gotten past the whole claiming dibs."

"I can't. As much as I wanted to stay with her…I couldn't do it."

"Why the fuck not?"

"Why haven't you?"

"I haven't met the person who makes me *want* to stay the night, and have breakfast in the morning, and spend the day with. If I did, I sure as shit wouldn't have walked away from her for no goddamn good reason."

I jumped up, nearly knocking the stool over. "I have a goddamn reason!"

"What is it, Mitch? Why did you leave Corina when you really wanted to stay?"

My heart pounded, and I fought to find the answer. Why had I left the person who woke up my heart for the first time in my life?

My phone buzzed with a text. Pulling it out, I said, "I've got to go, I just got called in. Looks like they found a body earlier this morning in the Frio."

Cord frowned. "Life of a cop."

"Yeah. Sometimes I get tired of it." I headed to the door. "Thanks for the coffee and ear."

"Hey, Mitch?"

Stopping, I glanced over my shoulder. "Yeah?"

"Don't lead her on. She's a sweet girl, and she deserves more than a guy playing with her feelings."

I swallowed hard and stared at the floor. I knew my brother was right. When I looked back up, I nodded. "Guess it's a good thing I didn't stay then, huh?"

The moment I shut the door I felt sick.

Corina Miller deserved someone who wouldn't end up destroying her heart. A guy who was willing to give her the life she wanted.

I wasn't that guy.

CHAPTER 1

Mitchell

"So, this is your place, huh?"

I dropped my keys on the coffee table. "Yep. This is it."

Cassidy spun around and took in the loft apartment I owned in the building above Lilly's restaurant. I had bought the entire fourth floor and had it remodeled two years ago.

"I'm glad you finally invited me back to your place and not the back seat of your truck," she said.

A sharp pain hit me in the middle of my chest.

Cassidy grinned as she placed her hands on my chest. "It's been awhile since we fucked, Mitch. All that teasing at Cord's Place the last few months has been driving me crazy. I was glad when I got your call tonight."

I forced a smile and stepped back. "Want a beer?"

She nodded and made her way to my sofa. "Sure."

Entering the kitchen, I took a deep breath and opened the refrigerator. What in the hell was I doing? I had tried this once already—

with this same chick. It hadn't worked then, and I was fooling myself to think a redo would change things.

I pulled out my phone and sent a text.

Me: *What are you doing?*

Robert and I had been best friends since high school, so I knew
it wouldn't take him long to respond.

Robert: *About to castrate a bull. You want in on it?*

With a smile, I replied.

Me: *Yes. On my way. Do me a favor and call me.*

Robert: *Why? You want to hear my sweet voice?*

Me: *Something like that.*

I grabbed two beers and headed back into the living room. It
was time to get rid of the mistake I had almost made.

As I handed the beer to Cassidy, my phone rang. I was going to
owe Robert big time.

"This is Mitch."

"Okay. So I called. Now what?"

"Yes, sir. I understand."

"Aw, we've got a chick we don't feel like sticking to?"

I turned away from Cassidy and rolled my eyes. "That's af-
firmative."

"You owe me, you prick. Get your ass over here. Mary will be
glad to feed your face."

I nodded. "Leaving now."

I hit *End* and looked back at the woman sitting on my sofa.
"Sorry, Cassidy. I've got to go into work."

She jutted a lip out. "Are you serious? Can't we just...you know? Really quick?"

Jesus, how do I get myself into this shit?

Grabbing my keys, I headed to the stairs and motioned for her to follow. "Sorry, duty calls."

She groaned and snatched her purse off the table. "Seriously, Mitch? I'm tired of this. You feel me up at the bar and then you switch off when I mention sex. Are we ever going to fuck again?"

I laughed and placed my hand on her lower back. "Cassidy, you know there is no chance of an *us*. Ever."

"That's fine! But my panties are tired of being wet and not getting any relief. I don't need a relationship, Mitchell. I need your dick."

By the time we got to her car, she was finished giving me hell

"I'll see you around?" I said, kissing her on the cheek.

"Fine. Be careful."

She slipped into her car and a part of me felt guilty that she thought I was going to work. I sighed as I walked to my truck.

Fucking hell, I needed to stop this shit. For the last six months I kept getting close to fucking, only to throw on the brakes.

I couldn't get her out of my head.

Corina.

I closed my eyes and went back to the night we'd spent together. I'd only slept with one person since the night I'd spent with Corina. And that was Cassidy, a failed attempt at meaningless sex to wash away the memory of Corina.

All it did was make me feel worse.

By the time I pulled up to Robert's, Cassidy had sent three pictures. Fuck, I hated selfies. What did she think I did with them? Jack off to her tits and duck lips?

Hardly.

I got out of the truck and walked up the drive.

"Well, look who the cat dragged in. Mitchell Parker. To what do we owe the honor?" Mary stood on the front porch of their small farmhouse. Her hands were resting on her seven-months-pregnant stomach.

"Well, I was about to screw a girl and needed an out so I had Robert call me. Pretended it was work and all," I said with an evil grin.

She laughed. "Why do I think you're telling the truth?"

Leaning down, I kissed her cheek. "Because I am."

With a blank look on her face, she stared into my eyes for the longest time. "You're in love with someone, Mitchell Parker. Admitting that to yourself saves a lot of rescue calls in the future, ya know."

Frowning, I laughed. "Yeah, no. This was a random hook-up that I wasn't into."

She shook her head. "You weren't into her because you're in love with someone else."

I let out a groan. "Oh, man. Mary, you always were the matchmaker. Not this time, sweetheart."

She waved her pointer finger back and forth. "Tsk-tsk-tsk. If you think you can hide it from me, go ahead. I know that look, Mitchell Parker and even if you aren't ready to admit it, your heart already has. Those 'random hook-ups' you aren't that 'into' are going to become more and more frequent, just you wait and see."

"Is my wife giving you hell, Parker?" Robert called out.

I stared into Mary's light brown eyes before I let a smile cross my face. Giving her a wink, I replied, "Nah. She's trying, but it'll never work."

She simply shrugged and turned to Robert. Giving him a kiss, she said, "I'll make us up some biscuits and gravy. I'm craving it."

"Sounds good, baby. We'll be down in the barn."

I followed Robert over to his Mule and jumped in the passenger side.

He started it up and we headed down to his barn. Jumping out, I followed him into his office. Robert ran the dairy farm that had been in his family for the last two generations. His daddy had an office built into the barn and spent most of his time there; he pretty much lived in the damn thing. That was until Robert's mom finally had enough of it and divorced him.

"Beer?" he asked, tossing me a Bud Light.

"Thanks," I replied as I sat down in one of the chairs.

"Want to talk about it?"

"No."

He exhaled a gust. "Seriously, Parker? You need to figure this shit out. When was the last time you got laid?"

Pressing the bottle to my lips, I took a long drink before answering. "February."

His mouth dropped open. "Dude! It's fucking August."

I stared at him. "That's why I had Cassidy French in my damn living room earlier."

"Why couldn't you go through with it?"

"Because I don't want Cassidy. And I don't want the bleach blonde who had her tits all pressed up against me the other night at the club in San Antonio. I don't want the girl who offered to blow me in the bathroom at Cord's Place. I don't fucking want any of them."

"Because you want *her*."

"I don't know what in the fuck I want, Robert. That's the problem."

Robert and Cord where the only two people I'd talked to about Corina, and I'd mentioned it to Wade once. Fuck if I wasn't driving myself mad.

"What are you going to do when she moves on, Mitch? When she gets tired of you waiting to figure out your shit?"

Taking another drink, I half-shrugged. "She was with some asshole at Steed and Paxton's shower. Philip, or some pussy name like that."

Robert laughed. "Damn, dude. Harbor any ill feelings for the guy?"

I rolled my eyes.

"She's better off without me. At least, I keep telling myself that."

"Why?"

With a look that said he should already know, I replied, "My job, for one thing. The fact that commitment scares the piss out of me. Plus she deserves a guy who hasn't slept with nearly all the single women in Oak Springs."

Now he really laughed. "For Pete's sake. All of you Parker boys have slept with all of Oak Springs and beyond. I wouldn't doubt if one of you put the moves on my wife at some point."

I held up my hands. "That was Tripp who put the moves on Mary. Not me."

He frowned. "Are you kidding right now? When the fuck did he do that?"

Oh, shit.

"Um, what?"

He lifted his brows. "Did Tripp fuck my wife? I mean, before she became my wife."

Aw, fuck. "What?"

Robert stood. "I'll kill him."

I walked over and put my hand on his chest. "Christ, Robert. Tripp was in a bad place, Mary had just lost her parents. It was one time."

He let out the breath he was holding. "I wasn't dating her then."

"No joke. You know Tripp wouldn't do that, and you know damn well Mary isn't the type to cheat. Dude, please don't bring it up to her. She's married to you now and expecting your first child. Leave the past in the past."

"Leave the past in the past? Do you hear what you just told me, Mitch? Here you are worried about what Corina will think about the women of Oak Springs and the next second you're preaching to me about forgetting something from a while back. Pot, meet kettle."

Fuck, why did he have to turn this shit around on me? "You know what I mean, dude. Just don't say anything to Mary. She'll never let me eat over here again."

He shook his head. "I'm not going to bring it up. Hell, I slept with plenty of girls before I settled with Mary. Just knowing she was with a Parker brother makes me feel sick. Y'all have golden dicks."

It was my turn to laugh. "*Golden* dicks?"

He shrugged. "I heard a girl say it once after Cord got it on with her at the bar. She was bragging to her friends."

I lost it laughing, holding my side. Robert joined in. When I was able to speak, I said, "I'm making a T-shirt for Cord that says that!"

He rolled his eyes and wiped his face. "Dude, you all need one. I'm serious."

"What's so funny?" Mary asked, walking into the barn.

Robert stood quickly. "Hey, why didn't you call? You don't have to be driving down here on that bumpy road."

When she smiled at him, I could feel the love between them. They were soon lost in a kiss, and I found myself looking away, an ache in my chest I was trying to ignore.

When they were finished, she said, "I tried to call. Your phone must be turned down or something."

Robert pulled out his phone and glanced at the missed call. "Damn. I'm sorry, baby. Mitch, you hungry?"

"For biscuits and gravy? Hell, yeah."

"Sausage gravy. I had a hankering," Mary said, wiggling her brows.

I walked behind the two of them. "Beggars can't be choosers."

Watching Robert and Mary walk hand in hand to the truck, my heart continued to ache in that strange, building way. Maybe it was time I admitted to myself what I really wanted.

CHAPTER 2

Corina

Paxton placed Gage in my arms as I sat in the oversized chair.

"Isn't he pretty, Corina?" Chloe asked, staring down at her baby brother.

"He is. Just like you, Chloe. How do you like being a big sister?"

She stood a little taller. "Oh, I love it! I'm a great big sister too. Mommy says she couldn't do it without me."

Paxton sat down on the sofa, a wide smile across her face. I was so happy for my best friend. She'd found her happily ever after.

"I bet she couldn't," I said. "Daddy helps too, right?"

Chloe nodded. "Yes, but he gags when Gage goes number two. He said he did with me too!" She covered her mouth and giggled. "It's stinky!"

Laughing, I glanced over to find Steed and Paxton lost in each other's eyes. The emptiness in my chest grew a little more as I looked back at Gage.

"Have you heard from Amelia again?" I asked as I ran my fingertip over Gage's cheek. He was sound asleep and the most precious thing I'd ever seen.

Paxton sighed, "No! Have you?"

I shook my head, "Nope. She only sent me the one text that said she had something big to tell us when she got home from New Orleans."

"Yeah, she sent that to Waylynn and me as well."

"Let's hope she didn't do something crazy and get married," Steed said with a light-hearted chuckle. My eyes lifted to meet Paxton's. Neither of us had to say a word. We both knew that was *exactly* what had happened.

Paxton smiled bigger. "You never know with Meli."

Steed tossed his head back to laugh, but stopped abruptly. "You don't think they did, do you?"

Paxton shrugged. Steed looked at me. I laughed and added, "I'm not saying anything."

"Do you think Wade and Aunt Meli will bring back a surprise for me and Gage?"

Steed gazed down at his daughter. "I bet so, pumpkin."

Chloe jumped up, her face lighting up like she'd remembered something important. "Corina! I drew you a picture. It's in my room. I'll go get it!"

I giggled and nodded. "I can't wait to see it!"

Watching Chloe run off, I turned back to Steed. He stood and paced the floor. "They got married. I have this weird feeling they did. Pax, do you think Amelia would do that?"

She nodded.

"Mom and Dad will freak out!" Steed said.

Paxton stood and took Steed's hands. "Steed, calm down. Your folks are not going to care if they *really* did get married, which I *really* think they did. All they want is for y'all to be happy."

"Besides, if they *did* get married, we could always throw a reception," I added. "So much more fun, and less stress!"

Steed nodded. "You're right. This would totally be something I could see both of them doing."

Paxton sat down, pulling Steed with her. "Especially with everything that has happened with Wade. Knowing his history, I have a feeling he likes to live in the moment and not waste a second of it."

"That's true," Steed said, "but if they did get married, we have a problem bigger than my parents."

"What's that?" Paxton asked.

"Chloe," Steed and I both said at once.

Paxton's eyes grew wide. "Oh, shit."

"Hell! Shit! Fuck!" Chloe shouted as she came running back in.

"Chloe Lynn Parker, what did I tell you about saying bad words?" Steed cried out.

Stopping in front of me, Chloe covered her mouth and giggled. "Sorry, Daddy!"

She leaned in and whispered in a rather loud voice, "I need to be careful or Santa won't bring my horse."

"Your horse?" I asked.

Chloe nodded. "Aunt Meli said if I was good Santa would bring me a horse!"

Steed buried his face in his hands. "I'm going to kill her."

Feeling my phone buzz on the desk, I glanced down to find a text from Amelia.

Amelia: *Wade and I should be home around seven. Can you come over to my parents' place for dinner? I want everyone there for our big announcement.*

My heartbeat quickened at the thought of seeing Mitchell. No matter how hard I tried to forget him and move on, I couldn't. I was going to have to soon. It was clear he wanted nothing more than the night we'd shared together. But *was* it clear? The way he looked at me sometimes…as if he longed to pull me into his arms. It was confusing, and one of the reasons I couldn't let myself move on.

Me: *Of course! I'll see you then.*

Staring at my phone, I took a deep breath and thought about asking Philip if he'd like to join me. We were only friends, two-of-towners who bonded while working together at the school, but I wouldn't mind a repeat of Mitchell's reaction when he saw Philip with me at the shower.

I dropped my phone. "For the love of Pete. Don't play games, Corina."

"Do you always talk to yourself?"

My head lifted. A handsome guy stood in the doorway of my classroom.

When I opened my mouth, nothing came out. I slowly stood. "Excuse me?" I finally managed to say.

"Oh, good. You've found Corina's room," our new principal, Lance Moreland, said as he walked into my room.

"Mr. Moreland, how are you this morning?" I asked, rounding my desk. School was starting in a few weeks and I was one of the first teachers to head back and prepare. What else did I have to do? It wasn't like I had a distracting love life.

"I'm fine, thank you. Ms. Miller, I'd like for you to meet Lane Lewis. Mr. Lewis, this is Corina Miller. You'll be taking her place in the first-grade classroom."

"Wait, what?" I asked, my smile dropping from my face.

"Ms. Miller, Mr. Lewis will be teaching first grade this year."

My heart sank. "I teach first grade!" When I swung over to Lane, he seemed just as surprised as I was, but he forced a smile. Ugh. If he wasn't so gosh darn cute I'd be even madder.

"Well, we've had to make a few changes," Lance said.

"Mr. Moreland, I was under the impression you didn't have a first grade teacher," Lane said, clearly feeling awkward.

"You're firing me?" I cried out.

Mr. Moreland wore a shocked look. "What? No! You're moving to kindergarten."

"W-what?"

"Oh, no," Lane said as he looked at me with eyes that said he knew exactly how I was feeling. "Been there. Done that."

Yep. He knew.

"Kinder? You want me to take Paxton's place? But…they'll tear me to pieces!"

Mr. Moreland chuckled. "Don't be silly. You teach first grade. Kinder is just one below."

I shook my head. "No, first graders are broken in! They know the ropes. Kinders are…new and they're scared, and the parents are insane."

"Ms. Miller! We do not call the parents insane."

Lane leaned in. "Kinder parents *are* harder to deal with."

My head was spinning. I needed a drink. A hard drink.

Lane took me by the arm. "Maybe you should take a seat, Corina."

I nodded. "Yes. Sitting would be good."

Taking a few deep breaths, I pulled myself together and looked at my boss. "And if I refuse to teach kindergarten?"

Mr. Moreland seemed surprised. "Well, if you refuse, I guess we'll have to see if another teacher will do it. I've gotten such amazing feedback from the parents who are on the PTA, though. Your name was the first and foremost to replace Paxton."

I forced a smile. It was nice to know the parents thought so highly of me.

Lane cleared his throat. "First grade is right next door. Correct, Mr. Moreland?" The principal nodded. "I've taught kinder before. I'm sure Ms. Miller and I will work together during the transition, especially since I'm coming from teaching almost six years of tenth-grade biology."

My eyes widened in horror, and my jaw fell open. "When did you teach kindergarten?"

With a wide grin, he said, "My first year of teaching."

Laughing, I stood. "Oh, my gawd! They are going to tear *you* to pieces. You have no idea what you're walking into."

Now it was Lane Lewis who blinked like the room was spinning.

Mr. Moreland clapped his hands, causing both Lane and me to jump. "I see you two are going to be great working partners. Lane, I'm glad you decided to head on back into town. Tell your folks I said hi."

And like that, our new boss—and the man who just set us both up for failure—quickly walked out of the room.

"I need a drink," Lane whispered.

"That makes two of us."

CHAPTER 3

Mitchell

"Mom, will you please stop pacing?" I asked.

My mother stopped and turned to Tripp. "Where is she? She said she was almost home and what's this *big* announcement?"

The doorbell rang, and my mother flew through the living room to the front hall.

"It's not Amelia!" my mother shouted.

Laughing, Tripp made his way to the bar in the back corner of the family room and poured a drink. "Anyone else need one? I have a feeling Meli is about to drop a bomb on us all."

With a long groan, my father dragged his hands down his face. "Please, Lord. Don't be a baby."

"Why not, Daddy? What's wrong if Amelia is pregnant?" Waylynn asked as we all directed our gazes to my father.

Looking at each of us, he smiled. "Nothing would be wrong if she was pregnant, but I'd rather she and Wade get married first."

"Look who's here!" my mother said in an overly cheerful voice.

When I glanced at the entrance of the family room, my breath caught. Corina was so damn beautiful. Her smile made my chest constrict, and yet feel light at the same time. How the fuck could that happen?

"Hey!" Paxton said, walking over to her best friend. "She texted you, too?"

Corina nodded, trying with all her might to ignore me as she glanced around and said hello. When her eyes finally met mine, she held her smile in place, but it looked a little painful. "Hey, Mitch."

With a quick nod, I said, "How's it going, Corina?"

She shrugged. "It's going."

Chloe rushed over and dropped on the floor. "I can't wait until you're my teacher!"

Corina's smile faded. Big time. "Chloe, I was so looking forward to that, but I've got some bad news."

My heart seized. My breathing was at a standstill. Was she moving back to Chicago?

"What's the bad news?" Chloe asked while I leaned forward.

"They moved me down to kindergarten."

"What?" Paxton and Chloe said at once.

"Why in the world did they do that?" Paxton asked.

"The new principal thinks I'm a good fit for the position. Well, definitely a better fit than the new teacher they hired for first grade." Corina looked down at Chloe and smiled. "You'll like him, Chloe."

"He? My new teacher is a *he*?"

Corina nodded. "Yep. His name is Mr. Lewis."

Paxton shook her head. "Where is he from?"

Chloe had her face buried in her hands bemoaning that a man teacher wouldn't be able to draw.

"I'm sure he draw perfectly fine, Chloe. You'll see."

Chloe looked up and nodded, not really sure if what Corina had said was true.

"He's from Oak Springs, but he's been teaching in Austin for the last few years. He wanted to move back here, but he has to teach elementary until they open a position for a high school biology teacher."

Waylynn jumped into the conversation. "Hold up. You said his last name was Lewis? *Lane* Lewis?"

Corina gave her a wide grin. "Yes! Do you know him?"

Paxton and Waylynn started laughing before Waylynn said, "Yes, Corina! I went to school with him. He was a year younger than me. Please, tell me he is just as gorgeous as he was in high school."

"Oh, he is!" Corina added, peeking at me before turning back to Waylynn.

Waylyn shook her head. "Man, oh man. Lane Lewis is back in town. This ought to be interesting. Remember he had a thing for Harley, Tripp? He actually asked her to prom y'all's junior year 'cause he thought you had broken up with her."

Tripp huffed. "Yeah, that fu…ahh…jerk."

"Good save," Steed said with a chuckle.

Corina smiled at Chloe. "I think you're going to like your new teacher. I'll be right next door, so I'll still get to see you."

Chloe stood up. "Aunt Corina, I have something important to ask you!"

I pulled back, turning to Cord. "When did Chloe start calling Corina her *aunt*?"

He shrugged. "Beats me. It's cute, though."

"Ask away!" Corina said as she pulled Chloe onto her lap.

"This is important."

Trying to hide her smile and look serious, Corina replied, "I'm ready."

I couldn't help but think what an amazing mother Corina would be.

Chloe used her hands to ask her important question. "Is my new teacher cute like Wade?"

"What?" Steed cried out as Paxton covered her mouth, trying to muffle her laughter as Gage slept in her arms.

"Chloe, that is *not* an important question!" Steed said. His face was as white as a damn ghost. It was near impossible for the rest of us not to start laughing.

"Actually, Steed, this might help with the present situation you're fixin' to face, if you get my drift," Waylynn said.

Steed sat back and raked his hand down his face. "Christ Almighty, I need strength."

Corina cleared her throat and looked at Chloe. "Well, I'd have to say *yes*! He is very much as cute as Wade. Maybe even more handsome."

Corina and Paxton looked at each other. When Corina wiggled her eyebrows, I rolled my eyes and took a drink of my iced tea. Lane Lewis was a dick, and I couldn't stand the motherfucker. Now he was going to be teaching my niece and playing teacher with Corina.

This fucking sucks.

"Yay! I can't wait to meet him!" Chloe clapped her hands. How Gage slept through Chloe's outburst was beyond me.

Cord bumped my arm. "You remember Lane. Don't you, Mitchell?"

Glancing over, I shot him a dirty look. "Yes, I remember him. Why?"

"Oh, I don't know. Just wondering how you feel about the woman you secretly pine over getting cozy with a guy who, back in high school, stole your clothes when you were in the shower and ran them up the flagpole."

Keeping my voice low, I replied in a hushed voice, "She isn't getting *cozy* with him. They work together."

"I give him less than a week before he asks her out."

Looking at the rest of them, I realized we'd missed some of the conversation.

"We actually had a couple of drinks before I headed over here," Corina said. "Tried to nail our game plan for the school year."

They'd had drinks already?

"I'd started my lesson plans, so I told him I would let him look over them. You don't happen to have a copy of your lesson plans from last year, do you?" Corina asked Paxton.

"Yep, I sure do. They're in the file cabinet. I left it all there for the next teacher."

Corina and Paxton got lost in shop talk, lesson plans and where the crayons were stored.

With a chuckle, Cord shook his head. "Well, hell. The bastard moves fast. I'll give him that much."

I tried to tune in to what Corina and Paxton were talking about. Not two seconds later, my mother yelled as Amelia and Wade walked in.

"We're home!" Amelia said with a huge smile.

"Oh, hell yeah. She's married," Cord whispered as we all stood. "Look at the blush on her cheeks. It's killing her not to shoot it out."

I let out a chuckle and nodded.

Pulling Amelia in for a hug, my mother said, "Welcome home! How was the trip?"

Amelia drew back. "It was amazing. Beyond amazing. I love that town and now I have a reason to love it even more!"

Wade slipped his arm around Amelia's waist.

Waylynn slid next to Amelia. "Tell us already, Meli! We're all going to crazy trying to guess what it is!"

Lifting her hand, Amelia let out a scream. "We got married!"

Cheers erupted, and I couldn't help but notice my father mumbling a silent *thank you* prayer to the good Lord above.

Laughing, I walked over and hit him on the back. "Well, you know what they say."

He looked confused.

With my best smirk, I said, "First comes marriage, then comes a baby carriage."

His confused look turned to one of horror.

"Bite your tongue, Mitchell Roy Miller. It's hard enough knowing my baby is married. Let me get used to that."

Amelia was the apple of my father's eye. It was going to be hard for him to let her go. I'm sure that was one of the reasons my parents had never complained about Amelia still living at home.

"Well, at least she's sort of still here. She'll be living on the ranch."

He nodded and took a drink of rum and Coke.

"When's the baby coming?" Chloe shouted and everyone laughed.

My father groaned. "Oh, Christ Almighty."

When the call came over my radio I let out a frustrated sigh. "Jesus Christ. I'm trained in Special Weapons and Tactics. I handle murder investigations! Not missing pies from Mrs. Johnson's window!"

Marilyn's voice responded over the radio. "Sheriff Miller can't get to it, Mitchell. He asked if you could go on over and talk to her. She likes you and all."

I closed my eyes and shook my head. "She wants me to date her granddaughter, Marilyn! That's why Miller wants me over there. He thinks it's funny."

"Well, things are quiet on the front. Sure you can't handle it for the sheriff? He's dealing with loose cattle over on Ranch Road 37."

"Fine, I'll take care of it."

I did a U-turn and headed back to town. By the time I pulled up to Mrs. Johnson's house, I'd gotten six text messages from Robert. It didn't help that our dispatcher was his sister, and I was positive Marilyn told Robert about the pies. When I stopped my car, I noticed I had a message from him.

Robert: *Hey, while you're there, get me an apple pie.*

Me: *Fuck you, asshole.*

Robert: *Make it a cherry. Mary is craving it.*

I rolled my eyes and got out of my squad car. Don and Nancy Gates's teenage boys watched me. They looked scared as hell, and I knew they must have expected the sheriff to show up and not me. I decided to have some fun with the little troublemakers.

Turning on my heel, I headed their way. Even though I was dressed in my normal uniform of dress pants, a white dress shirt, and cowboy hat, you could see my gun belt as clear as day. I didn't need to be dressed like the sheriff for these boys to know they were in a shitload of trouble.

With a tip of my hat, I nodded. "You boys know what happened to Mrs. Johnson's pies?"

The one with the bright red hair smirked. "What if we do?"

I slowly grinned. "Well, hell, if you do you just made my job easier. The faster I make an arrest the better."

His smirk faded. "Arrest?"

"They stole property; that's a crime. Mrs. Johnson said it's happened before, so I'm guessing it's the same thief. They've brought me in to handle it. Think it might be linked with some other robberies in town."

Sheriff Miller handled most of the things that happened locally. My jurisdiction was a hell of lot bigger than Oak Springs. As a Texas Ranger, my job was special investigations, apprehending wanted felons, suppressing larger disturbances, and assisting local law enforcement with crime and violence. For a small, almost crime-free town like Oak Springs, stealing pies off a windowsill was almost a fucking felony.

"Th-thief?" the light brown-haired kid said.

Narrowing my eyes, I stared them down. "You steal something from someone, you're a thief. There are two types of people I can't stand. Thieves and liars. You boys aren't either of those, are ya?"

They both took a step back. "N-no, sir. We ain't either of those."

With a slow nod, I looked them over. "Good. Glad to hear it. I'm going to go interview Mrs. Johnson. See if she turned on those security cameras Sheriff Miller told her to put in."

"Cameras?" they said at once.

"What's the matter, boys? You done look like you've seen a ghost."

"Um, we've got to go, officer," the red-haired kid said.

"It's Lieutenant Parker," I said

They stumbled over each other and took off to their backyard. I was positive that if I followed them I'd find the damn pies.

Heading back toward Mrs. Johnson, I shook my head. "I don't have time for this nonsense."

As I crossed the street, I saw Corina. She was walking down Mrs. Johnson's sidewalk, heading to her front door. I paused and waited until she was invited inside. Something was up, but I didn't seem to mind. Smiling, I made my way to the house.

Mrs. Johnson answered the doorbell with a wide smile. "Mitchell Parker, what in the world are they doing sending you over here for some pies?"

I wanted to laugh. "Your pies are just as important as any other stolen items, Mrs. Johnson."

She tossed her head back and laughed like I'd said the funniest damn thing. "Now, don't be sweet-talking an old woman, Mitchell Parker. Come in and have some sweet tea. I have company, but I'm sure she'll enjoy the view."

My mouth nearly dropped open as Mrs. Johnson winked and headed toward her kitchen.

"Corina, darlin', pour Ranger Parker a glass of iced tea, will you?"

Her blue eyes met mine.

"Hey, Corina. Long time no see."

Forcing a smile, she replied, "Twice in one day. I'm a lucky girl."

"Oh my!" Mrs. Johnson exclaimed. "You are indeed."

Glancing at the older woman, Corina went about pouring another glass of tea.

"What brings you over to visit Mrs. Johnson?" I asked while setting my cowboy hat on the table.

Corina answered without looking at me. "We met a few months back at the butcher's, and Mrs. Johnson has been kind enough to give me cooking lessons."

My brows pinched. "You don't know how to cook?"

I didn't even see Mrs. Johnson's hand lift up, but the back of my head sure felt it.

"Mitchell Parker, your momma didn't raise you to be rude. You say you're sorry to Corina this instant."

Rubbing the back of my head, I turned to Corina. She was trying to hide her smile and doing a piss poor job of it.

"I'm sorry."

She shrugged. "No worries. I would expect you of all people to think every woman should be born knowing how to wash clothes, keep a clean house, and cook for her man."

My head jerked. "I don't think that way. I was only surprised, that's all. My sisters learned early on with my mom and grandmother."

"God rest her soul," Mrs. Johnson whispered.

"And granddaddy taught us boys to fish and hunt—"

"God rest *his* soul," Mrs. Johnson added with more fire. Corina and I looked at her. "When you speak of the dead, it's best to pay yer respect."

"Yer?" Corina asked.

Laughing, Mrs. Johnson said, "Boy howdy, that's the back woods country in me. Mr. Johnson, God rest his soul." She looked at us expectantly.

"God rest his soul," Corina and I said together.

"He rescued me from the swamps of Louisiana. I had no school-in', no knowledge of nothin' but helping ma and pa around the farm."

"I didn't know you were from Louisiana, Mrs. Johnson," I said.

She grinned. "Oh, yes. I met the mister in New Orleans. I went for a job cooking in a restaurant. That's how I learned to cook so well, Corina."

We grinned at each other and then turned back to Mrs. Johnson. "He promised me a life I could never have in New Orleans. He was studying to be a dentist. I thought that was kind of gross to be lookin' in people's mouths all day, but who was I to judge? I was making the food that went into them. Might as well marry the man cleaning 'em!"

"Did you get married in New Orleans?" Corina asked. "Mitch-ell's younger sister, Amelia, was just married there. She came back today."

Mrs. Johnson's eyes widened. "Amelia Parker is married? Heavens to Betsy, you don't say. I thought that girl was still in high school."

Laughing, I shook my head. "No, ma'am. She's twenty-two years old. She writes books."

"I love to read. Just ask that nasty old mean librarian we got at the public library. Ornery thing, that woman."

Corina chuckled. "Now, now, Mrs. Johnson, that's not nice. She's just…old fashioned."

With a huff, she looked at me. "She refuses to carry *Fifty Shades of Grey*!"

My cheeks heated. "You do know what type of book that is, don't you?" I asked.

Flashing me a look that said I was insane, she brushed me off with her hand. "Just because I'm eighty-two years old doesn't mean I don't like a little naughty in my life, Mitchell Parker."

Corina busted out laughing. "You're making him blush, Mrs. Johnson."

"Good, the boy needs to get some color on that face. You should read the book. Try some of the moves out on Corina here."

And just like that, Corina stopped laughing. We tried not to look at each other and failed. Corina Miller was as innocent as they came. Her honesty with me about her sexual inexperience had actually turned me on. There were so many fucking things I wanted to teach her. Do to her.

My cock grew in my pants as we stared at each other. Corina was looking at me with a heated stare.

"Hell, maybe you *have* tried some of the moves on her, with the way you two stare. I feel like I'm watching a porn movie!"

Corina's head snapped to the older woman. "What? No! No, I think we're just both shocked, Mrs. Johnson, that you know what the book is about."

The old woman shrugged. "We watched the movies at our monthly quilting meeting."

Christ Almighty, as my father would say. I needed to change the subject fast.

"About those pies. When did you notice they went missing and where were they, Mrs. Johnson?"

She slowly stood. "If that wasn't a change of subject, I don't know what is."

Corina pressed her lips together to keep from laughing as I followed Mrs. Johnson to the dining room window.

"Look here, one of the pies is back!" Mrs. Johnson exclaimed.

"I'll be," I said, shaking my head. With a glance out the window, I couldn't help but notice one of the Gates boys leaning over to throw up. That's what the little bastard got. "I have a feeling I know who took your pies."

Mrs. Johnson glanced out the window and covered her mouth.

She placed her hands on her waist. "Well, if karma ain't a bitch."

CHAPTER 4

Corina

I dropped my keys on the coffee table and collapsed on the sofa. I was exhausted. I closed my eyes and thought about my day. It had started with finding out I was going to be teaching kindergarten.

Oh joy.

Then I'd seen Mitchell. Twice. Then a flat tire on the way home from Mrs. Johnson's.

A cracking sound made me open my eyes.

"What is that?" I walked to the wall that separated the living room and the dining room. I had bought an old house that was in need of serious renovations. Paxton had talked me into it, and I'd regretted it every darn day.

"Cheese and crackers, what is making that noise?"

I pulled my phone out and hit Tripp's number.

"Hey, I heard you had a flat," he said.

Snarling, I asked, "From who?"

"Karen had the day off. She said she drove by and noticed you changing it. I'm super impressed you can change a tire, Corina."

With a roll of my eyes, I huffed. "Yes, Tripp, I can change a tire. And you let Karen off?"

A low, tumbled laugh came though the phone. "I *do* let my poor secretary take days off, ya know."

"So you're not a cold, heartless boss who works his legal secretary to the bone?"

"I wouldn't go that far."

We both laughed. "How are you doing, Corina?" he asked, more seriously.

Leaning against the kitchen counter, I sighed. "I'm okay."

"He's just afraid. You know that, right?"

I squeezed my eyes for a quick second and tried to push Mitchell out of my mind.

"What is he afraid of, Tripp?" I asked. Some might think it was weird for me to talk to my ex-boyfriend about his brother, whom I'd had a one-night stand with. But even if he wasn't the right man for me, Tripp was surprisingly easy to talk to.

"Mitchell is afraid of commitment. The same thing most guys are scared shitless of."

I smiled. "Are you?"

His silence was my answer.

"Maybe if the right girl came along, but she's long gone."

My heart ached for Tripp. He'd told me about his high school love, Harley, one night when we both decided to be honest. I was head over heels for his brother, and he was in love with a woman who'd left Oak Springs to follow her dreams.

"You never know, Tripp. I heard the town vet is retiring soon."

Tripp let out a long sigh. "I'm perfectly fine with the way my life is. Besides, with me looking to run for mayor, the last thing I need is woman drama."

"Hey!"

"You going out with the girls tonight?" he asked, changing the subject.

"I am. You gonna be there?"

"I'll probably show up later. I've got a case I'm working on, and I need to get with Mitchell on some things."

"Is it a criminal case?"

"Yeah, that's all I can tell you though."

"That's okay, I get it. Listen, I'm going to get ready to head out tonight. Mrs. Johnson had me making roasted garlic, and I swear I won't get the smell off of my hands for months."

Tripp chuckled. "Wait, the whole reason I called. Are you driving with the donut tire on your car?"

"Yes, I'll take it to the shop tomorrow and have them put a new one on. Amelia's picking me up."

"The less you drive on that small tire, the better."

I grinned. "Yes, Dad."

"Ha ha. Later, kid."

"Later, Tripp."

I hit End and stared at my phone. A part of me wished things had worked out between Tripp and me—but it never could. We made better friends than anything. Heck, we'd never even made it past third base. Tripp had held back because of Mitch. So had I.

My cat chose that moment to come over and nudge my ankle. "Hey, buddy," I said, bending down. "Are you my favorite big boy?"

"Meow."

I hugged Milo close. He was a rescue cat, mostly white with a little bit of orange sprinkled in. His blue eyes reminded me of Mitchell's. It was the reason I'd stopped at his cage. Then he *meowed*, and I was lost to him.

I giggled. "What would Mitchell think if he knew I picked you because your eyes reminded me of him?"

Milo purred.

Heading up the stairs, I set Milo down and made my way into my bedroom. The crackling sound started again. This time it was louder. I would have to tell Tripp about it tomorrow.

My phone rang and Amelia's name popped up on the screen. I answered quickly. "Hey, what's up?"

"You're going, right?"

Laughing, I said, "Yes! I'm not backing out. I need a night out."

"Good! Dress sexy."

Rolling my eyes, I headed to my closet. "Why do you want me to dress sexy?"

"'Cause I happen to know a certain brother of mine will be there. I just heard Wade talking to Mitchell."

I chewed on my lip. "Sexy, huh?"

"Yes! It's time my brother opens his damn eyes."

I scanned my closet and stopped on the outfit I knew I was going to wear. "I think I found the perfect thing."

"It'd better show skin!"

Laughing, I pulled out the dress Amelia had talked me into buying a few weeks back. "Oh, it does." The red form-fitting dress wasn't something I wouldn't have purchased normally, but Amelia wouldn't stop going on about it. I pretty much bought it to shut her up. Or maybe it was because it pushed my boobs up and made them look even bigger, and the open back made me feel sexy.

"See you soon," Amelia said.

Hitting End, I spun around to find Milo sitting on my bed and giving me the evil eye.

"Sorry, Milo, but I refuse to be an old cat lady. Tonight I'm going to give Mr. Parker a run for his money."

The bass rattled against my chest as I danced with Amelia, Paxton, and Jenn. It was Paxton's first night out since the baby, and we were celebrating Amelia's surprise wedding. It was honestly the last place

I wanted to be, but the thought of running into Mitchell outweighed my desire to stay in bed with a pint of ice cream and a good movie.

"It feels so good to be able to dance again!" Paxton yelled over the music.

We laughed, and Amelia spun Paxton around a few times.

"Paxton, you look amazing!" I yelled.

Her cheeks blushed. "Look at you, Corina! I don't think that dress could hug those curves any tighter! Girl, you are looking hot!"

"Look at how freaking perky her tits are!" Jenn screamed.

My face heated as a few guys turned, and I instantly regretted my outfit.

Of course, the only reason I wore this dress was because I knew Mitchell had tonight off, and Amelia had mentioned that he would probably be at Cord's Place.

A cowboy wouldn't stop ogling my breasts, so I gave him the stink eye.

I turned and immediately felt a different stare. It only took me two seconds to shift my gaze to the bar and see him.

Mitchell.

My heart raced like it did every time our eyes met, every time I even found myself in the same room as him. But no matter how excited he seemed at first, he would eventually look elsewhere and act like he hadn't seen me.

Tonight he didn't.

Tonight his gaze stayed on me, and I could practically feel him burning a hole right through my slutty dress that I was *really* wishing I hadn't worn.

"Corina, are you okay?" Paxton yelled.

I nodded. My eyes drifted back; Mitchell was still watching us. "I need to use the restroom and splash my face. I'll be right back."

She gave me a concerned look, so I flashed a fake smile. "Honest. I'm hot, that's all. I haven't danced this much in a long time!"

Paxton laughed, accepting my answer.

Before I turned to head to the bathroom I peeked at Mitchell.

Big mistake. He was talking to the same girl I had seen him dancing with a few months back. He looked to the left, and our eyes met again. The girl leaned in and whispered something into his ear, but he never took his eyes off me.

Spinning on the heel of my boots, I pushed through the crowd. The room felt like it was closing in, and I was about to lose the turkey on rye sandwich I'd for dinner.

"Hey, beautiful, want to dance?" some cowboy asked.

"No, thanks. I feel like I'm going to puke."

He jumped out of my way, allowing me to keep moving. Each breath grew harder and harder to take as I tried to get to the hall.

What in the heck is wrong with me? Why can't I forget about him?

Once I broke through the crowd, I dragged in a deep breath, my hand clutching my chest, trying to calm my racing heart.

I fought the tears that threatened to spill. I wasn't sure how much more of this I could take. Seeing Mitchell, not knowing if he left with some girl he would screw in his truck and then never call again…

Maybe that's all I was to him. Another notch on his belt.

I wiped my tears and started for the ladies' restroom just as someone grabbed my arm from behind.

"Hey! Let go of me!" I yelled, hitting the guy with everything I had.

"Corina, stop fighting me."

Mitchell had taken me by the arm.

He pulled me toward Cord's office, unlocked the door, and guided me in as I jerked my arm free.

"Are you crazy, Mitch? You scared the crap out of me. It's dark in that hall, and I had no idea it was you!"

Before I could say another word, his lips pressed against mine. His hands pushed through my hair, and he held me gently even as he kissed me urgently, like he needed my kiss to breathe.

It was the first time he'd kissed me since the morning he'd stood at my front door. Leaving me to hope for something that would never be.

I should have pushed him away. Or told him that he couldn't drag me into a room and kiss me like he hadn't ripped my heart out and kicked it to the side all those months ago. But my heart was in control right now, and it loved every moment of Mitchell's kiss and the feel of his hands on my body. He tasted like peppermint and a hint of alcohol. It made me dizzy with desire.

A soft moan slipped from my lips. I grabbed his strong arms while they moved down my body, pulling up my dress.

Stop this, Corina.

He moved his lips along my jaw, then my neck, making his way to the sensitive area behind my ear. His hot breath and hands on my ass had me instantly wet.

"Corina." His whisper sounded so pained that my chest squeezed.

My mouth opened, but no words came out. The room was spinning, and as much as I knew I should tell him I couldn't do this without wanting more, I didn't want to break the moment. I wanted him to keep going.

"You look so goddamn sexy in this dress."

I smiled, no longer regretting my decision to wear it. Mitchell's hands pulled me up and my legs wrapped around his waist. He pushed me against the wall, his erection pressing against me in the most delicious way. This man brought out an inner goddess in me and I longed to explore that side of me with him.

"Mitch, yes." My breath was needy and rough, but I didn't care. I was in his arms and that was all I could focus on.

His breath was hot against my ear. "You drive me crazy. Do you know how much I want you?"

Hope bubbled in my chest. I shook my head, my chest rising and falling while his blue eyes stared into mine.

When I smiled, something in his eyes changed. He dropped his head and buried his face in my neck, kissing me in the most tender way. My skin was on fire beneath each kiss.

He pulled on my earlobe with his teeth, sending a zip of energy straight between my legs. He softly whispered, "You're so precious. I'm sorry. I never meant to hurt you."

Closing my eyes, a tear rolled slowly down my cheek. When I felt him pull back, I met his gaze.

I was positive the sadness in his eyes mirrored mine. He let my body slide down his until my feet touched the ground. He wiped away my tears with his thumbs, then pulled my dress back down.

He stepped away and dropped his hands to his side. "I can't do this, not like this. You don't deserve to be fucked against my brother's office door."

My mouth opened while I nodded, but then I realized what he was saying.

He took another step back and reached for the door. Before he opened it, I grabbed his arm. "Why are you doing this to me?"

He stared.

Anger raced through my body as I glared in disbelief. "Do you have any idea how fucked up this is?"

He winced at my use of *fuck*. Anyone who knew me knew I rarely swore. "You can't ignore me for months, and then haul me into your brother's office, feel me up for your own cheap thrill and walk away. Were you using me to warm up for the brunette?"

"What? No!"

I hit him as hard as I could on the chest. "You bastard! How could you?" Tears streamed down my face. I covered my mouth as I stumbled back. "How could you do this to me...again?"

"Corina, I—"

I hit him again. "I hate you, Mitchell Parker. Just go! Go fuck whatever flavor of the month you're into, but don't you dare ever touch me again!"

"It's not like that, sweetheart. Please, let me explain."

He reached out, and I screamed. He stopped. A look of horror moved across his face.

The door to Cord's office opened, and Amelia and Cord stood there.

"What's going on?" Amelia asked as she glanced between her brother and me.

My chin trembled as I looked at Amelia and Cord, then back to Mitchell.

Mitchell's eyes were pleading. "Corina."

I'd never in my life felt so defeated and broken. I'd foolishly believed that Mitchell Parker might care about me. I didn't bother to look at him as I took in a deep breath and blew it out. "You're right. I deserve someone who actually cares about me and wants to be with me. Someone who will cherish my heart."

Looking up, my breath caught when I saw his tears. "I'm tired of waiting for something that was never mine in the first place. I'm finished waiting for you, Mitch."

As I walked out, Mitchell called out, "Corina! Wait!"

I tried to hold back my sobs as I pushed my way through the crowd. I needed air. I needed to leave and get home.

My eyes met Tripp's. His brows drew together as he held out his arms, and I rushed into them.

The last ounce of strength I had left my body when he wrapped his arms around me.

"What in the hell happened?" he asked.

"Please take me home, Tripp. Please."

He lifted my chin. "Why are you crying, Corina? Tell me what happened."

His eyes drifted over my shoulder. From the look on his face it was clear Mitchell must have been standing there.

Tripp looked back down at me and forced a smile. "Let's get you home."

He placed his hand on my lower back and guided me through the bar. The farther I walked, the worse I felt. I could feel Mitchell's eyes boring into me. One glance over my shoulder proved I was right.

Looking straight ahead, I made the decision I should have made months ago.

It was time to move on and forget about Mitchell Parker.

CHAPTER 5

Mitchell

"Fuck!" I cried out as I watched Tripp leading Corina out of the bar.

Cord pulled me by the arm. "Get back to my office, now!"

I followed him back to his office and took a seat in one of the chairs. I buried my face in my hands.

"Totally just fucked that all up," I groaned.

"Mitch, what happened?" Amelia asked. "What in the world did you do to Corina?"

"Nothing! I mean, things got a little hot and heavy, and I stopped because I didn't want to fuck her against a goddamn office door. I wanted to get her out of here and take her back to my place to talk…she thought I was trying to back out. She wouldn't even let me explain."

Cord sat on his desk and lifted his hands with a confused expression. "Why would she think you were leaving?"

I dragged my hands down my face. "I don't know. I don't think she was really listening to me once I stopped kissing her. I told her I couldn't do this and that she didn't deserve to be fucked up against the door. I wanted to get out of here but when I went to open the door, she freaked the fuck out."

Cord and Amelia looked at each other. Glancing back at me, Cord said, "Dude, she thought you were blowing her off."

I jumped up. "I fucking know that now, Cord! I got that much when she started hitting me and saying she hated me. She wouldn't even let me get a fucking word in. She took off and ran straight into Tripp's arms." My voice cracked and I dropped my head. "She left with him."

"Oh, stop it."

Lifting my eyes to meet Amelia's, I frowned.

"You know damn well Tripp is not going to do anything. He's her friend and that's all. The one guy who doesn't push her away and pretend he doesn't have feelings for her."

"Don't fucking start with me, Amelia."

Cord put his hand on my chest. "Dude, you don't talk to our sister like that."

I closed my eyes and blew out a breath. Focusing on Amelia, I said, "I'm sorry, Meli. Do you have any idea how many times I wanted to just walk up to Corina and tell her I had feelings for her?"

"But you never did, Mitch. You danced and flirted for months with other women. How many times have you had sex since that night with Corina? How many women have you been with?"

I swallowed hard. My stomach felt sick.

"Once."

Amelia pulled her brows together and jerked her head back. "Once what?"

Combing my fingers in my hair, I answered. "I've had sex *once*, and it was with Cassidy."

"I knew it!" Amelia cried out. "I knew that skank got to you."

"I was drunk. I don't even remember the night."

"Nice," Amelia spat out as Cord jumped in.

"Alright, Amelia, you got your jab in. Let's cool it, okay?"

"Cool it? Cord, this girl has been pining over him for months. And he thinks just one night he can walk up and kiss her senseless, and *bam*, she's gonna take him back? Fuck that!"

Amelia walked over and sat down next to me on the loveseat. "Mitchell, I love you, but you don't know shit about women. And no offense, but none of my brothers do."

"Hey!" Cord said.

Looking up at him, Amelia rolled her eyes. "You know how to make a girl cry out your name and beg you for more. That's about all you know, Cord. Sorry."

I let out a chuckle.

"Don't laugh, Mitch. You're the same way. You guys have been able to get any girl by smiling at them and saying hi. But you know what? The one girl who really matters, the one you're going to want to spend the rest of your life with, that girl is going to take work. She's going to need to know she's more than a quick fuck in the back of your truck. Mitchell, you're doing this all wrong."

Letting out a frustrated sigh, I turned to my sister. "Then tell me what I need to do, Amelia. I can't stop thinking about her. Every time I see her all I want to do is pull her into my arms and kiss her."

An evil smile grew across my baby sister's face. "You're going to *swoon* her."

"Swoon her?" Cord and I said at once.

Amelia looked between us. "Have neither one of you read one of my books?"

Cord and I shrugged. Cord replied, "I've *bought* them."

"Yeah, me too," I said. "But I'm sorry, sis, I'm not really into romance, and I'm for sure not into reading sex written by my baby sister."

"A-fucking-men," Cord added.

Her body slumped. "Okay. I'll give y'all that. I've got some good books I'm going to send you both. They're on audio so you can listen to them. I'm going to teach you two what it means to swoon a woman and make her fall, not because you're going to screw her brains out, but because you're showering her with romance and respect."

Cord laughed. "Please. Amelia, I think I know how to romance a woman if I want."

I stood. "That goes for me too. I don't need some damn book to tell me how to win a woman's heart."

Amelia slowly stood. "Is that right?"

"Yes!" Cord and I said together.

Taking her phone out, Amelia pulled up Amazon. "Let's see, Jennifer Probst, Sydney Landon, Marie Force, oh, yes. Erika Kelly."

She tapped a few things on her phone and then looked up at us. "If you'll excuse me, gentlemen. I've got some dancing left to do."

Turning to leave, she let out an evil laugh and disappeared out the door.

"Why do I have a feeling we are about to be schooled on romance by our baby sister?" Cord asked.

"You think she ordered each of us the audiobooks?"

Cord gave me a *what-the-fuck* look before rubbing the back of his neck and heading toward his office door. "She better have."

I followed Cord back into the bar. Pulling my phone out, I sent Tripp a text message.

Me: *She misunderstood me. I wanted to take her back to my place and talk.*

Tripp: *Yeah, she is pretty pissed. I think she is making an effigy of you right now.*

My head pulled back as I stared at the phone.
"What?"

Me: *What in the fuck?*

Tripp: *Dude, when I say she's pissed…I mean she is PISSED. I don't think I've ever head Corina curse and she's called you an asshole six times.*

I let out a groan.

"Shit."

Tripp: *My advice, don't come over here or call her tonight.*

Me: *Why?*

Tripp: *Image*

Opening up the picture, I stumbled back. "What in the living fuck!"

"What's wrong?" Trevor asked as he handed me a beer.

I stared at the image before looking at Trevor.

"Corina. She…she made a doll of me, and I'm pretty sure that is a piece of my windbreaker I left the night we were together. I was wondering where that jacket went."

It only took him about five seconds before Trevor burst out laughing.

"Awe, hell. I always did like that girl."

When the lights of Tripp's truck came around the corner, I let out a sigh. I was almost positive his uptight neighbors were fixin' to call the sheriff.

The garage door opened and Tripp pulled in. Shutting off his truck, he looked at me and smiled.

"She made a fucking doll?" I asked.

"Dude, it was so true to life, too. She's going to make a great kindergarten teacher. She's totally crafty." He pulled in a deep breath through his nose and exhaled. "Maybe I shouldn't have let her go. She'd a been a good wife for the mayor."

"Oh, fuck you, motherfucking dickhead son-of-a-bitch traitor bastard asshole cocksucker of a brother!"

Tripp stopped walking. "Wow. That was something there, baby brother."

"Fuck off! I'm not your baby brother!"

"Um, yeah, you are!" he said as he reached up and shut his garage door. "I'm older, you're younger. Need I explain it further?"

"I hope you lose your bid for mayor."

Clutching his chest, Tripp tossed his keys onto his kitchen island. He lived in a huge house—over four thousand square feet. How in the hell he got paid so much for being a small town lawyer was beyond me. Of course, he did work for a firm in San Antonio, as well.

"That really hurts, bro," he said. "Hurts deep."

Guilt flooded my veins. "Shit, I didn't mean that."

Reaching into the refrigerator, he grabbed two beers. "I know you didn't. Just like I didn't mean it when I said I hope you misfired and shot yourself in the foot."

The beer froze at my lips. "When did you say that?"

He smiled. "When I found out you slept with Corina."

I rolled my eyes. "Whatever. By the way, your wish could have caused bodily harm, mine wouldn't have."

He looked up in thought and then glanced at me and smiled.

"Asshole," I said.

"Takes one to know one, Mitchell."

I sat at one of the stools at his large kitchen island. "Is she okay?"

He leaned against the counter and took a long drink. "You want me to be honest?"

"Of course."

"No. She's nowhere near okay. Angry, hurt, feeling rejected... again."

"I wasn't rejecting her! I didn't want to fuck her in Cord's office. I wanted to take her back to my place."

"To fuck."

"No! Well, maybe after we talked, but I wanted to talk to her first. To tell her I've been so damn stupid. Ever since I saw Mrs. Johnson showing Corina how to cook, I couldn't stop thinking about how much I needed to talk to her."

Tripp stared at me like I had grown two heads. "It was a pie crust that got you to realize you've been an ass?"

"Yes. No. Hell, I don't know." I gripped my hair with both hands as I let out a groan. "I didn't want to leave her today. I wanted to watch her stupid cooking lesson, then take her to Lilly's to get something to eat and tell her I wanted another shot."

He lifted a brow. "Another shot at what?"

"Us. This thing I feel in my chest about her. I can't eat or sleep because of it. My focus is all kinds of screwed up, and I'm afraid I'm going to accidently shoot myself in the foot."

Tripp held up his hands when I gave him a fuck-off-and-die look. "Okay, listen. I'm the last person to give you advice, but I'm going to do it anyway."

I leaned closer. "Okay."

He set his beer down and rested his hands on the island. "This is what you need to do."

"I'm listening."

"Go ask Dad."

I sat there, staring at my older brother. "That's all you got?"

He shrugged. "That's all I got."

"What happened to the 'I'm older and wiser' bullshit you always used to say?"

"Yeah, that was all bullshit. Hell, Mitchell, you've always been the wise one. The one with your head on right. The thinker. But this time, I guess I was."

"You were not, you asshole! You told me to go talk to Dad. How is that being a thinker?"

"I *thought* you should go talk to Dad. Thought is what happens after someone thinks."

Closing my eyes, I exhaled a frustrated breath before scrubbing my hands over my face. Then I gave him one last look. "You suck, Parker. I hope your skills at being a lawyer are better than your advice."

"Oh yeah? Well, I hope your cop skills are better than your... your..."

Waiting for his reply, I tilted my head and smirked.

"Yeah, I've got nothing."

Heading toward his front door, I said, "I didn't think so. Night, Tripp."

"Honestly though, Mitchell. I know you care about Corina, and I know that no matter how ticked off she is right now, she cares about you. I think you need to take things slow. Prove to her you know you fucked up and you deserve another chance."

I nodded. "Good advice, bro."

Starting down the steps, I hit the button to unlock my truck.

"Hey, Mitch!" Tripp yelled after me. "You remember what Corina said about Lane Lewis?"

I stopped walking and looked back over my shoulder. "Yeah."

"Maybe don't move *too* slow with Corina."

A knot formed in my stomach. "Why?"

Tripp ran his hand behind his neck and frowned. "He sent Corina flowers and said he was looking forward to working with her."

Anger raced through me.

"Talk to Dad in the morning. Just go home and get some sleep. You look like shit."

My jaw hurt from clenching as I headed to my truck. I made a mental note to get to my folks' place first thing in the morning. There was no way I was going to give up now. I'd pushed Corina away, and I wasn't doing it anymore. And I sure as hell wasn't going to let her run into the arms of the little prick who hated me in high school.

"Fuck that," I mumbled as I started up my truck and headed to the one place I knew I shouldn't be going.

Corina's.

CHAPTER 6

Corina

With a clink, I placed my cup on the dish and pushed it to the waitress.

"Thank you," I said as she took my coffee cup and then Lane's.

"It was really sweet of you to send the flowers."

He smiled. "It was nothing." Motioning between us, Lane laughed. "But what about this? I can't believe I ran into you here and on a Friday night. I figured you'd be out on a hot date."

If he thought I was stupid, he was insane. I knew he was fishing to see if I was dating anyone. "I was out earlier but had to call it an early night."

He nodded like he accepted my answer, but I knew he didn't. I could see it in his eyes. "Lucky for me you called it an early night."

"No hot date with the high school crush who got away?" I asked.

He laughed. "Hardly. All the girls in this town were not worth my time."

My eyes widened.

"I don't mean it in a vain way. It's just most of the girls in my high school pined over the Parker brothers. It would have been hard enough to compete with one, but I had three I had to deal with in high school."

I lifted a brow. "One of my very dearest and best friends is married to Steed Parker, and I dated Tripp for a while. He's a good friend, so I'd tread lightly."

He lifted his hands in defense. "Treading lightly." Glancing down, he played with the fork on the table. "You dated Tripp, huh?"

I shrugged. "Yeah. We both did it for stupid reasons, though. We make better friends than lovers."

Lane stared at me. Crap. I had made it sound like I'd had a sexual relationship with Tripp.

Glancing at my Apple watch, I cleared my throat. "Well, I should get going."

"Yeah, sure. You want me to walk you back to your house?"

"I drove over here. I know it's only a couple of blocks, but you know, it's still kind of scary being out this late at night. Small town or not."

"I'm glad you drove. It is safer. Let me pay for this and I'll walk you to your car."

We both stood. "You don't have to pay for mine."

Lane gave me a wink and a sexy-as-hell smile. "I know I don't have to. I want to."

I returned his smile. "Thank you. I'll meet you outside. My car is parked out front."

The second I walked out and looked at my car, I groaned.

"Are you kidding me?" I yelled.

"Corina."

Mitchell's voice made all the hairs on my body stand up. Of course, my heart also fluttered and my stupid stomach dropped. I had to take in a deep breath and replace my silly emotions with anger. I glared at him. "What do you want, Mitchell?"

"I went to your house, but you weren't home. I started driving around town looking for you. Not sure how I missed your car sitting here, I drove by five times."

Crossing my arms over my chest, I let out a gruff laugh. "Some cop you are." He frowned, and I regretted my harsh words. "I'm sorry, Mitch. I didn't mean to say that."

But you did! You're angry with him. He played with your emotions again! You. Are. Angry!

"Actually, I did mean that. I meant it very much, and I don't care if it hurt your feelings. You deserve it."

He flashed me that damn panty-melting smile and winked.

Lord. Help me be strong.

"Please, can we talk?" he asked. "I need to explain what happened at Cord's Place. I didn't do a good job of explaining things and…"

I glanced into the café; Lane was almost finished paying.

"Not now. I'm busy."

"When?" Mitchell asked.

"I don't really know, Mitch. Honestly, I'm not sure when I want to talk to you again…*if* I ever do want to talk to you."

Peeking back into the restaurant, I couldn't help but notice that Lane was talking with our waitress.

"You're with Lane?" Mitchell asked.

I wasn't sure why I lied, but it came out of my mouth before I could stop it.

"Yes."

Mitchell looked at Lane and then focused on me. Even though it was dark, I could see the sadness in his eyes, illuminated from the café window.

"Right. Goodnight, Corina. I hope you enjoy your evening."

Wait. That's it? He's going to give up just like that?

He walked to the door on the other side of the Lilly's café window, which led to the apartments above the diner. Panic mixed with my anger. I don't know why I spoke, but I did. "You live here? At the restaurant?"

Mitchell turned the key and opened the door. "I live on the third floor and part of the fourth. It's a nice place. The owner had it remodeled and kept all the historical features."

I smiled as he stepped inside the door. "I bet it's nice."

He shrugged. "It's home...for now."

My head tilted. I wanted to ask what he meant. Was he planning on moving? Leaving Oak Springs? More panic built in my chest. We stared at each other. A small part of me wished he would ask me up, but I knew he wouldn't, since I'd so stupidly said I was with Lane.

Mitchell smiled and was about to say something when Lane walked out.

"Let's get you home, shall we?" Lane asked. "I bought a couple slices of pie. Figured we could eat them on the front porch of your place."

Forcing a smile, I replied, "Actually Lane, I think—"

When I turned back, Mitchell's front door was closed. He was gone.

Swallowing hard, I pushed my disappointment in Mitchell deep down and let the anger resurface. "I'm going to call it a night and head home to bed. Can we eat the pie tomorrow, maybe?"

"Tomorrow?" he said with a huge smile. "A second date. I like it."

I laughed and hit him in the stomach. "Seriously though, my tire is flat." I looked at my car. "And my spare tire is flat too."

Lane stared at it for a few seconds. "Looks like we're walking."

As we made the walk back to my house, I took a chance at looking behind me and up to the third floor of Lilly's café.

My breath caught when I saw his lights turn on and a figure walk to the sliding glass door. He stared down at us and then turned away. The sinking feeling in my stomach grew.

I focused on the sidewalk before peeking up at Lane. He was going on and on about how scared to death he was of the first graders. I couldn't help but laugh and tried to let myself enjoy the moment.

My phone went off and when I read it I could practically feel the steam coming from my ears.

Mitchell: *Lane Lewis is a dick. You deserve better.*

I tuned out Lane as I typed my response.

Me: *You're one to talk. I'm surprised you didn't have some girl on your arm tonight. Oh, wait, you probably already screwed her in the back of your truck. Am I right?*

I was livid; only Mitchell got me so upset I swore.

Mitchell: *If you hadn't gone home with that asshole, I could have asked you up to my place and explained myself. I wasn't leaving you back in Cord's office. I wanted you to come home with me.*

I practically laughed out loud. Peeking up, Lane was *still* talking. Something about the class pet.

Me: *So, instead of doing me against your brother's office door, you wanted to do me at your place. Nice. Classy move. I'd rather let Lane take me against any door than have you touch me ever again!*

I stared at my phone for a minute, but it was clear he wasn't texting back. Fine by me.

I'd almost let my emotions take control again earlier. From this moment on, I was putting a wall around my heart, and Mitchell Parker was not going to break through.

Mission move-on-from-Mitchell-Parker begins tonight.

"Hey, you okay?" Lane asked as he stopped walking.

I forced a smile. "Yes, sorry I was being rude."

He glanced down at my phone. "I didn't even notice. Guess I was talking too much!"

We both let out a chuckle.

"If you need to text them, go ahead."

"No, it doesn't matter anymore."

Lane flashed me a huge smile. "People who don't make you happy don't belong in your life, Corina."

His words hit me hard. I dragged in a shaky breath. "I know, but sometimes it's hard to let them go."

He nodded like he knew what I meant. "When you do let them go, you'll find you can breathe easier."

I looked at the ground. The idea of letting Mitchell go didn't cause me to breathe easier; it was the exact opposite. My chest pulled with an ache so strong it felt like it kept the air from moving in and out of my body. I needed to let him go. It was clear he didn't want the same things I wanted. Which was us. Me and him, exclusively. The future that I longed for was not the same future Mitchell wanted.

Pulling in a breath, I glanced back up at Lane. "You know what?" I asked with a wide grin. "I think I do want to eat those pies on my front porch."

I don't think I'd ever seen a guy's eyes light up like Lane's did. At some point I was going to have to inform him that we needed to keep things on a friendship level only. I wasn't going to risk my job by dating another teacher.

Lane laced his fingers with mine as we started walking again. Peeking down, I looked at our hands. I knew I needed to say something, but a part of me wanted to pretend things were different—that I hadn't just had one of the worst nights of my life by being rejected by Mitchell yet again. Mitchell's words hit me newly. He had wanted me to go back to his place. And he seemed so pained when I left him at Cord's. The way he called out. Had I jumped to conclusions?

Sirens lit up in the distance as we kept walking. A truck raced by, and I had to do a double-take because I swore it was Mitchell's truck.

"Was that Mitchell?"

"Is that smoke?" Lane asked.

My heart dropped as I followed his gaze. "Yes! It's coming from the direction of the street I live on. I hope no one's house is on fire."

Lane picked up his pace as I joined him. We rounded the corner, and I let out a gasp.

"No," I whispered. I stared at my house; the second floor was in flames.

"Milo!" I screamed as I started running toward the front door.

"Corina! Wait, where are you going?"

Running as fast as I could, I screamed out my cat's name. Onlookers turned to see me running like a bat out of hell. The fire department was there and so was…Mitchell?

It *had* been Mitchell's truck.

I didn't stop. I focused on getting to Milo. Strong arms grabbed me, and I knew in an instant who had me. "Mitchell, let me go! Milo is in the house! Milo's in there."

He cupped my face and forced me to look at him. "Corina, I need you to calm down."

Tears streamed down my face for the second time tonight as I looked at him.

"But…Milo."

He glanced at the house and then back to me. "Wait here."

Mitchell ran up to the front porch. The firefighters ran after him, calling out for him to stop.

"Mitchell!" I screamed as he kicked in the door and disappeared. Two firefighters went in after him.

"Holy shit, did Mitchell just go into the house?" Lane asked.

"He did what?"

Spinning around, I saw Tripp. "Oh my God, Tripp, he went in after Milo!"

Tripp placed his arms around me as I buried my face against his chest. "I'll never forgive myself if something happens to him," I cried out.

"There he is!" Lane called out.

I pulled away from Tripp to see Mitchell coming out along with a firefighter. He had something in his arms, and I struggled to see what it was.

"Milo," I whispered.

"What a damn idiot! He could have gotten killed for a cat!" Lane said.

"Shut up, Lane," Tripped said in an angry voice.

I ran to Mitchell, and he handed Milo over, but I threw myself into Mitchell's body. I was so relieved he was okay.

He wrapped his arm around me. "He's okay. A little scared, but he's okay."

Stepping back, I took the cat and wrapped him in my arms. I didn't want to look, but I couldn't seem to stop myself. I turned around and watched my house going up in flames.

CHAPTER 7

Mitchell

My lungs burned as I coughed.

"Mitch, are you sure you're okay?" Travis asked, looking at me with a concerned expression.

"Just breathed a little smoke. I'll be fine."

Before I knew it, an oxygen mask was being pushed on my face. I took it only because my lungs felt like they were on fire. I glanced to Corina talking to Tripp and Captain Smith, the fire chief.

"Damn shame about the house," Lane said. His voice was like nails down a chalkboard.

With a yank, I took the oxygen mask off. "Yeah, well, it can be fixed. Looks like it's mostly the top floor."

He stared at the house. I couldn't shake the feeling I got. "Why in the fuck are you smiling?" I asked.

Looking my way, he shrugged. "I didn't realize I was. Maybe I'm happy that Corina was with me tonight and not home when the fire broke out."

My blood boiled as I tossed the oxygen mask down. As I walked past him, I made sure to bump his shoulder…hard. "Asshole."

"What was that, Parker?"

"You heard me," I replied with a smile of my own.

As I approached her, I heard Corina ask, "Where am I supposed to live now? I have nothing. All of my clothes, everything I owned was on the second story of that house."

My heart ached for her.

"Can you stay with friends?" the Captain asked.

Corina's body slumped.

"You can stay with me if you want," Lane said. A part of me wanted to grab him by the T-shirt and knock the hell out of him. He didn't even know Corina that well, and he was asking her to move in with him.

Tripp stepped in front of Lane. "I'd say you could stay with me, but honestly, Corina, it wouldn't look right. Especially with me running for mayor soon."

She nodded and held onto Milo tighter. "You could stay with my parents," I suggested.

Clearing his throat, Tripp added, "Our folks love Corina, but they did mention how happy they were that the house would soon be empty."

My head pulled back as I gave Tripp a what-in-the-hell look. I knew for a fact they would love to have Corina at the house.

"Oh," Corina said with tears building in her eyes.

Tripp cleared his throat. "I think it's best if you stay with Mitchell."

"Mitchell?"

"Me?"

Corina and I had spoken at the same time.

"It makes sense," Tripp said. "You have three bedrooms, Mitch, and you're only a few blocks from Corina's place. When they start fixing it back up, she'll want to be close by." The way Tripp looked at me, I knew exactly what he was doing.

"It would probably be the most convenient, Corina," I added.

Her eyes dashed back and forth between Tripp and me.

"Well, I live close by too." Lane added.

Corina turned to him. "Lane, I hardly know you. It wouldn't be appropriate for us to live together."

He frowned. "But it would with you and Mitchell?"

She chewed on her bottom lip. It looked like she was actually thinking about this asshole's proposition.

I went to speak, but Tripp beat me to it. "Seriously, Lewis, how long have you been gone? You want the kindergarten teacher and the first grade teacher living together? Mitchell's a cop and has earned respect in the community. Plus, he's Corina's friend. People won't think twice that he's offered her a place to stay."

Corina looked at Milo, then back up at me. "I guess it makes the most sense to stay with Mitchell. I mean, Lane you said you were in a small, one-bedroom place."

When I glanced over to Lane, he looked furious.

Finally, he grinned. "Hey, I'm renting out a place at the old Riley house. You could look at getting something there."

Tripp nodded. "Oh, yeah, I heard they converted it into a bed and breakfast. Shame they don't take pets," he said, nodding at Milo in Corina's arms. Lane's face dropped; he knew what was happening too.

With a clap of hands, Tripp added, "Well, that settles it. No way you two can stay in a one-room together without the cat. Tongues would be wagging, and I'm sure you wouldn't want that for Corina."

"No, not at all. Staying with Mitchell until she can make other arrangements is probably for the best."

I wanted to laugh. *Other arrangements? I don't think so.*

One quick glance to Corina showed her eyes bouncing back and forth amongst the three of us. I was a bit surprised she didn't speak up. After all, we were basically deciding where she would live, and she wasn't uttering a word.

I reached for Milo. "I had them call the Oak Springs shelter. They brought a cage for Milo."

Corina handed me the cat, still not saying a word as she watched a young lady open the cage for me. After slipping Milo in, I asked, "Kim, would you mind taking Milo to Doc Harris? I'm sure Corina will want to make sure he's okay."

The girl who worked at the shelter nodded. "Of course. I'm sure Doc 'll want him to stay the night. You can pick 'im up in the mornin', if you want."

Tripp let out a chuckle as Corina stared at Kim with an open mouth. The girl's Texas accent was heavy as hell and even hard for me to understand.

"Thanks, Kim. Either Corina or I'll be by to pick him up."

She took the crate and started talking to Milo. Corina looked worried now, on top of being scared. She still didn't say a damn thing about the living arrangements, which gave me hope that maybe she secretly wanted to stay with me. "Will he be okay, Mitch?" she asked in a voice barely above a whisper.

Lane wrapped his arm around her shoulder. "He'll be fine, Corina."

Taking me by the arm, Tripp guided me away. "Listen, I know what you're thinking. I'm thinking it, too; he's a slimy fucker. But what you need to concentrate on is helping her through this."

"Did you say Mom and Dad wouldn't want her at the house because you wanted her to stay with me? Why would you do that?"

He grinned. "As bad as this shit is, it's almost a blessing in disguise, Mitch. This is your second chance with her. You'd better not fuck it up."

Looking past Tripp's shoulder, I couldn't help the tug at the corners of my mouth when Corina stepped out of Lane's hold. She glanced over her shoulder and looked at me. For about five seconds she stared into my eyes, and I knew Tripp was right.

This was my second chance. No way in hell was I letting Lane Loser Lewis steal the only woman I'd ever cared about.

No way in hell.

I stumbled into the kitchen, then stopped on a dime when I saw her.

My dick instantly went hard while I scanned Corina's body. She was dressed in one of my old T-shirts and a pair of shorts she had pulled to the side and tied a hairband around to keep them up.

Sexy. As. Fuck.

Getting my head out of my ass, I spoke. "Hey, I figured you'd be exhausted."

Corina stood in front of my coffee maker, waiting for it to dispense its liquid gold. "I can't sleep."

She turned around and looked me over. I had on a pair of sweats. And that was it.

I wanted to smile as she took in every inch of my body. She lingered a little long on my chest before snapping her eyes to mine. "Are you going to make it a habit to walk around half-naked?"

I shrugged. "What? Normally I walk in here butt ass naked. So, compared to my *normal* attire, this is a one-hundred-percent improvement."

Her eye twitched, and I could tell she was holding back a smart-ass reply.

"Are you going to let Milo live here or is that why you had that girl take him away?"

I narrowed my eyes as I made my way over to the coffee. Corina stepped away. It was almost like she was scared to let me breathe on her.

"Of course he's welcome here, Corina. And I didn't let Kim take him away. She took him to Doc Harris. We can head over there now and get him, if you want."

She let out a sharp laugh. "We? So, what are *we* now, Mitch? Best friends? Buddies?"

I took out a coffee mug, filled it to the brim, and handed it to her. "The way I see it, Corina, we're roommates. If you'd rather go shack up with your new friend, have at it."

Her eyes widened. She opened her mouth and shut it just as quickly. My phone rang.

"This is Mitch."

"Mitchell, it's Dr. Harris."

"Doc Harris, how is Milo?"

Corina reached for the phone, but I pushed her hand away.

"He's doing great," Doc Harris said. "Sitting on the front desk flirting with all the women."

I laughed. "Smart cat."

"Must have learned that from you."

"Not this time, Doc. Corina, Milo's mom, and I will be heading down soon to come get him."

Corina stopped trying to take the phone from my hands and took a step back. She turned and sat down at the bar.

"Sounds good, Mitchell," Doc Harris said. "Shame about the young lady's house. Chief said something was suspicious about the fire this morning at the café."

That comment pulled my eyes off of Corina. "What?"

"Don't be saying anything to anyone. I wasn't supposed to repeat that."

My hand went to the back of my neck where I tried to rub the instant tension away. Turning my back to Corina, I asked, "What makes him think that?"

"I'm not sure. You'll have to talk to him about it. He said he was gonna give you a call about it."

A knot formed in my stomach at the idea of someone setting Corina's house on fire. My mind drifted back to Lane standing there, smiling at the burning house.

"Right. Thanks, Doc. We'll see you in a bit."

"I'll have the girls put some things together for the young lady. I'm sure she won't have anything for the cat."

I turned and looked at Corina. "That's awfully nice of ya, Doc. We are sure lucky to have you."

"Well, the plan is to retire soon, but I won't leave Oak Springs until I have a replacement I feel worthy of the town."

My brows lifted. "You're retiring? The town will sure miss you."

He laughed. "I'm not leaving Oak Springs anytime soon. You'll still see me around, and I'm sure I'll come in and help out the new vet."

"I'm glad to hear that. Better get going. See ya soon."

"Sounds good, Mitchell."

The line went dead, and I was about to say something when my doorbell rang.

"Mitchell?" Blue eyes locked with mine before a pissed-off look washed over Corina's face. "Who is that?"

"Before you go accusing me, it's Amelia. She has a key." Her face relaxed. "She brought you some stuff. I called her last night and was hoping she'd be here before you woke up."

"Oh, that was really nice of you." Her eyes drifted away, like she felt guilty about whatever she'd just been thinking.

"Any decent person would have done it."

Amelia walked into the kitchen, a huge smile on her face. I couldn't get over how my sister practically glowed.

"Hey," I said, pulling her into a hug. "You look beautiful. Do you know that?"

Drawing back, Amelia looked up at me. "I do?"

"Yes," I said as I tapped her nose. "You look good in love."

She blushed. "Thank you, Mitchell. Wade makes me the happiest I've ever been." Spinning on her heels, Amelia faced Corina. "Waylynn and I raided our closets and have bags of clothes for Mitchell to bring up. I stopped at the store and got you some shampoo, a toothbrush, and some deodorant. I hope I got the right kind. I tried to think of everything you'd need right now."

Tears filled Corina's eyes. She buried her face in her hands and lost it crying.

Amelia shot me a dirty look. "What did you do to her, Mitchell Parker?"

My mouth dropped open. "What? I didn't do anything!"

Corina dropped her hands to her lap. "He...he's been...w-wonderful. It's just me. I don't know what to do. I lost everything. Pictures, memories. Everything I owned is...gone."

Amelia hit me on the chest and motioned for me to go over to her. I pointed to myself with a 'Who? Me?' look, and she nodded.

Looks like Amelia was in on the plan for me to win Corina over.

I motioned I had no shirt on, and she gave me the stink eye. Making my way over to her, I lifted her off the stool and pulled her into my arms. She melted against my body. It took every ounce of willpower I had to keep my dick from going hard.

"All that is replaceable, Corina," I said. "I know it hurts to lose all of it, but on the bright side, you saved Milo. And you can really make that house amazing with the insurance money!"

Amelia's eyes widened before she slowly shook her head in disappointment. Corina pulled back and looked up at me. It killed me to see her crying. Using my thumbs, I wiped her tears away.

"Please, don't cry," I whispered.

Something moved across her face as she stared at me. "You saved Milo. You ran into the house to save him. Why would you do that?"

My heart was pounding. I wanted to tell her I did it for her. That there wasn't anything I wouldn't do for her. Instead, I said, "Instinct. Guess it comes with my job."

I could practically feel Amelia's eyes burning a hole in me.

"Oh," Corina whispered.

Fuck. Fuck. Fuck. Recover!

I shrugged. "Plus, it was Milo. He was yours, and I know how much you love him."

"So really what you're saying is, you did it for Corina?" Amelia asked in an annoyed tone of voice.

We turned and stared at Amelia. Now it was my turn with the daggers.

CHAPTER 8

Corina

There was no way I was going to let Mitchell see my reaction when Amelia spoke.

"Yes, Amelia. Thanks for clearing that up."

Amelia smiled. "Sure, no problem. Okay, so if you need anything, let me know? I'm late for a conference call with my agent."

Walking to her, I pulled her tight and whispered, "Thank you for everything."

Her hold tightened. "You were there for me, and I promise I'll be here for you. No matter what."

When we stepped back, we both had tears in our eyes. I never imagined when I moved to this small town I'd make such amazing friends. Paxton had been a gift in my life, but the addition of Amelia and Waylynn was like icing on top of my favorite cake.

"I'll call you later," Amelia said. "Maybe we can all head into San Antonio and do some shopping."

I nodded. "I'm meeting with the insurance company around noon, so I'll let you know when I'm finished."

"I'm glad they're not making you wait until Monday."

My chest tightened as I thought about the phone call last night. I could hardly talk when I called the insurance company. Mitchell ended up telling them what happened while I sat on his couch and held my knees into my chest. I'd had my few moments of weakness, and now it was time to pull my big-girl panties up and handle this like an adult.

Yes, I lost everything. But no one died. Milo was safe. I was safe. And currently standing in Mitchell's kitchen with him half-naked. As much as I loved the view, I would never let him know. I needed to remember the wall I'd built. He might have been acting all sweet and kind, but if I let him in, I'd risk being hurt again.

A part of me knew he was trying, but I needed more time to figure things out. The last thing I needed was to let my guard down.

Hurt me once, shame on you. Hurt me twice...shame on me.

"Hey, you okay?" Amelia asked, touching my arm.

With a forced smile, I nodded. "Yeah, tired and ready to see Milo."

Leaning in, she kissed me on the cheek. "Alright, talk to you soon. Later, Mitchell."

"Bye Amelia."

The second she disappeared I felt a tingle move across my body. Mitchell had walked up behind me. I wanted him to touch me...anywhere. I wanted something to ease the ache. But I also wanted to run like crazy.

"I'm, um, I'm gonna go get dressed so we can get Milo," Mitchell said. "Doc isn't usually open for long on Saturdays."

I swallowed and watched him walk past me with his cup of coffee, into his bedroom. He'd given me a quick tour of his place last night, but I took these few moments to myself to really explore.

I'd already checked out the entire kitchen earlier. It was obvious Melanie had a hand in the design. Plus, Mitchell had every kitchen gadget known to man. I didn't even think the man knew how to cook, but he was well stocked.

The kitchen opened into the living room, which lead to the terrace. I stepped out and took in a deep breath. It was a corner balcony that went around the side of the building. Glancing down, I looked at Main Street and all the people walking toward Lilly's Café.

I sat down on one of Mitchell's chairs and sipped my coffee while I people-watched. Lane walked up and I went to call out his name but he stopped in front of Lucy, Lilly's daughter who worked at her mom's café. I watched as they talked and couldn't help but notice how much Lane flirted with her. It wasn't like I cared—I didn't have those types of feelings toward him. He was good looking, but there was something about him I didn't like.

I also wasn't sure he would last as a first-grade teacher.

He smiled, and then walked in the other direction while Lucy headed into the café. I shrugged. Of course, I could have Lane pegged all wrong. I doubted it, though.

I headed into the house and made my way through the living room. The décor was simple, classic with a slight ranch feel to it. His sofa and love seat were both made of a beautiful, soft leather. Running my fingers over it, I smiled. "This screams Mitchell Parker."

I made my way down the hall and took the right turn that led to either the guest room on the left, or the office on the right.

"Which way do I go?" I asked myself. "Right. Office."

I smiled at the large desk. I instantly fell into a fantasy of Mitchell taking me from behind as I laid across the massive oak desk. The things I wanted Mitchell to teach me. I closed my eyes and squeezed my legs together.

Ugh, stop this Corina.

After pushing my naughty daydream away, I glanced around the office. Everything was neat and in its place. Not really what I was expecting, but then again, why not? Mitchell was a cop; he was a responsible kind of guy, except when it came to my heart.

My eyes lifted to the bookcase behind the desk. Mystery books. I let out a chuckle while I made my way over to them.

"Let's see, James Patterson, John Grisham, Agatha Christie... nice pick there." I bent down to read the others. "Patricia Cornwell, David Baldacci, Frank Peretti." Reaching for the Peretti book, I stood up and looked at the title. *This Present Darkness.*

"It's a great book. You should read it."

I jumped and let out a small scream. Spinning, I looked at Mitchell. "You scared me."

He grinned. "Sorry, I didn't mean to. Frank Peretti is an amazing writer. Christian mystery."

"I'll have to read it."

"Are you ready to go?"

Glancing down, I said, "Um, no. I need to get the bags Amelia brought."

"I already did. They're in your room. I'll give you a few minutes to get ready while I run down to Lilly's. Want a breakfast taco?"

I couldn't help the smile that tugged at my mouth. *I knew he didn't cook!*

"That would be great. Just a bacon and egg. I'll meet you down there?"

He nodded. "I've left you a house key on the dresser in your room. Just lock the door when you leave."

I watched Mitchell retreat. Letting out the breath I hadn't noticed I was holding, I made my way into the guest room, the book still clutched in my arms. It wasn't lost on me that Mitchell referred to it as *my* room. Once I found out how long it would take to get my house back, I would make the decision on what to do.

After finding something to wear from the clothes Amelia had brought, I washed my face, applied a small bit of make-up and pulled my hair into a pony. I slipped on my sandals I had worn last night and made my way downstairs.

"Dang it! The key!"

Dashing back into the room, I grabbed the key. My phone was sitting on the dresser, as well. Fully charged, thanks to Mitchell finding an extra charger for me last night. I hit the home button and saw I had a text from Lane.

I chewed on my lip for a few seconds before heading out of the room, leaving behind the phone and the unread text.

The drive to the vet's office was relatively quiet, which left me wallowing in my own silence. I had nothing to do but think. And, boy, did I think.

Why was Mitchell being so nice? What did he hope to gain? How did he get to the fire so quickly last night? That last one had kept me awake all night.

"How did you get to the fire so quickly?" I asked.

He didn't bother to look at me. "I heard it over the radio. As soon as they said your address, I knew it was your place and I ran to my truck and raced over there."

"Oh."

Wringing my hands, I took in a deep breath and exhaled. "Why are you helping me? Why are you doing this, Mitchell?"

Before I knew it, the truck was pulling into the St. Andrews Catholic Church parking lot. Mitchell put the truck in park and turned to me. "The other night, I wasn't trying to stop because I didn't want to be with you."

I narrowed my eyes at him. "You said—"

"Wait. Let me talk, damn it."

My mouth snapped shut.

Closing his eyes, Mitchell shook his head, took in a deep breath, and blew it out.

"I wanted to talk to you, I didn't want to just fuck you against my brother's damn office door. Well, I did, but I wanted to talk to you first. Tell you I was sorry for what I did. I haven't been able to stop thinking about you since our night together. It takes every ounce of strength I have not to pull you into my arms and kiss the living hell out of you every time I see you. I've been fighting my feelings and I'm tired of it."

My heart was pounding so hard I had to place my hand over it. "Why did you leave that morning and ignore me?" I asked, barely above a whisper.

His eyes looked sad. "I was scared."

"You were scared?"

"Yes. I'd never spent the night with a woman before. Let alone felt the things I was feeling for you."

I stared at him, trying to process his words. "So, you decided the best thing to do was to ignore them? It didn't bother you, at the time, that I started dating your brother?"

"Of course it bothered me! Drove me fucking crazy."

"Yet you did nothing. Why?"

He faced the windshield, running his hand through his beautiful brown hair. He sighed. "I don't know why, Corina. Like I don't know why I do some of the shit I do do when it comes to you. When I'm around you, I feel twisted inside, and I don't know which way is up or down. I was confused, things happened too fast, and I didn't have the balls to admit how I was feeling. I fucked up."

The urge to crawl onto his lap was overwhelming. I had to dig my fingernails into my hands to stop myself.

I wanted Mitchell Parker. There was no denying it. And I could tell by the way he looked at me that he wanted me as well.

Turning away, I stared out the passenger window as he pulled out of the parking lot. An evil smile grew over my face as my plan unfolded before my eyes. I was not going to let him simply walk into my life or capture my heart again like nothing had happened.

Oh. No.

Mitchell Parker was going to have to fight his way back in, and I was *not* going to make it easy. Or at least that was my plan. When it came to this man, my heart seemed to win out over my head.

"I'm sorry I make you uncomfortable, Mitch."

He parked in front of the vet clinic.

"I never said I was uncomfortable around you. It's the opposite, Corina."

"What do you want me to say? 'Oh okay, yay! Let's go back to your place and have sex'?"

He grinned, a sexy smirk as he looked me up and down. "No, I don't expect that at all. I wouldn't argue if you wanted to do that…but no, I don't expect it."

I searched his face. "Then what do you expect?"

"To win your heart."

I let out a gruff laugh and looked away to catch my breath and calm my racing heart. "Do you have any idea how hard I've tried to get over you, Mitchell? I finally decided to push you out of my heart and move on. If you think you can simply smile at me and say something sweet, rescue my cat, give me a place to stay, and think I'm going to back down, then you've got another thing coming."

His grin grew into a wide smile. "Has anyone ever told you that you're sexy as hell when you get pissed off?"

My jaw dropped. "You are unbelievable, do you know that?"

"I do know it, and you find it cute. I see it in your eyes."

I couldn't help the smile that spread across my face. Mitchell Parker was good at this game, but I intended on being better. He just had no idea how much harder I could play.

CHAPTER 9

Corina

We walked into Dr. Harris's office, and I smiled when I saw Milo sitting on the counter at the front desk. "Looks like he made himself at home," I said.

The girl behind the desk jumped up. "He's a sweetheart! I fell in love with this cat."

Milo did his little bark meow that was special to him. I scooped him up into my arms. "I'm so glad you're okay." Snuggling under my chin, Milo purred.

"So, you're going to be okay with the cat at your place, Mitchell?" the girl asked.

My eyes snapped up to her.

"News really travels fast," Mitchell said with a slight chuckle.

With a shrug, the girl winked. "Small town, big mouths. Lilly told me at breakfast this morning."

Standing there with a stunned expression, I got my crap together and cleared my throat. "There is nothing between Mitchell and me except friendship. That's all."

The girl grinned before focusing back on Mitchell. "Does this mean you need a date for the Pecan Street Honky Tonk?"

Mitchell looked at the receptionist, then me. "Sorry, Julie. I'm going with someone else."

I made a mental note of her name. I was positive her disappointed face matched mine. How could he say all that to me in the car, only to have a date to one of Oak Springs' biggest summer events?

"Bummer, who's the lucky girl?" she asked.

"Corina."

If I had turned my head faster, I would have broken it.

"Me?"

Mitchell laughed. "Yeah, Paxton said you didn't get to see it last year and asked me to make sure you went this year, so, yeah, I guess you're my date to the Pecan Street Honky Tonk."

I didn't know whether to be excited or pissed that he would assume I'd go with him. I wanted to tell him I already had a date, but if I said it now, that would leave it open for Julie to go with him.

Oh, no. I needed to play this right.

"How much do I owe you, Dr. Harris?" I asked, changing the subject.

"Nothing. It was my pleasure to take care of the little guy."

The kindness of the people in this town never ceased to amaze me. You wouldn't get this from a vet back in Chicago.

"Thank you so very much. I truly appreciate it." I extended my hand to the vet.

"I've put together some items to help get Milo settled," Dr. Harris said, handing two bags to Mitchell.

Tears filled my eyes, but I somehow managed to keep them at bay. "Thank you so much. Your kindness is overwhelming."

The doctor waved it off. "That's what we do in small towns. Take care of each other."

"Well, I certainly appreciate it. Thank you."

Julie brought over a cat carrier and helped me put Milo in. "See ya around, handsome boy!"

I thanked her for all her help and followed Mitchell out the door as a round of goodbyes took place.

Mitchell walked to the passenger door, and I opened it for him to put the bags in, followed by Milo.

"What did Julie mean when she asked if you'd be okay with Milo at your place?"

Mitchell gently put Milo's case in and shut the door. "I'm allergic to cats."

My hand came up to my mouth. "Oh no!"

Leaning closer, Mitchell smiled as he whispered, "Don't worry, I'm sure I can handle a little pussy being at my place for a while."

I felt the heat in my cheeks and the pulse between my legs. Swallowing hard, I kept a straight face, or at least I tried to. "I'm sure Milo's not the first pussy to stay at your place."

His eyes turned dark, and he slowly rolled his tongue over his mouth. I had to press my lips together to keep from moaning. "Nope, you were."

And like that, he was walking around the front of his truck as I let out a breath. My head was spinning from this latest development.

Mitchell had never had a girl stay at his place.

Interesting.

With a quick shake of my head, I got into the truck. I needed to remember the plan.

"By the way, how do you know I don't already have a date to the Pecan Street Honky Tonk?"

Mitchell pulled out into the street and asked, "Do you?"

His eyes met mine for the briefest of moments before he focused on driving. I couldn't do it. I couldn't lie. As much as I wanted to tell him I was going with someone like Lane, I couldn't. "No. But you never know. Someone might ask me."

"What you're saying is, I have to ask you officially, to make it so you won't say yes to anyone else?"

I half shrugged. "I'm not sure I'd want to go with you."

He pulled over and threw his truck in park. "Why not?"

Turning to face him, I answered. "For starters, you broke my heart."

"Are we always going to come back to that?"

"Probably. It's kind of a big thing for me."

His brows pinched. "And? Why else wouldn't you go with me?"

I folded my hands in my lap. "You might have a disease or something."

Mitchell's expression was priceless. "Excuse me?"

"You know, from all the women you sleep around with."

He narrowed his eyes. "You weren't so worried about that when we fucked practically everywhere in your house."

I pointed to him. "You're crass."

"You like it."

"I do not."

"You do."

Shaking my head, I emphasized each word. "I do not."

Mitchell stared at me hard for a minute. "When I was making love to you and I whispered how I loved that your pussy squeezed my cock, and you came, you didn't like that?"

Oh. Dear. God. He's gonna play dirty, huh? I've underestimated his game-playing skills. Well, two can play at that game.

"*That* I liked. A lot." I paused for a second and added, "I wonder if Lane's a dirty talker."

Mitchell's face went white.

Score one for me.

His reaction went one step further; a step I wasn't expecting, and it had me regretting my outburst. He turned away, put the truck in drive, and pulled back out onto the street. Not a single word was spoken until we got back to his place.

I sat on the sofa, trying to concentrate on the paperwork the insurance company wanted me to fill out after my meeting with the adjuster. Mitchell hadn't said a word, and I knew my little stunt earlier had gone too far. I wanted him to hurt like he'd hurt me, but deep in my heart I knew that I was being cruel.

Blowing out a frustrated breath, I found Milo sleeping in a little ball on the recliner. "Hey, buddy, don't you want to snuggle with me?" My cat stared at me before getting up and turning around. My eyes widened. "Milo!"

"Looks like he's pissed at you."

I jumped at Mitchell's voice. When I looked over, I let my eyes trail over his body. He was wearing a dress shirt, jeans, and cowboy boots. "You look nice."

He smiled. "Thanks."

Watching him walk into the kitchen, I tried not to stare at his perfect behind. *Ugh. Why does everything about him have to be so sexy?*

Milo jumped up and headed into the kitchen. "Hey, buddy, you want something to eat?"

Milo jumped on the counter, something he was never allowed to do at my house, but I guess he thought he would see how far he could get here.

"No way, little dude." Mitchell picked up Milo and set him on the floor. Then sneezed. For some reason, that made my stomach flutter. "Not on the counters, buddy."

I smiled and had to hand it to Milo for trying.

Mitchell pulled out a small can of cat food that I had bought at the store. "Can he have some?"

I kicked off the blanket I'd wrapped up in on the sofa and made my way to the kitchen. "Sure. He loves that stuff more than he likes his crunchy food."

Mitchell glanced at me then fumbled with the cat food. It dropped to the floor, and when Mitchell tried to pick it up, he hit the corner of the counter.

"Ouch!"

"Oh God! Mitchell, are you okay?"

Rushing to him, I pulled his hand away and gasped. "Cheese and crackers, it's swelling and turning black and blue already."

"Yeah, I hit it hard."

"Do you feel dizzy or sick to your stomach?"

"No, just a massive fucking headache."

I grabbed a towel and filled it with ice. "Here. Put this on the corner of your eye and go sit down."

"It's alright. I'll be fine."

With a tilt of my head, I glared at him. "You are not alright. You hit the corner of your eye, hard. It's swelling as I speak."

He touched it and winced.

Pushing the ice toward him, I said, "See, I told you." Mitchell took the ice and pressed it against his eye. "Now you can have an interesting story to tell the guys at work."

"Shit, I'm not telling them I hit my head on my own counter trying to get cat food."

I peeled the lid of the cat food back and dumped it in Milo's dish. One quick pet from me, and Milo was in heaven.

"What even happened? You started fumbling the cat container in your hand like you were playing hot potato."

His eyes scanned my body. One quick peek at myself, and I knew why. I was wearing shorter-than-all-get-out shorts and a super tight tank top. I was a little more blessed in the chest area than Amelia. Most of her tops were too small.

"I need to go clothes shopping. With the insurance lady taking longer than I thought, Amelia and I decided to go into San Antonio tomorrow."

The only thing Mitchell did was nod.

"Sorry," I said.

He shook his head. "You don't have to apologize for being drop-dead gorgeous, Corina."

I couldn't help the grin that moved across my face or the heat that flushed my cheeks.

"You look pretty good yourself," I said. "Where are you off to?"

"Dinner."

My stomach twisted when he didn't say who he was meeting. "Well, enjoy your evening."

Mitchell opened his mouth to say something, but his cell phone rang.

"This is Mitch."

He turned away, a clear hint he wanted privacy. I headed back into the living room.

A date. He must be going on a date. Darn it. I went too far with the Lane comment.

"No, I don't mind if she comes to dinner."

Two women? He's going out with two women! Ugh. Asshole.

I got off the sofa and headed to the guest room. I hadn't even bothered to check my phone all day. Picking it up off of the dresser, I read Lane's text from earlier.

Lane: *Hey, next weekend is the Pecan Street Honky Tonk, you free to go?*

I rolled my eyes. Crap! Mitchell had never officially asked me.

I decided to deal with that later as I tossed my phone onto the queen-size bed. One quick glance around the room, and I wanted to cry. I was living with a man I was secretly in love with—but pretending not to be in love with—and it was slowly pulling me apart.

Admitting I was in love with Mitchell was nothing new. I had admitted it to Tripp—told him I was in love with a man whom I'd spent one amazing night with. Who'd kissed me goodbye the next morning and never looked back.

How stupid am I?

I jumped up and headed to the closet of clothes I had hung up earlier. Paxton had thrown in some of her clothes, and one of them was a little black dress that would be perfect for tonight. If Mitchell was going out on a date, I'd go out on one too. Although, I had no idea who my date was gonna be.

My phone buzzed on the bed. Glancing down, I saw Paxton's name.

"Hello?"

"Hey, has your day gotten any better?"

I wanted to laugh. "No. It has gotten worse."

"I'm sorry. Listen, really quick, will you do me a favor and tell Mitchell that Steed forgot his phone, and he and Chloe just left to meet him for dinner. Can he ask Steed to pick up milk on the way home? I tried calling him, but got his voicemail."

"Wait. What?"

"Wait what, why?"

My brows pulled together as I dropped onto the bed. "Huh?"

"What are we talking about, Corina?"

"You said Steed and Chloe are meeting Mitchell for dinner?"

"Yeah, Melanie and John too. They wanted to talk to Steed and Mitchell about a birthday party for them."

"A party?"

Paxton chuckled. "Yeah, Chloe is insisting on throwing them a birthday party for their twenty-ninth birthday together since they're twins. We tried to tell her thirty would be better, but she wants to be different."

I giggled. "That's so cute."

"Not if you heard what she wants to have Patches do."

Covering my mouth, I laughed. "Let me see if Mitchell's still here, and I'll let him know."

"Thanks! Hey, got to run. Gage is crying."

"Okay, talk soon."

"Kay, bye and love you!"

The line went dead before I could respond. I walked into the living room to find Mitchell standing on the terrace, still holding ice on his eye. I tapped on the glass door, and he looked my way. "Steed doesn't have his phone and Paxton asked if you could tell him to pick up milk on the way home."

He nodded. "Sure."

It was clear Mitchell was still hurt about the whole Lane comment. If we were going to be living together for a few weeks, I needed to play nice. "I'm sorry for what I said earlier. I was trying to hurt you, and I think I went a little far."

Not bothering to look at me, Mitchell replied, "Not sure what you're talking about. Everything's fine."

Sitting next to him, I let out a sigh. "I'm talking about when I wondered out loud if Lane was a dirty talker."

He tossed the ice on the coffee table. "No worries. If you want to date a douche like him, have at it. Who am I to stop you, right?"

"How can you call him a douche when you had a one-night stand with me and never even called me again? It took you months to even look at me, Mitch!"

"That's different. I care about you."

I laughed. "You *care* about me? Well, if this is you caring about me, I think I'll pass. I'd hate to see what you loving me would be like."

His whole body slumped, and I wished I could take back my last comment. This was never going to work. I was fooling myself.

Again.

CHAPTER 10

Corina

Mitchell stared at me for the longest time. He opened his mouth twice to speak, then shut it.

I stood and gazed down at him. "This isn't going to work. Us living together like this. I'll start looking for a place tomorrow."

Not saying a word, he got up and walked back into his place.

I followed him, my hands shaking as I grew angrier by the second. "That's it? You're going to let me move out?"

Mitchell reached for his keys, then turned to me. "I can't force you to stay here, Corina. If you're unhappy, then yes, you should leave. Do I want you to? No, I don't. I know I fucked up, but if you're going to throw it in my face every goddamn chance you get, then you're right, this won't work."

He headed to the stairs that led down to his front door. My heart raced, and I knew I couldn't leave it like this. Closing my eyes, I called out to him. "Mitch! You never asked me to the Pecan Street Honky Tonk."

Stopping, he looked back up at me. "What?"

I swallowed hard and took in a quick breath. "The dance, you never asked me. And well, Lane asked me."

Sadness swept over his face. "What did you tell him?"

Wringing my hands together, I answered, "I haven't responded...yet. I was waiting for you."

Mitchell rushed back up the steps and stopped in front of me. I don't think I'd ever felt my stomach dip like it did when he raced toward me. He cupped my face and leaned in. My chest rose and fell with each breath as I waited for him to speak. His touch sent a flurry of butterflies through my chest.

"Corina, will you go with me to the street dance next weekend?"

My teeth sank into my lip, and I watched as his eyes filled with lust.

"Yes." I smiled and added, "But only as friends."

The corner of his mouth rose into a sexy smirk. God, how I loved that smile of his. "It's a date, then."

"As friends," I added.

He leaned down and pressed his lips to mine. Before I could even process his lips, they were gone and he was stepping back. "I'll take it. For now."

Turning on the heel of his boot, he headed down the steps. Once I heard the door shut, my fingers slid across my tingling lips, and I couldn't help the huge smile that formed.

I flopped down on the sofa and dropped my head back as I stared up at the ceiling. My emotions were everywhere. I was still angry at Mitchell, but I could feel the wall slowly beginning to fall. Milo jumped up next to me and meowed.

"Shut up. I know I said I was mad at him and I am."

Milo added more to the conversation with one of his bark meows.

Lifting my head, I stared at him. "Keep your thoughts to yourself, buddy. I know what I'm doing. I think. Besides, you're a traitor."

Milo tilted his head and stared at me with his blue eyes. "That's right. I saw you rubbing all up against his leg."

He looked away.

"And the guilty shall prove they are guilty by avoiding eye contact!"

When he jumped off the sofa, I let out a chuckle. *Goodness, I'm talking to my cat.*

My cell rang, and I quickly ran into the guest room to get my phone.

"H-hello?"

"Please tell me you're out of breath because you and my brother got your shit figured out and did the dirty deed…again."

Laughing, I shook my head and laid back on the bed. "Nope, sorry to disappoint you, Waylynn. I'm still angry with him."

She sighed. "Well, one of these days he'll get tired of using his hand, and you'll get tired of using a dildo, and y'all will bump uglies like you did all those months ago."

I shook my head to erase the image that had appeared. Not because it was something that I didn't like, quite the opposite. It was an image I could obsess over.

"How do you come up with this stuff?" I asked.

"You've never heard that before?"

"No!" I replied with a chuckle.

"Jesus, you're more innocent than I thought. Put on that little black dress I saw Paxton slip into the bag. We're going out."

"We are?"

"I've had a hellish week, and yours has been even worse. We are going to dinner, getting halfway to drunk, then going to Cord's Place tonight. It's karaoke night, and we are going to sing and drink our sorrows away."

"Yikes, what happened?"

Waylynn sighed. "The damn city won't approve my application for the dance studio because old lady Hopkins thinks I'm going to be doing something inappropriate on the side."

"Why does she think that?"

The phone went silent before Waylynn said, "It might be because she walked in on Jonathon and me releasing a bit of pent-up energy."

Oh, no.

"Waylynn, you weren't."

She laughed. "Hell yes, we were, and let me tell you, it was the best screw I'd ever had. Probably because he's younger and the man knows how to use his tools…if you know what I mean."

"Eww! Oh, my gosh I don't want to know that!"

Waylynn let out an evil laugh. "Come on, Corina. If you go out, then that pansy ass sister of mine will go. Right now she's probably riding her cowboy and having a good evening. I want a good evening, too."

I ignored her comment about Amelia and Wade and stared at the dress already on the bed. "Fine. I'll go, but only because I really need the night out."

"Yay! I'll meet you at Marco's."

My stomach rumbled. "I love that little restaurant."

"Yeah, it's one of my favorites. Remember, dress *sexy.*"

Walking into Marco's, I took a deep breath. "It smells so good in here."

Waylynn nodded and looked around like she was searching for someone.

"Are we meeting Amelia here?" I asked.

She stopped and turned to me. "What? No, she's going to meet us at Cord's Place."

"Who are you looking for, then?"

"Huh? No one."

I glared. She was lying. Waylynn was not a good liar. It was one of the first things I had learned about her.

The owner, Marco, approached us. "Good evening, Ms. Parker, Ms. Miller. Table for two?"

I waited for Waylynn to answer. "Um. Ah."

"Yes," I said with a smile. "Table for two."

Marco grabbed two menus and headed into the restaurant. Waylynn was still looking around. "Look! My parents!"

My stomach dropped when I glanced at where she was pointing. The first person I saw was Mitchell.

"Marco, we'll be joining my folks," Waylynn said.

Grabbing my hand, she dragged me behind her. "Waylynn, did you set this up?" I asked as we made our way to the table that oh-so-conveniently had two empty seats. The moment Melanie saw us, she smiled ear to ear.

"You and your mother set this up, didn't you?" I whispered.

"I have no idea what you're talking about," Waylynn said with an evil grin. The same evil grin that her mother wore. "Hey! Fancy meeting y'all here."

"Corina!" Chloe cried out.

With a smile, I leaned down and kissed Chloe on the forehead. "Hello, sweet pea. How are you?"

"Granddaddy is promising me a new goat!"

"Patches will have a friend. How fun!"

John, Steed, and Mitchell all stood as Waylynn and I took our seats.

"Steed, move down one so that Corina can sit next to Chloe," Melanie said.

Doing as his mother asked, Steed moved, and I went to sit between him and his daughter.

"NO!" Melanie and Waylynn cried out.

"Chloe, honey, slide over so you stay next to your daddy," Waylynn said. "I want to sit across from you."

I was positive I was shooting daggers at both Waylynn and Melanie.

Once everyone had moved, I took my seat. The men sat, and I couldn't help but chance a look at Mitchell. He was, of course, smiling as his blue eyes met mine.

"Fancy meeting you here," he said.

With a grin, I focused on Waylynn. I was trying hard not to give her a look that said I was going to kill her later.

"We just ordered," Melanie said.

Steed laughed. "And now I know why you kept stalling, Mom."

Melanie cleared her throat and took a drink of water. "I have no idea what you mean, Steed."

"Uh-huh."

John picked up his glass of wine and took a drink. "Boys, there are some things in life you just accept. One of those things is women butting into other folks' business."

Melanie hit John on the arm. "You hush up, John Parker. There is no harm in giving two people a little push."

I was positive my eyes grew wide at that. "Are you talking about me and Mitchell?" I had no idea why I asked that out loud.

"If the shoe fits," Waylynn added.

My body caught fire as Mitchell's leg pressed against mine. It suddenly got really hot in Marco's.

"First off, y'all both need to keep your noses out of my business. And Corina's." Mitchell reached for my hand. "We're friends, isn't that right, Corina?"

Dizzy with desire, I tried to ignore his leg. His hand on mine. I tried not to focus on the way his eyes lingered on my lips, like he wanted to kiss me again.

His *kiss*. My lips tingled. The kiss he had given me on the stairs was so simple, yet it had nearly knocked me off my feet.

For Pete's sake, Corina! It was a quick peck, not even a kiss.

Mitchell leaned in and asked in a hushed voice, "Are you okay?"

His thumb swept over the top of my hand, leaving a burning path.

Pulling my eyes off him, I glanced around the table. Melanie and Waylynn were leaning in, trying to hear my response. Chloe giggled. "Why is everyone staring at Corina?"

I swallowed hard and pulled my hand away from Mitchell. "Excuse me, I need to use the ladies' room."

When I stood, John, Steed, and Mitchell all got up from their chairs. *Oh, Lord. Why do they have to be so chivalrous?*

Quickly making my way through the restaurant, I rushed into the ladies' room. I placed my hands on the sink and pulled in a few deep breaths.

"Corina?"

I spun around. The same girl I'd seen Mitchell with at Cord's bar was standing in front of me. I was pretty sure I'd heard Amelia say her name was Cassidy.

"I'm sorry. Do we know each other?" I asked with a confused expression.

She smirked. "We have a common interest."

My stomach dropped. "We do?"

"Yes. Mitchell Parker. Rumor has it you're living with him now."

The room started to spin. *Oh God. He's been sleeping with this girl, and now she thinks I'm a threat.*

"My house caught fire. Mitchell was nice enough to let me crash at his place until I can find other arrangements."

She stared at me with nothing but hate in her eyes.

The bathroom door flew open, and Mitchell was standing there. "What in the fuck do you think you're doing?"

I took a few steps back, not sure who he was talking to.

"Don't get your jockstrap in a twist, Mitchell. I only wanted to meet my competition."

"Competition?" I asked, my eyes darting between the two of them.

Mitchell took her by her elbow and led her to the door. "Get out and stay the fuck away from Corina, do you understand me?"

"Is she the reason we haven't had sex in so long?" Cassidy asked.

Covering my mouth, I tried to hold back a gag.

"What in the hell are you talking about?" Mitchell asked.

"You bring me to your place the other day to have sex, then you have her move in? What game are you playing?"

I turned around. My head dropped as I tried to take in one breath after another. Mitchell had lied. He'd said he'd never had a girl in his place.

He lied.

This was not happening. Not with his parents sitting on the other side of the door. "Get. Out. Now." With my eyes closed, I tried to get ahold of my emotions. I would not show weakness.

When his hands touched me, I jumped.

"Corina."

"You lied to me."

"What?"

Spinning to face him, I repeated myself. "You lied when you said I was the only woman to stay at your place. You had her in your bed."

"No, I didn't! She was in my place for all of ten minutes."

My lower lip trembled, and it made me so mad. I didn't want Mitchell Parker thinking he had this power over me. His words rattled my brain as I let them settle. "What?"

"I never slept with her, or anyone else, at my place. I've never had a woman in my bed, Corina."

Lifting my chin and trying not to let his words affect me, I asked, "Why not?"

Mitchell blinked. "I don't know how to explain that."

My arms folded over my chest. "Now would be as good a time as any for you to try."

He stared for the longest time before swallowing hard. "I don't know. I've never met a woman I felt like I wanted to share a bed with. Until I met you."

An instant heat rushed over my body.

"W-what did you say?"

"You're the only woman I've ever spent the night with, Corina. The feelings I have for you are new. I didn't know how to deal with them, and I'm trying so fucking hard not to mess up again."

My heart raced, and I was left breathless. A part of me wanted to jump into his arms and kiss him. Tell him how I wanted him, how much I needed to be with him again. The idea of getting lost in his kiss was almost overwhelming.

But I didn't.

Mitchell Parker was going to know that I wasn't another girl willing to follow him around any time he smiled at me. Dragging in a deep breath, I took a step closer. His entire body seemed to quiver as I grew closer. The hint that I had such a strong effect on him did crazy things to my heart.

In a soft whisper, I asked, "Would you let me share your bed, Mitchell?"

His eyes lit up and my stomach fluttered. I had my answer before he even opened his mouth. His hand pushed a piece of loose hair behind my ear. "You're the only woman I want in my bed, Corina."

I lifted on my toes, and Mitchell leaned down, our lips inches apart.

"Nice to know," I said. "Let me get back to you on that one." Dropping down, I walked around him and left him alone in the women's restroom.

I couldn't hide the smile on my face as I walked back to the table.

Corina one.

Mitchell zero.

CHAPTER 11

Mitchell

What in the fuck just happened?

I held my chest and tried to get it to settle down, while also trying to figure out what in the hell Corina just did to me.

The bathroom door opened and an older woman walked in. She let out a gasp and looked around.

"I'm...I'm sorry," I said. "I walked into the wrong restroom."

She gave me a polite smile and stepped out of my way, allowing me to retreat. I was pretty sure that was Mrs. Hathaway, my English teacher in twelfth grade.

By the time I made it back to the table, I was twisted completely around inside. Corina Miller was going to be the death of me.

As I sat down, Corina smiled. "You get lost?"

"Something like that."

Her smile dropped for a moment before it returned.

"Well, let's get back to the party planning!" my mother said with a light clap of her hands. Everyone soon got lost in the plans. I replied every now and then. My head was still spinning, and I couldn't concentrate. Especially with Corina sitting next to me. Every now and then our legs would touch, or I'd get a glimpse of her perfect tits in that black dress.

"Mitchell? Mitchell!"

Lifting my eyes, I looked at my mother. "Yeah?"

"Does that sound good to you?"

I had no damn clue what she was asking me. "Does what sound good?"

Her head shifted to the side. "Have you even been listening?"

"If the boy is smart, he learned the art of tuning out long ago," my father said with a chuckle.

"Sorry, Mom. My mind was somewhere else."

Her eyes seemed to sympathize. She probably thought the distraction was a case I was working on. In a way...it was.

Operation Win Corina's Heart.

"We're going to have the party at our house," Mom said. "Chloe wants it to be Halloween themed."

With a smile, I replied, "Wouldn't it be easier to just have a Halloween party?"

"That's what I said!" Steed added.

"No! Daddy, please!"

Chloe stared up at Steed with those blue eyes, and I knew he was toast.

"I think a Halloween birthday party sounds perfect!" I said, saving my brother the embarrassment of caving to his daughter, yet again.

Chloe jumped up. "Yay! I'm so happy!"

The rest of dinner was filled with two different conversations. The girls talked about Corina's ideas for remodeling her house, and I talked to Steed and my father about the embezzlement case that was being investigated, involving Dad's former best friend. I had to bring in another Texas Ranger due to the fact that it was my father's business that the money had been stolen from. This case had been going on for quite a while and we were finding out that the embezzling went deeper than anyone could have imagined.

"Uncle Mitchell, can I spend the night at your house?" Chloe asked out of the blue.

"Of course you can, squirt."

Her sweet little face lit up. "Yay! We can have a *Frozen* party."

I smiled. "That sounds good."

"Well, Corina and I are going to head out," Waylynn said.

"Where are you girls headed?" my mother asked.

"Cord's Place. We both need a night out on the town."

My eyes drifted over Corina. She looked hot as hell and for a brief second I wished I hadn't said Chloe could spend the night. I wanted to go and make sure no asshole put his hands on Corina.

"Well, be careful girls," Mom said. "Don't drink and drive!"

Waylynn said, "Trust me, Mom. I would never do that. Besides, I don't want my own brother arresting me!"

"That might be kind of fun!" I said with a laugh.

"Yeah, you would think that. Good thing you're off tonight."

"It was so wonderful seeing you again, John and Melanie," Corina said with a beautiful smile. "Chloe, I'll see you later?"

Chloe smiled. "Okay! Bye, Aunt Corina." She had no idea Corina was living at my place. I couldn't help but notice how Corina's eyes lit up when she talked to Chloe. I wondered if she'd want to have kids right away or wait.

I choked when I realized where my thoughts had taken me.

"You okay, Mitchell?" my father asked.

With what must have been a look of horror, I nodded. "Yep. Sorry."

Steed stared as if he knew where my thoughts had been.

"What are you staring at?" I asked sharply.

A slow smile built as he said, "Nothin' at all."

I shot him a dirty look. "Good!"

"Night, y'all," Waylynn said.

Jumping up, I reached for Corina's arm. "You'll call me if y'all need a ride home, right?"

She stared blankly. I couldn't read her at all. *What in the hell?* My job was all about being able to read people, and this woman had me all kinds of messed up.

"I'm sure we'll be fine."

Letting out a frustrated sigh, I sat back down before she spoke. "If we need you, I'll call, Mitchell. Always."

Giving her my best smile, I replied, "Thank you. Y'all have fun and be safe."

Waylynn walked past me. "Now where would the fun be in that?"

I watched as my sister, and the woman who was slowly driving me insane, walked out of Marco's.

"They'll be fine, Mitchell," Dad said. "Cord will keep an eye on them."

Nodding, I focused on my father. "I know. Trevor's working tonight. I know he'll call me if he thinks I need to come get them." I turned to Chloe. "Hey, how about I follow y'all home and you pack an overnight bag?"

She fist-pumped. "Come on, Daddy! Let's go so I can have my princess party with Uncle Mitchell."

My smile dropped. "Princess party? I thought we were watching *Frozen?*"

Chloe turned to me and shook her head. "Oh, Uncle Mitchell. You're so funny."

Snapping my head to my parents, I asked, "What did I say that was funny?"

They both attempted to hide their smiles and failed miserably.

"You sure you don't mind her spending the night, Mitchell?" Paxton asked as she handed me Chloe's bag.

"No, not at all. I never get tired of spending time with her. It'll be fun."

Chloe came walking into the kitchen. "Let's go get Patches!"

"Patches?" I asked as I looked back at Steed and Paxton.

"Pumpkin, Patches can't spend the night with you. Uncle Mitchell lives in the city, remember?"

"But he has a yard. It's big enough for Patches."

I laughed. "Patches needs more space than my yard, squirt."

"Ah, dang. That's okay, we'll still have fun without Patches."

"Gee, I hope so! I'd hate to think the goat was more fun than me!"

Chloe giggled and took my hand. My heart dropped and something strange hit me right in the middle of my chest. I ignored it.

I glanced at our hands then back up to Steed. He was wearing the same damn smile that he'd had at Marco's earlier.

"What?" I asked.

He shrugged. "I think you're starting to want it."

I pinched my brows.

"Want what?" Paxton asked.

"Yeah, what do you want, Uncle Mitchell? A goat? A horse? Oh, I know, a giraffe? Cuz I really wanted one of those too."

I chuckled. "No, kiddo. I don't want any of those things."

"What about a kid?" Steed asked as I shot him a dirty look.

Chloe gasped. "You want a baby goat?"

Meeting the big blue eyes looking up at me, I shook my head. "Don't listen to your father, Chloe. He's delusional."

We started toward the door. "What does that mean?"

"It means your dad thinks he knows the truth, and he is far from it."

"I thought Daddy was always right?"

"I am," Steed said.

"He isn't," Paxton and I both said at the same time. Laughing, I kissed her goodbye on the cheek. "I always knew you were secretly on my side."

She bent down to face Chloe. "You have fun and listen to Uncle Mitchell, okay?"

Chloe nodded. "I will, Mommy. Kiss Gage for me, okay?"

"Of course I will. I love you, Chloe Cat."

"I love you too! Love you, Daddy."

Steed squatted down and pulled Chloe in for a hug. "I know Uncle Mitchell looks like me, but remember, Daddy is smarter, more handsome, and a better singer."

Covering her mouth, Chloe chuckled. "Oh, Daddy. You are *not* a good singer!"

Everyone laughed as I guided Chloe out of the house and to my truck.

"Let me know what time you want her home!" I called out. I lifted Chloe into the backseat and buckled her in. Steed had already put Chloe's booster seat into the truck for me along with a checklist of other Chloe-related things. I rolled my eyes and set it in the seat next to Chloe. It wasn't like it was my first time having my niece over.

"You ready to get our *Frozen* on?" I asked.

She nodded her head. "Let's do this!"

When I walked around my truck, I glanced over at my brother. He smiled and called out, "I'm right and you know it!"

"Delusional. That's all you are."

As I slipped into the truck, I turned back to see my precious niece, and I knew in that moment who the delusional one was.

Me.

CHAPTER 12

Mitchell

Chloe and I spun around the room as we belted out the lyrics to the songs from *Frozen*.

"Sing it louder, Uncle Mitchell!"

I jumped onto the ottoman, spread my arms, and sang like I never had before. The Elsa braid I had clipped in my hair swung around and hit me square in the face. Chloe had a huge smile as she sang with me. She handed me my "magic wand" and we both made pretend ice everywhere we pointed.

"This is the best night ever!" Chloe cried out. I had to admit, it had my heart soaring to know she was having fun.

Hopping to the ground, I sang the lyrics while I spun around and came to a stop.

"Why did you stop singing, Uncle Mitchell?" Chloe asked.

Corina stood with her hand over her mouth, trying not to completely lose it laughing.

When I pointed, Chloe screamed so loud I was sure my eardrums would burst.

"Aunt Corina! What are you doing here?"

Corina bent down and caught Chloe as she jumped into her arms. "I live here."

"Whaaat?" Chloe asked dramatically.

"She is indeed a Parker woman," I said as I rolled my eyes, and Corina laughed.

"My house caught on fire, and your Uncle Mitchell was nice enough to let me stay here for a bit."

Setting Chloe down, Corina grinned. We watched Chloe make her way over to the TV. Picking up the remote, Chloe hit pause. Spinning around, she glanced between the two of us.

"So, are y'all boyfriend and girlfriend?"

I don't know what surprised me more—hearing my little niece say y'all for the first time, or the fact that she totally called us out.

"No, but I like Corina. A lot."

I could feel Corina's eyes pinning me.

"Oh!" Chloe squealed. "Aunt Corina, do you like Uncle Mitchell?"

Facing her, I waited for her answer. I cocked my head to the side and gave her a shit-eating grin. If looks could kill, I'd have been flat on the ground.

"Well, it's complicated," Corina said.

"Why?" Chloe asked.

Corina glanced between the two of us. "It's hard to explain, Chloe."

My sweet little niece shrugged and gave Corina a confused look. "I don't see why. You either like him or you don't. Like how I like Timmy. I know I like him. So, do you like Uncle Mitchell?"

Kicking her shoes off, Corina sighed. "He's okay."

Chloe looked at me. "That's girl talk for she likes you."

"Chloe!" Corina said with a laugh.

"Come on, Aunt Corina. Dance with us!"

Hitting the play button, Chloe started to sing. Corina peeked at me and waited to see what I would do.

What the hell. She's already seen me, so I might as well have fun with my niece.

I started to sing again. It didn't take Corina long to join in. I don't think I've ever had as much fun as I did dancing and singing with Chloe and Corina. *Thank you, Disney.*

At one point, I picked up Chloe and spun her around. Her foot hit a picture frame, causing it to hit the ground and shatter everywhere.

"Oh no!" Chloe cried out.

"Not a big deal. We can clean that up fast," I said, setting Chloe on the sofa. "Here, squirt. Stay up on the sofa while I get it cleaned. Corina, don't move."

She jumped up next to Chloe. Both girls snuggled on the sofa as I cleaned the broken glass. Every now and then they would whisper and giggle. Each time I looked at them, they stopped.

"Something funny, ladies?"

"Nope. Just girl talk," Corina said with a beautiful smile. I loved seeing her with Chloe. It was clear she loved kids.

She's going to make an amazing mother to our kids.

My eyes widened as I took a few steps back.

Where in the hell did that thought come from? Kids? Our kids? Me with kids? Corina having my kids?

What's wrong?" Corina asked.

My heart pounded, and I felt myself sweating.

Corina stood, a concerned look on her face. "Mitchell, are you okay?"

"I...um..."

"Spit it out, Uncle Mitchell."

My eyes jerked to Chloe. I wanted kids. Holy shit. I wanted kids, and I wanted them with Corina. *Holy fuck.*

Swallowing hard, I turned fast, causing the broom to hit a lamp and knock it to the ground. Both girls screamed out.

"Shit!" I said.

"Hell, shit, fuck!" Chloe cried out.

"Chloe!" Corina and I both said.

I took one step and felt the pain. "Fuck! Fuck! Fuck!"

Chloe decided to put a spin on my outburst by singing everything I said, *Frozen*-style. "Fuck! Fuck! Fuuuuck!"

"Chloe Parker, stop that this second. You know better," Corina said in a firm voice.

"I stepped on glass!" I cried out.

"Come sit down," Corina said. "Give me the broom and let me clean this up."

"Tweezers, I need tweezers! They're in my bathroom! Stat!"

Corina stared at me like I had grown two heads. "Chloe, sweetheart, just stay on the couch. Don't move."

With a nod, my sweet, bad-mouthed niece sank down and reached for her iPad and was soon lost in a story, like nothing had happened.

My foot throbbed as I waited for Corina.

"Here's the tweezers. Let me clean this up before someone else steps on glass."

I worked at getting the glass out of my foot while Corina cleaned. When I glanced up, Chloe was passed out on the sofa.

"I'll vacuum in the morning, but I'm pretty sure I got it all," Corina said. She sat on the ottoman and watched me.

"Shit! I can't reach it with these damn tweezers. They suck! Do you have any better ones?"

Looking at me like I was stupid, she shook her head. "Mine burned up in a house fire."

I held onto my ankle. "Jesus, why is it throbbing?"

"Because you have glass in it?"

Letting out a frustrated groan, I dropped against the chair. "I need better tweezers."

With a quick glance at her watch, Corina said, "Everything is closed. It's after ten."

"Why are you home so early?" I asked.

She half shrugged and looked down at my foot. "I don't know. I wasn't much in the mood for going out, and Waylynn was having enough fun without me pulling her down."

I didn't say anything, even though I wanted to tell her I was glad she came home early.

"What should we do?" I asked.

"I don't know. Do you have any of that black tar stuff your mom puts on everything?"

Shaking my head, I replied, "No. Christ, it's throbbing."

"The glass splinter doesn't look that big. Maybe soak your foot in Epsom salt?"

"I don't have any of that."

Corina sighed.

"There is the ER at the Oak Springs hospital," I said.

She stared at me, her mouth open. "For a tiny piece of glass?"

"It hurts! And I can't get it out. I think it's in there deep. What if it moves into my bloodstream?"

Her lips pressed together, and I knew she was holding back a laugh. "Your bloodstream?"

I rolled my eyes. "It could! I mean…it's possible…ish."

The corner of her mouth twitched as she fought to keep from smiling. "Do you think we need to go to the ER?"

"Well, unless you can figure out a way to get it, I don't know what to do."

"We could go over to Tripp's place. I'm sure he has decent tweezers. Maybe a needle so I can try to get it out."

"You want to poke around for a piece of glass with a needle?! You'll push it in farther."

Corina walked over to me, dropping to her knees. She looked into my eyes. "Mitchell, how in the world did you become a cop if you can't take a piece of glass in your foot?"

Shooting her daggers, I pushed her away. She fell onto her ass and rolled over laughing. "Oh. My. Gosh. I'm sorry! It's just so funny!"

"I'm going to the ER, and I need you to drive because it's in my right foot."

She sat up. "Wait, you're serious. You want to go to the ER?"

"Just get your ass up and get the kid."

Corina looked back at Chloe. "You want me to wake up your niece so that I can take you to the ER for a piece of glass that can honestly wait until morning."

"It's getting deeper!"

She covered her mouth and tried not to laugh. Once she was composed, she held up her hands. "Okay, doesn't Lilly live right around the corner?"

I nodded.

"I can call her, and see if she has tweezers."

Rolling my eyes, I sighed. "Fine. Call her."

"Hey, Mitch?"

I lifted my brows. "Yes?"

A smile covered her face. "You might want to take off Elsa's braid before Lilly comes over."

With a sigh, I pulled the damn thing off my head and tossed it to the floor.

"I can't believe you pushed it farther in."

"You wouldn't stay still, Mitch! Even Lilly said you were acting like a baby."

Turning to face her, I replied, "She did not say that."

With a smirk, Corina replied, "Oh, sorry. She said that to me when you weren't listening."

My eyes widened. "You bitch!"

Corina lost it laughing as she put on the turn signal and pulled into our small town hospital.

"Looks like parking won't be a problem," she said while pulling into the first spot by the ER entrance.

"Ha ha."

I pushed open the car door and got out. I walked on my heel, being careful not to put pressure on the glass.

Corina walked next to me in silence until we got closer to the door. "You need to lean on me." She peeked over. "You know, make it look worse than it really is."

"Shut up! It hurts!"

Her hands covered her mouth for the hundredth time tonight.

As we walked in, Bobby Jo, the nurse who worked the night shift in the ER on the weekends, jumped up.

"Mitchell! What happened? Did you get shot?"

That's when Corina lost it. I don't think I'd ever heard her laugh so much.

"Bobby Jo, this is going to sound crazy, but I've got a piece glass stuck in my foot and I can't get it out."

The nurse stopped walking and stared at me. Then she grinned. "You're kiddin', right?"

Cue Corina's laughter again.

With a long, frustrated groan, I shook my head. "I can't get it with tweezers, and Corina here pushed it in even more."

Bobby Jo's eyes bounced between me and Corina. There was no doubt in my mind she was waiting for one of us to say we were kidding. Finally, she walked back around the desk. "Well, let's get you to fill out some paperwork."

I leaned in closer. "Bobby Jo, is that necessary?"

She gave me a hard look. "It is, Mitchell Parker. If you want to be seen, you've got to fill out the paperwork."

Corina bumped my arm. "You need me to do it? You know, with the pain and all?"

I shot her a go-to-hell look. "I've got it. Thanks."

Ten minutes later I was sitting in the small nurse's station getting my blood pressure and temperature taken. When Bobby Jo held up the name bracelet and asked me if I was Mitchell Parker, I thought for sure Corina was going to pass out from lack of oxygen while she was doubled over laughing.

"Does she really need to be in here?" I asked.

Bobby Jo looked at Corina and smiled. "Yes, I think it's best."

I endured five more minutes of endless questions that had nothing to do with my foot or the glass.

"Okay! Let's get you into a room," Bobby Jo said. "Do you need a wheelchair?"

"I think I can walk fine, thank you."

Once Bobby Jo put us in the room, I pointed to Corina. "Payback is a bitch, my friend."

She opened her mouth to speak, but at the exact moment a doctor walked in—who looked like he was Amelia's age.

"Hello, I'm Dr. Hackerman. So, you've got a piece of glass stuck in your foot?"

I nodded. He put on a pair of gloves and took a look. "Bobby Jo, let's get an X-ray."

"Wait. What?" I asked.

"Don't know how big it is. We need to get a look."

Corina turned her back, but I saw her shoulders bouncing in a rhythmic motion.

"Dr. Lackerman—"

"HACkerman. Dr. Hackerman, is my name."

"To be frank, that's sort of a scary name for a doctor." I laughed, but no one else did. No one but the little blonde traitor sitting in the corner, wiping tears away. "Um, is an X-ray really needed?"

In that moment I realized I wasn't going to win. When they brought the wheelchair in to cart me over to the X-ray machine, I reluctantly got in it.

"Wait! Mitchell, smile through the pain!"

Glancing up, I frowned as Corina snapped a few photos of Bobby Jo taking me to X-ray in the wheelchair.

"I'll make sure they're ready for you, Mitchell," Bobby Jo said as she vanished on the other side of the door that read X-ray.

"If you so much as breathe a word of this to anyone, I will arrest you, Corina!"

Corina pouted. "Oh, come on. You have to admit it's funny."

"It's not funny!"

She took another picture of me. "It really is."

"Whatever feelings I once had for you…they're gone! Vanished."

Her smile slowly faded as she bent down and placed her hands on the arms of the wheelchair. My heart began to beat faster, which made my foot throb more, but having her lips so close to mine kept my mind off the pain.

"That's a shame, Mitchell. I was hoping to share your bed tonight."

I swallowed hard. "You were?"

Her lips brushed lightly over mine as she spoke softly. "I *wasn't*. I thought it might take your mind away from the pain."

The door handle moved, and Corina stepped back. Slowly shaking my head, I stared at her with a hard look. That was twice today she had my cock jumping in my pants.

Bobby Jo interrupted my thoughts. "Ready, Mitchell?"

I pointed to Corina. "Payback! Oh, it's coming!"

With a wiggle of her fingers, she waved to me as I was taken into the X-ray room.

"Payback, Corina Miller! And stop taking pictures!"

CHAPTER 13

Corina

"I like your socks. They're sexy."

Mitchell glanced at the hospital socks. "You laugh, but I actually like these. I think I'm going to keep them."

A small giggle slipped out as I parked my car next to Mitchell's truck.

Mitchell pushed open the car door and got out. "I'm going to owe Lilly because she stayed with Chloe."

"At least we weren't there for more than an hour."

Mitchell groaned and started up the stairs to his place.

"Good thing you've got those anti-slip socks on. So you don't get a splinter in your other foot and land us back in the ER." I needed every ounce of my willpower to say that with a straight face.

He didn't say a word as we climbed the steps and saw Lilly sleeping on the sofa. Chloe was still passed out on the love seat.

Mitchell gently tapped Lilly's shoulder. "Hey, we're back."

Sitting up, she asked, "How big was the glass?"

Mitchell shot me a look that dared me to say something. I forced myself not to laugh.

"It wasn't that big," Mitchell said.

"They couldn't even see it on the X-ray," I quickly added.

Lilly stood. "X-ray? They took an X-ray?" It was clear she was also fighting to keep in her laughter.

"Lil, I owe you big time," Mitchell said. "You want me to walk you back to your place?"

She glanced down to his feet. "You want to put shoes on first?"

Mitchell held his head high. "I actually like these socks."

"What if you step on something else? Two trips to the ER could be costly," Lilly said with a huge smile.

"Fine!" Mitchell went to his room to get shoes.

"Please tell me there was an on-duty cop there tonight," Lilly said.

I shook my head. "Nope. He'd just left."

"Damn. News will get out fast with Bobby Jo there."

I agreed. "I think she was on the phone with someone when we were leaving."

We both busted out laughing. My stomach was going to be sore from the hilarity of this evening.

"Let's go," Mitchell bit out.

Lilly's eyes widened as she followed Mitchell down the steps. "Someone is a grumpy bug."

Once I got my giggling under control, I walked over to Chloe. "Chloe, sweetheart, do you want to sleep in my bed or in Uncle Mitchell's?"

Sleepy blue eyes met mine. "Uncle Mitchell's."

I scooped her up and carried her up the steps to Mitchell's room. It was the only room I hadn't been in yet.

The moment I walked in, I smiled. I knew in an instant Mitchell had his hand in designing this room. It had a masculine feel, with gray-blue walls and a dark gray comforter set. The furniture was huge, yet had a classic look. Everything was clean and neat. Not even a piece of clothing on the floor.

"Totally opposite of me," I whispered.

Lilly must have woken Chloe up to put her pajamas on. I smiled as I set her on the bed and looked at her Disney princess PJs. Pulling the covers back, I lifted Chloe's legs and covered her up.

"Aunt Corina?"

"Yes, sweetheart?"

"Will you lie down with me?"

My heart started beating twice as fast as normal. "You want me to lie down with you? Um, Uncle Mitchell will be back any second."

"Please, Aunt Corina? I had a really bad dream and it scared me. I want to be between you and Uncle Mitchell."

Her little eyes looked so scared, and I didn't have the heart to tell her no.

"Of course. Scoot over, sweetie."

I felt him the moment he walked into the room.

"Uncle Mitchell, I had a bad dream. I need a happy sandwich."

"Oh no, pumpkin. We can't have you scared."

Peeking up, I looked at him. "She asked me to lie down next to her. She wants you on the other side."

He nodded. "Let me get my PJs on."

I realized I had yet to get myself into pajamas. Chloe looked at me and yawned. "Do you have PJs here, Aunt Corina?"

"Um, yes, I do. I'll let Uncle Mitchell get ready for bed first."

Mitchell headed into his bathroom. I couldn't read him at all. Was his heart racing like mine? Was the idea of both of us being in the same bed making him think of the night we'd spent together?

When he walked out of the bathroom, I let my eyes travel over his body. He had on sweats and a T-shirt.

My gosh, he is so handsome.

"I'll, um, be right back, Chloe."

"Hurry, Aunt Corina! There's a monster in the house."

Mitchell sat down on the bed. "I promise you, squirt, there are no monsters."

Chloe chewed on her little lip.

"Uncle Mitchell is a police officer, Chloe. No monsters would dare come in here. You'll be safe with him."

She nodded. "I still would feel better if you laid down with me. I miss Mommy and Daddy."

My heart broke a little. "Why don't you go get ready," Mitchell said to me. "We'll say our prayers."

I swallowed hard. "O-okay. Be right back."

In the guest room, I changed into the pajamas one of the girls had given me. Thank goodness they were modest! A pair of cotton pants with a matching shirt from Victoria's Secret.

After brushing my teeth and washing my face, I headed back to Mitchell's room. If I was lucky, they would both be asleep and I could sneak back down to my room.

I heard Chloe's sweet little voice as I walked up the steps.

Dang it.

When I stepped into the room, Mitchell was lying on his side, singing a song to Chloe.

Boom. There went my ovaries. This man was going to test every ounce of strength I had. Just when I thought I had my emotions in check, he went off and did something like this. Never mind earlier, when I walked in to find him singing and dancing. If he asked me right now to sneak out in the living room and have sex I'd probably do it.

Chloe looked at me, her eyes barely staying open. "I waited for you."

I rushed to the bed and crawled under the covers. Mitchell had a California king-sized bed so there was no chance of even getting near him, and then there was Chloe, my safety buffer.

"Go to sleep now, Chloe." I whispered. "Dream of happy things."

She yawned. "Like what kind of happy things?"

I rolling onto my side, and my eyes met Mitchell's. "Your mommy and daddy. Patches and all the ranch animals. Butterflies and kitty cats."

"Where's Milo?" Chloe asked.

As if on cue, he jumped up and made his way over to Chloe where he flopped down and began purring.

"Keep going," Chloe whispered.

"Flowers in a meadow," I added. "Golden retriever puppies."

Mitchell lifted his brows in question. I shrugged and whispered, "They're my favorite."

He smiled.

Chloe mumbled, so I kept talking. "Princess games, playing in the rain, singing songs, family."

When I heard Chloe breathing heavier, I knew she'd fallen asleep.

Mitchell and I stared at each other for the longest time before a sexy grin spread over his face. "Looks like I got you in my bed tonight after all."

I scrunched my nose up. "I'm only in your bed because your niece asked me to sleep next to her."

He pouted, and my stomach dropped. I'd never grow tired of looking at him. "Is that the only reason?"

My eyes fell to his soft lips. "Well, I also wanted to keep an eye on you. Make sure you didn't need any pain meds in the middle of the night."

The corners of Mitchell's mouth rose into a full smile, and my chest pulled with a familiar ache. "Goodnight, Corina."

I softly whispered, "Goodnight, Mitchell."

I couldn't pull my gaze off of him as he drifted off to sleep. Tears filled my eyes as I let the truth settle in my heart. I was in love with Mitchell Parker, and there was no denying it. This man came rushing into my life like a storm surge. He'd left a permanent mark on my heart that could never be erased. The only problem: could Mitchell love me like I needed him to?

Right before I closed my eyes, Mitchell looked over at me. It was as if we were both silently trying to figure this out. He lifted his arm and laid it across the pillows above Chloe's head. His eyes pleaded as he motioned for my hand. I swallowed hard as I moved closer and laced my fingers with his. It felt like a million bolts of electricity raced through my body. It was clear Mitchell felt the same as he quickly took in a breath at our touch.

When he smiled, I was lost in a world I had imagined a million times in my head.

After a few minutes of gazing into each other's eyes, I let sleep take over.

Rolling over, I took in a deep breath.

"Hmm."

The heavenly smell of Mitchell. My eyes snapped open as I sat up in bed. One quick look around proved I hadn't been dreaming last night. I had slept in Mitchell's bed, with Chloe tucked in between us.

Chloe's laughter rose from downstairs, followed by Mitchell's voice. I pushing the covers off and made my way into Mitchell's bathroom. I splashed my face and was about to leave when I realized this was the perfect opportunity to be a bit nosy.

Chewing on the corner of my lip, I took a look around. The man was a neat freak. I opened the cabinet under his sink to reveal nothing shocking. Cleaning supplies, extra shaving cream, soap, and shampoo. I turned to face the massive shower. I stepped inside and spun around while looking at all the heads. There must have been eight in there.

I closed my eyes and pictured Mitchell making love to me in the shower. A slow smile moved over my face before I shook my head and said, "What are you doing, Corina? Get a grip, for Pete's sake."

Leaving the bathroom, I looked at the side tables next to the massive bed. One peek at the door and I made my way over to the side I'd slept on. "What are you doing, you idiot? You are *not* a snoop."

I spun on my heels and went to leave, but froze. "Maybe one little peek."

Turning back, I pulled the drawer open. I could hear Chloe and Mitchell downstairs. My eyes widened in shock at what I saw: a gun sitting on top of a men's Bible study book.

"*Not* what I was expecting," I whispered as I covered my mouth to hide a giggle.

Okay, enough of that. What did I think I'd find? Condoms?

I started for the door when I remembered the other side table drawer. My pace slowed and some unseen force brought me to the other side of the bed.

Taking a deep breath, I pulled the drawer open. It was filled with stuff. Chargers, a notebook, money. Money? Who puts money in a side drawer of their bed? I pushed the notebook to the side and saw a small blue box. My heart dropped when I realized it was a jewelry box.

Should I look at what was inside? Had Mitchell planned on asking someone to marry him at some point? Why did he have a ring box in his bedside drawer? If it was a ring, shouldn't it be in a safe or something?

I rolled my eyes. This was Oak Springs, not Chicago.

My curiosity got the better of me. I picked up the notebook and set it on the nightstand as I reached for the ring box. Holding my breath, I opened it to see a beautiful emerald ring.

"Oh my," I whispered.

A loud bang from downstairs scared me and I shut the jewelry box and put it back. When I reached for the notebook, I accidently bumped it, causing it to fall to the ground. It had opened face down on the floor. Grabbing it, I turned it over and went to close it when I saw my name.

I started to read what was written on the page. Covering my mouth, I sat on the bed and got lost in the words.

Corina is in my house. She's sleeping in my guestroom and it's playing havoc with my emotions. It took every ounce of strength I had not to kiss her tonight. Hold her in my arms and tell her how much I missed the feel of her body against mine. Tell her I knew she was scared about her house, but that I would be there for her every single step of the way. But I can't. I need to go slow and not mess this up again. I need to prove to her that I care about her. Going slow is going to be hard... especially when I can hardly think straight when she's in my presence.

Corina Miller...
what have you done to me?

I closed the notebook and slipped it into the drawer. Standing, I attempted to calm my racing heart. Mitchell had feelings for me too. He was as affected by me as I was by him. And he wrote about it in a journal. If that didn't make me fall head over heels, I don't know what would. Taking in a few deep breaths, I made my way downstairs to the kitchen. I needed to pretend I hadn't just read his thoughts.

"Be cool, Corina," I whispered as I headed down the hallway. Rounding the corner, I saw Chloe sitting on the kitchen island. Mitchell stood with his back to me. He had a giant paper hat and apron on.

"Good morning, Aunt Corina!" Chloe shouted in the happiest of voices.

I smiled at her. "Good morning, sweetheart."

When I forced my eyes to Mitchell, all I could do was stare. He was holding a spatula and his apron said, *I turn grills on.* His dark hair was messy and he had on a muscle shirt that nicely showcased every ripped and defined part of his anatomy.

"You…um…cook?"

Okay, is that the best you could come up with, Corina?

Mitchell pulled his head back in surprise. "Heck yeah, I cook. And good morning to you too, sleepyhead. Chloe already watched a movie while I went for a run, and you slept in."

Focusing on Chloe, I said, "You've already watched a movie this morning?"

She nodded. "Uncle Mitchell promised me French toast when he got back from his run."

"What time is it?" I asked.

"Ten."

"Ten?" I practically shouted.

Laughing, Mitchell asked, "Do you have plans or something?"

"Oh, I hope not. Uncle Mitchell was gonna take me ice skating. Please come, Aunt Corina."

Chloe was making it very hard for me to pretend to be angry with Mitchell. "Ice skating? Where could you possibly find ice skating in the middle of summer?"

Mitchell let out a rumbling laugh that moved through my body. "We do have ice rinks in Texas, Corina."

I rolled my eyes. "I know that, but near Oak Springs?"

"Yep."

Did I want to spend more time with Mitchell? Or to stick with my original plan of being pissed off at him? Who was I kidding? I was far from angry with him. Still, as much as I wanted to, I wasn't ready to let him in.

At least not yet.

CHAPTER 14

Mitchell

I pulled up to the rink and put the truck in park.

Corina helped Chloe out of the truck. "I had no idea Uvalde had a skating rink," Corina said.

"It's the most fun ice rink ever!" Chloe practically shouted.

"How about 'this is the best ice rink ever'," Corina said.

"Yeah! That too!" Chloe shouted as she took our hands and dragged us to the front door.

I let out a chuckle. "*A* for trying, Ms. Miller."

Corina rolled her eyes.

"Follow me, Aunt Corina! I know where to go. Uncle Mitchell and I have been skating here lots of times."

We followed Chloe to the counter were we all rented skates.

"Does Chloe stay with you often?" Corina asked.

Tying my shoes, I nodded. "She stays with me a few times a month. We have fun together."

The way she smiled made my stomach do a weird dip. "It's obvious she loves spending time with you. You're so good with her."

With a shrug, I stood. "I guess 'cuz I'm a little kid at heart."

Laughing, Corina stood on her skates. "You sure your foot is okay to skate?"

I shot her a dirty look. "My foot is perfectly fine, thank you very much."

There was no way I was going to tell her all four of my brothers had already found out about the damn glass incident, and so had a few guys I worked with. I could thank Trevor for that one. Little bastard.

"By the way, how did Trevor get a picture of me in the hospital?" I asked.

Corina's face turned red. "I don't know what you're talking about."

"Come on, y'all! Let's skate! Aunt Corina, wait until you see Uncle Mitchell skate. He's good!"

"Really?" Corina asked, her brows lifted.

With a smirk, I blew on my fingers and shined them on my chest. "Not to brag, but I did play a little hockey when I was younger."

Making a face like she didn't believe me, Corina said, "You don't say."

"I bet I can skate better than you."

Shit. That came out before I actually thought about it. Corina had grown up in the north. I bet kids there ice skated all the time.

"I'll take that bet, Mr. Parker."

"Oh! What are y'all bettin' on?" Chloe asked as she stepped onto the ice very carefully before she started skating. She was actually pretty good.

Corina tilted her head and gave me the sweetest smile I'd ever seen. What I wouldn't give to see that smile every damn day...

"What *are* we betting on?" she asked.

"I'll let you decide."

"Okay. If I can skate better, you have to make me dinner."

I stepped onto the ice and spun around. I had this in the bag. Corina's eyes widened. "And if I win?"

Glancing to Chloe halfway down the rink, Corina looked at me. "I'll share your bed with you again tonight."

Now it was my turn to look surprised.

"Chloe's not going to be there tonight," I reminded her.

She let a sexy grin grow across her face. "I'm aware of that."

That was all it took. I lost every ounce of coordination. I somehow tripped over my own feet and landed straight on my ass. And I didn't even care because all I could think about was Corina in my bed. With no six-year-old niece between us. The thought of holding Corina in my arms made me go temporarily insane.

"Are you okay?" Corina asked, as she attempted not to laugh and failed.

"I'm fine!" I shouted, jumping up.

"You're not starting off too well," she said with a wink.

I stumbled again and looked down at the ice. "Jesus, when was the last time someone used the Zamboni on this ice?" I called to no one.

"Uncle Mitchell! You fell," Chloe said as she skated up to me.

"There was something on the ice."

"Your Uncle Mitchell was just about to show me how great he can skate," Corina said.

Chloe started clapping and calling my name.

Pointing to my niece, I smiled. "I have my own little fan club."

Corina rolled her eyes and motioned for me to skate. With a little spin, I took off around the rink, going as fast as I safely could. There weren't a whole lot of people skating, but there were enough that I couldn't go full speed. Corina got the picture.

As I circled around, I turned to the side and shot ice at Corina. Chloe laughed, but Corina gave me a dirty look.

"I guess it's my turn," she said, chewing on her lip. Oh, yeah. She was nervous now.

"Looks like I'm going to have a warm bed tonight," I said.

"How come?" Chloe asked.

Staring at her, I tried to think of an answer but Corina beat me to it.

"He's already cold and thinking of all the ways he can heat up his sheets!"

My dick jumped at the thoughts Corina had just placed in my head.

"In the dryer," she added on quickly

With a smirk, I replied, "We'll see about that. Now show us what you got."

The second she flashed me that smile I knew I had been played by a master. Corina Miller knew how to skate.

She took off and skated perfectly.

"She's good." Chloe gasped. "I think you lost your bet, Uncle Mitchell."

With a smile, I nodded. "Maybe."

Corina made her way to the middle of the rink. Picking up a bit of speed, she did some kind of double salchow, fancy jump, spin thing.

"Yep. You for sure lost," Chloe said.

I put my hand on her head and ruffled her hair. "I've been tricked!"

With a sweet giggle, Chloe nodded and skated over to Corina. I watched as Corina took my niece's hands, and they skated in a circle. I loved seeing Chloe laughing and having so much fun. Skating my way over to them, I shook my head. Corina wore a huge, shit-eating grin.

"You sly little thing," I said.

She half shrugged. "I like Italian food, by the way."

Laughing, I held up my hands in defeat. "Italian it is."

By the end of our skating session, Chloe had learned how to do a few little spins that Corina had taught her.

We sat on the bench and took off our skates. "So…how do you know how to skate?"

With a chuckle, Corina lifted her shoulders and gave me that sweet innocent smile. "Lessons from the age of two to sixteen."

My head dropped forward, and I sighed. "You *did* play me!"

"What does that mean, Uncle Mitchell?"

I grabbed Chloe and pulled her onto my lap as she let out a small laugh. "It means she tricked me into thinking she couldn't skate, but she knew all along she could skate better than me."

Chloe made a shocked face and looked at Corina. "You played with Uncle Mitchell."

With an uncaring shrug, Corina stood. "I really enjoy playing with your Uncle Mitchell. And I got myself a dinner out of the deal. So it was a win-win."

Chloe glanced up. "I'm so sorry, but I'm kind of glad she won! I had so much fun."

I kissed Chloe on the nose and whispered, "I'm glad she won too, squirt. Come on, your daddy sent a text. He misses you."

Chloe jumped off my lap. She reached for Corina's hand as they walked back to the rental booth.

There was no denying that I felt something strong for Corina, and the more time we spent together, the more it grew.

Now the only thing I had left to figure out was how I was going to get Corina back into my bed.

Corina and I walked into the fire marshal's office and sat down. While we were dropping Chloe back off at home, I'd gotten the call that they had found the source of the fire.

"Hey, Mitchell, Ms. Miller, thanks for coming down," the fire marshal said.

With a nod, I reached to shake Jack's hand. Corina did the same, except her hand was shaking like a leaf.

"What did you find out?" I asked.

"Electrical fire."

I let out a relieved sigh. The last thing I wanted was for someone to have purposely set a fire and still be walking the streets of Oak Springs. When I glanced over to Corina, she was white as a ghost.

"Old wiring in the house caused a spark on the inside wall of the master bedroom. The whole second floor is a total loss, as you both know, but it looks like the first floor only sustained water and smoke damage."

With a forced smile, Corina said, "Can they start work on the house now?"

"Yes, I've already let the insurance adjuster know about the cause of the fire."

Corina's voice shook. "Th-thank you so much. If you'll excuse me."

She quickly got up and made her way out of the office. Standing, I reached out for Jack's hand once more. "Thanks, Jack."

"No problem. I'm glad she wasn't home. It could have been a lot worse."

I nodded. "Yeah, it could have been. Thanks again. I'll see you around."

As I made my way back to the truck, I sent Tripp a quick text to let him know it had been an electrical fire.

Stepping outside, my heart dropped. Corina was up against my truck, crying. I made my way over to her and gently cupped her face in my hands. "Hey, what's wrong?"

Tears streamed down her face, and I would have given anything to make them stop.

"What if…what if I had been home? What if you hadn't gone in and saved Milo? What if…"

I wrapped my arms around her. "Stop. No *what ifs* allowed. You weren't home. I got Milo out, and everything else can be replaced."

She pulled back and looked up at me. "I don't want to move back into that house."

My brows pulled together. "Why?"

Her lower lip trembled, and I knew she was simply scared. "Listen, that whole house is going to be re-done. Wiring, plumbing, everything is going to be stripped out, and I promise I'll make sure there's nothing unsafe in your house."

I brushed away a piece of hair that was stuck to her tear-soaked cheek.

Her teeth sank into her lip, and she closed her eyes before dropping her head against my chest.

"Why are you making it so hard to be angry with you?" she asked, grabbing my shirt.

"Don't worry, I'm sure I'll fuck up somehow, and you'll find another reason to be pissed."

She sort of chuckled, knowing I was most likely right. She pulled back and looked into my eyes. "Thank you…for everything you've done and are doing for me."

I ran the back of my hand down her cheek. "That's what you do for people you care about, right?"

"Mitchell, I wanted to tell you—"

Another male's voice interrupted mine. "Corina, is everything okay?"

Taking a step back, Corina faced Lane.

"Lane, hey. How are you?"

The little fucker flashed her a smile, then glanced at me and replaced it with a smug expression. "Mitchell, how are you?"

"I'm doing well, you?"

"Doing great. Life is good."

"I'm sure it is, Lane."

"What are you doing here?" Corina asked, clearly noticing that the exchange between Lane and I was forced.

"I wanted to see how you've been," Lane said. "I've texted you a few times, and you haven't answered."

When he looked my way, I shot him a smug grin. *Think on that one for a little bit, asshole.*

"I'm sorry, Lane," Corina said. "Things have been a bit crazy the last few days. I meant to respond and I forgot."

He looked disappointed.

Good.

"No worries," Lane said. "Did you want to go with me to the street dance in town?"

Corina glanced back and gave me a sweet little smile before turning to the dickhead. "I'm sorry. I'm actually going with Mitchell."

Lane's eyes snapped back at me. "I thought y'all were only friends."

"Well, um, we have…"

Corina was struggling with her words, so I thought I would help.

"I'm not allowed to take a friend to the street dance? Wouldn't that be what you were doing by asking her? Or were you hoping for something more?"

The look on his face said he'd love to punch the living shit out of me. Then he shot me a smirk. "Now that you put it out there, Mitch, I *was* hoping to move things a little further with Corina."

"What?" From the tone of Corina's voice, I could tell she wasn't shocked by his admission. "Lane, we work together and I've already expressed that I don't think it is a good idea for us to be anything other than friends."

"I heard you went out with Philip," Lane said.

Now her hands moved to her hips, and I knew she was pissed. Corina pissed off was one of the sexiest things I'd ever witnessed, and I'd witnessed it a few times already. But it was even better now that she was pissed at someone other than me.

"Excuse me? Are you snooping around my business, Lane?"

He shrugged. "I've heard a few rumors."

"Hell, you gone off and done it now," I said with a chuckle.

Corina turned to me. "You be quiet." She faced Lane again, poking him in the chest. "How dare you dig into my personal life. What I do and whom I'm doing it with is none of your GD business."

Damn, if she wasn't cute when she tried to swear and couldn't.

Lane stepped forward. "Corina, I only—"

"I'm not finished talking. I don't know what rumors you've heard, but Philip was in need of a friend. I was there for him."

"And what about Tripp Parker? Seems like you're making your way through the brothers, from what I've heard. Does Cord come after Mitchell?"

My fists balled, and I started to step closer, but Corina beat me there.

Corina slapped the living shit out of Lane. And that wasn't enough. Her knee hit his crotch so hard the poor guy didn't stand a chance. Correction: he wasn't standing at all now.

"I've heard a thing or two about you, as well, Lane Lewis," Corina said.

Lane was on his knees, bent over in pain. Corina leaned down and whispered into his ear before she walked around him and climbed into my truck.

There was no way I could have wiped the smile off of my face even if I'd wanted to.

I held a hand out to Lane. "You need help standing up, dickhead?"

He jumped up. "If this is your way of trying to pay me back for high school, you won't win."

I tossed my head back and laughed. "Dude, I don't live in the past. But that woman sitting in my truck is someone I care about. And I'm warning you now, stay the fuck away from her. You understand me?"

A smirk moved over his face. "Well, I'm going to be working pretty closely with her, asshole…what are you going to do about that?"

I let myself scan him up and down before I met his eyes. "You'd be surprised at the things I'm capable of doing without it linking back to me."

"Are you threatening me, Parker?"

I slapped him on the side of his arm and smiled. "Hell no. That's a promise."

CHAPTER 15

Corina

My heart was racing as I looked out the window at Lane and Mitchell. I had no idea what was being sad, and I didn't care. I was *angry*.

How dare Lane Lewis say those things. And what rumors had he heard? Maybe people were talking about me staying with Mitchell. After all, how would that look on the outside? First I'd dated Tripp, now I was living with his brother…

Crap! I wasn't helping the rumors by telling Lane the only Parker brother I'd slept with was Mitchell. Why did I tell him that just now?

Ugh.

I buried my face into my hands and let out a scream. The driver's side door shut, and I jumped when I felt Mitchell's hand on my leg.

"Are you okay?"

Dropping my hands, I looked to see if that jerk was still there. Lane was walking away with something of a limp. I was glad I'd kicked him where it counted.

I looked back at Mitchell. "No! I'm not okay. I'm…I'm pissed off!"

His eyes widened as he let out a soft chuckle. "I'd say so. Easy with the language there, dove."

My heart dropped, and I was instantly taken back to the night Mitchell and I spent together. My chest rose and fell as I fought for each breath as the memory hit me.

Sitting on Mitchell, my legs wrapped around his body as he held me tightly. He was buried so far inside me. Our breathing labored as we both came down from our orgasms.

"I've never felt like this before," he said. "What are you doing to me, dove?"

My stomach clenched when Mitchell called me dove. *It made our moments seem even more amazing, if that was possible. I'd never experienced such passion in my life. I would never forget the feeling of him inside me. It was clear that I'd given this man a piece of me that I'd been guarding. It would forever be his.*

"Why dove?" I asked.

With a sexy smile, he moved his hand up my arm and around the back of my neck, pulling me closer to him. When his lips brushed mine, I felt the fire ignite between us again.

"Doves are my favorite bird. They're pure, fragile, beautiful creatures. They have a soft and beautiful call, which reminds me of how you sound when you come with me inside you."

With a wide smile, I pressed my lips against his. "That's beautiful."

Mitchell brought us to the bed and held his body over mine. "You're beautiful."

He kissed me and I was lost again to him. To his touch, his kiss, his slow, sweet way of making love to me.

Mitchell Parker would forever hold a piece of my heart, whether I wanted him to or not.

Finally finding my voice, I asked, "What did you just say?"

Mitchell winked. "I said easy with the language."

I shook my head. "No, that's not all you said."

He started the truck, and I realized how flipping hot it was inside the cab.

"That's all I said."

He pulled out onto Main Street and I tore my eyes off of him. Staring straight out the window, I swallowed hard and dug down deep to speak.

"You called me dove."

From the corner of my eye, I saw him look at me before turning straight ahead again. He didn't remember, did he? Or maybe he called all of his women *dove.*

His silence made my emotions go all over the place. Scared, angry, hurt, sad. *I don't know what I was thinking. Mitchell Parker isn't going to change.*

I looked back at him. It was obvious he couldn't do commitment, and I needed that. I needed to know that the man I gave my full heart to was going to give me his in return. "Mitchell, I don't think this is going to—"

"Wait. Before you say a word, please give me ten minutes."

My brows pinched. "What?"

He reached for my hand and looked at me. His eyes were pleading. "That's all I'm asking for. Please."

I nodded as I whispered, "Okay."

Mitchell headed out of town and toward his family's ranch, but he took a left turn on Ranch Road thirty-seven. He drove for about ten minutes before pulling down a long driveway.

"What is this place?" I asked as I glanced at the beautiful scenery. I loved the Texas hill country so much. I loved living in Oak Springs, but being farther out, away from everything, was so peaceful.

An old house came into view. It was stunning. "Wow, what a beautiful house. Who lives here?"

"No one anymore. This used to be the old Robinson place."

He parked the truck and we both got out.

"It's in beautiful shape," I said.

"Yeah, it is. Was built in nineteen twenty-three."

"Wow! Have you shown it to Amelia?"

Mitchell laughed. "No, I haven't shown it to anyone other than my father and Tripp. I bought it a few weeks ago."

My mouth fell open. "You bought this place? How much land comes with it?"

"A hundred acres. Not very much, but enough for me right now."

My head was spinning. "How can you say that's not a lot of land?"

He laughed. "Well, considering what I grew up on…"

I felt the heat in my cheeks. "I guess that's true. What are your plans?"

"I'm not sure just yet."

Spinning around, I shrieked with sudden excitement. "You could get a dog!"

Mitchell looked at me like I was insane. "A dog?"

"Yes! A dog. Look at all this land! She would love it."

"She?" he asked.

"Yeah. Come on, you have to let a woman into your heart one of these days, Mitchell. You can't be a player for the rest of your life." The words were out of my mouth before I could stop them.

His eyes turned dark, and I wasn't sure if he was angry or if that look was something else. He took a step toward me. I stepped back.

"What makes you think I haven't already let someone into my heart?"

An awkward laugh bubbled out. "I would bet the farm you haven't. I see it so clearly. You're afraid to open up, and I get it, I do. Maybe it's your job, or other insecurities. I just don't think I can wait around to see who the lucky girl is going to be." Turning back to the house, I forced my tears away. "I'm sure someday you'll be ready to fill this house with love and the person who wins your heart will be lucky to be a part of that."

"Why in the fuck do you assume I'm not ready to open my heart? And why in the hell can you not give me a chance before you run your mouth off?"

Spinning on my heel, I stared at him. "Run my mouth off?"

"Yes! You jump to conclusions and accusations before you even let me speak. You're acting like a teenage girl, creating drama for no reason. I brought you here to show you this house for a reason."

"Why? What's your reason?" I shouted back.

"Because, damn it! I want to share this with *you*, Corina. I want us to be together and I don't know...maybe someday *we* can fill it with kids and dogs and all that...stuff."

I was stunned. I hadn't expected Mitchell to come back at me with those words. He thrust his fingers in his hair. "I don't know what in the fuck I'm doing anymore. Let's just leave."

We hadn't even seen the house yet. I glanced back at it and didn't move.

"Corina."

"I want to see the house."

"Yeah, well, the mood's kind of ruined, don't you think?"

My chest ached. Why was it so hard for us? It shouldn't be this hard. At least, I didn't think it should be. Was it because I was keeping Mitchell at arm's length—because I didn't believe him?

Wrapping my arms around my chest, I stared at the house. It was perfect. Old, yet in beautiful condition. The wraparound porch was my favorite. I could see us sitting in rocking chairs, getting a baby settled, as we looked over the land. Finding our places in this world, together.

Was that what Mitchell pictured when he looked at this house? I desperately wanted to ask him.

I made my way back to the truck. Mitchell was already sitting inside. It was clear the Parker men had short fuses. I'd witnessed Tripp losing his cool a time or two—never with me, but with other people.

I shut the truck door, reached for my seat belt and waited for him to drive off.

He took a deep breath and let it out. "I'm sorry I hurt you. I didn't know how to deal with my feelings for you then, and I'm not doing a bang-up job of dealing with my feelings now. A million and one things race through my mind when I think of us together."

I stared at my hands while he spoke.

"I don't know if I can make you happy and give you the things you want, Corina."

My eyes met his. "What if all I want is you?"

He swallowed hard. "My job…"

"Is dangerous. I *know*. I've understood the risks of falling for you from the very beginning. And it didn't stop me."

The corners of his mouth lifted slightly as he reached for my hand and ran his thumb across the top of it. Crackles of fire danced across my skin as he swept back and forth. "I want to show you I'm serious about making us work and that I'm not filling your head with bullshit to get in your pants."

I raised my brows.

His smile grew bigger and his dimple popped, causing a pull in my lower stomach. "Okay, correction, I want in your pants more than you could ever fucking know, but I want more than that. I want to make this work...but I don't know how to go about doing that."

My teeth sank into my lip. "So if I said I wanted to sleep in your bed tonight, but no sex, what would you say?"

"I'd say okay."

"Really?"

"I'll do whatever I need to do, dove."

My entire body became hyperaware of Mitchell. Each breath he took. Where his eyes traveled, the way his lips parted slightly. When he ran his thumb over my hand, an electric jolt started there and raced through me.

My voice sounded like I had a frog stuck in my throat. "Do you mean that, Mitchell?"

He gently kissed the back of my hand. "I've never said truer words before in my life."

My stomach fluttered, and I knew the words he'd spoken were the truth.

Our eyes were locked on one another. "What do we do from here?" I asked with a grin.

Mitchell laughed. "You want to go get something to eat?"

I replied with a flirting grin, "I *am* hungry, but I was hoping for something else."

His eyes danced with a brilliant light before he opened the truck door and got out.

Good grief. He thinks I want to see the house. I need to work on my flirting skills more.

He walked with purpose as he rounded the front of his truck. I opened the door and went to get out when he grabbed me and gently drew me to him.

Moving from the door, he pressed me against the truck. Cupping my face with his hands, Mitchell pressed his lips to mine. It didn't take long for me to relax into the kiss. Opening my mouth to him, his tongue explored mine in a perfect, rhythmic dance.

We both moaned at the same time when he pressed his body close. The kiss turned hungrier as I took hold of his strong arms. My head spun as my body was wrapped in the euphoria that only Mitchell Parker could deliver. A strange feeling of peace settled into my chest as I let the wall I'd built around my heart fall. I was letting him in, and nothing was going to be the same from this point on.

CHAPTER 16

Mitchell

My heart thundered in my ears as I kissed Corina. Her arms moved over my arms and wrapped around my neck, drawing me closer to her body. It felt like an eternity passed as we kissed, until we both needed to breathe.

Leaning my forehead against hers, I whispered, "I've missed you so much, dove."

Corina drew back and gazed into my eyes. A single tear slipped from her beautiful baby blues. I gently brushed it away.

With a breathtaking smile, she placed her hands on my chest. "What took you so long?"

"I was a fool, plain and simple." I chuckled, gently running the back of my hand down the side of her face. "I swear to you, I'll never hurt you again. Please believe me when I say that."

Her hands grabbed at my chest as she took a shaky breath. Her eyes were screaming that she wanted to say something, but she looked down for a brief moment before gazing back into my eyes.

"I believe you, Mitch."

Placing my hands over hers, I laced our fingers together. "You know I'm going to mess up."

She giggled. "I know."

"Can we make a promise to each other right now that if something bothers us, or we're unsure, we'll talk about it and not jump to conclusions."

Corina nodded. "I like that promise."

Squeezing her hands, I kissed her on the forehead. "So do I. Now, let me show you the house before we get some food."

We walked toward the house, hand in hand. Never in a million years had I thought want something like this, but I did…and, most importantly, I wanted it with her. Every time I thought of Corina, my mind wandered off in a million hopeful directions.

Stepping on the porch, I watched Corina look around. "It's huge! I can totally see a porch swing with some rockers sitting out here."

I made a mental note. There was no doubt in my mind that I was going to be sharing this house with her. I wanted it to be perfect in every way.

I unlocked the door and we headed inside.

"Oh my!" Corina gasped. "It's so true to the time period."

"The previous owners were the original owners. They never changed a thing. When Mr. Robinson passed last year, his son came in and had everything restored, but made sure to keep it exactly the same. The wallpaper in here…"

I led her into the parlor.

"It's the exact same pattern. He took a piece of the original wallpaper and had it reproduced. It was important for him to restore the house to look the way it did when he grew up. The colors, the fixtures, the flooring…everything is either original to the house, or a reproduction."

Corina took everything in. "Did they open this wall between the dining and living?"

"It was built with stained-glass doors originally. Seems like Mr. Robinson was the first to come up with the open floor plan."

"I'd say," Corina replied with a chuckle.

We toured the rest of the house and ended up on the second floor back balcony.

"Wow. Look at the view."

"It's pretty," I admitted. "Not as pretty as Amelia and Wade's place, but still good."

She turned to me and tilted that pretty little head. "I think it's perfect."

I placed my hands on her hips and drew her a little closer. With a grin, I replied, "Good, I'm glad you think so. I really hoped you'd like it."

When her teeth sank into her lip, I had to keep myself from dragging her in for another kiss. "Hungry?"

"I am starved! All that ice skating worked up an appetite."

With her hand in mine, we made our way to my truck. Opening the passenger door, Corina paused before getting in.

"Mitchell?"

"Yeah?"

She worried her lower lip before those beautiful blue eyes met mine. "I didn't mean it when I said I hated you that night in the club. I was angry, and I shouldn't have said that."

My throat grew thick as I placed my hand on the side of her cheek. "I'm the one who needs to be apologizing for being a complete and utter asshole." I took a step back. My heartbeat quickened, and I knew I had to tell her the truth. I didn't want anything false between us.

"Corina, I need to tell you something."

Her smile faded, and she looked away. I was pretty sure she knew what I was about to say.

"Cassidy?" she asked, not looking at me as she spoke.

Fuck. How did she know?

"It was only once, and it was last February, and I felt like a complete jerk for doing it."

The way her breath hitched made me feel sick.

"We weren't together, Mitch. You shouldn't feel like that."

"I do, and it doesn't matter because it wasn't fair to you or her. I couldn't get you out of my head and all I wanted to do was get it over with once it started. It meant nothing, and if I could go back and undo it I would, you have to believe me."

Her head lifted and she pinched her brows together as she held up her hand. "Wait. You only slept with Cassidy that one time? You haven't…I mean…you haven't had…"

Her eyes fell to my dick before snapping back up.

I shook my head. "No, I haven't slept with anyone since then. It's the longest I've ever gone without sex, and believe me, I've thought of taking you in every position I can think of. I've rubbed my cock practically raw thinking about you."

Her mouth dropped open and that sweet and beguiling smile moved across her face. She hit me on the chest. "You are so bad, Mitchell Parker."

"Want me to tell you some of the positions?" I asked with a wiggle of my brows.

She licked her lips, and I knew she wanted to play along with my naughty game. Corina Miller might have been innocent, but after spending one night with her, I knew she had a naughty side that was begging to come out.

"If I say yes?" she asked.

"I'll tell you one."

"Just one?" she asked, her cheeks blushing. It made her look adorable as hell.

"Just one."

She looked me over from head to toe before piercing my eyes again. "Okay, tell me one."

"Reverse cowgirl, in a canoe."

Corina stood there with a stunned expression before she busted out laughing. "What? You lost me with the canoe!"

I shrugged. "Don't you think it would be kind of hot to have sex out in the open? Plus, think about the rocking of the canoe."

She pulled her lower lip into her mouth before she bit down, causing my dick to jump.

"I'm sure you, of all people, have had sex in public before," she said.

"The backseat of my truck doesn't count."

She snarled. "Note to self: never have sex with you in the back seat of your truck."

I moved closer. "What if I got a new truck? Would you do it then?"

Her chest rose and fell as I narrowed my gaze to her lips. "Maybe."

I smiled. "Really?"

"Um, Mitchell. I haven't had sex since last fall and all this talk of positions is starting to make me a little…um…"

With a tilt of my head, I stared into her eyes. "Horny?"

Corina closed her eyes and whispered, "Yes."

"You want me to take care of that for you?"

Snapping her eyes back open, she opened her mouth, but nothing came out.

My hand moved to her jeans and when she didn't stop me, I unbuttoned them. Her entire body trembled when I ran my finger along the edge of her panties.

"Jesus, do you have any idea how fucking sexy you are, dove?"

She shook her head as I pulled her jeans down and slipped my hand into her panties. I let out a long, low growl when I felt how wet she was.

Moving my mouth to the side of her head, I whispered into her ear as I pushed my fingers deeper inside of her. "I can't wait to hear you scream my name when I make you come."

Grabbing the truck to hold herself up, she whispered, "Oh God."

I moved slowly at first, fighting with everything I had not to take her right there.

"Mitchell," she cried out as I picked up speed and pushed another finger into her tight pussy.

"That's it, dove. Let it go."

Her body shook, and I could feel her pulsing on my fingers. She was close, and I knew just the thing to push her off the ledge. "I want to bury my face between your legs and taste you, baby."

"Oh God!" she cried out.

Moving my mouth closer to her ear, I whispered, "I can't wait to make love to you, but baby, I need you to come. Now."

"Mitchell…I'm coming. Mitchell!"

The sound of her calling my name was almost more than I could take. I'd been waiting so fucking long to hear it. When I pushed on her clit, her body trembled again. This time she grabbed onto me and held on with everything she had. When I no longer felt her pulsing against my fingers, I slowly withdrew them.

Corina's chest rose and fell with each labored breath. She watched as I brought my fingers to my mouth. That beautiful mouth of hers fell open. I smiled while sucking hard on my fingers.

I let out a moan before gazing into her shy expression. "Look at me, dove."

She did as I asked. Our eyes locked, and I drank every single second of it before leaning down and kissing her. Corina wrapped her arms around my neck. The kiss nearly brought me to my knees. It was soft and filled my body with a warmth I'd never experienced before. This woman was my everything.

When I withdrew my mouth from hers, I rested my forehead against Corina's.

"I'm sorry it took me so long. I swear to make it up to you every single day."

Corina let out one of her sweet innocent giggles before crinkling that cute little nose of hers. "That was a nice start."

Laughing, I kissed her forehead. "Come on, dove. Let's go eat."

Music came from the bar as I knocked on the door. Less than thirty seconds later, the door unlocked and I followed Cord in.

"What's the big emergency, Mitchell?" Cord asked, walking over to the bar. A pile of receipts was laid out on the surface.

"Corina and I are together."

He stopped and looked at me. A huge smile took over his face. "No shit? It's about damn time."

I grinned. "Yeah, well, I was a stubborn asshole."

"I'll second that."

As I turned, I saw Tripp walking from the back offices. "Define *together*."

He reached for my hand, and I quickly shook it. "Well, we haven't slept together and that's why I'm here. I need advice from both of you and this is one time I don't want to go to Dad for it."

They both laughed. Tripp jumped onto the bar and spun his baseball cap around. "You mean you don't want to ask Dad how long you should wait to sleep with the woman you're in love with."

I nearly choked before letting out an awkward laugh. "I'm not in love with Corina. I care about her...a lot. But love? Hell, we only spent one night together and that was almost a year ago. I feel something, but I'm not ready to call it love."

Tripp and Cord looked at each other. "You don't have to be having sex with someone to fall in love with them, Mitchell," Tripp said before taking a drink from a bottle of water.

"Can you let me get used to the fact that I actually *want* to be with one woman first?"

Cord chuckled. "Yep, you're in love."

Rolling my yes, I turned to walk away.

"Okay, okay. Stop. We'll cool it with the love talk," Tripp said. "But, Mitchell, I do need to tell you that Corina has already told me she's in love with you."

I could feel my cheeks burn as I smiled.

A look of horror moved across Cord's face. "Jesus, you've turned into a fucking pussy! If this is what love does to you, no thank you. I'll keep my bachelor ways."

Tripp slapped Cord on the back. "Dude, your life is going to turn upside down when the right woman comes along."

He huffed. "Well, I'm certainly not going to stand here with a damn Smurf-looking smile on my face."

"Smurf?" I asked with a chuckle.

"Yeah, you know the little blue people."

I looked at Tripp, and he shrugged his shoulders.

"I know who they are. Why did you pick *Smurfs*?" I focused back on Cord.

Cord stared. "I don't fucking know, dude. They're happy little creatures who are full of love and all that shit. That's what you look like with that goofy smile on your face. Like a Smurf."

I pulled my head back. "I look like a Smurf?"

Tripp laughed harder.

"Fuck you, Mitchell. You know what I mean."

Laughing, I replied, "I don't. Should we call Smurfette and ask her? And if I look like a Smurf, does that make you Grumpy Smurf cuz, well, you see where I'm going with this?"

Cord shot daggers at me. "Don't you have someone to arrest or some shit?"

Placing my hand over my holster, I looked at Cord as seriously as I could. "I don't know, have you spotted Gargamel and Azrael?"

Tripp fell back on the bar, laughing. I couldn't help but join in while Cord shot me the finger.

"I hate you both."

Hitting my brother on the back, I jumped over the bar as I sang, "la, la, lala, la la" and helped myself to a beer.

"First off, it's Sunday and I'm off," I said. "I don't arrest people when I'm off."

Cord rolled his yes.

"Second, I really do need y'all's advice. I don't want to fuck up again with Corina. Last night we stayed up nearly all night talking. She ended up falling asleep on the sofa, and I didn't have the heart to wake her up so I sat there beside her for the rest of the night sleeping sitting up."

"Wow," Tripp said with a slight grin. "Papa Smurf would be proud of you."

Cord groaned.

I grinned before rubbing the back of my neck. "Yeah, my neck is killing me. I bet I only got an hour of sleep."

Cord smiled. "I take having her in your arms was worth the lack of sleep."

I could feel my grin turn even bigger. "Let's hope I don't have to go arrest anyone, I'm so damn tired. But, yeah, it was worth it."

"Alright, listen," Tripp said. "I don't feel like spending my whole morning off with you two, so here're my thoughts. Take it slow. Don't push her into anything to make up for lost time."

"I agree," Cord said.

I looked back and forth between my brothers, nodding. "The no sex thing I had already planned on. I want Corina to see that's not all I care about. I mean, we started out doing that and look where it got us. So, you think I need to date her, show her how much she means to me?"

"Yep, that's what I think," Tripp echoed.

"What if she wants sex?" Cord asked.

I shook my head. "Yeah, I thought about that. She was sort of hinting about sex last night. I did the only thing I knew to do."

"You ran?" Cord asked with a smirk on his face.

"No, dickhead. I made popcorn and put a movie on."

They looked at each other before laughing their asses off. When they finally stopped, Cord jumped over the bar and reached for a bottle of whiskey. He poured himself a shot and drank it. "Jesus, dude. Don't put me down for love. I'd like to keep my man card."

I reached for my cowboy hat and shot Cord the finger. "I cannot wait until the day a woman walks through that door and knocks you flat on your ass."

As Tripp and I headed for the door, Cord shouted, "That's never gonna happen! Ever!"

CHAPTER 17

Corina

"Hello? Earth to Corina?"

Fingers snapped in front of my face, pulling me from my memory of last night with Mitchell.

"What did you say?" I asked as I looked from Paxton to Amelia, and then to Waylynn.

The three of them stared.

"You and Mitchell did the deed, didn't you?" Amelia asked with a squeal.

"What?"

"Oh, my God! They did!" Waylynn added.

"No, we didn't!"

My voice cracked, and I knew Paxton caught it. Pointing to me, she exclaimed, "Corina Miller. You better talk, woman!"

I could feel my cheeks heating, which made all three of them jump up and fall to the floor in front of me.

"Forget talking about the reception, I want to hear what happened with you and my brother!" Amelia squealed.

I let out another awkward laugh. "Nothing happened. I mean, we had a lot of fun with Chloe, and well, we decided to…to…"

"To fuck like rabbits after you dropped her off because the sexual tension was so crazy you couldn't keep your hands off each other?" Waylynn called out. The three of us all looked at Waylynn with shocked expressions.

She half shrugged. "What?"

"No, that would be you and *Jonathon*, Waylynn." Amelia chuckled.

"Hey, it was a moment of weakness. It can't ever happen again."

"Why?" all three of us asked at once.

Now it was Waylynn's turn to look like we were insane. "Um, he's six years younger than me, for starters."

"So?" Amelia replied. "He's hot, has a rocking body, and you said he knows how to use his tools."

Waylynn wiggled her brows. "He's got a really big SCREW-driver , too."

I covered my mouth to hide my chuckle. The Parker girls could be so dirty.

Paxton hit both Amelia and Waylynn on the arm. "You two are so bad, I swear."

Brushing Paxton off, Waylynn focused on me. "We are not changing the subject. Corina, spill it."

With my hands over my flushed cheeks, I smiled. "We haven't had sex again…*yet*."

All three of them screamed like middle school girls.

Paxton pointed. "But something happened. I can tell by how red your cheeks are."

Peeking at Paxton, I nodded. "He might have relieved some of my pent-up tension."

"O to the M to the holy shittin' G!" Amelia shouted. "What did he do?"

"Wait!" Paxton cried out as she flailed her arms around to stop the talking. "I don't know if I want details. I mean, he is my brother-in-law and y'all's brother!"

"Screw that, I want details!" Waylynn said. "Did he use his hand or mouth?"

I rolled my eyes and looked away.

"Both!" all three shouted.

Picking up the sofa pillow, I threw it at them. "No! His hand."

Waylynn stood. "Ugh. I thought my brothers were better than that. Maybe all those rumors about the Parker boys aren't true."

Paxton smiled. "Trust me, they're true. At least they are for Steed."

We fell into a giggling fit as Chloe walked into the living room. "What's so funny?" she asked.

"Nothing, sweetheart. What are you doing?" Paxton got up and picked up her daughter, giving her a kiss.

"I'm waiting on Daddy. He said he was gonna take me to town to buy Aunt Meli and Uncle Wade a weddin' gift."

Amelia stood up. "Oh, Chloe Cat. That's so sweet of you."

Chloe beamed with pride. "Aunt Meli, can Patches come to the party?"

Pressing my lips together, I tried to keep from laughing, especially seeing the shocked look on Amelia's face.

"Well, um…I…Patches?"

Chloe nodded.

Waylynn walked to Chloe and kissed her on the cheek, then faced her younger sister. "I vote yes!"

Chloe clapped. "Yay!"

"Wh-what?" Amelia said, giving her sister a death stare.

"I mean, if Patches was at Steed and Paxton's wedding *and* my welcome home party, it's only fair he gets to come to the reception."

Amelia turned to Paxton, who was desperately trying not to laugh. Focusing back on Chloe, Amelia forced a smile. "Of course Patches can come. We'll have him sit next to Waylynn."

"Thank you, Aunt Meli!"

Paxton put a very excited Chloe down as she ran out of the room calling for her father.

Waylynn turned from watching Chloe to face Amelia. "You think you've won this round, but wait, little sister. You forget who your teacher was."

After I left the ranch, I stopped by and checked my house. The entire second floor had been gutted and work had already begun. It was Sunday, so the workers were absent.

I headed back to Mitchell's place. Standing in the middle of Mitchell's living room, I looked around for something to do.

Milo jumped onto the back of the sofa and meowed.

"Hey, buddy. You want some food?"

Another loud meow signaled he was more than ready. He followed me into the kitchen where I poured him some kibble. Milo stared at it before looking up at me.

"Don't tell me you want soft food."

He gazed at me with those big blue eyes.

"Fine. I need to get something for dinner anyway. What time do you think Mitchell will get home?"

With a tilt of his head, Milo answered with his little bark meow.

"No, I'm not texting him to ask. The last thing I want to do is be a pushy girlfriend."

I paused to smile. Reaching down, I lifted Milo and snuggled him. "Is it too soon to call myself Mitchell's girlfriend?"

Milo struggled to get out of my arms.

"Don't be jealous, Milo."

He ran to Mitchell's bedroom. Traitor. Milo hadn't slept with me since I'd moved in, preferring Mitchell's bed.

"I'm going to get cat food!" Rolling my eyes, I headed down the stairs. "I cannot believe I'm letting the cat know I'm leaving."

Stepping outside, I locked the door. When I turned around, I let out a small scream. Cassidy was standing there with a smug expression. "Still haven't found a place to live yet?"

Ugh. I hated drama, and the last thing I wanted to do deal with was a crazy woman who had the hots for Mitchell.

Another voice came from my side. "Hey, Corina. I've tried calling you."

I looked over, surprised to see Lane. He was the second-to-last person I wanted to talk to right now. "If you'll both excuse me, I'm in a bit of a rush." It was a lie, but they didn't need to know that. Besides, I was still pissed at Lane.

"Corina, please," he said. "Let me apologize."

Glancing over my shoulder, I called out, "No worries, Lane. See you at work soon!"

I made my way across the street, catching a glimpse of Mrs. Johnson trying to put something into the backseat of her car.

"Mrs. Johnson?" I called out. She peeked up and smiled. "Oh, Corina."

"What are you doing?" I asked as I got closer.

"Trying to get this body into my car."

My brows pulled tight. "What?"

"This scarecrow I made with my crafting group. Darn thing won't get in."

I let out a sigh to see it was just a stuffed scarecrow. Leaning down, I helped her get it into the back seat of her car.

"May I ask why you have a scarecrow?"

"It's for the fall festival pie eating competition."

Okay, now I'm lost.

Once we got the thing into the car, I shut the door and faced Mrs. Johnson. "You need a scarecrow for that?"

"Now, Corina, I know this isn't your first fall festival."

I laughed. "No, ma'am. But it's actually the middle of August and the festival isn't for another month."

"And I'm a month ahead of schedule. Now, come with me, I have a new pie for you to taste. I'm entering it into the contest."

Mrs. Johnson's house was two blocks from the main square on Orcher Ave, a block over from my house. The ride was quick and Mrs. Johnson went on and on about the pie contest. She was positive she was going to win this year.

After pulling up to her house, she got out of her car and ordered me to help her. "Help me carry this fellow in."

Getting the scarecrow out of the car was easier than getting him in. I walked behind her, carrying him as we made our way to her garage. "Just set him in the corner there, Corina. Then come on in. I'll put a pot of coffee on."

"I can't stay long, Mrs. Johnson," I called out from over my shoulder.

She waved her hand and shouted. "One cup!"

After securing the scarecrow in the corner, I made my way into her house.

"You haven't been by the last week," she said.

I nodded. "I know, I'm sorry. With my house catching fire and trying to get things ready for school, it's been sort of busy. I lost most of my school supplies in the fire."

The older woman made a *tsking* sound while she filled up a pot with water to boil on the stove. She was the only person I knew who still made coffee this way.

"Have you seen those coffee machines where you put the little plastic cup in and fill the pot with tap water? About a minute later you have a perfect cup of coffee."

She stared at me like I'd gone mad. "That's insane. Why would you want something like that?"

"Well, it's good coffee and super-fast. Plus, it's perfect when you only want one cup."

"What do your guests do?"

With a shrug, I replied, "They make a cup too."

She rolled her eyes. "Pish posh applesauce. I ain't got no time for that."

I covered my mouth to hide my smile, deciding not to tell her that by the time she boiled the water we could have made and drunk two cups. Making a mental note, I decided to buy her a coffee maker for Christmas.

She took a pie from the windowsill and brought it over to the table. "This one's been cooling."

I chewed on my lip. I wasn't sure how she thought putting a pie in the window when it was almost a hundred outside was cooling it. At least she didn't have the window open.

"What flavor is this one?" I asked while I watched her slice a piece and put it on a glass plate.

"This one is blueberry lemon lavender."

I took one bite and closed my eyes. With my mouth full, I tried to speak. "*Ohmygawd.*"

Mrs. Johnson took a seat. "Good?"

Nodding, I smiled. "I taste the lemon in the crumble crust. It's so amazing."

"Good. I think that one has a chance at winning this year."

Moaning in pure delight, I took another bite. "So. Good. You'll win for sure."

"Anything need to be added?"

I shook my head. "No! Don't change a thing. It's heaven in a slice of pie. Almost orgas…mmm…umm."

She lifted a brow. "I was hoping Mitchell Parker would be helping out in that area."

I inhaled the pie that was in my mouth, causing a coughing fit.

"Oh come, child. You don't think I saw the way that boy was looking at you the last time you were both here? Besides, the ladies in my crafting group like to talk. Rumor has it you're living with Ranger Parker."

She waggled her eyebrows.

"Water!" I said, still coughing.

Setting the water on the table, she started pouring our coffee. My eyes were watering from swallowing the pie wrong. Once I got myself under control, I spoke.

"Mrs. Johnson, I'm not sure what you heard, but Mitchell...Ranger Parker was nice enough to let me stay with him after the fire. We're friends and that is what friends do. Plus, I have a cat and all so it was hard finding a place that would take care of—"

"Your pussy?"

I was positive my eyes popped out of my head. I dropped the fork, jumping when it clattered against the glass plate.

"Pussy cat," she corrected with a wink.

"I'm...I'm not even sure I know what to say after that."

Mrs. Johnson laughed as she handed me the coffee. "Darlin', let me school you on men."

"I know men," I replied, a defensive tone laced in my voice.

She frowned. "Child, you have innocence drippin' off of you. I wouldn't be surprised if you were still a virgin, but I know that's not true because Mrs. Winsten saw Mitchell Parker go into your house one late night last fall, and he didn't emerge from the house until early the next mornin'. So, that would lead me to believe that you bumped uglies with him on at least one other occasion."

My mouth hung open. "What is it with you southern women and the 'bumping uglies' thing?" I asked when I finally found my voice.

"Do you think a man's dick is pretty?" she asked.

"Um, I've never been asked that before."

She shook her head. "Well, I don't. Don't know any woman who says a man's dick is pretty. Oh, in those fancy romance books they say they are." She rolled her eyes. "Please. I ain't ever looked at my husband's dick in all the years we were married and thought to myself, 'now there is a beautiful long, thick shaft glistening with a bead of his cum that I can't wait to lick off.'"

My body shuddered at the mental image.

She took a sip of her coffee, then she set it down and shook her head. "Instead, I thought, Jesus Christ, the man's got himself another hard-on. *A-gain*. And it's leakin' all over my nice new clean sheets."

I tried so hard not to laugh, but lost the battle. Mrs. Johnson smiled and took another sip of her coffee.

"Mrs. Johnson, I needed that laugh."

"No, what you need is to get yourself back to your *friend's* house. Slip into something sexy and jump that man's bones."

I pressed my lips tightly together.

"No giving me that shy look. Corina, take the situation by the ropes and lead that stallion into the barn. Ride him like a good cowgirl."

"I'm from Chicago, remember?" I stood, trying not to laugh. "I'd better get going."

She stood. "Would you like to bring some pie home for Mitchell?"

And just like that, she flipped the switch and was a sweet old grandmother again.

"Sure! I'm sure he'd love it."

Soon I was racing down the sidewalk, pie in hand, as I made my way back to the small grocery store right off the square. I couldn't get Mrs. Johnson's words out of my head.

Slip into something sexy and jump that man's bones.

CHAPTER 18

Mitchell

I set the grocery bags down on the kitchen island with a loud clank. "Corina?" I called out.

"*Bruff.*"

Glancing down, I found Milo. "Dude, are you confused as to whether you're a dog or a cat? Your meow sounds like a bark sometimes."

The blue-eyed cat tilted his head and gave me what I swore was a *fuck off* look before he started bathing himself.

"Be careful what you wish for."

Milo ignored me.

"Where's your momma? I've got some goodies here to make the dinner I owe her from yesterday's bet."

The cat continued to bathe himself as he ignored me.

"Fine, but I'm shutting my fucking door tonight. I've had to double up on allergy pills because of you."

Emptying out the grocery bags, I turned the oven on and got ready to make my famous garlic parmesan wings. Slipping the bottle of wine into the fridge, I got to work. I wanted to text Corina, but I didn't want to come across as one of those guys who had to know where his girlfriend was every second.

I dipped the wings in my secret sauce, then dropped them into the parmesan coating. Stopping, I glanced to Milo. He was sitting his ass on my dining room table.

"Get off of there, you little dick."

He meowed and jumped off, making his way over to me. "I don't drop food, so you're wasting your time."

Milo reached up like he was stretching and tried to pull food off the counter.

"Dude! Seriously, go eat your own food. You have a bowl full of it."

His blue eyes stared into mine. I swore he was trying to use some sort of mind power on me.

Looking back at the wings, I frowned. "Do you think it's too soon to call her my girlfriend?"

Meow.

I started to toss the wings in the bowl. "Yeah, I don't think it's too early either. I mean, I did make her come up against my truck yesterday."

The memory of hearing her fall apart made my dick hard.

Meow.

I peeked down at the cat. "What? It was fucking hot watching her come. I want to hear her call out my name again, but I have to play it cool. Maybe I'll go down on her tonight."

Milo did the little bark thing again. *Bruff.*

"I think it's a good idea too. Maybe I won't wait until tonight. Maybe when she walks in I'll take her right here. Those pretty pink lips against my mouth."

My eyes closed, and I groaned as my dick grew harder. Fuck, it had been a long time and my mind was going dizzy at the thought of fucking Corina.

No. At the thought of making love to her.

The oven beeped that it was ready, pulling me out of my fantasy.

I quickly dumped the wings on the cookie sheet and slid them in. I reached for the potatoes, washed them, cut them up, and seasoned them before putting them on their own cookie sheet and sliding them in next to the wings.

"I think we're good to go. Wine. Check. Famous wings. Check. Mom's homemade fries, check."

I searched the pantry for the candles I'd used for the birthday party we threw Chloe's teddy bear one time when she was staying over. She insisted we make him pizza by candlelight. I had no idea that shit was bred into girls, but it was. She wanted to make the night romantic for her favorite teddy bear.

I placed the candles carefully, then grabbed a few dishes and set the table. The front door opened and closed, and I heard feet hitting each step.

"Cheese and crackers! What is that heavenly smell?"

My smile grew wide. I loved how my girl didn't swear.

"It's dinner," I said as she came up the last step. She stopped and stared at me.

"What? I told you I could cook."

Her eyes moved down my body before they trailed back up. The hunger on her face, and the fact that she wasn't trying to hide it, made my dick hard once again.

"Everything okay?" I asked, a grin still on my face.

Corina's teeth sank into her lower lip. "What did you do?" she asked in a whisper.

"I, um, I made dinner. That was the bet, right?"

She nodded. "Yeah. It was…the bet."

I narrowed my eyes and tilted my head. "You sure you're okay, baby?"

She licked her lips. "You look...I mean, I've never seen you in a baseball cap."

Lifting my hand, I felt my cap. I had spun it around when I started cooking.

"Oh, I went to the gym and worked out. I always wear a baseball cap to the gym."

Corina eye-fucked the hell out of me—like a hungry beast who hadn't eaten in days and was staring at her next meal. My body actually fucking trembled from the intensity of her gaze.

"You look so..."

I glanced down. I had on a muscle T-shirt and gym shorts.

"Sweaty?" I asked, laughing as I focused back on her.

Closing her eyes, she took a deep breath. "Mitchell, I need you to fuck me. Right now."

My stomach dropped, and all I could hear was my own damn heart pounding in my ears. "W-what?"

Her hands went to her T-shirt. Pulling it over her head, she stood there looking sexy as fuck in a white lace bra.

No, no, no! She wasn't supposed to come on to me! No sex! No sex! Date her first. Shower her with attention.

"I am...fuck, wait a second." I shook my head to clear my thoughts. "I wanted to date you! Show you it wasn't all about..."

She pulled her pants off and kicked them to the side. Who was this girl and what had she done with my sweet, innocent dove? I salivated as I took in the matching, white lace panties. Her body was perfect, and her breasts spilling out of her bra were begging to be sucked. A flat stomach led to curvy hips that drove me almost insane with lust.

I forced words out. "I wanted to show you it isn't about the sex. I want to be with you for so many other reasons and..."

She walked up to me. "You're driving me insane. The baseball cap is so hot. Please. I want to feel you inside of me, and I can hardly stand it."

I swallowed hard. "I'm never taking this fucking cap off ever again."

With a sweet smile, her head dropped. A blush moved over her cheeks, and I knew she was losing her newfound nerve. With one swift move, I reached over my back and pulled my shirt off, bringing the cap with it.

Corina took in my body with a hungry, lustful stare. She reached out and touched my chest gently, almost like she was worried I'd break.

"Dove, you're not going to hurt me."

Her eyes lifted to mine. With a sexy-as-fuck smile, her hands moved down to my workout shorts. She pushed them down and gasped when she saw my hard dick pressing against the black boxer briefs. When she trailed her finger over it, I let out a groan.

"Christ, don't make me come in my damn underwear, baby."

She giggled, cupped my hard cock and peeked back up at me.

"Too slow." I yanked my briefs off, letting my dick spring free. I wrapped my hand around my shaft and stroked it. Corina watched, her teeth biting so hard into her lip it was turning white.

"Mitch," she whispered.

I leaned over, brushed her hair from her neck so I could kiss below her ear. "Corina, tell me what you want me to do, and I'll do it."

Her hands grabbed my arms, and she held on tight, almost like she was afraid she would fall if she let go.

"I want… I want…" Her voice cracked.

Moving my hands behind her, I unclasped her bra, letting it fall down her arms. Moaning, I cupped both tits in my hands. They fit perfectly.

"Need them in my mouth," I panted. She dropped her head back and whimpered when I sucked on her right nipple and twisted the other with my fingers.

"*Mitch*. Mitch, I'm so horny."

Groaning, I slipped my hand down her perfectly toned stomach and into her panties.

"Not your fingers. I want you…inside of me."

My heart slammed against my chest.

I was dreaming. That's what this was. A fucking dream come true. A dream I should be stopping so that I could follow the advice of my brothers.

Corina whimpered, and all my sense went out the door.

One tug and I ripped her panties off her body.

"God, yes," she panted. "It's been so long."

"I want my mouth on your pussy first."

Corina's body swayed while her eyes lit up like a sunny Texas sky. She wanted my mouth there too, and if I was an asshole, I'd make her tell me so. Make her say out loud that she wanted to fuck my face. But I couldn't wait. I needed to taste her.

Lifting her, I set her ass on the kitchen island and ran my hands along her inner thighs, spreading her open. Her body trembled, and I knew it was going to be hard to keep myself from fucking her until we were both spent, our bodies covered in sweat.

Corina leaned back on her hands, ready for me to devour her. Spreading her legs even wider, I looked at the blonde landing strip that was waiting…no, *begging*…for me to take off. As I slipped my fingers into her, we both moaned.

"You're so wet."

With a nod, she closed her eyes. "Please, don't make me beg, Mitchell. Please."

My dove would never have to beg me to eat her pussy.

Dropping my head, I buried it between her legs as I pulled her to the edge of the island. My tongue slid right through those pink lips and dipped into what I could only remember as pure fucking heaven. I knew for a fact I was the only man who'd ever given her oral sex.

Or did I?

And like that, the wind was knocked out of me. Had she done this with Tripp?

I tried to ignore the nagging question. I licked and sucked on her clit. Corina cried out, "Oh, God."

I pulled back, wanting to ask her if my brother had done this. I wasn't sure how I would feel if he had.

"Mitch, please. It's been so long."

I pushed a finger inside her. Massaging her. "How long has it been, baby?"

Her hips started to lift; she wanted more. She needed more.

"Since that night with you. Please. Please, I need more!"

Smiling, I felt my stomach drop in a weird way. She hadn't let Tripp go this far and that did all kinds of shit to the organ pounding in my chest.

My mouth was back on her, sucking, licking, tongue-fucking her with everything I had. It didn't take long before she screamed out my name. Her pussy grinding against my face. I loved this side of Corina. The one where she let go and let herself enjoy it. There were so many things I wanted to do with her...do *to* her. I lifted my eyes and groaned when I saw her squeezing her tit.

Jesus. I was going to come I was so damn turned on.

I slipped my fingers inside her again. Another orgasm raced through her body. She trembled from head to toe

"Mitch! Oh God, I'm coming again!"

Her hips lifted and pushed her against my face. I was going to lose my fucking mind soon. I needed to stop this before it went too far.

"Can't...take it...anymore."

I stood and pulled her to me. Corina wrapped her legs around me, drawing me closer. Her eyes dropped to my mouth before she leaned in and kissed me. I was taken aback for a second, surprised that she would let me kiss her after going down on her.

"I want more," she whispered, pulling her body closer to mine.

That's when my other head kicked in. The one that felt her warm, wet pussy up against the head of my cock. She dug her heels into me, pushing me into her. We both moaned.

Corina's hands grabbed at my hair, pulling me closer. Our kiss turned frantic as I slipped farther inside. My heartbeat was through the fucking roof. I'd stop it in a second...I would. But right now, I wanted to taste her, feel her body against mine. It had been so fucking long.

"Oh God, Mitchell. More. *Please.*"

Her begging was enough to make me lose my shit. I spun us around and walked over to the sofa.

Stop. Stop this now, Mitch.

"Yes," she whispered as I sat down. She moved over me. Before I had time to think, she sank down on me, filling herself with my dick completely.

"Fucking hell, Corina! We need...oh, fuuuck, you feel so good." *Holy shit.* I went straight to heaven on a one-way ticket, and I didn't want to come back down. Ever.

She rocked her hips and all my common sense went out the door. Reaching up, I pulled one of her nipples into my mouth and sucked hard while Corina rode me even harder. So fucking hard I had to force myself not to come.

Dropping the nipple from my mouth, I gripped her ass, pushing myself deeper into her. "That's it, baby. Rock into me. Fuck me hard. I've missed you so goddamn much."

Her eyes blazed with a fire I hadn't seen since the last time I was balls deep inside of her. With her hands on my shoulders, she lifted and slammed back on me, grinding herself as she mumbled words I couldn't even understand. I loved seeing her let loose like this. And I loved it even more knowing I was driving her to this place.

Bringing her head forward, she pushed against me, her body glistening with sweat as the sounds of our fucking echoed through the room.

"Mitchell, I'm going to come again," she said softly. Corina wasn't one of those women who screamed out when they came.

When she looked into my eyes, I lost it. "I'm going to come, too, baby."

Her pussy pulsed around my cock, pulling my own orgasm out of me so fucking hard I saw stars exploding. It felt like it went on for an eternity. My hand slipped behind her neck, pulling her lips to mine as she continued to ride me. Whimpers spilled from her mouth into mine as we fell blissfully together.

Then it happened.

The oven timer went off. It was like a shot of reality rushed through my veins.

Cupping her face with my hands, I pulled her gently from my mouth. We stared at each other for the longest time as the oven timer continued to give its warning. A warning that came way too fucking late.

I saw the horror in her eyes, and I was positive it matched mine. We'd gotten so damn carried away that we hadn't used protection.

Her hand flew to her mouth. "Oh, Mitchell."

My hands fell to her hips, and I gently lifted her off of me. Never taking my eyes from hers, I helped her so she was sitting on my lap. Tears formed in her baby blues before she buried her head into my neck. I wanted to kick my own ass for being so damn careless. For not taking care of her like I knew I should have. For letting my own weakness lead us to this moment. I had never in my life forgotten to wear a condom. I was *never* this irresponsible.

"I'm so sorry, dove. I'm so sorry I didn't… I didn't stop us."

She shook her head. "No, don't say that. I wouldn't take that back for anything. I've never felt so amazing. So connected to anyone in my entire life. And it was my fault. I threw myself at you and…and I said all those things…and…"

More tears.

My chest tightened, and I felt the strangest ache. What in the hell was this? Was I scared because we'd just had sex without protection? Was I upset because she was scared and crying? Or was I hoping that…*no*.

I shook the thought away.

"Please don't cry, baby. I can't stand to see you cry."

Placing my finger on her chin, I drew her lips to mine. The kiss was soft, slow, and so damn perfect. The urge to pick her up, bring her to my bed and make love to her the right way was overwhelming. So overwhelming I let the thought linger longer than it should.

Seconds turned into minutes as we kissed like we would never see each other again.

When we both needed a breath, Corina gave me a smile that changed everything for me. I wasn't sure in what way, but I knew something deep inside of me was different. Her eyes had the most brilliant light to them. She had just taken me on a ride that was a million times better than any fucking amusement ride I'd ever been on, and it wasn't just the amazing fuck. It was the connection, a connection to her that I'd never experienced before in my entire life.

She pulled her lower lip between her teeth. "I think the oven is trying to tells us to take the food out."

"Shit!" I said, moving her off of me and running into the kitchen. I was well aware I was butt ass naked as I rushed over and pulled out the wings and fries.

"They're not burnt!" I cried out with glee.

Turning, I stood there frozen as I stared at Corina. She had wrapped her body up with the blanket I kept on the back of the sofa.

"Would it sound crazy if I said I wanted you again?" she asked shyly, her beautiful cheeks a soft rose color.

Slipping the oven mitts off my hands, I made my way to her. I pushed her hair back from her face. My hand slipped into her hair, drawing her head back, and we stared into one another's eyes.

"We have to be careful, dove. Are you on the pill?"

When her eyes drifted from mine, I felt a sickness take root in the pit of my stomach.

"I'm on the pill, but I've missed the last few days. With the fire and all…my pills were on my bedside table. I've been meaning to get the prescription refilled."

I swallowed hard and leaned my forehead against hers. "Cord and Tripp are going to kick my ass. I had a *no sex* rule in place."

Covering her mouth, she whispered, "I guess I took Mrs. Johnson's advice to heart."

"Mrs. Johnson gave you advice? On sex?" I pretended to tremble in fear.

Corina giggled. "She told me to come home and jump your bones. When I saw you standing there…looking all hot with your baseball cap on backwards, the muscles showing." She shrugged. "I lost all control."

"Wait, *Mrs. Johnson* told you that?"

She nodded.

"Well, fuck, my dick just went limp."

Corina reached out and took my cock in her hand. "Bet I know how to fix that."

Boy, did she ever. We spent the rest of the night in my bed, taking old lady Johnson's advice to heart..

CHAPTER 19

Mitchell

I stared out the window of my patrol truck, lost in memories of this past week. My dick was exhausted. Corina and I couldn't keep our hands off each other. Every day when I came home from work, she was there, waiting in a different outfit that she must have known would drive me out of my damn mind.

It didn't help that she'd gone into San Antonio on Monday and bought new clothes. After a trip to some fancy lingerie store that Waylynn knew about, I was good as gone. No way a man can resist a beautiful woman sitting on his kitchen island dressed in a pink lacey nighty, or a black one. Or a red one.

I'm only so strong!

I tried. I tried so fucking hard to stop the sex, take it slow. But we were like two horny teenagers trying to have sex every spare moment. We'd used condoms every single time since the first, to both of our displeasure. Once I'd taken Corina bareback, it was hard to go back. She was heading to the doctor next week since she was overdue for her appointment, and they had insisted she come in for a pregnancy test before prescribing more pills.

My body shook at the thought of her being pregnant. What if she *was* pregnant? What would we do?

We'd barely gotten our relationship going. Truth be told, we hardly knew each other—at least the things that two people who were having a baby together should know. Over the last week we'd tried talking, but somehow ended up making love, or fucking like we couldn't get enough. Sure, there were those intimate evenings when I held her in my arms, and we talked about our dreams. I asked her to move into the new house with me, and she said she'd think about it. After all, we had been thrown together in this living situation. I think Corina wanted to feel like it wasn't something she had to do…but something we both wanted.

The crackling of my radio pulled me from my thoughts.

Suspicious person. At Corina's address.

I pulled my truck onto the highway and headed into town. It was rare for dispatch to call me before calling Sheriff Miller, but this was a small town and by now, everyone knew Corina and I were together. I felt sure the late nights sneaking down to Lilly's Café and tucking ourselves in a corner booth to eat because we were too tired from making love or fucking—depending on the mood—might have had something to do with the rumors flying. I'd already gotten three text messages from my mother wanting to know why she was the last to find out about my new relationship.

As I pulled up to the front of Corina's house, I spotted Sherriff Miller, Tripp, and Mr. Knight, Corina's neighbor.

"What's going on?" I asked.

All three turned to look at me. Tripp was the first to talk. "Someone broke into Corina's house. The construction foreman said he couldn't get ahold of you. Turns out he had your number wrong in his phone."

I frowned. "How hard is it to put a number in a phone?"

Tripp shrugged. "He called Sheriff Miller and then me when he couldn't reach you."

I turned to Mr. Knight. "Did you see anything?"

With a nod, he pointed toward the back of the house. "I saw someone running from the building. I was out walking Minnie, my border collie, when I saw 'em. I've done told the sheriff I thought it was a young one. Not very tall or big."

"What did they do?" I asked.

Tripp and Sheriff Miller looked at one another and then back to me.

Sheriff Miller spoke as he started walking toward the door to the house. "It's probably best we just show you. I told the foreman to hold off doing anything until we got prints and investigated a bit more."

I followed them into the house. We made our way to the kitchen and I froze. Giant red words had been spray-painted across the back wall that had once housed the kitchen cabinets.

Lieutenant's whore.

Swallowing hard, I stared at the message. "What in the living hell?" I finally managed.

"Seems like someone is pissed at you and knows you and Corina are together," Tripp said while pushing his hand through his hair. "I don't think you should tell Corina. This will freak her out, and I'm sure she's stressed as it is."

I didn't answer Tripp because I had no idea what to do. I walked over to the back door. There was no sign of a break in there.

"How did they get in?" I asked.

Sheriff Miller looked somber. "The foreman swears the house was locked up tight. When he got here this morning, the back door was wide open. They've already begun to re-build the second story, but the windows are still boarded up. The front door was double locked, so the back is clearly how they got in."

"Fuck," I whispered as I looked back at the message. Turning to Tripp, I asked, "You honestly think we shouldn't tell Corina?"

He nodded. "She's got a lot on her plate. Why bother her with what is probably just some kids screwing around?"

Corina was already stressed because of the fire, her job, and now the worry of possibly being pregnant. The last thing I wanted to do was tell her some nutcase broke into her house because they were pissed at me and knew she was a part of my life.

"You could tell her, but you could also wait and find out more information before you say anything," Tripp added.

I nodded, trying to decide what to do.

I made the decision I thought was right. "Let's keep this between us for now. Roy and I will dust the place for fingerprints and take a look around. Tell the foreman he and his crew can take the rest of the day off."

A part of me knew keeping this from Corina was wrong. I pushed the thought to the side and decided to deal with it later.

"So, are you going to work all night or are you going to take me dancing?"

I swung my office chair around, and my breath caught in my throat as I took in Corina from top to bottom. She was dressed in a one-piece outfit that looked like a dress. On closer inspection I noticed it was shorts with a long black skirt that barely swept across the floor. She was wearing the new cowboy boots she had bought in San Antonio last Monday on her shopping trip with the girls.

I took three steps toward her, getting as close to her as I could. My hand rose and I played with the one piece of hair that had fallen from her ponytail.

My chest ached with a desire to tell her how I felt about her. How she had made me feel things I'd never thought I could, and it wasn't just the incredibly hot sex we'd been having all week. It was the moments when we talked about where we saw ourselves in five years. Or the type of swing that we should put on the porch of the new house. How Chloe was the sweetest little girl we'd ever had the pleasure of knowing and how scared we both were at the idea of Corina being pregnant.

It was those moments that made me realize I was in love with her. That no matter what, I would never leave her side.

"In case you didn't know, Corina. I'm crazy about you."

Her eyes lit up. "Oh yeah?"

Tracing my finger along her jaw, I replied, "Yeah."

The pace of her breath increased as she looked up into my eyes. "I'm crazy about you too."

I knew she had another set of words she wanted to let fall from her lips, but she held back. In a way, I was glad she did. I wasn't ready to tell her I loved her yet. Deep in my heart, I knew without a doubt that I did, but saying the words out loud scared the living hell out of me.

"You ready to go dancing, dove?"

With a nod, she smiled. "I'm so ready."

"This will be our first official outing as boyfriend and girlfriend."

She lifted her brow. "So we are officially calling ourselves that?"

"Hell yeah, we are. No one else gets to put their hands on my girl."

Her head tilted. "You know, I never did say I wasn't mad at you anymore."

I bent down to look at her, leaning in so I could whisper. "I'm pretty sure when my face went between your legs and licked up your pussy you got over being mad at me."

She blushed. "You have such a dirty mouth, Mitchell Parker."

With a wink, I leaned in against her lips. "You know you like it."

Her arms wrapped around my neck. "I do. So very much." Our mouths pressed together into a soft, sweet kiss.

"Come on," I said. "Let's get on out of here before this kiss turns into something else and you're doing the two-step in my bed instead of on a dance floor."

Corina giggled as I laced my fingers with hers. We headed out of the office and made our way to the Pecan Street Festival.

As we stepped out of the building, I couldn't shake the heaviness I'd felt in my chest ever since deciding to keep the break-in from Corina. With everything she had on her mind, the last thing I wanted to do was worry her. Especially if she was carrying our child.

Our child.

My body trembled at the idea. I couldn't tell if it thrilled me or not. Corina rarely mentioned it, so neither did I. I guess we both figured we would deal with it when we had to.

Pushing away my thoughts, I smiled. "You can already hear the band."

Pecan Street was a block over and served as the main street that separated the west side of town from the east. Massive amounts of people walked along the street. Everyone in Oak Springs would be at the dance, including folks from surrounding areas. One thing we knew how to do in this town was throw a street party.

Corina and I walked hand in hand, making small talk as we went.

"Do you think Amelia and Wade are excited about the wedding reception?" Corina asked.

"I do," I answered with a smile. "Mom and Amelia have been busy all week with party planning."

Corina's grin spread wide. "I can't believe they got married. You think people will wonder if Amelia is pregnant?"

With a shrug, I replied, "Who knows. I don't think Amelia cares what people think."

I could see the worry on Corina's face. I was still kicking myself for letting things get so out of control that we forgot to use protection. Then there was my job. I was worried sick by the idea of having someone in my life worrying about me, the risk of leaving her and possibly a baby behind if anything happened...

Fuck.

My hand raked through my hair. I'd already had three good friends die in the line of duty, each leaving behind a family who loved and needed them. If Corina was pregnant with our child, would I want to keep putting my life on the line every day?

I wasn't so sure. I wasn't sure about anything anymore. When I was younger, my dream had been to work on the ranch, but things hadn't turn out like I had originally planned.

"Hey, are you okay?" Corina asked.

The soft touch of her hand on my arm drew me out of the downward spiral of my thoughts.

"Thinking about something with work. Sorry. Bad habit."

She gave me the sweetest smile. "You know, if you ever need to talk about anything, I'm always here for you." My chest tightened. I was so damn stupid to push her away.

We had stopped walking and were now facing each other. This beautiful woman standing before me blew me away. I didn't deserve her. She could have kept me at a distance and made me fight harder for her, but her heart was so forgiving. Her house had been destroyed, her job had changed at a moment's notice, her entire life had turned upside down. And she was worried about me. The urge to tell her I loved her pulled on my heart, but my head was telling me it was too soon.

Cupping her face within my hands, I smiled. "Do you have any idea how much you mean to me?"

Her cheeks flushed slightly. "I have an idea."

My gaze searched her face. Her eyes were the most beautiful I'd ever seen. My heart melted into the ocean of blue staring back at me.

"No matter what happens, Corina, I'm never leaving you."

Tears pooled in her eyes. When she opened her mouth, I knew she wanted to tell me she loved me, but she held back. In a way, I was still relieved.

She finally let some words slip free. "I'm scared, Mitchell. I don't know what to do if I'm pregnant."

The fear in her voice sent me off the edge. Leaning down, I covered her mouth with mine. It didn't matter how many people were around to see us. I needed to take her fear away. Nothing else mattered.

Corina wrapped her arms around my neck as she opened her mouth to me. Her lips were warm and soft as a cloud. We both let sounds of pleasure slip out as we deepened the kiss.

Someone standing next to us cleared their throat. We ignored it; the kiss was too perfect to break.

"Y'all might want to take it back to your place if you want to suck face like that in front of the whole town."

Stepping back, I dragged in a breath. Corina did the same. A smile spread over her beautiful face, followed by a pink flush on her cheeks.

"Hey, Waylynn," I said, pulling my eyes off of Corina and looking at my older sister leaning against the building. I hadn't realized we had stopped in front of the place she had chosen for her dance studio.

With a wide grin, she stepped closer. "Hey there, love birds. You keep up the PDA and tongues are gonna be waggin'."

I laughed. "They already are."

Waylynn's gaze moved between the two of us. She lingered longer on me, and I couldn't help but wonder if she had heard what Corina said about possibly being pregnant. If she had, she didn't mention it.

"Well, this town needs good gossip." She lifted her brows. "Maybe now they'll move on from my sad story of being cheated on and having to crawl back home to Oak Springs from New York."

"Fuck what people say, Waylynn," I snapped.

Her stare pierced me. "Remember your words of advice, little brother."

Amelia let out a scream when she saw us. Running up to our small group, she grabbed Corina and hugged her before doing the same to Waylynn. I reached down and gave her a kiss on the cheek, my gaze still fixed on my older sister.

"The Parker family is all together!" Amelia said with a clap.

Waylynn turned to Amelia. "I say we show this little town the proper way to have a good time."

Amelia laced her arm with Corina's as they walked. Waylynn fell in step next to me. As we approached my father's barbecue pit for the annual Pecan Street barbecue contest, Waylynn pulled me to a stop.

Our eyes met, and we didn't have to exchange words. I knew she had heard Corina.

"Do you know what you're doing?" Waylynn asked.

I let out a sigh. "No fucking clue, but if she is pregnant, we'll figure it out."

She looked over to Corina and then back to me. "Well, I can tell you one thing, Mitchell, y'all better figure it out fast."

As my sister walked over to our family, I shoved my fingers through my hair.

"Yeah, I sure as fuck better."

CHAPTER 20

Corina

Everyone was enjoying themselves. There was something about a street dance that made me feel good—small town country at its best. Kids ran through the crowds, playing and exploring. High school kids danced in the middle of the street while older folks sat at tables and enjoyed one another's company.

This was one of the many reasons I loved Texas.

Waylynn let out a *yee-haw* as Cord spun her around and did some flip move before they took off two-steppin' again. Amelia and Wade were lost in each other, dancing slowly even though it was a fast song. I couldn't help but smile at the love between them.

On one side of the street, Steed held a sleeping Chloe while Paxton cradled Gage. My heart melted as I took them in. I wanted desperately to tell Paxton what had happened with Mitchell and the night of the forgotten condom, but I knew the first thing she would do: jump all over me for not being careful. Even though she and Steed ended up with Gage for the very same reason.

A breath slipped from my lips as I tried not to think about it. Mitchell's laughter pulled my head to the right where I saw him with his father and Trevor, joking about something. I watched Mitchell's every move, loving everything about him. The dimple that came out when he smiled. The way he whispered sweet and tender things in my ear when we made love. The way he placed his hand on my lower back to guide me through a room. Even the way he pretended to despise Milo, yet secretly loved him.

Another laugh from Mitchell broke my stare. My stomach tightened as a new round of thoughts hit me.

If I was pregnant, how would Mitchell react? He was still getting used to the idea of being in a relationship. There was no way he would be able to handle a kid thrown into the picture. Or would he? Deep in my heart, I knew his words from earlier were his way of telling me he was in this for the long haul.

Tears stung my eyes as I forced them back.

He said he wouldn't leave, no matter what. Did that mean he wouldn't leave me? Or the baby?

My gaze dropped to the ground, and I tried to push the thoughts away. I wasn't even sure I was pregnant. Touching my stomach, I held my breath.

Was *I* ready for all of this? I had a career. A life I had planned that didn't include a baby—at least not yet.

Then there was the problem with my brother. He was getting married, and if I announced I was pregnant, he'd say I was trying to steal his thunder.

Crap. Why did I lose control that day? I threw myself at Mitchell, knowing he wouldn't be able to resist. Did I subconsciously want this?

"Corina?"

My head popped up to see Vi, Mitchell's aunt.

"Hi, Vi. Having fun?"

She sat down next to me and let out a sigh. "I'm too old for this shit."

I let out a chuckle. "Why are you here then?"

With a drawn-out sigh, she replied, "On the search for a man."

Nearly choking on my own breath, I stared at her. "Are you serious?"

Vi turned to look at me. "Of course I'm serious. I'm a woman. I have needs, my dear."

I didn't like where this was going. I frantically looked for Mitchell. My heart dropped when I saw him talking to another woman. I couldn't tell who she was from behind. I willed her to turn around. Was it Cassidy?

"He's only talking to her. Stow the fears," Vi whispered.

"I'm not worried," I said, my voice sounding weak. Truth was, a small part of my brain wondered if Mitchell could settle down and be with one woman for the long run. He hadn't been with anyone in months, so I wasn't sure why I was worried…but I was.

"You don't sound convincing to me, so I know you aren't convincing yourself. The one thing you're going to have to get used to, Corina, is that you are with a man who is terribly good looking. Women are going to stare, flirt, and yes, attempt to slip into his bed. Do you trust him?"

It didn't even take me a second to answer.

"Yes. It's her I don't trust." I threw that last sentence in because I assumed he was talking to Cassidy.

"Spoken like a woman who isn't naïve," Vi said.

Mitchell lifted his eyes and looked at me from across the street. Almost as if he knew my gaze was on him. He smiled and my stomach dropped and instantly fluttered. When he looked back to the woman, his smile slipped off his face.

A moment ago when he was looking at me and smiling, now he seemed angry. He went to step around the woman and she reached for his arm. It *was* Cassidy. Pulling his arm free, he said something that caused her to take a step back. I wondered if he'd put her in her place, like that day in the ladies' restroom.

"Aunt Vi, don't you look beautiful this evening," Waylynn said.

I looked up at Mitchell's sister. "She's on the hunt for a man," I offered.

Waylynn's brows lifted. "Me too! Let's go hunt together."

Vi let out a laugh and stood. "You always were my favorite, Waylynn."

I focused back on Mitchell and Cassidy, but they were both gone. My heart started to race and my mind wandered to a place it shouldn't.

Did they go off together?

No, I know better.

Cheese and crackers, Corina. Settle down.

I suddenly felt sick. Standing, I took in a deep breath and came face to face with Mitchell.

He looked concerned, reaching out for me. "What's wrong?" he asked.

My mouth opened but nothing came out. What was I going to say? *I'm jealous because you're talking to a woman you slept with a while ago?*

Like that would go over well.

"Nothing. I felt a little sick. It's pretty warm out, and I don't think I've had enough water today."

Mitchell frowned. "You need to make sure you're drinking water, dove."

His pet name felt like a cool breeze over my hot skin.

"I know," I barely replied.

Mitchell wrapped his arm around my waist and led me to one of the food booths. My mind was racing with what I should do next: ask him what he and Cassidy had talked about? Or ignore it and let my curiosity fester?

I knew what to do. I wasn't into playing games, and I knew Mitchell wasn't either. Before I had a chance to ask, he spoke first. "Cassidy was asking how serious we are."

A lump formed in my throat. I looked up at him as we waited in line.

"I told her we were serious *and* exclusive. You're my girlfriend and I am your boyfriend."

My body tingled as he spoke. "What did she say after that?"

He rolled his eyes. "Some smart-ass remark about me not being able to stay with one woman."

The tingles vanished. "Is she right?" I asked, deciding to voice my worries.

Mitchell looked hurt. I regretted asking the question, but then again, I felt like I needed to.

"She's far from it. I know I didn't start things off right with us, and I regret it. I can't change that, but the last thing I want is for you to think I might cheat on you. I would never do that to you, Corina."

Lifting up on my toes, I wrapped my arms around his neck. I had already known the answer in my heart, but my head was being a bitch and wanted reassurance.

Our lips pressed together. Mitchell's hand moved up my back and into my hair, tugging me closer to him.

He pulled back and gave me a sexy grin. "I have another position."

Lifting a brow, I asked, "Really? I'm listening."

Mitchell looked around, then back at me. "I say we sneak behind this food trailer and see how quiet we can be in public."

My eyes widened in surprise. "Are you serious, Mitchell? Sex in public? You're a cop!"

He laughed. "That makes it all the more fun."

I chewed on my lip as I thought about it. Mitchell grabbed my hand and pulled me around the food truck. It was darker and no one was around, but we could hear the voices of everyone around us.

"I can't do this!" I whispered.

When he gave me a sexy-as-sin grin, I knew I was about to lose this battle.

Mitchell unbuttoned his pants and pushed them down. My eyes moved down to stare at his impressive length. Taking a breath, I leaned over and took him into my mouth. Mitchell hissed and dug his fingers into my hair. How did this man have such an effect on me? He brought out my naughty side, and I loved it!

Reaching with my other hand, I played with his balls before slipping my fingers and applying light pressure around his shaft. Mitchell let out a groan, tapped me on the head, and said, "Baby, I'm going to come."

You can do this, Corina!

And did I ever. I swallowed every drop of Mitchell's cum. When I stood up, I wiped my mouth and looked at him. His eyes were glassy, and he had a smile on his face.

"Fucking hell. That was amazing," he gasped as he tucked himself back into his pants and zipped up.

With a smile of my own, I made a check motion with my finger. "Not really a position, but we can check off blowjob in public."

Mitchell laughed. "Yes, we can."

His hand went behind my neck, crushing my mouth to his.

Time seemed to stand still. I felt him pour everything he had into that kiss, and I knew no matter what happened next, Mitchell Parker would never hurt me again.

When he broke the kiss, he leaned his forehead against mine and his mouth fell open. Words were on his lips, but he didn't give them to me. They were probably the same words I wanted to say. I was just as nervous to admit it aloud. So I whispered the truth in my mind.

I love you, Mitchell Parker.

CHAPTER 21

Corina

Excitement was in the air at the Parker house. Melanie and John floated from person to person like the perfect hosts that they were. My cheeks hurt from smiling so much at all the stories that had been told throughout the evening. Amelia and Wade's wedding reception was turning out to be the party of the year, although Chloe informed everyone that her daddy and Uncle Mitchell's party would be better.

I glanced around, my eyes landing on Amelia. I'd never seen her so happy. I thought back to a few months ago when she'd been scared that she might have lost Wade. Things could really change in the blink of an eye.

Heck, look at me and Mitchell. Last month we were barely able to look at one another across the room. Now I was sitting next to him, our hands laced together and I might possibly be...

I let the thought slip away. The less I thought about it the better.

"What do you think about the bodies showing up between here and Uvalde?" an older gentleman asked Mitchell. I couldn't remember if he was someone Amelia's dad worked with or an old family friend.

"It's unsettling, that's for sure," Mitchell replied.

"Murders?" the man asked.

I could feel Mitchell tense. "Looks to be that way."

Now I tensed. "How many bodies have they found?" I asked.

He looked at me, and I could tell he wasn't in the mood to talk about his job. He rarely ever was. "Enough to cause concern."

I swallowed hard.

"Lloyd Gillory said they are all runaways," the man added. "Young women, most under the age of thirty."

Mitchell cleared his throat. "Lloyd Gillory shouldn't talk about things unless he knows the facts."

Taken aback at Mitchell's sharp tone, I quickly changed the subject. "Can you believe how insanely hot this summer has been? I'm hoping September brings a few early cold fronts. Especially with school starting next week and the fall festival a few weeks away."

The older man, his wife, and Aunt Vi all looked at me.

"You couldn't change the subject to something other than the weather, Corina?" Vi asked with pinched brows.

I managed a half-smile and shrugged.

A bell rang from the kitchen area, and everyone turned their attention to Melanie and John..

Mitchell leaned over and his hot breath brought goosebumps to my entire body. "I love your help, but the weather? We need to find some more interest subjects."

I licked my lips before pressing them together. "Like?"

His mouth ran across my neck, causing a pull in my lower stomach. "Like how boring this party is and how I want to take you home and try a new position."

I pulled away slightly to look at him. "You want me to bring up new sex positions next time I need to change the topic?"

He shrugged. "Might give the old bastards something good to talk about."

I couldn't help but smile. "I hardly think your mother would approve."

He nodded, flashing a sexy grin. "She wouldn't, but I would."

I pushed his shoulder, then put my finger to my lips while his mother spoke.

"Thank you to everyone who came to help us celebrate Amelia and Wade's wedding! Two down…five more to go!"

Cheers rang across the rooms as Trevor, Cord, and Tripp all held up their hands as if trying to reject their mother's words.

"Never!" Trevor shouted.

Cord and Tripp both uttered something under their breaths. I was almost positive I heard a curse word or two.

Laughing, I looked at Mitchell. He stared with a goofy smile, and I wasn't the only one who noticed. A few of the younger folks shot off a comment or two about how it looked like Mitchell had gotten bit. When Cord shouted something about Mitchell looking like a Smurf, everyone laughed.

Mitchell stood, taking a glass of champagne from one of the young ladies who had been walking around with a tray.

"I'd like to propose a toast to my baby sister," Mitchell called out, glancing around the room. When he locked eyes with Amelia, both of their smiles lit up. "To see you so happy and in love is a beautiful thing. I've never been so proud of you for following your heart."

Tears built in Amelia's eyes as Wade pulled her close.

"To Amelia and Wade," Mitchell said, lifting his glass. "May you both have a lifetime of happiness and here's to all your dreams coming true. And may you give dad a new grandbaby soon!"

"What?" John shouted out as everyone else cheered, "Here-here!"

I pretended to take a drink. Until I went to the doctor on Monday, I was playing it safe, but I also didn't want to draw any attention to myself. I'd given Mitchell a knowing look when I took the glass of champagne earlier. Not a single person, other than Mitchell, had noticed I'd had the same glass all evening.

Everyone moved outside under a giant white tent. The Parker family was all sitting at one table while friends sat at nearby tables. News of Mitchell and I becoming a couple had spread fast among the Parker family's friends, so I was seated next to Mitchell at the family table, with Cord on my right.

Dinner was served and soon mini-conversations started at each table. Mitchell and his father talked about the ranch and some new horse that would be arriving in the next few days. I hadn't realized how much Mitchell was involved with the ranch until the past week. There wasn't anything he didn't know about horses, and he pretty much ran the horse stables on some days. We had stopped by three evenings in a row so he could check on two new horses and a filly that had been born last week. I loved seeing him with the horses. Of course, the Parker ranch was a cattle ranch, but I could see something in Mitchell's eyes when he was in that barn with the horses. I wanted desperately to ask him about it but decided to wait.

"I heard you got shot at work on Thursday," Tripp announced. My fork froze at my lips and my hand started to shake.

Mitchell let out a half-hearted laugh. "Yeah, good thing I had my vest on."

This time, the fork dropped and clattered against the plate. Everyone at the table looked at me.

"You okay, Corina?" Waylynn asked from across the table. Our eyes met, and I wasn't sure what to say. I could tell she knew exactly why I was having a panic attack.

She gave me a knowing look before focusing in on Mitchell. She made a face then jerked her head toward me.

Mitchell turned and took my hand. "I'm sorry. I didn't even think to mention it."

I stared at him. "You didn't think to *mention* it?" It's not like I wanted much from him. To be faithful. To be honest. And to tell me if he got shot at!

"Everything was fine. It wasn't a big deal." He looked agitated.

"Mitchell, you said it was a good thing you had your vest on. Does that mean he actually hit you with the bullet?"

"Shit. Sorry, Mitch," Tripp said with a slight laugh. I glared at him. He stopped laughing on a dime.

Swinging my eyes back to Mitchell, he frowned. "It's part of the job."

He turned to his father and started talking about harvesting or something while I tried to make heads or tails out of what I had heard. I stared at my plate, my breath not the least bit controlled no matter how hard I tried.

"Corina, will you help me get something in the kitchen?" Waylynn asked.

My eyes lifted, and she raised her brows before motioning for me to get up and follow her.

I was on automatic. I stood, turned, walked to the kitchen.

Waylynn took my hand and pulled me into the family room. "Breathe."

I shook my head as I let Mitchell's words replay in my mind.

Her hands gripped my shoulders. "Corina Miller! Breathe, goddammit!"

I looked into Waylynn's blue eyes and sucked in a breath.

She nodded. "Good. Let it out."

Exhaling, I sat on the leather sofa.

"Corina, I know being a cop was one of the reasons why Mitchell never wanted to settle down. Now with you possibly being *in the family way* and the fact that he is head over heels in love with you, I think he was only trying to shield you."

Staring at her, I opened my mouth. "You think he feels that way about me too?"

Waylynn laughed. "Hell, yes. Girl, don't you see the way he looks at you? I mean even before y'all were together he had puppy dog love eyes. He may not be saying it yet, but Mitchell is head over heels."

A smile lifted my face as I let her words sink in. Then they slipped away. "I knew it was dangerous to be in a relationship with a cop, Waylynn, but if he's going to hide this type of thing from me, I don't know how I feel about that."

She nodded. "And if he had told you, what would have happened?"

"I…I'm sure I would have been worried."

Pointing to me, she said, "Bingo. You would have worried, freaked out a little, then when he left the next morning for work, what would have happened?"

With a shrug, I replied, "I would have worried a little bit more than normal, I guess."

"Yes! And do you think Mitchell wants you to worry right now?"

I looked down at my hands in my lap, feeling like an idiot. "No."

Waylynn reached for my hands. "Men aren't always right, but I know Mitchell's heart is always in the right place."

Feeling foolish, I closed my eyes and sighed. "Everything is happening so fast, Waylynn. I told myself I wouldn't fall back into Mitchell's arms and then I did. I promised myself we would take it slow, only to have us both be reckless the first time we were back together. And now…now…"

My eyes stung with tears.

"Now you might be carrying his baby. Do you want to keep it?"

"Yes!" I said without even having to think about it. "Am I ready? No. I mean, I want kids more than anything, but I don't want them because we were stupid and careless. I want them when we decide it's time. This is not how I saw my life playing out. I mean, I love your brother with my whole heart, and I think he loves me, but he isn't even ready to say it. What does that mean if I *am* pregnant? Will he love the baby or will he feel like he's trapped? The last thing I want is to make him feel trapped."

"Hey, it takes two to tango and I know Mitchell. He will love this baby with every ounce of his being. The same way he loves you."

I forced a smile. It was nice to hear Waylynn saying what I so desperately wanted to hear Mitchell say.

"Come back outside and finish eating," she said.

Nodding, I replied, "I will. Give me two minutes."

Waylynn stared at me for a few seconds. "Two minutes. Now I have to go figure out what we needed in the kitchen and bring it back out with me."

We both chuckled. Waylynn headed out of the family room, and I took a few moments to breathe and calm my racing heart.

Mitchell had a dangerous job. I was okay with that. No matter how much he tried, he wasn't going to be able to protect me from all the bad stuff that came with it. Tonight I would tell him that. Let him know that I wanted all of him. The good, the bad, the dangerous job, the fear of opening himself up. I wanted all of it, and I wasn't going to push him into anything. No matter what happened on Monday.

I loved him, and even though only a few weeks ago I set out to forget about Mitchell Parker, my heart had other plans. Now I needed to be there for him, let him know that I wasn't ever going to leave him either. That he could trust me to know that whatever happened I would be strong enough to handle it.

I headed back through the house. As I stepped outside, I forced a smile and headed to the family table. All the other guests were engaged in conversations. I couldn't help but notice Mitchell's voice as I grew closer.

"Mom, please don't do this."

"I'm just saying, being in a relationship is a two-way street, Mitchell. If you start off hiding things, it's not good."

Pushing his hand through his hair, Mitchell let out a groan. "You think maybe I had a good reason for not saying anything to her?"

Tripp saw me and cleared his throat. "Mitchell, Mom. Let's put this away. Y'all are getting loud and this *is* Amelia and Wade's reception dinner."

"Have you said the L word yet?" Melanie asked, peeking in my direction.

What in the heck? Is she trying to put him on the spot?

I shook my head and walked faster toward the table. I wasn't going to let someone make Mitchell utter those words until he was ready.

"Momma, please let it go," Waylynn said, making her way to her seat after setting down a bottle of wine.

Melanie shrugged and looked my way again. She quickly let an evil smile play over her face. "Well, someday when you fall in love you'll be ready to say it."

Mitchell let out a small, frustrated laugh. "I *am* in love, Mom."

I froze.

"I'm pretty sure I was in love with Corina when I met her. Then I fell in love a little more when I heard her laugh for the first time. I fell harder when she kissed me. When she got pissed at me, hated me, and then loved me again. Through all of it, I was in love. I just didn't know how to admit it to myself."

I covered my mouth and didn't even attempt to hold back my tears. Amelia, Paxton, and Waylynn looked at me, each of them wearing a goofy grin.

"I knew you were, Mitchell," Melanie said with a wink. "You just needed a little push to say it out loud."

Standing, he shook his head. "You're an evil woman, do you know that?"

The whole table erupted with laughter. Mitchell looked back and our eyes met.

His smile faded, and his face filled with disappointment. There might have been a touch of sadness, but not because of what he had said. It was because I knew this wasn't how he wanted me to hear it for the first time.

"Hey," he softly said.

"Hey," I replied.

He took my hands in his. "That wasn't how I wanted to tell you."

I couldn't help my smile. "I know. I wanted you to say it when you were ready." I shrugged. "It's still kind of soon, maybe."

Mitchell shook his head, leaned down, and gently kissed my lips. It was a sweet kiss—short and simple—a kiss I would remember the rest of my life. "What do you say we blow this popsicle stand?" he asked.

My eyes widened. "What about Amelia and Wade?" I asked, peeking over to them. They were lost in conversation.

"I hardly think anyone will notice if we sneak away. I mean, can they blame us after the bomb I just laid out for everyone to hear?"

A giggle slipped from my lips. I glanced around at the tables. No one was paying any attention to us. Well, except for John and Melanie. I could practically feel their eyes burning into us.

"Your parents are staring."

Mitchell laughed. "My father is probably trying to figure out if the cameras are going to come out and say *gotcha*! And my mother, well, I'm sure we can guess what she's thinking."

A flutter rose in my chest as we gazed at one another.

Mitchell placed his hand on my lower back and guided me into the house. We were in his truck and driving down the long driveway faster than I could wrap my head around everything.

Mitchell loves me.

He's loved me the entire time.

Warmth radiated throughout my body. My heartbeat picked up, and I swore if Mitchell listened hard enough, he would be able to hear it.

When I peeked at him, he glanced my way and winked. Everything was going to be okay.

Simply because…

He loves me.

CHAPTER 22

Mitchell

I couldn't be angry with my mother even though I wanted to be. That shit she pulled at dinner had pissed me off, but at the same time, it had lifted something off my shoulders I hadn't realized was there. Sure, I had known deep down I was in love with Corina. It had been on my lips more than once…especially this past week.

But there was something about hearing myself say the words. It hit home and made everything so damn clear.

I was in a committed relationship, and I fucking loved it. And the woman I was in the relationship with might be carrying my child.

Okay, so that bit of information still freaks me out.

We drove in silence for a bit before Corina finally said, "I think we need to talk."

The old me would have flipped if a girl said those words, but I knew it wasn't a *Dear John* type of moment, where Corina was going to say things weren't working out between us. It was the opposite.

"I'm heading to the old house," I said. "I've got a surprise for you. How about if we talk there?"

I chanced a look her way, only to be greeted with the most radiant smile I'd ever seen. "I like surprises."

A small laugh slipped from my mouth. "So I've been told...by Paxton."

Corina chuckled and told a story about when she and Paxton were in college.

"Paxton discovered my love of surprises by accident. One of our neighbors had a cookie bouquet delivery, and they weren't home to get it. So, Paxton took it and told the delivery guy she'd make sure they got it that evening."

I grinned like a fool. "Why do I have a feeling I know where this is going?"

She giggled and the innocence made my heart skip a beat. "I came home from classes. Did I mention it was finals week?"

My smile grew bigger. "No, you didn't."

"Yep. I was super stressed. Paxton always played it so cool and never made it seem like that week bothered her in the least. I was on the phone with my brother that morning and he told me he would send me something to get me through the week."

"Oh, Corina. You didn't."

"I did!" she replied, laughing hard. "I walked in and saw the cookies. The whole apartment smelled amazing! I ripped open the card and read it."

"What did it say?"

"Good luck on finals. Don't stress! We love you."

"That was it?" I asked.

"Yes! I figured they were from my brother and Mom. I mean, who doesn't sign the card when they send something?"

I shrugged. "I wouldn't think very many people."

"Right? So anyway, I must have eaten half the cookies by the time Paxton got home. She freaked out and went into full-on panic mode. She was sure the neighbor was going to fall into a major funk because she didn't get the cookies."

"What did y'all do?"

Corina looked off in the distance and smiled. She was lost in the memory. Finally, she shook her head and laughed. "We stayed up nearly all night making cookies and decorating them, studying in between batches. The next morning, Paxton gave our neighbor the cookie bouquet. Her parents had sent the original basket, and she was so happy she cried. She offered some to me and Paxton and I felt so guilty I broke down right there in the hall and confessed my cookie-eating sin."

I let a roar of laughter out. "Why does that not surprise me? What did the girl do?"

"Well, after she looked at us like we were insane, she busted out laughing. We all had a cookie-eating party that night and celebrated finals week being over. Turns out she was pretty cool."

"That's awesome. Y'all still friends?"

Corina shook her head. "We lost touch shortly after that. Paxton and I came back from summer break, and she was gone. Never did find out what happened to her."

"That's a bummer."

She shrugged. "Yeah, she was a nice girl."

I pulled into the driveway that led to my house. Corina's cheeks flushed, and I knew she was thinking about me making her come against my truck. I was going to see more of that blush in a bit when I pushed balls deep into her.

Corina jumped out of the truck and started for the front porch while I grabbed a few things out of the back seat.

"There's a light on in the house, Mitchell."

Walking up behind her, I leaned in next to her ear. "That's because I was here earlier today."

She turned to me, a sexy little grin on her face. "This is where you went off to earlier for your errand."

With a quick kiss on the cheek, I replied, "Yep. Come on, I want to show you what I did."

I unlocked the door and we stepped inside. The smell of roses filled the air and Corina gasped. "Mitchell! You did all of this?"

Glancing around the living room, I smiled. Red roses were everywhere. They were in vases, some in small baskets, petals were carefully sprinkled across the floor, stems laid across the fireplace mantel. *Everywhere*.

"I did."

She spun around. "You have no idea how many nights I dreamed of the two of us together like this."

I set the stuff in my arms down and drew her to me. "I promise to never walk away from you again. I need you to believe me when I say that."

"I believe it with my whole heart. I truly do."

A single tear slipped from her eye. Leaning down, I kissed it away.

"I had a few things delivered to the house over this past week."

Her brows lifted. "You did?"

"Yep. Figured we might be needing them if we planned on staying out here more. I hope you don't mind, I sort of picked out a bedroom set for the guest room. I didn't want to pick out ours without your input."

I started to walk toward the kitchen to show her the new appliances. She was frozen in place.

My breath caught in my throat. What if she didn't want to move in here with me? I had assumed since she was living with me, she'd move right on into this place when I did. Shit. We hadn't even talked about it.

"I mean, that's if you want to pick it out. I figured once your place is put back together we'll be spending time between the two houses."

She took in a deep breath and slowly let it out. "That's one of the things I wanted to talk to you about."

I swallowed hard. "Do you want to go sit on the back porch?"

Corina nodded. I took her hand and we started through the house. When we walked into the kitchen, she gasped.

"Mitchell! You got the appliances I said I loved!"

Smiling, I rocked back and forth on my feet. "You said you wanted them for your place, but you loved them so much, I wanted you to have them here too."

She shook her head, and then our eyes met. "I don't know what to say. You did all this for me?"

My finger went to her chin. Lifting her eyes to meet mine, I answered. "There isn't anything I wouldn't do for you, Corina. I've got a lot of making up to do, and I plan on making you the happiest you've ever been and spoiling you every day of your life."

Her lower lip trembled. "I am happy, Mitch. So very happy. And all I need is you."

I rested my hand against her face, and she leaned into it. "I know you want to talk, and one of the things we need to discuss is why I didn't tell you about the shooting this week."

Corina's gaze fell to the floor, and I knew it was because she didn't want me to see the fear in her eyes.

A few seconds later, her gaze was back on mine. "Let's go outside. I'm feeling a bit queasy, and I'm not sure if it was something I ate, or nerves."

We sat on the rocking chairs that had been left by the previous homeowners. The sun had already dipped below the skyline, but there was still a touch of daylight.

The silence between us wasn't awkward or worrisome. It felt natural.

"Mitchell, I've been thinking the last few days. One of the things I've been thinking about is your job. I know one of your biggest fears was to fall in love only to have something happen to you, leaving behind the person you fell for."

My heart dropped in my chest.

Corina turned in the rocking chair, her legs pulled up so that she could sit sideways.

"I knew you were a cop when we spent that night together. I knew your job was dangerous and even though things didn't work out right away, I still gave you my heart that night. Call me crazy, but something beautiful happened between us and I..."

She looked down at her hands. "I knew when you made love to me that morning, before you left, that there was something between us. I told myself I was stupid to be in love with a man who would walk away and never look back, but there were so many times I saw it in your eyes—I knew you had to feel the same thing I felt that morning."

Corina chewed on her lip then took another deep breath. "There's a reason neither of us truly moved on after that night."

I nodded. "I agree."

"But that's in the past, and like you said, it only brings out hurt feelings when we revisit those memories. I just wanted you to know that I knew what I was getting into the first time we were together, and I know what I'm into now. I know your job is dangerous and I know there are going to be days when it puts your life at risk. But I don't want you to hide that from me, Mitchell."

My stomach dropped. "I didn't tell you because—"

Her finger came to my lips. "I know why you didn't tell me. That makes me love you more. But even if I am pregnant, we've got nine months of this. You can't hide everything from me. I want our relationship to be built on trust. I trust you and you trust me. If I'm feeling a certain way, I want to communicate that with you, and I want you to do the same. Like your parents. I've watched them together and they're not only in love, they're partners in every sense. I want that for us."

Guilt ripped through my body. I knew she was right, and I wasn't about to start our relationship with secrets.

With a somber look, I nodded. "The past few weeks have been so damn amazing, Corina. I guess I was afraid something would happen and you'd leave."

Her eyes filled with tears. "Mitch, I'm not going anywhere. I swear to you."

I reached for her hand and rubbed my thumb over her soft skin. "If anything ever happened to you, I'd never forgive myself."

Her hand covered mine and our gazes connected. I could hear every sound around me. The wind blowing the branches up against the window of the house. An owl calling out as the sky grew darker. The sound of my heart beating in my chest.

"Talk to me, Mitchell. I see something in your eyes."

I didn't know how to start, so I just went for it. "Someone broke into your place the other day. They spray painted something on the kitchen wall."

A look of pure terror moved over her face. "W-what did it say?"

I swallowed hard. My mouth went dry and I had to force the words out. "It said…um…"

"Just tell me, Mitch."

Closing my eyes, I whispered, "Lieutenant's whore."

Corina's gasp made my eyes snap open. A small part of me wished I hadn't told her. The fear in her eyes was evident. I also couldn't help but notice that her arms were wrapped around her stomach. Was she doing it because this made her sick to her stomach? Or was she worried about the baby she might be carrying?

She had to know that I would never let anything happen to her or our baby.

CHAPTER 23

Corina

I opened my mouth to speak. Nothing came out. Mitchell picked me up out of the chair and carried me through the house and upstairs to a bedroom. Not the master, but one of the other rooms. There was a bed, dresser, and a few other pieces of furniture.

He set me down, and I glanced around the room. It didn't look like new furniture.

"Where's this furniture from?" I asked.

"It's the bedroom set from my old room at my folks' place. I asked them if I could have it."

After scanning the room, I placed my eyes back on Mitchell. He looked nervous. Scared, even. I wanted to ask more about the break in. A part of me wanted to know if he had any leads. I thought about Cassidy. He seemed agitated with her. Did he think she'd done it?

I closed my eyes. I wanted to forget all of it. None of it mattered. This whole 'let's communicate openly' now seemed like the stupidest idea I'd ever had. Even though I knew it was important, it didn't seem so important right now. The last thing I'd expected was a sudden bomb like this.

Mitchell's hand pushed through his beautiful dark hair, and he cursed under his breath. "I should have waited to tell you."

"No," I said, finding my voice. "I'm glad you did. Do you know who did it?"

He wore a somber expression. "We dusted the place for fingerprints and came up with nothing. I'm almost positive the stupid ass foreman left the back door unlocked."

"I don't really have anything left in the house. Were they trying to steal something?" All of my important papers that had made it through the fire had been taken out when I met with the insurance adjuster. Everything upstairs was a total loss. The furniture downstairs needed to be sent out for smoke and water damage. The rest of the house was going to be gutted so there really wasn't much left in the house.

"I don't think anyone was going in to steal, Corina. I think it was a prank. Most likely some local kids I've picked up for stuff trying to be funny."

I looked directly into his eyes. "And if it wasn't?"

He smiled so sweetly, and I could almost read his thoughts. He would never let anything happen to me. "Then I'll take care of it. I promise no one will ever hurt you."

His eyes burned into my soul. He'd spoken each word like it was an oath.

"Mitchell," I whispered. My eyes closed as his hands moved over my body.

"I don't want to think about anything other than us right now, Corina."

I nodded.

Mitchell's lips found their way to my neck where he peppered me with the softest kisses. I let out a small whimper when our fingers slipped under each other's clothes. I was soon pressed against the mattress. Mitchell's hands pushed mine over my head while his kisses turned more passionate. Hungry, almost. My body felt like it was floating, and I hadn't even had an orgasm yet. The feel of him pressing against me was pure heaven. I wanted more. Needed more. Mitchell's heated breath mixed with mine as he teased me with his dick.

"Mitchell, please. Make love to me."

He moved so quickly I hadn't even realized what he'd grabbed until I watched him sliding the condom over his impressive, hard length.

Each breath I took made my chest rise. I craved Mitchell inside me constantly. There was no way I could have pushed this man away—not when I needed his touch to breathe.

"I want to stay like this forever, Corina. You and me...alone ...as one."

We both moaned when he pushed all the way in. Neither of us moved. It was as if we were both afraid the intensity would end if we did.

My fingers moved slowly over his back while he stared into my eyes.

"I can't believe I was such an idiot," he said.

I smiled and bit my lip. "There were so many moments I could pinpoint. You are going to have to clarify which you're talking about."

His head pulled back with a shocked expression before we both started laughing.

Mitchell quickly rolled us over so that I was now on top of him. His hands cupped my breasts while he pulled and pinched my nipples. I felt like a completely different woman when I was on top of him. Mitchell had this way of bringing out another part of me. A daring and carefree part, not only with sex, but with life in general.

And he had paid attention and knew how much I enjoyed this position.

Heck, I loved it.

I had control and could go as slow or as fast as I wanted. Plus, Mitchell had a tendency to talk dirty to me when I rode him, and it spurred me on even more. Some of my best orgasms were with me on top and him talking naughty.

"Fuck me, Corina. Hard and fast, baby. We've got lots of time for lovemaking."

I did exactly as he commanded. By the time we were finished, it was well into the middle of the night. After some serious making out in a hot shower, I curled up next to the man I loved and drifted off to sleep. I'd never felt so at peace or so happy in my entire life.

My gynecologist wasn't in Oak Springs. She was in Uvalde, and I had never been so thankful. Tongues would have wagged for sure had they seen Mitchell walking into a local Ob/Gyn office hand-in-hand with me.

I signed in and sat down in the waiting room. Mitchell sat next to me, his hand still wrapped in mine.

So much had happened in the short amount of time since we had gotten back together.

Back together? I really couldn't even say that. We were never truly together before. We had both desired each other from a distance, but in all honest truth, we had only been a couple just shy of a few weeks. And here we were…sitting in my doctor's office about to take a pregnancy test.

Sickness moved over me like a thief in the night. It hit me so fast, I had to cover my mouth to keep it from coming up.

"You okay, dove?"

His words were like silk over my skin, and they calmed my nerves. All I could do was nod.

When the nurse called my name, Mitchell stood and I stayed frozen in my seat.

Was this really happening? Why were we doing this? We could just keep using a condom, pretend we never had the slip up and just act like a normal couple.

A normal couple? Oh, my gosh. We are so far from that. We had both been secretly in love with each other for months, neither of us willing to admit it. And now? Now everything was about to change.

Oh. My. God. *I might be pregnant, and we've barely even started our relationship.*

Leaning over, Mitchell placed his mouth next to my ear. "Do you want to leave?"

I shook my head and stood. If I wasn't pregnant, I still needed to get my pills prescribed.

"I'm okay," I said as I slowly stood. Mitchell wrapped his arm around my waist and led me through the door. It wasn't lost on me how the nurse was checking him out.

Really, lady? Ugh.

Thirty minutes later, the door to the exam room opened and the doctor walked in. My breath caught and Mitchell sat up, straight as a board.

What was he thinking? Was he as scared as I was? A baby could change everything. When the doctor closed the door, my urge to jump up and run out of the room was overwhelming.

"Ms. Miller, Mr. Parker. I'm so sorry to have kept you waiting. I had a patient who thought she was in labor, and it took some convincing to get her to see that she was only having false contractions."

I let out a fake laugh that caused Mitchell to look my way. His eyes filled with concern, and I wanted to ask him exactly how he was acting so calm and cool when I was freaking out on the inside.

"Ms. Miller."

"Corina," I replied with a tight smile.

The doctor returned the gesture. "Corina, your results came back negative. You're not pregnant."

I let out the breath I had been holding. When I snapped my eyes to Mitchell, I could see the relief all over his face.

"How do we both feel about this?" the doctor asked.

I swallowed hard. "Honestly? Relieved. I don't think Mitchell and I were ready to jump into parenthood just yet."

We were still staring at each other as I spoke. He smiled, softly adding, "Someday a baby will be an amazing addition. Right now, I think the two of us sounds like the perfect plan."

My hand landed on my stomach as I felt that familiar dropping sensation when Mitchell did or said anything sweet or romantic.

"If that's the case, then let's get you back on some birth control, shall we?"

I nodded. "Yes. Let's do that." The idea of feeling Mitchell inside with no condom was making me horny. Or maybe it was the relief of knowing we hadn't really messed things up by being careless…

Peeking at Mitchell, my breath caught. Nope. I was horny, and by the way Mitchell was staring at me, I could tell he was thinking the same exact thing.

Sex. Bareback. As soon as possible.

CHAPTER 24

Corina

There was a knock on my classroom door. I lifted my gaze to see Mitchell standing with a huge bouquet of fall flowers.

"A little birdy told me fall was your favorite season."

One quick glance at the calendar, and I smiled. September 22nd. First day of fall.

So much had happened in the last month. Mitchell and I had both moved into the house he had bought. My house was coming along, with the second floor rebuilt and drywall in. No one else had broken into the house, and Mitchell and I agreed it had most likely been teenagers.

Pushing away from my desk, I stood. "It *is* my favorite time of year."

He made his way over to me, dressed in jeans, cowboy boots, a long-sleeve shirt, and a cowboy hat. The whole package caused a pulse between my legs. My top lip dug into my bottom one, and I held my breath, waiting for the kiss I knew would make me weak in the knees.

Lane called out, "Corina, are you free tonight?"

My head turned as Lane walked into my room from his class next door.

He stopped when he saw Mitchell. "I, ah, I wanted to go over the lesson plans you made up."

I sighed. Lane had no business teaching first graders. He hated it, and it was beginning to show. Even Chloe had mentioned how all the kids in the class didn't really like Mr. Lewis.

"Lane, you taught high school," I said. "Why is first grade throwing you?"

Mitchell chuckled, and I shot him a look that warned him to behave. Even though Lane knew I was with Mitchell, he still tried his best to get me to spend time with him. It was getting annoying.

"They're not," Lane said. "I just had a simple question."

"You don't need her to be free for the evening to ask a simple question," Mitchell said, his eyes daring Lane to argue.

"Where are the spelling books?"

The spelling books? He can't come up with something better than that?

"In the cabinet, under 'spelling lessons.'"

Lane frowned. He had totally made himself look like a fool not only in front of me, but Mitchell as well.

"Right. Thanks."

When he turned to leave, I called out. "Remember, I won't be here next week. Paxton will be, though. I'm sure she can help you if you need anything."

Lane smiled. "That's right. Your brother is getting married. Are you looking forward to the trip?"

"I am." I couldn't help the smile that spread across my face.

Mitchell walked up to me, wrapped his arm around my waist and kissed me on the forehead. "I'm looking forward to it, too."

Lane let out a harsh chuckle. "Wait, you're going? To the wedding?"

"Of course I am. I'm looking forward to meeting Corina's family."

Lane huffed a little before he forced a smile. "Right. Well, y'all have fun." He hightailed it out the door.

I faced Mitchell. "The flowers are beautiful. Thank you." Our lips pressed together, but before things got heavy, I drew back, remembering I was still at work.

Mitchell leaned his forehead to mine and whispered, "I could kiss you all day and never get tired of it."

"Hmm, I feel the exact same way."

"You ready to head home?"

"Are you off already?" I asked, glancing up into his beautiful blue eyes.

"I am. I took the rest of today off so we could finish packing. Mom and Dad want to have dinner over at their place before we head out."

"Oh, that will be fun. I haven't seen the whole gang in a few weeks."

Mitchell laughed. "Yeah, Mom was pretty happy knowing she got all the kids rounded up for the evening. Two weeks without a family dinner was longer than she could take."

"I bet. What time do we have to be over there? I need to run by Mrs. Johnson's and pick up a pie for Paxton."

"I told her we'd get there a bit early. I figured you'd need to get Milo all set up and let Mom know the little bastard's routine."

"Don't call him that! He loves you."

"He loves me? I wake up in the middle of the night, and he's sitting on my chest *staring*. It's like he's plotting to take me out or something. That little fucker is amazing at intimidation tactics."

I chuckled as I reached up and kissed Mitchell again. He was so allergic to Milo, and Milo loved him so much. He slept either on Mitchell's chest or somewhere near his head every single night.

"Just think, a week with no cat."

He closed his eyes and let out a delighted moan. "No sneezing. No hair on my uniform. No missing food from my plate when I turn away. It's going to be fucking heaven."

My hands covered my mouth in an attempt to hide my laughter. Milo had gotten into the habit of reaching his paw up and taking food off of Mitchell's plate. He never did it to me, only Mitchell. I was convinced Milo was messing with the man I loved out of pure jealousy.

"Let me finish up really quick, and we can head on out. I want to make sure Paxton has everything for the little monsters."

"And I'll just sit here and admire my beautiful girlfriend doing her thing."

My stomach fluttered. Sometimes I had to pinch myself to make sure I wasn't dreaming. Mitchell was mine and I was his. Life was beautiful. Perfect in every single way.

"Come on, Milo. Get into the carrier. You're such a good boy."

Milo sat on the sofa and stared at me like I was insane. He did his little bark meow thing and turned his head from me.

Bruff.

"Milo. Don't ignore me. You're going to have so much fun exploring Melanie and John's house. It's huge!"

"Why don't you just grab him and push him into the thing?"

My mouth dropped open as I turned to Mitchell. He was leaning against the kitchen bar with his arms folded across his massive chest. He looked absolutely yummy in a University of A&M baseball cap.

"I'm not going to push him into it. It will scare him."

Mitchell rolled his eyes. "He'll get over it."

Milo meowed, and I focused back on him. He was staring at Mitchell like he wanted to pounce on him and scratch his eyes out.

"See, he doesn't like the idea of being shoved into the crate," I said.

"Corina, he's a cat. I doubt he knows what you're saying."

Milo stood, stretched his back and slowly made his way into the crate. He turned around and laid down, but not before letting out his signature bark meow.

"Oh, my gosh! He just showed you!"

Mitchell huffed. "He did *not* show me. He was curious and walked into the damn thing!"

I started laughing. "He totally proved you wrong!" I shut the crate and leaned over to look at my handsome boy. "He's a smart kitty cat. Isn't he? Yes, he is! Milo is a smart kitty cat!"

Mitchell's body was next to mine in an instant. The way I reacted to this man was insane. He took my arm and pulled me to face him.

"Do you have any idea how fucking sexy you are?"

My cheeks heated. I'd never get used to his compliments.

"You think it's sexy when I talk to my cat?"

His eyes turned dark. "Yes."

With a tilt of my head, I asked, "Why?"

The corners of his mouth rose into a sexy grin. My insides were melting, and I was mentally trying to figure out if we had time for this.

"Why?" he asked, his hands moving up my skirt.

I nodded, but I was dizzy with the anticipation of his touch.

"I think you're sexy all the time. No matter what you're doing."

My teeth dug into my lip, and I tried not to whimper when he slipped my panties to the side and pushed his fingers inside of me.

"There's a new position I want to try."

Swallowing hard, I asked, "Now?"

His smile grew bigger, and he turned his baseball cap around on his head. "Now."

I was going to lose this argument. "Your parents. We'll be late."

Mitchell's other hand moved up my back. My entire body trembled as he pushed into me more, pressing against my clit.

"Who cares? I want you, dove. Now."

Each breath I took was faster than the one before. "Wh-what…position…are we…"

I couldn't even form words. Mitchell's other hand was now up my shirt where he was pinching one of my nipples through my bra.

I gasped. "Mitchell, I want you."

Before I knew it, my shirt was off, my bra pushed over my breasts and my panties were gone. My skirt was still on, and for some reason that turned me on even more. Mitchell quickly took off his boots, jeans, and boxer briefs.

"The pick-me-up," Mitchell said as he lifted me up.

"What?" I asked between gasps.

"The position. That's what it's called. Put your feet on the sofa."

He held onto me by my upper legs and ass while he backed up against the sofa. Once I rested my feet on it, he positioned himself at my entrance. His bare dick against me was one of my favorite feelings in the world.

Mitchell guided me onto him, filling me so completely I let out a long, low moan.

"So deep. So fucking deep," he whispered against my neck.

"Yes. Mitchell, yes."

I wasn't sure if I was supposed to move my body, but I started to. I pushed with my feet and lifted up, then back down. The movement was amazing and the feeling so new and thrilling I was already beginning to feel my orgasm build.

"Feels so good," I said. "Oh my gosh."

Gripping my body harder, Mitchell pulled me closer to him. His dick was hitting something inside that made my eyes roll to the back of my head. The feel of his body rubbing against my clit added to the jolt of electricity that raced through me, letting loose the most amazing orgasm ever.

I wasn't normally a screamer when I came, but this orgasm hit me fast and hard. "I'm coming!" I cried out as I pushed my legs to make my body go faster, harder. Pushing him deeper.

"That's it, baby. Fuck, I feel your pussy squeezing my dick."

Mitchell's dirty talking was my undoing.

"Oh God!" I screamed. Another orgasm—or maybe it was the same one—pulsed through my body. My eyes closed, and all I saw were bursts of light behind my eyelids as my body drifted up and I enjoyed the euphoria.

When I opened my eyes, I was on the sofa, Mitchell over me, my legs over his shoulders as he pounded into me so deliciously hard and fast another orgasm hit me. I felt him grow bigger. He was about to come with me.

Leaning closer, he put his mouth to my ear. "Dove, I'm going to come."

I covered my mouth with my hand, holding back the scream of pleasure I wanted to let out as we both fell apart together. I don't know why I cared; we no longer lived above Lucy's place. No one would hear me even if I did scream.

Mitchell buried his face against my neck as we both attempted to catch our breath.

"Holy. Fuck. That was hot as hell," he said between breaths.

I let out a small laugh. He was still buried inside of me, his dick twitching every now and then. "That was amazing. It felt so incredible that way."

He lifted his head and stared into my eyes. I couldn't help my smile as I stared into his blue eyes. They sparkled like diamonds.

"Are you happy, Mitchell?"

His hands framed my head, and he stared at me with such intensity. It made my entire body break out in goosebumps.

"I've never been so happy in my entire life. Are you happy?"

Tears burned while I tried to keep them down. I lost the battle. Nodding, I let one slip free as I whispered, "So incredibly happy.

And scared at the same time. I'm scared that I'm going to wake up and the last few months will have been a dream."

He slowly lifted himself out of me, and then pushed back in. I wasn't sure if he was still hard from our first round of hot sex or if he was getting hard again. Either way, I didn't care. It felt amazing.

"It's not a dream, dove. I promise you that."

We laid there, lost in each other, neither of us wanting to move.

Milo's angry meow finally broke the connection. I managed to get out the words I really didn't want to say. "We should clean up really quick and head out. We still have to stop at Mrs. Johnson's place."

Mitchell pouted, and I couldn't help but giggle. He looked adorable.

"Pick this up later?" I asked, raising my brows.

"I like that idea. A lot."

CHAPTER 25

Mitchell

Laughter filled the living room and I couldn't help my smile. I took in each person in the room. Each one so special to me. My gaze finally landed on Corina.

Corina.

The last few months had been the most amazing time of my life. Corina and I spent every spare second with each other. Of course, Lane was still trying to go out with her and that pissed me off, but I quickly learned to let that jealousy go. Corina had zero interest in him, and I knew that deep within my heart.

"So, Mitchell, are you excited to be heading up north?" Steed asked.

My head lifted to face him. "I'm excited because Corina is."

He grinned and sat down across from me. "Good answer."

I let out a huff. Heading to Chicago wasn't something I really *wanted* to do. I hated big cities, and truth be told, I was scared shitless of meeting Corina's mom. But I was looking forward to what I had planned after the wedding.

"Does she have any idea about your side plans?" Cord asked, taking a seat in one of the chairs that flanked the two sets of couches.

I smiled big. "Not a damn clue. She thinks we're only going to be gone a week. Paxton made the arrangements with the principal for the additional week off."

"Canada? You're really going, huh?" Cord asked.

"Better believe it. Banff is a place Corina has always wanted to go. I want to make that happen. To be the one who makes one of her dreams come true."

Both Steed and Cord studied me for a few seconds.

"Fuckin Smurfs," Cord said with a laugh.

"What?" Steed asked, turning to Cord. "What do the Smurfs have anything to do with this?"

Cord pointed to me. "Look at his face. He's wearing a stupid ass Smurf smile. He's been Smurfed. Like you've been Smurfed. All happy and in love."

Steed's brows pinched together in confusion.

"Don't be too jealous, Grumpy Smurf. Your Smurfette will be along soon," I said with a chuckle.

Cord rolled his eyes. "Listen, I don't have anything against love. I honestly don't. I'm only saying that I'm having fun living the single life. Like Tripp and Trevor. Will I want to settle down some day? Yeah, I'm sure when I've gotten it all out of my system. But for right now I like pussy too much to only stick with one."

I stared at my younger brother. To think I used to feel the same way, until I saw Corina's smile and those beautiful blue eyes. Corina Miller turned my world upside down.

"There's nothing wrong with wanting to be single and having some fun," Steed said.

Nodding, I added, "But I sure as shit cannot wait until the day you meet a woman who knocks you flat on your ass."

Steed laugh and so did Cord before he shook his head. "Well, I don't see that happening for a *long* time. I can honestly say I'm not looking and don't plan on looking for another five years, at the soonest. Plus, I know for a fact it won't be a local girl."

Steed let out a chuckle. "Why? 'Cause you've fucked all of them?"

Cord shot Steed a dirty look. "Go to hell. I haven't slept with *all* of them." He lifted a beer to his lips and smiled. "Almost all of them, but not all of them."

"What are you boys talkin' about?" Waylynn asked, flopping down next to me on the couch.

"Guy talk," Cord said, tipping the bottle back and finishing it off.

Waylynn laced her arm with mine as she tucked her feet up under her. "Hmm, guy talk translates into y'all were talking about how many women Cord has slept with."

"Hey, you're a smart cookie," Cord said with a chuckle.

Waylynn shot him a smug look. "I know my brothers."

Glancing across the room, my breath stalled as I watched Corina holding Gage. The way she was looking at him made my chest ache in a good way. A wanting way.

"I'm going to ask her to marry me."

I wasn't sure why I said it out loud, but I did.

"What?" Waylynn asked.

"Dude, did you hit your head or something? We went from me screwing half of Oak Springs to you mindlessly saying you're asking Corina to marry you? Where did that come from?"

I continued to stare toward Corina. She was rocking Gage. Every now and then she would look down at him and say something with the most breathtaking smile I'd ever seen. My heart felt like it was about to combust inside my chest.

There was no denying how much I loved her and wanted to spend the rest of my life with her. The need to see her belly growing bigger with a child was so overpowering, it nearly brought tears to my eyes. The thought alone had me making one of the biggest decisions I'd ever made in my life. I knew what I needed to do. What I *wanted* to do.

Swallowing hard, I shook my head. "For the first time in my life, I actually know what I want."

"Hell, this just got good," Steed said.

Cord leaned forward. "Holy shit, is it just me or is he for real turning blue?"

I shot Cord a dirty look, then followed it up with my middle finger.

Waylynn took my hand. "Mitchell, are you being serious? You're going to ask Corina to marry you?"

Smiling, I looked at my older sister. "I've never been more serious in my entire life."

Waylynn's eyes searched mine. It was almost like she was looking deep into my soul. "That's not the only thing you've decided."

With a wink, I replied, "No, it's not."

"Are you sure you've got everything?" I asked. Again.

Corina stood in line at the ticket counter and stared at me. "What is going on with you? Yes! I've got everything." She let out a sweet chuckle.

Leaning down, I kissed the tip of her nose. "It's our first time traveling together and all. I want everything to be perfect."

"It's going to be amazing. You know, Cord would say you're acting like the girl in the relationship."

I let out a light-hearted laugh. "Yeah, and he'd mention something about the Smurfs."

She stared at me with a blank expression. "The who?"

Stepping back, I asked in horror, "You don't know who the Smurfs are?"

She shook her head. "Nope. Oh wait, there was a kids' movie about them! The little blue people."

My mouth dropped open. "I have so many things to teach you, young grasshopper."

Corina rolled her eyes. We looked up when the ticket agent called out, "Next." As we stepped up to the counter, we handed over our driver's licenses.

"Heading to Chicago?" the ticket agent asked.

"Yes! My brother is getting married."

It was clear the agent couldn't have cared less. She forced a tight smile and kept typing. "How many bags?"

"Two each," Corina answered. I would have only had one, but Corina needed extra space for her bridesmaid dress and all of that.

My phone buzzed in my pocket. When I pulled it out, I saw that it was my boss. *Shit*. I quickly sent him a text.

Me: *About to get on my flight. Call you after I land.*

Sliding my phone back into my pocket, I didn't bother to look at his response. I knew what it was going to say. Probably something along the lines of call me now or I'll have the plane delayed.

"You're both set. You can head over to security and proceed through to gate sixteen. Enjoy your trip."

We both said, "Thank you," and made our way through the air-port to the security checkpoint. I was TSA pre-approved so I made it through first, giving me enough time to call the boss man.

"Michael, it's Mitch."

"Do you want to explain to me what in the fuck I'm looking at on my desk right now?"

I winced when he yelled.

"I believe it's pretty clear, sir."

"Mitch, have you thought about this? Have you talked to your father about it?"

Anger raced through my body. How dare he even ask that—like I was a kid who couldn't make a damn decision on his own. It wasn't like it was in the beginning, when I was young and not sure what I wanted to do. It killed me to give him my answer.

"Yes, I did speak to him about it. Last night. In great detail."

I wasn't going to let Michael know my father was over the moon about my news.

"We need to talk this over when you come back."

Pushing my hand through my hair, I watched as Corina stood with her hands over her head while they scanned her.

"Sir, I need you to know I won't change my mind. This is something that has been weighing heavy on me for a number of months."

He huffed. "I go through this more than you think. It's a phase. You'll get over it. Enjoy your trip, have fun, relax. Just know that when you come back, shit is going to get real."

The line went dead, and I pulled the phone away from my face. Security was taking Corina off to the side for an additional check. Sitting on the bench, I thought back to last night and my conversation with my father.

His glass froze at his lips. Moving around in my seat, I glanced at Trevor and Steed. They both wore huge smiles.

Turning back to my father, I said, "Dad? Are you okay?"

Trevor let out a hearty laugh. "Hell, yes, he's okay. He's in shock, like I am. Happy, but in shock."

"Can't say I didn't see this coming," Steed added.

After taking a long drink, my father set his scotch down onto the table and focused back on me.

"Do you know how long I've waited to hear those words from your lips? I have to ask though, why now?"

I swallowed. I'd become a cop for so many reasons. The main one was proving to my father that I wasn't going to take Steed's place at the ranch. Once Steed left for Colorado, my father assumed I would fall in line. Hell, at the time I wanted to work on the ranch. At least, I thought I did. I had big ideas, things I wanted to try, ways to branch out—until my father mentioned I was going to have to take Steed's place. I didn't want to work on the ranch to take someone's place. I wanted to work on it because my father saw something in me. A place for me.

"So, you went off to college and became a cop because you thought I expected you to take Steed's place?"

I nodded. "Yes, sir."

My father stared at me for the longest time. "Mitchell Parker, this ranch has a place for each of you kids. From the day you boys first climbed up onto a horse and rode out into those pastures, it was in your blood. Waylynn and Amelia have it in them, too. Do I want all of y'all here working? Call me selfish, but yes. I do. Will I force you? No, I won't. But if you for one second think I don't believe you belong on this ranch..."

His voice trailed off. He closed his eyes and then looked back at me. "Boy, I'd like to slap you upside your damn head."

Trevor and Steed laughed as I jerked back. "Excuse me?"

My father leaned forward, his arms resting on the tops of his legs, his blue eyes blazing as he stared into mine. "Mitchell, I can't run this ranch without you boys. Whether you're here full time or part. Steed, Trevor, and Wade do a hell of a good job, but son, I need all of you boys. I'll take whatever your heart wants to give."

I felt the tears stinging my eyes. "I love being a Texas Ranger, Dad. I've put everything into it. A hundred and ten percent."

"Good. That's how your mother and I raised you."

Smiling, I took a look over to Trevor. He sat quietly off to the side, yet every now and then, he'd bob his head and give me the encouragement he knew I needed to do this.

Focusing on my father, I continued. "But things have changed. Corina made me see what I really want in life. I want to marry her, start a family, and—"

My voice broke. "I want to work on the ranch full time. And it's not because I'm worried that something's gonna happen to me. I know the risks of my job and so does Corina. I won't lie and say that's not one of the reasons, though."

With a lift of his brows, my father asked, "What's the main reason?"

My hand went over my chest, where for the last few years I'd felt empty. "I'm missing something. There's a hole in me, and it took me a little bit to figure out why it was there. Corina has filled most of it...but it's still a hole."

The corners of my father's mouth rose into a smile. His eyes brightened, and I swore they cast a light into the room. He reached for his drink, finished it off and stood. I followed his lead, as did Trevor and Steed.

"Well, son, dust off your old work boots and get you some good gloves. There's a shit ton of work to be done on this ranch. If my memory is correct, I believe you wanted to talk to me about horses."

"Mitchell? Hello? Mitch?"

Lifting my head, I found Corina standing in front of me.

"Wow! You were in deep thought. What was that all about?"

I grinned. "Nothing. I was thinking about my conversation with Dad last night."

"He sure seemed happy after you guys came out of his office. I don't think I've ever seen him so gleeful."

Standing, I pulled her to me and kissed her on the lips. "Me neither."

I took her hand, and we started toward our gate. One of the things I loved about Corina was that she didn't push. She could have asked what we had talked about, why Dad had been so happy, but she didn't. She respected the fact that we'd talked in private. I loved how she always let me come to her with things and didn't pressure me. It reminded me of my mother. When I was little and our father would be upset about something, my mother would always say, "When he's ready to talk about it, he will. Until then, wait patiently until he feels like he's ready to let the burden go."

Corina and I were lucky to learn that lesson quickly in our relationship. We would never hold anything back from one another, but we would also never pressure each other.

We took a seat at our gate and Corina wrapped her arm under mine. When she looked up at me with those big blue eyes, I couldn't help but smile.

"What?" I asked.

"Let's people watch!"

Letting out a half-laugh, I took her hand in mine. I couldn't wait to slip the ring I was carrying in my backpack onto her finger. I couldn't wait to make Corina my wife.

My gaze took in her beautiful face as she looked around. I'd never in my life felt so complete. Everything was falling into place.

CHAPTER 26

Corina

Pam, my brother's fiancée, sat next to me while we got our nails done. She was silent as all get out and for some reason, I didn't get the feeling it was nerves.

"Do you need me to help with any last-minute things?" I asked.

With a dumbfounded look on her face, she turned to me. "What?"

"Do you need help with anything?"

Pam was the one who had suggested we get our nails done. She felt like she needed to spend more time with her future sister-in-law, which was strange since we had grown up together. She had only lived a few blocks from us and was always at the house, even before she and my brother, Rick, started dating.

"Um, no. Everything is ready to go. My mother made sure of that. I'm sure Lori has mentioned what a pain in the ass my mother has been."

I gave her a weak smile. There was no way I was going to tell her that my mother had indeed filled me in on Pam's over-the-top mom and her antics.

"She hasn't mentioned it."

Pam huffed. "Then she is a saint. I'm losing my mind, Corina. All I wanted was a simple wedding. Marry the man of my dreams. My mother is making it a nightmare."

"Why don't y'all elope?"

Pam froze and I quickly realized what I had said.

"Wait. Did you just say...*y'all*?"

I shrugged. "I guess I've been in Texas long enough for it to rub off on me."

She winked. "Or you're spending a lot of time with that hunk of hotness you call a boyfriend."

"Pam! You're marrying my brother. You can't say that about my boyfriend."

Pam rolled her eyes. "Please, I'm still allowed to look, and honey, when a man that handsome comes around women are going to *look*."

My chest felt heavy. It was hard to deny that no matter where we went, women stared at Mitchell. I'd even heard them say things about him—things that made my stomach tight with disgust. Of course, Mitchell seemed to be clueless about it all.

"You don't get bothered by all the eyes staring at him?" Pam asked.

I shrugged. "I don't know. Sometimes it bothers me, but I don't blame that on Mitchell. He doesn't even seem to notice."

Pam grinned from ear to ear. "Oh trust me, Corina. That man only has eyes for you."

My cheeks heated.

"Don't pretend like you don't know that man worships the ground you walk on. The way he looks at you? It's like he breathes when you breathe. Moves when you move. It's utterly romantic."

I smiled. "Well, we had a bit of a long journey to get where we are now. Things happened slowly, then *really* fast."

"Have you guys said the L word yet?"

When I didn't answer right away, she grabbed my hand. "Oh. My. Gosh. Corina! Have you?"

I covered my mouth to hide the silly young-girl giggle that was threatening to come out.

"You have!"

"You probably think it's too soon, but we've known it for so long. Mitchell denied it at first, but by the time he got around to realizing it, I had started to push him away. In the end, I couldn't resist."

Pam wiggled her brows. "Well, who would be able to? That body! Those piercing blue eyes. Holy shit, I bet he's good in bed."

All eyes turned to us, and I could feel my cheeks getting even redder. "Sorry! She didn't mean to say that," I said, glancing around to the women now totally in tuned to our conversation.

"Oh yes, I did."

I hit Pam on the arm and we lost our composure. "Stop talking about my boyfriend that way! You're about to get married!"

"Hey, I'm only speaking the truth. Although, I don't know how you stand the idea of him being a cop."

My breath hitched. "What do you mean?"

Pam nonchalantly lifted her shoulder. "I don't think I could deal with it if I knew Rick was leaving for work every day with the risk of him being injured or killed."

I swallowed hard. It wasn't like I didn't know the risks of Mitchell's job. I knew. *Very* well. "You would. You'd stand by his side and support him no matter what he did."

I could feel her eyes on me so I turned to face her.

"Corina, are you prepared if something happens to him? Are you ready to be left alone, possibly with a child, or God forbid, more than one child?"

My heart knew the answer to that question instantly. My brain, on the other hand, wouldn't allow me to speak. Finally, I found my voice.

"Of course I am. If it means being with Mitchell, I'm prepared for anything that could come our way. After all, anything could happen to any of us no matter what we did for a living."

Pam stared as if she felt sorry for me.

"Did my mother put you up to this?" I asked.

She looked away.

"I knew it. She has an issue with Mitchell being a cop, and she needs to get over it. And she has to stop sending other people to talk me out of having a relationship with the only man I've ever truly loved."

"Oh Corina, I wasn't trying to do that. I see how you look at Mitchell. It's no different than how he looks at you. Your mom is worried, that's all."

I turned away and stared down at my feet. My nails were being polished with a beautiful, soft pink. "Well, she doesn't need to worry. I'm not."

An aching filled my chest, causing me to drag in a deep breath.

Pam and I fell into lighter conversation about the wedding. I laughed, got teary eyed, and laughed some more. Talk of Mitchell being a cop was long forgotten, and I hadn't realized how much I had missed home and my family. A small part of my heart broke knowing in a few short days I'd be leaving to go back to Texas.

Mitchell's arms were wrapped around me as we slow danced. It felt like I was on a cloud. Being in Mitchell's arms was one of the most amazing feelings in the world and something I would never get tired of.

"So, your mom had a little chat with me earlier while I danced with her," Mitchell said.

I held my breath. If she had said anything to Mitchell about him being a ranger, I was going to be so upset. "Oh, yeah? What did you guys talk about?"

"She mentioned coming to Texas. I told her a little bit about the ranch and when would be the best time of year for a visit."

I let out the breath I'd been holding. "I've been begging her to come for a visit, and she always says 'soon'."

"Well, you never know. She may have a good reason soon enough."

My brows pinched together. "What do you mean?"

With a shrug, he leaned down and brushed his lips over mine. "Nothing, dove. Have I told you how beautiful you look in your pink gown?"

I hit him playfully on the shoulder. "You can call a spade a spade, Mitchell. I look like a bottle of Pepto-Bismol. I have no idea why Pam picked this color."

Mitchell pulled me closer. When his hot breath touched my neck, my body fired up.

"I want to make love to you, Corina. Desperately."

A slight whimper slipped from my lips. Mitchell had been the perfect gentleman the last few days, with us staying at my mother's house. Even though we slept in the same room, he wouldn't make love to me, although he'd used his fingers to make me come a few times. It felt naughty doing something like that in my mother's house, but I enjoyed the daring.

An idea came to mind. "We could always sneak off later. Go to the beach."

Mitchell's hand moved lower as his fingertips teased my exposed skin. "I like that idea."

I buried my face into his chest. His smell was like a drug. I couldn't seem to get close enough to him.

"I love weddings," he said.

His statement caught me off guard. Leaning back, I looked up at him. "Really?"

"Why do you seem surprised by that?"

I let out a chuckle. "I don't know. Maybe because you were so against relationships until recently."

Mitchell's eyes turned sad. "I've never been against relationships. I simply didn't think I was ready for one...until you. You changed the way I think about everything, Corina. I hope you know that. Every day you make me want to be a better man."

Tears threatened. Reaching up, I pressed my lips to his.

His hands cupped my face while he deepened the kiss. I swore I could feel every ounce of his love pour into me. I was dizzy with love. Happiness. The feeling of having this amazing man love me like he did was beyond thrilling. It was magical.

When we finally broke the kiss, I was aching to have him make love to me. "I think we need to sneak out of here, grab a blanket, and head to the beach."

Mitchell raised his brows. "I like it when you think naughty."

My tongue ran along the bottom of my lip as I replied, "And I'm thinking it's time for a new position."

Mitchell swallowed hard, then took my hand and pulled me toward the house. "Come on. Let's go before anyone notices we're gone."

This made two weddings we had snuck out of for the sheer purpose of having sex. I couldn't help the giddy feeling bubbling up in my stomach as we snuck away from my brother's reception and down to the beach.

"How about right here?" Mitchell asked.

Glancing around, I could barely see the lights coming from the beach house. No other houses were nearby, so I suspected we had walked far enough into the state park area.

"This is perfect!"

Mitchell laid out the blanket and sat down. He reached up for my hand and gently pulled me into a sitting position next to him.

"It's beautiful here," he said,

I leaned my head against his arm and let out a soft, contented sigh. "Beautiful and cold."

"Not for long," Mitchell said as he grabbed the backpack he had quickly packed up. He pulled out a sweatshirt, helped slip it over my head and then put one on himself.

"I want to show you something," he said in that sexy voice.

"Oh, yeah? Is this a 'you show me yours and I'll show you mine' kind of thing?"

Laughing, Mitchell pulled me back so that we were both lying on the blanket.

"Naughty little thing. When did you get so dirty, Corina Miller?"

I stared up at the star-filled sky. "Mmm, let me think about that. I would have to say it was when this amazing guy showed up and swept me off my feet and taught me a few things in the bedroom I had never experienced before."

"Sounds like a great guy."

"He was sort of lost at first."

Mitchell laughed. "Really? Why?"

"Well, he seduced me one night. Made mad, passionate love to me."

"Sounds like a stud."

I couldn't help the smile that spread across my face.

Clearing his throat, he asked, "So, what happened after he seduced you?"

I rolled onto my side and ran my finger along Mitchell's jaw. The last thing I wanted to do was bring up the past, especially since I had promised Mitchell I wouldn't keep throwing it in his face.

"He got spooked."

"Spooked, huh?"

I nodded.

"Then what happened?" Mitchell asked.

"Well, after a few months of both of us acting like fools, everything changed. He changed, and I changed."

Turning to face me, Mitchell smiled. "He was a stupid asshole for not seeing what was right in front of him."

I sat up and crawled on top of him. I could feel his hardness pressing into me. "No, he's the most amazing, caring, incredibly romantic—"

"Funny."

I raised a brow. "Stubborn."

"God-like in bed."

I squirmed on top of him, and he let out a low growl.

"I will totally agree with *that*. He is very gifted in the area of lovemaking."

His smile made my stomach drop.

We stared at each other for a few moments before I started laughing. "I totally forgot what I was talking about."

Mitchell's laughter filled me with so much happiness as he lifted his hips. "Distracted, dove?"

Leaning over, I kissed his neck. "I am very distracted and curious to know about this position we are going to try."

His hand lifted to my face gently. The warmth of his touch spread heat through my body. "Do you know what I really want to do?"

I shook my head. "Tell me," I whispered.

"Make love to you under the stars with the sound of the waves gently crashing on the shoreline behind us."

My teeth sank into my lip. "Did I say incredibly romantic?"

"I believe you did."

"I meant to say *insanely* romantic."

Mitchell's hand reached down and slipped under my dress. A crooked grin appeared on his face.

"Please tell me you haven't been panty-less all day because had I known, I'd have snuck you away a hell of a lot earlier."

"Nope. I slipped them off when you were packing your back-pack."

Mitchell rolled us over so that I was on my back and he hovered inches over me. His hand slid back under my dress. When his fingers slipped inside me, I let out a soft moan.

"Mitchell," I gasped, pushing my hips into his hand, silently demanding more.

"You're so fucking sexy. Do you know that?" he whispered against my ear. His unshaven face brushed against my skin, causing another rush of excitement, fueling my building release.

"Oh God, Mitchell, I'm so close. Faster, please."

When he slipped another finger in, pressed up and hit the exact spot I needed him to, I came undone. His name flowed from my lips as my orgasm rippled across my body. It felt like it went on forever. Mitchell's mouth was everywhere. On my lips, my neck, whispering into my ear. Before I could come back to my senses, he pushed inside me. Slowly moving in and out, the two of us became one, kissing passionately. Our bodies pressed as close as we possibly could with two layers of clothing between us.

It was heaven on Earth.

Mitchell's hips rocked against mine, another orgasm building.

"I'm going to come, baby."

I wrapped my arms around him, drawing him closer. The moment I felt him grow bigger, *harder*, I softly called out his name before his mouth crashed against mine, and we fell together with thousands of stars shining above us.

CHAPTER 27

Mitchell

"I've got sand in my ass," I said.

The silence over the phone was priceless. There weren't many times I could render my brother, Tripp, speechless.

"Do I want to know why you have sand in your ass?"

I let out a chuckle. "Romance on the beach, my good brother."

"Oh, hell. Sex on the beach is not one of my favorite things."

"Well, when you're with the woman you love and she says she wants you, it means fucking sand in your ass and between your bal—"

"Stop right there, bro. Sounds like y'all are having fun. Does she think you're leaving today or did you break down and tell her?"

I walked over and shut the bedroom door. Corina and her mother had gone for a walk along the beach, but I didn't want to risk her coming back and overhearing.

"She is clueless. Thinks we're heading back to Texas today. Her mother knows, of course, because I asked for Corina's hand in marriage."

"Awe, look at you being all traditional. Cord's right, you have turned into a fucking Smurf."

I laughed and pushed my hand through my wet hair. "It was the least I could do. Corina's family is amazing. Her mom is great. I'm not sure how she did what she did as a single mom after Corina's father died. I think she and Mom would get along."

"Yeah, I have the highest respect for single parents. I've seen a sad case or two come through our San Antonio office. I'd like to rip the heads off of some of these loser dads who knock up a girl and then take off. Dicks."

Walking to the window, I saw Corina and her mom sitting on the beach, staring out over the water.

"Do you think I'm moving too fast, Tripp? Asking Corina to marry me?"

"Not at all. Nothing says y'all have to turn right around and rush to have the wedding."

I let out a deep breath. "I don't want to fuck this up. I always feel like I'm walking on water, so afraid to screw up again."

"Mitch, Corina loves you. She trusts you one hundred percent and I have no doubt that if you asked that girl to marry you, she would jump into your arms screaming yes. From the moment the two of you laid eyes on each other, it was obvious. Trust your heart, dude."

Smiling, I leaned against the windowsill. "You been taking lessons from Dad or something?"

Tripp laughed. "Let's just call it personal experience. Had I listened to my heart back in the day I would probably be…"

His voice trailed off. I knew what he was going to say. He would probably be with Harley right now.

"You're right about Corina," I said, changing the direction of the conversation.

"You giving her grandma's ring?"

My heart soared at the idea of Corina wearing our grandmother's emerald ring. When dad's mom passed away two years ago, we all drew for the ring. Waylynn and Amelia had passed on it, giving us guys the chance to someday give it to the person we wanted to marry. I lucked out. It had been in my safe until the night of the fire when I'd taken it out and was looking at it, dreaming of someday giving it to Corina. When I heard the call about the fire, I put it in the side drawer of my nightstand. My mother would have killed me if she had known.

"I hope she likes it," I said. "I mean, if she wants to go and pick out a diamond, I'll understand."

"Nah, not Corina. She'll love it and treasure it, especially when she hears the story. How you going to do it?"

I let out a gruff laugh. "Shit, I don't know. I've been trying to think of different places, times of day, what would be the most romantic. I'm coming up with nothing."

"Why don't you just do it when the time feels right?"

"So, you're saying carry the ring with me everywhere I go until the mood strikes me and then pop the question?"

Tripp let out a chuckle. "That's exactly what I'm saying."

Huh. He has a good point.

"I like that idea. Go with the flow. Let it come naturally."

I glanced out the window to see Corina and her mother standing on the beach. They were embracing, and I couldn't help but watch them. My heart broke when they wiped tears off their faces.

"Listen, Corina is headed back in. Tell everyone hey for me. Oh, did Waylynn get the permit to start back up with the dance studio?"

Tripp groaned. "Fucking hell, what a damn nightmare. Old lady Hopkins was convinced Waylynn was going to be running some sex shop in there. At one point, Waylynn leaned over and told me she was going to open a sex toy store in Oak Springs just to piss off the old woman. Then she smiled and said the locals would probably all enjoy it and was going to pitch the idea to Dad as an investment opportunity."

I trembled at the mental image my brother had given me. A shop full of Mrs. Johnson and Mrs. Hopkins and their friends shopping for sex toys.

Blah.

"Does Waylynn want to give him a heart attack? Jesus."

Tripp laughed. "Anyway, Judge Hill sided with Waylynn and informed Mrs. Hopkins that just because she walked into the building while a private sexual act was being performed, didn't mean anything illegal was going on in the building."

"*Please* tell me Dad was there."

My brother laughed harder. "Dude, I had to look at his face. It was fucking priceless. He was white as a ghost. Waylynn slid down in her seat almost to the floor."

I couldn't help but laugh. "Damn. That would have been a moment to see."

The bedroom door opened, and Corina walked in. She looked beautiful, her cheeks slightly chapped from the cold wind coming off the lake. When she smiled, my heart felt like it grew ten times larger in my chest.

"Hey, Corina just got back from her walk. Tell Mom and Dad I said hey and that we'll see them soon."

"Will do. And, Mitch, follow your heart. Don't overthink it too much."

"Gotcha. I'll talk to you later, bro."

"Later."

The call ended and I slipped my phone into my pocket. My heart ached when I looked into Corina's eyes. She'd been crying.

"You okay, dove?"

Her chin trembled, and I knew she was trying to hold back her tears. I held out my arms and she rushed into them, pressing her body against mine.

"I'm going to miss my mom so much. I can hardly stand the thought of leaving her."

Wrapping my arms around her, I pressed my lips against her head. "I know. I'm so sorry, baby."

Corina's buried her face in my chest as she cried. I honestly couldn't imagine living away from my family. My parents were my rock—the solid foundation that kept everything together.

"She's going to be all alone."

I lifted Corina's chin so she met my gaze. "What do you mean?"

"Rick took a job in New York City. They're moving when they come back from the honeymoon."

My heart dropped. "Oh. That really sucks."

"I wish she would come to Texas and visit Oak Springs. I think she'd love it there. She told me this was her home, and she couldn't leave it. Mitchell, I hate the idea of her being so alone with her kids so far away."

The pounding of my heart nearly rattled my brain. "What are you saying?"

Corina's eyes widened. "No! I'm not saying I want to stay here, gosh, no. I want to be with you, in Texas."

I let out a huge breath and closed my eyes.

Thank God.

When I opened my eyes, I watched a tear roll down her beautiful face. I brushed my thumb across her cheek and wiped it away.

"Don't cry, baby. I can't stand it when you cry."

"Maybe we can come back for Christmas? We could have a white Christmas."

Smiling, I started hatching a plan in my head. "That sounds like a great idea. Let's do it."

Her face lit up and a breathtaking smile covered her face.

"I love you, Mitch. I love you so much."

With my hands on her face, I leaned down and kissed her softly. "We should probably get the luggage in the car and head to the airport."

With a slow nod, she chewed on her lip. "Yeah, we should."

After I loaded up the car with our suitcases, I turned to see Corina and her mother hugging.

Stepping back, Corina took her mother's hands. "I'm so sorry I'm leaving you."

Lori wore a brave grin. "Corina, I'm not crying tears of sadness. These are happy tears. I'm so happy that both of my kids found love and happiness. That is all I ever wanted. Stop worrying about me, sweetheart. I'll be fine. Now I want you to stop feeling sad."

When she glanced at me, Lori's grin grew even bigger. "You take care of my little girl."

I nodded. "Yes, ma'am. I will."

Turning her attention back to Corina, Lori kissed her on the cheek. "I love you, my sweet girl. Now go on before you miss your plane."

Corina hugged her mother again. "I love you too. I'll call you when we land."

Lori walked over to me and opened her arms for a hug. "It was so nice to meet you, Mitchell."

"The pleasure was all mine, Lori." As we hugged, I whispered in her ear, "Thank you for your blessing."

She squeezed me harder and whispered back, "You make her happy."

We stepped apart and looked at each other. I wanted to tell her I would do everything in my power to make sure her daughter was always happy. Instead, I nodded and smiled.

I opened the door for Corina and held her hand while she got into the car. My heart raced along with my mind.

This was it.

In the next few days I would be asking Corina to marry me.

Holy shit.

Panic started to take root in my gut—not because I was afraid of asking her to marry me. Far from that. It was because I so desperately wanted to make it special for Corina. A memory that would last us a lifetime.

As we drove down the streets of Chicago, I took in all the trees that were beginning to change colors. Glancing to my right, I noticed Corina doing the same.

"You okay?" I asked, taking her hand in mine.

She nodded. "I will be once we get back home and settled. Work will take my mind off things.

Little did she know we were not heading back to Texas. We were going to Banff.

Gripping the steering wheel, I took in a deep breath.

This was it.

Time to fill Corina in on the change of plans.

CHAPTER 28

Corina

"*Canada*? We're going to Canada?"

I stood there staring at Mitchell. I felt sure I had a dumbfounded look on my face.

He was holding out my passport as we stood in line to check in.

"We're staying outside of Banff at a place called The Post Hotel. Hopefully the weather stays nice and no crazy storms roll in."

My mouth opened slightly as I tried to form the words.

Canada. Banff. The one place I've always dreamed of going and Mitchell is making that dream come true.

"How? What about my work?"

He reached for my hand. "I already worked it out with Paxton for you to take more time off. I was pretty sure she was going to ruin the surprise. I'm glad she didn't."

I shook my head. "She didn't utter a word! Banff? Oh, my gosh! Are you serious?" Excitement bubbled inside of me, and I nearly screamed. People were starting to stare, but I didn't care. I'd never been so excited.

"I've never been more serious."

I jumped into his arms while I cried out, "Oh Mitchell!"

He laughed as he picked me up off the ground and kissed me. When he set me back down, I wasn't only dizzy from the idea of going to Banff, but from Mitchell's kiss as well.

"You little sneak. How in the world did you manage to find somewhere to stay? I figured a room would need to be booked way in advance."

A crooked smile appeared on his face, and my knees grew weak.

"When I was in college a group of friends and I went on a ski trip near Banff. Actually, we went every year. The place we stayed was amazing. One of the guy's parents knew the owners of the hotel. They met through business or something. Each time we stayed they upgraded us. Anyway, I gave him a call to see if he might be able to hook us up. He contacted the owners' daughter and she got us a cabin."

"A cabin! Oh, my gosh! Are you serious?"

Mitchell nodded. "Lenny said there was a catch, not sure what it is just yet. He told me I'd find out when we got there."

"Who cares what the catch is! We're staying in a cabin in Banff!"

"Well, it's about forty minutes or so from the town."

I did a weird little jig in line and let out a squeal. "This is going to be so amazing! I hope it snows just a little!"

"Do you know hard it was to pack your winter jacket in my suitcase? I was scared to death you would see it."

I playfully hit him on the shoulder. "You sneaky man." The corners of his mouth curved into a sexy-as-sin smile, causing my lower stomach to pull. "I've never been so happy in my entire life, Mitchell."

He leaned down and kissed the tip of my nose. "Good. That was the plan."

Magical. That was the only way I knew how to describe our location. The Post Hotel was beautiful. No, it was stunning. A dusting of snow covered the ground, but higher in the mountains everything looked as white as I'd imagined it would be.

I gasped as Mitchell opened the door of the rental car. Well, Jeep. Mitchell didn't want to chance being caught in a storm without four-wheel drive.

"The pictures don't do it justice, do they?" Mitchell asked.

"No! Where did y'all go skiing?"

Mitchell pulled me into his arms. "Did you just say y'all?"

My cheeks heated. "I guess I did."

"I like it. Now I just need to get you saying *fixin'*. Like 'I'm fixin' to ride you all night long, Mitchell' or 'I'm fixin' to do a strip tease for you, Mitchell.'"

I glanced around to see if anyone had heard him. "Stop that!" I whispered.

He shrugged. "So what? We'll never see these people again."

We walked to the back of the Jeep, and a bellhop came out with a cart, waiting to take our luggage.

"What if we come back with our kids?" I asked.

It was out of my mouth before I could stop it.

Mitchell didn't freeze, or freak out, or even stumble on his words.

"People will be so enchanted by our beautiful children they won't even notice we were the young couple talking dirty to each other so many years ago."

This time someone definitely heard him. The bellhop. He cleared his throat and asked, "Can I get a last name, sir?"

"Parker."

Mitchell had said that sentence before the bellhop cut in like he couldn't have cared less. Meanwhile, my heart raced like a hummingbird's wings as I thought about his words.

Our beautiful children.

I couldn't help but wonder if Mitchell had thought about the future. Things were serious between us, and they had moved at lightning speed. One day I was angry with him, the next I thought I was pregnant with his child.

My hand went to my stomach. Carrying Mitchell's baby suddenly seemed like something I wanted to do sooner rather than later.

"Ready?" Mitchell asked, taking my hand in his.

I smiled. "Yes! I can't wait to see the cabin."

He dropped my hand, slipped his arm around my waist and pulled me close. "I can't wait to make love to you in the cabin."

Mmm… Delicious heat pooled between my legs. It didn't matter if he was being romantic or talking dirty, Mitchell made my body ache for him in ways I had never dreamed possible.

As we walked toward the lobby, I took in the exterior of the hotel. Large river rocks were mixed with wood, giving it that rustic lodge look. The inside of the hotel was just as amazing—beautiful wood everywhere. Next to a large wall of windows that offered a view of the beautiful scenery sat large, chunky pieces of furniture.

"Wow. This place is stunning."

"It is nice, isn't it? We loved coming here in college."

I did a quick glance around. A woman about our age sat at one of the large, oversized chairs. Her face lit up when her eyes landed on Mitchell. One of these days I would get used to women ogling him.

Focusing straight head, we approached the front desk. "Good evening. Welcome to The Post Hotel. Your name, please."

"Mitchell Parker."

The young girl behind the desk tried really hard not to gawk at Mitchell. His arm was still wrapped around my waist, pulling me against him. Almost like he was claiming me. And I liked it. No, I loved it.

"You'll be with us five nights?"

I sucked in a breath. "*Five* nights?"

Turning, Mitchell shot me the smile that made me weak in the knees. When he wiggled his brows, I couldn't help but giggle like a schoolgirl.

Oh, the fun we are going to have.

"One key or two?"

Mitchell held up two fingers. "Better give us two, just in case."

The girl chuckled like he had told a joke. I wanted to roll my eyes, but I knew how the poor thing felt. That had been me a year ago when I first laid eyes on Mitchell Parker.

"Mitchell Parker? Is that you I see standing in my daddy's hotel lobby?"

I turned to face the woman I'd noticed earlier. Her light brown hair was pulled up into a tight bun that sat neatly on top of her head. She was dressed in business attire, but her breasts were practically spilling out of her shirt. My eyes drifted down her perfectly-shaped body to her Jimmy Choo shoes.

She looked like she belonged in New York City, not a small town in Canada.

Mitchell laughed. "It's been a long time, Kristi. Thank you for getting us booked."

Her eyes seemed to light up when she looked at Mitchell. For a moment I thought she was going to walk right through me to get to him.

"Of course! When Lenny called and said you needed a favor, I was more than happy to accommodate. Especially with our..." She looked right at me as she said, "past friendship."

"Yeah, I really appreciate it," Mitchell said. "I forgot how beautiful it was here."

Her gaze went back to Mitchell. Talk about staring a hole right into him. "Yes…very beautiful."

My brows pulled in tight. *Okay, this girl is openly flirting with him.*

"Here are your keys, Mr. Parker," said the girl at the desk.

Mitchell dropped his arm from around me and reached for the keys.

When he faced Kristi, he laced his hand in mine. "Kristi, I'd like you to meet my girlfriend, Corina."

Her eyes widened in shock as she looked between the two of us, and I got a smell of her over-the-top perfume. *My goodness, did she bathe in it this morning?*

"Girlfriend? Mitchell Parker has a *girlfriend*?"

With an uncomfortable chuckle, Mitch ran his hand through his hair. "Sure do."

Kristi tilted her head and made a *tsking* sound with her tongue. "Well, it's going to be awkward since you promised to have dinner with me while you're here."

Mitchell stiffened next to me. "What?"

"Lanny told me you promised to have dinner with me if I worked some magic to get you into a room. I got you into more than a room. Although, I hadn't realized you were bringing a…*friend*… along."

My mouth dropped open. *She did not just go there.*

"Well, um, I'm sure we can arrange to have dinner with you one night."

The air was beginning to drip with not only tension, but the lust-filled waves Kristi was shooting Mitchell's way.

"The deal was dinner with *you*. I'm sure your girlfriend really doesn't want to be bothered hearing us talk about the days you and your college buddies came here to ski…among other things."

My heart dropped. *Oh, no. Please don't tell me Mitchell and this woman slept together.*

"Listen, Kristi, I never made that deal. Lenny said there was a catch. I didn't know what it was and if you want to have dinner together this evening we can, *all* three of us."

Anger washed over Kristi's face. "Jessica, did we accidentally double-book the Pipestone Cabin?"

Oh, for the love of all that's good. This girl is playing games!

"Mitchell, I don't mind if you have dinner with Kristi tonight," I said. "I'm exhausted and was going to suggest room service."

Mitchell's head snapped over to me, making me think he did not want to have dinner with Kristi tonight, or any night.

"No," he said, anger clearly in his voice. Turning, he set both keys on the counter, took me by the arm and spoke to Kristi.

"I don't play games, and I sure as fuck am not about to go to dinner with you and leave my girlfriend alone in our room. We'll find somewhere else to stay."

We started walking away, and Mitchell motioned for the bellhop to take our things back outside.

"Mitchell Parker, stop being so dramatic. I'm kidding! I'd love for Lorina to join us."

We stopped walking, and Mitchell looked back at her. "It's Corina, with a C."

Kristi tapped her finger against her lips. Her nails were perfectly manicured. "Right. Corina with a C. How about you both meet me in the dining room at eight sharp."

Her eyes lingered on Mitchell before she turned to me. "It's casually elegant. More on the elegant side."

I forced a smile. "Sounds wonderful. Right, Mitchell?"

Knowing Mitchell really didn't want to go to another hotel, I tried to make nice between the two of them. Lucky for me I'd gone shopping with my mother and bought a dress for a special night out with Mitchell. Looks like tonight was the night I was pulling out the little black dress.

CHAPTER 29

Corina

Mitchell was silent as we made our way to the cabin in the Jeep. I didn't want to push, but there was no way I was having dinner with that woman until I got some information.

"Did you sleep with her?" I asked as he pulled into the cabin's parking spot.

With a deep sigh, he dropped his head back against the seat. "Yes."

I swallowed the lump in my throat. "More than once?"

When his hand raked aggressively through his hair, I had my answer. I felt sick to my stomach.

"We came up here all four years of college."

I stared out the window at the flowing river. I was already regretting that I had agreed to dinner tonight. I was going to have to sit at a table with a woman who had slept with my boyfriend on more than one occasion. *Lord knows how many times.*

My morbid curiosity got the better of me.

"Are you saying you slept with her four times or multiple times on each trip."

"Does it really matter, Corina?"

I let out a gruff laugh. "Well, considering I now have to sit with this woman at dinner, I'd kind of like to know if she was a causal fuck or someone you liked to fuck often on your trips up here."

He winced at my use of the word *fuck*, and I didn't care. I was suddenly pissed off. I had expected this to happen at some point in Oak Springs, but in Canada? No.

"It was more than four times."

Just like that, the air left my lungs, and I was regretting asking him. Pushing the door to the Jeep open, I jumped out and headed toward the cabin.

"Corina, wait."

"Not right now, Mitch. I need a few minutes to process this. I could have dealt better with something like this in Oak Springs, but not in another country."

When he walked up behind me, I felt the warmth of his body, and I wanted nothing more than for him to wrap me in his arms and tell me how much he loved me—that no other woman before me meant anything. I knew they didn't, but I *needed* to hear it. This woman had invaded a space in my life, and I hadn't been prepared for it. Back in Oak Springs, yes. If I woman walked up and did this I wouldn't have been so caught off guard. I knew Mitchell wasn't a saint. I knew he had been with other women. Lots of other women.

Mitchell unlocked the door, and we walked into a completely enclosed sunroom. Nothing but floor-to-ceiling windows. It was stunning. Turning to my left, I stepped into the living room. A large, stone fireplace was in the middle of the outside wall. A sofa and two chairs sat in front of it. I could practically feel the heat as I daydreamed about Mitchell making love to me here.

Did he make love to her in front of a fireplace like this?

Ugh. I needed to get these thoughts from my head.

Walking farther in, I saw the steps that led to what I guessed was the master bedroom upstairs. I quickly made my way up them. Part of me hoped he would follow, but he didn't. I was behaving childishly, and I knew it. At the same time, I really needed some time to wrap my head around all of this.

Did he know this woman would be here? Did he know about the dinner and only decided to play it like he didn't?

My arms wrapped around my body.

No. I knew Mitchell would never do that to me.

When I stepped off the last step and I turned to my left, tears filled my eyes. It was the most amazing place I'd ever seen. Everywhere I looked I saw something that made me smile.

A massive king bed sat to the left. The white, shabby-chic bedspread had bits of light blue in it and made the room feel so cozy. The giant window showcased the snow falling softly outside. The vaulted, sloped ceiling was covered in wood planks, adding to the romantic feel.

To the right, a sofa sat in front of another beautiful stone fireplace.

Tears flowed down my cheeks as I made my way over to the sofa and sat. I buried my face in my hands. I didn't want to cry. I didn't want to let this Kristi situation get to me like it had.

So why was I letting it?

Dropping my hands, I stared out the window. I needed to snap out of this. Quickly wiping my face, I stood. There was no way I was going to let some rich snow bunny destroy my time with Mitchell.

I turned to head back down the stairs when I stopped. Mitchell was standing in the archway that led into the room. His expression was laced with worry and regret.

"I wanted to make this trip special for the both of us. Never in my wildest dreams did I think I'd be running into her. I haven't seen her in years, and the last I heard she lived in San Francisco. I need you to know that."

Nodding, I replied softly, "I know."

He moved closer. "The urge to pull you into my arms after you got out of the Jeep just now was insane. You asked me for time, and I gave you all I could, Corina. I love you. You are the only woman I have ever loved or will ever love. I don't even know how I breathed before you. You are my life. My now. My future. Please, don't let my past ruin something so special as our time here."

My hands covered my mouth. His heartfelt words made me fall even more in love with him. Mitchell closed his eyes and took in a deep breath. When he looked back at me, I knew he was waiting for me to speak, but I couldn't. The only thing I could do was show him how much I loved him.

I walked over to him and threw myself into his body. Strong arms wrapped around me and held me close. The sound of his heart beating was one of the most beautiful things I'd ever heard.

"I'm not angry with you, Mitch. I don't even know why I asked. I should have left well enough alone. I only needed a few moments to process it and to stop acting like a child."

He leaned back from me and looked into my eyes. The way his blue eyes stared into mine had my stomach dipping.

"You did not act like a child. I'm not a saint, and you know I've been with women. Oak Springs is one place for this to happen…but not here. We do not have to go to dinner with her. There are other places we could stay, Corina. She's being a bitch by forcing this."

I smiled. "No. I want to go to dinner. She needs to see she doesn't have control over either of us, and she needs to see we're in love and happy."

His hands cupped my face. "So very much in love and over-the-moon happy."

"Make love to me."

Mitchell's eyes danced with desire. "You don't have to tell me twice."

Holy crap. I look hot.

Standing in front of the full-length mirror, I took in the black cocktail dress I had slipped on after Mitchell and I took a hot bath together. Before that, we'd had a mind-blowing lovemaking session. The bath was all about me, with Mitchell massaging every single inch of my body. I felt so relaxed afterwards I almost told him I didn't want to go to dinner.

Almost.

I chewed on my lip as I took in my reflection. Thin spaghetti straps led down to a low-cut, sweetheart bodice that certainly showed off my breasts. Mitchell was going to pass out when he saw me. Of course, the push-up bra only made my chest look bigger. Smiling, I whispered, "One point for me. Zero for Kristi in the boob department."

Turning to the side, I blushed. The dress was sultry enough, but add in the sexy cutouts at the midriff, and it went off the charts. Not to mention the low, open back that dipped all the way to my waist. The design showed off my curves in the most delicious way. Sparkling sequins were the finishing touch to the mid-thigh hem.

"Okay, deep breaths. You can go out in a dress like this, Corina. Yes, you can."

Apparently talking to myself had become a new thing over the past few months. I reached for a black sweater and grabbed my clutch. I couldn't wait to see Mitchell's face when he saw me in this dress.

Slipping on the black heels, I gave myself another look. My blonde hair was pulled up into a French twist. Simple pearl earrings adorned my ears, and I decided to keep my neck free of anything. It looked sexier to me. I wanted Mitchell's eyes to travel down to the girls…not make a pit stop on a piece of jewelry.

My phone buzzed and I glanced at it.

Paxton: *Send us a picture!*

Amelia: *Yes! Picture, please!*

Waylynn: *It better be sexy as fuck.*

Smiling, I took a couple of selfies and attached them to the group text message. I'd filled the girls in on Kristi earlier as I was getting ready, and they were all fired up.

With a deep breath, I hit send. It didn't take them long to text back. Waylynn was first. Of course.

Waylynn: *HOT DAMN. Where is our little innocent Corina?*

I did a happy dance.

Paxton: *Wow. Oh…wow…holy crap. Mitchell is good for you, girl!*

Amelia: *Excuse me while I wipe the drool off my mouth. If I was into girls I'd be jealous of my brother right now!*

Paxton: *ROFL*

Waylynn: *Right?!?!?*

I loved those girls. They certainly knew how to build me up.

Me: *I love you guys. Okay, I'm heading downstairs. Wish me luck.*

Paxton: *You don't need it, sweetie. He loves you and will only have eyes for you.*

Waylynn: *If he does something stupid, tell us so I can kick his stupid ass.*

Laughing, I shook my head.

Me: *Night, ladies!*

All three texted back at once with their goodnights. One last look in the mirror and I headed downstairs.

Mitchell was sitting on the sofa watching TV. I cleared my throat, and he glanced over his shoulder. The second he saw me, he jumped up and took a few steps back.

"Holy shit."

My heart was racing. What if he didn't like the dress?

"Do you not like it?"

His mouth dropped open, and he stared at me. Not one single sound came from his mouth.

"Mitchell?"

He closed his eyes and shook his head. "Give me a second. I think I've died and gone to heaven."

I couldn't help the smile that spread across my face. "So, you *do* like it?"

"Turn all the way around…slowly," he begged. I turned at a tor-turously slow speed as I gave him the nickel tour of what was his.

His eyes were moving across my body with a hungry look. "Like it? All I can think about is fucking you in it."

A delicious pulse started between my legs as he stalked toward me.

"Fuck dinner. I want you."

There was no denying that I liked the way Mitchell was reacting to the dress. He couldn't tear his eyes off of me.

"Now, now. It's only a dress."

Snapping his eyes up, he pinched his brows together. "Only a dress? Only. A. Dress. You look insanely hot. Beautiful beyond words. Jesus Christ, Corina. My dick is damn hard. I may have to take it out and work it myself if you don't let me have you."

Placing my fingers on his lips, I narrowed my eyes at him. "Why, Mr. Parker, listen to that dirty mouth of yours."

"Did you look at yourself in the mirror before you came down here? If so, how do you honestly expect me to keep my hands off you?"

He moved his hands over my body, causing me to tremble. "See, even you know how hot you are."

Laughing, I pushed his shoulder back. "Behave, Mitchell Parker."

"I'm not going to make it an hour, Corina."

With a half-shrug, I winked. "Then I guess we'll be cutting dinner short."

His hand moved to my back where he lightly brushed his fingers across my bare skin. "Hell, yes, it will be cut short." He leaned down, his lips brushing across mine. "You taste like heaven, dove."

I placed my hand on the side of his face. "That's because I'm in heaven."

We looked into one another's eyes for the longest time before he groaned. "I guess we need to go."

With his hand on my lower back, he led me out of the cabin, toward the Jeep. We walked into the hotel and the restaurant the same exact way, Mitchell's hand possessively on my body. The few people who were in the restaurant turned to watch us walk in. I couldn't help but notice one guy staring. Normally I would be uncomfortable with the attention, but tonight was different. I felt sexy, strong, and full of confidence. It wasn't only the dress doing that. It was the man walking next to me. The one who kept telling me how beautiful I looked. How amazing I smelled. How much he wanted my body under his.

It was Mitchell who made me feel like this. It was Mitchell who would forever make me feel like this.

Kristi was sitting at a table, waiting for us to arrive. When she looked up, her smile faded and her jaw dropped. Her stunned expression was soon replaced with one seriously pissed-off look.

I internally fist pumped. Mitchell guided me to the table and pulled my chair out.

"Kristi." His voice was flat, no emotion in it whatsoever.

"Good evening, Mitch, Lorina."

I wanted to roll my eyes. Instead, I grinned and said, "Corina."

"Oh, goodness. That's right. I don't know why I keep thinking it has an L."

I picked up the napkin, laid it across my lap and didn't bother to reply. Mitchell sat next to me, so close I could feel his leg touching mine.

When the waiter arrived, Kristi said, "Walter, we'll have a bottle of Château Lafite Rothschild, Pauillac."

I wanted to chuckle when Kristi used her best French accent to say the name of the wine.

"I'll take a glass of water, please. No wine for me," I said with a slight grin.

Krisit turned to me. "What? This wine is amazing."

I forced a polite smile. "I don't care for wine, and I find spending over eight hundred dollars for a bottle isn't my thing."

"It's nearly a thousand, and it was on the house. I am, however, impressed with your knowledge of wine."

"Thank you," I purred as nicely as I could. "But I'll still pass."

Kristi flashed me a smug smile. "More for me and Mitchell then."

"No, thanks. I'm going to stick with a bottle of beer. I'll take a Blue Moon, if you have it."

The waiter nodded. "Yes, sir."

"Oh, that sounds good. I'll have one, too," I added.

Kristi huffed. "Seriously, you're both passing on the best wine in the restaurant for beer?"

Mitchell flashed her a fake smile. I knew his real smiles. They touched his beautiful blue eyes and made them sparkle like the stars.

"So, Mitchell, did you ever become a police officer?"

He nodded. "Yes, I did."

"Oh, I bet you look good in the uniform."

She. Did. Not.

"Lor…I mean, Corina, what do you do for a living?"

"I'm a kindergarten teacher."

Kristi chuckled. "That seems fitting for you. You have that innocent look. Classic kindergarten teacher."

I dislike this woman.

"Of course, I don't know what the parents of your students would think if they saw you dressed like that."

"I think she looks stunning," Mitchell said. "The most beautiful woman in the entire room."

Kristi frowned before forcing a smile that looked as fake as her boobs. *Okay, maybe her boobs weren't fake.*

Clearing her throat, she continued with her questions. "So how long have the two of you been dating?"

"Awhile now," Mitchell answered. I looked at him questioningly, but realized he didn't care to share much with Kristi based on how he was answering her.

"Where did you meet?"

"Oak Springs."

Kristi sighed.

"At a dance hall? At the school where she works? Give me something, Mitchell," Kristi said, laughing.

I took the opportunity to answer for him. "My best friend from college, and the person who talked me into moving to Oak Springs, is married to Mitchell's brother, Steed."

She raised a brow. "How sweet is that?"

The waiter brought out our drinks and set the bottle of wine in front of Kristi. He poured it into a glass and handed it to her. Of course, she needed to pull her eyes off of Mitchell to actually see the glass of wine being handed to her.

I really, really don't like this lady.

She looked at the wine in every possible way. She swirled it. Sniffed it. Once she was happy with the smell, she took a small drink and slurped it in her mouth. Mitchell and I looked at each other, and it was everything I could do to keep from laughing.

"Are we ready to order?" the waiter asked.

Waving him off like he was a bother, Kristi replied, "We're not ready to order yet."

"Actually, we can't stay for dinner. I figured we could have a drink, catch up some and leave it at that."

Kristi didn't look pleased. "No dinner? What's the rush?"

Mitchell took a rather long drink of his beer, then set it down and leaned forward. "If you must know, I'm taking my girlfriend out dancing, then plan on bringing her back to the cabin and spending the evening with her."

Kristi leaned back in her chair, her eyes darting between Mitchell and me. "Lucky girl." She focused in on me. "You know, once a upon a time, I was the girl Mitchell was bringing back to his room and...spending time with."

Oh. My. Goodness. This woman was something else.

I plastered on the fakest smile I could muster. "So I've heard."

"Dear me. Mitchell, you're rather open with your girlfriend." She turned to me. "You seem to be taking it well."

"I think it's time to leave," Mitchell said, about to stand up. I placed my hand on his leg to keep him sitting.

"Why should I be worried about someone from Mitchell's past? While he was in college, at that. I'm sure you weren't the only woman Mitchell...*spent time with.*"

Kristi's smug smile vanished. I stood. "It was a pleasure meeting you, Kristi. If you'll excuse me, I've had enough visiting for one evening."

Mitchell stood next to me and tossed a twenty onto the table. "Kristi, good seeing you. Thank you again for your help with the room."

She didn't say a word as we walked out of the restaurant. Anger raced through my veins as we headed toward the exit of the hotel.

"I'm sorry, Corina."

Lacing my fingers with Mitchell's, I turned and smiled. "I'm the one you're leaving with. Screw her."

His eyes widened before he started laughing. "Damn, I love you. Come on, let's go cut a rug and show these people how to dance."

My anger vanished. I spent the rest of the evening laughing and enjoying myself in the arms of the man I loved...and spent the early morning hours wrapped up in his arms even closer.

CHAPTER 30

Mitchell

I rolled over to find an empty bed. Sitting up, I glanced around. Corina wasn't in the room, and I didn't hear her in the bathroom. With a quick flick of the covers, I reached for my sleeping pants and slipped them on. As I made my way down the steps, I heard her. My heart felt full as I listened to her on the phone, talking to Chloe.

"I know you don't want to share kisses with Gage, but I promise to give you extra-long hugs."

I smiled. Chloe had reached the stage where the newness of her baby brother was wearing off and a bit of jealousy was making its way in.

"Wade made you a bed for your baby doll? How sweet of him. Yes, I know how much you love her. She'll be so happy to have a comfy bed. Yep. Okay. Yes, I am looking at the snow right now. Okay, I'll send you a picture. A snow angel? Yes, I'm an expert at making them. I'll have Mitchell take a picture."

I poured a cup of coffee and made my way to the sun room.

"No, Chloe, I'm not on my honeymoon. Your momma is right. Well, I do love your Uncle Mitchell so very much. Yes…someday… I hope."

I let my imagination run away and pictured Chloe asking Corina if we were going to be married someday.

"I'd love to make that title official, as well! Where did you even learn that, Chloe Parker?"

I stopped walking and stared at Corina. She was wearing gray flannel pants and a long-sleeve, pink flannel shirt. She looked beautiful as she stared out through the windows at the heavily falling snow.

I set the coffee cup down and rushed back up the steps and grabbed the ring box. Silently I crept back down the stairs. Corina was still on the phone with Chloe.

"I promise when I get back I'll read that book to you. Yes, I'll do the voice."

My heart was overfilled with love for this woman. She was everything I wanted in life. Everything I needed. Hearing her talking to Chloe only made it that much clearer to me.

This was the perfect moment to ask her to marry me.

"Okay, Chloe cat. I'll talk to you tomorrow. Yes. I promise to make sure Uncle Mitchell is awake before I call. You be a good girl and help Mommy with your baby brother. They both need you."

"Love you, too. Bye, pumpkin."

Corina pulled the phone away from her ear and hit End. She set the phone on the table and drew her knees into her body. With her chin resting on her knees, she let out a contented sigh while she watched the snow fall.

"Hey, beautiful."

Glancing back at me, she dropped her legs. "Oh, you just missed Chloe. She called to talk to us. I thought you were still sleeping."

I smiled and pushed the hand that wasn't hiding the ring box through my hair. "Just woke up. Someone kept me up half the night getting freaky with me."

Her cheeks flushed and my chest tightened. "I believe it was you, Mr. Parker, who was getting freaky with me."

I wiggled my brows. "Looks like we may be snowed in. We could get freaky again, if you want."

Corina pulled her legs up on the sofa and sat crisscrossed. "What I think we need to do is go get some food. Look at that snow coming down."

Looking out the window, I nodded. "We could get stuck in here. I knew there was a chance we could get an early storm."

She laughed. "Just our luck, huh? It's beautiful though."

I peered out the window. She was right. It was beautiful. Snow covered everything. The rushing river cut a path through all of it, large boulders covered in fresh snow rising in various spots throughout the river.

"I don't think I've ever seen anything so breathtaking in my entire life," she said.

"I have."

Corina was still looking out the window when I walked up next to her. "Really? Mitchell, look out that window and tell me that isn't the most beautiful thing you've ever seen."

Dropping to one knee, I took her hand in mine. Corina turned and faced me. Her blue eyes seemed to catch the reflection from the snowflakes falling from the sky. She smiled, and I lost the ability to breathe.

"You are so beautiful. You literally steal my breath when you look at me."

Her eyes filled with happiness. It was the perfect moment to ask her to marry me. The white backdrop, the soft music coming from the radio she had turned on. The fact that we were both in our pajamas, talking about the possibility of being stranded in a snow-storm.

Perfect moment.

"The first time I ever laid eyes on you I was mesmerized. You somehow managed to grab a hold of my heart, and I'm positive I loved you from that moment on."

A tear slipped from her eye and slowly traveled down her beautiful face.

"That first night we were together, I knew you were the one. I was stupid and scared and ran as fast as I could because I wasn't ready to admit what I felt in my heart. I'd never in my life experienced it before. Even then I knew I had fallen in love with you. It took me awhile to admit that you were the one I wanted to spend the rest of my life with. The woman I wanted to have children with."

Corina covered her mouth, trying not to cry harder, but losing the battle.

"I wanted to make this moment special for both of us. I'm not good at things like this, and Amelia's romance audiobooks can only help me so much."

Corina shook her head and let a slight sob slip from between her lips.

I swallowed hard and cleared my throat, trying to get my voice back. "I know this isn't the most romantic way to ask you to marry me, but I figured if you allow me, I'll spend the rest of my life working on the romance part. Corina, will you do me the great honor of becoming Mrs. Mitchell Parker?"

Dropping to her knees, Corina threw her arms around my neck. "Yes! Yes, I will marry you!"

I pulled her to me and held her tight. Her body shook as she cried.

"Mitchell, this is the last thing I ever expected!"

Drawing back, I wiped her tears from her face. "It's not too soon?"

She shook her head and her bottom lip trembled. "No. Not for me."

She looked down at the ring and gasped. I took it out and slipped it onto her finger while she stared at it.

"It was my grandmother's ring. She loved emeralds. My grandfather had this ring made for her. The halo of diamonds around it was to represent his unending love for her. She didn't like yellow gold, so he had it made in platinum. To represent the strength of their love."

"Oh Mitchell, that is so beautiful."

Grinning, I nodded. "My grandmother never took it off. She told me once when she would get upset or need clarity, she'd stare at her ring. The emerald would calm her...clear her vision."

Corina held the ring up and gazed at it. "It's the most beautiful thing I've ever seen."

My smile grew bigger. "I'm glad you like it."

Her eyes snapped to mine. "Like it? Mitchell, I love it and will treasure it for the rest of my days. You will never know how much it means that you gave me your grandmother's ring."

I pushed a piece of hair behind her ear. "Someday you can pass it down to one of our grandchildren."

Her eyes filled with tears again. When I placed my hand on the side of her cheek, she leaned into it. "I have something I need to tell you, dove."

Her grin faded some.

"It's nothing bad, I swear," I added with a lighthearted chuckle.

"Okay, what is it?"

I wasn't sure how she was going to feel about this. Would she think I was insane? Maybe she would think it was too soon. It didn't matter—I wanted to be honest with her and I knew she would want that too.

"I want to have a baby."

Her mouth parted and she sucked in a breath. "W-what?"

"A baby. I've been thinking about it a lot, and I mean…I want to start a family."

Corina sat onto the ground and stared at me like I had lost my damn mind.

Fuck. Maybe I had. We'd only been together since August, and we'd had a pregnancy scare the first week we were officially dating. It was only the beginning of October and I'd just asked her to marry me *and* have my baby.

Yep. I had lost my mind. But I knew this was what I wanted and prayed it was what she wanted too.

Corina stared at nothing, like she was trying to process everything that just happened in the last two minutes.

"Are you okay?" I asked as I sat on the floor in front of her.

"Mitch, did you hear what you just said?"

I nodded. "Yes."

"You want to have a baby?"

"I do. Very much so."

"Before we get married?"

I shrugged. "I don't care. If you want to run off like Amelia and Wade did, I'm game. If you want to have the biggest wedding known to man, I'm down for that too. I don't care how we do this, I just know I want all of it. With you."

She closed her eyes and took in a deep breath before focusing on me. "What about getting to know each other? Spending time together?"

"I know I love you. I know we started this relationship in a crazy-ass way, so why not keep up with it?"

Her hand went to her stomach. When I saw her beautiful blue eyes glass over, my heart about pounded out of my chest. I could see her answer in her eyes. It felt like I could look into them and read her soul.

Dropping her hand, she laughed. "Yes!"

Narrowing my eyes, I asked, "Yes to the marriage? Because you already said yes to that…or yes to a baby?"

She took my hands in hers. "Yes to a baby! Oh my God! Are we really going to do this?"

I smiled so big my cheeks hurt. "Only if you really want to."

"Do you? I mean, Mitchell, this is such a one-eighty for you. You're sure that you're not just caught in the moment of all this magic? Maybe it's the cold weather. It's gone to your head!"

I pulled her into my lap. "I'm positive. I want to marry you, and more than anything I want to watch your stomach grow with our child. I love you, Corina, and I don't want to wait another second to start this life with you."

"A baby? We're going to try for a baby?"

Placing my finger on her chin, I grinned. "I say we start practicing now."

Her teeth sank into her lip. "Practice makes perfect."

Corina and I spent the rest of the morning making love as the snow fell quietly all around us. I'd never been so content in my entire life.

There was no way life could get better than this.

We raced into the hotel and shook the snow off.

"Wow! Is all this snow normal?" I asked the bellhop.

"We are known for getting an early storm like this every so often. It is beautiful though, isn't it?" he said.

"It's breathtaking!" Corina answered. She still had a glow on her cheeks from all the lovemaking this morning. It had been amazing, being buried inside of her all morning. I had thought I was done for the day until I watched Corina throw her birth control pills away. Something came over me, and before I knew it, I had her on the counter in the kitchen and was fucking her like my life depended on it. By the time we both came, we were covered in a sheen of sweat, each of us breathing like we had just run a marathon.

After making our way to the restaurant, I looked around to make sure Kristi wasn't there. Corina ordered a water, and when she said "Just in case," it made my stomach dip like I was on a fucking roller coaster. I ordered a tea. If she wasn't going to drink, neither was I.

We ordered our meal and I reached across the table to take her hand. "I need to tell you something."

Her eyes sparkled with excitement. "Is it more big news? Because I think you've about reached your quota for today."

Laughing, I winked at her. "It is more news. Good news."

She smiled and my heart skipped a beat. *God, how I love her smile.*

"I probably should have told you this first before I asked you to marry me and tried to get you knocked up."

"Oh no! Did you quit your job or something, and now we have to live on my salary alone?" she asked as she let out a chuckle.

"Actually, yes. I gave my two-week notice that will go into effect when we get back from vacation."

Her smile dropped. "You did what?"

"I've been doing a lot of thinking the last few weeks. Being with you has really opened my eyes to the things I really want in life."

"Oh my gosh. Mitchell, what are you going to do for a job?"

I could see the panic in her eyes.

"Work for my father. That's what I was talking to him, Steed, and Trevor about last week. I want to work on the ranch. I've always wanted to. It just took me a few years to listen to my heart and go for the things I wanted."

A huge smile grew across her face. "I think this is amazing!"

The corners of my mouth lifted. "Yeah? You're not upset or angry?"

"What? No! Mitch, I've always known the worry that came with your job, and I was okay with it. But now…you've just lifted a huge weight off my shoulders!"

"Hey, ranching is dangerous work."

She laughed. "Not as dangerous as being a cop. Please, tell me you didn't do this because you thought it would make me say yes to the marriage and the baby."

I squeezed her hand. "Dove, you already agreed to that when you thought I was still a cop."

Her eyes widened. "That's right! I did!"

The waiter came up and set our bowls of soup down, followed by two salads.

Corina pulled her bowl closer. "Oh, yum. Soup sounds so good right now!"

"Is there anything else I can get the two of you?" the waiter asked.

Corina shook her head. I said, "No, thank you. I think we're good for right now."

I took a sip of the soup and wanted to moan. This Texas boy was not used to being so damn cold.

"I've got a bit of news to share with you as well," Corina said.

Looking up, I grinned. "Yeah? Share it with me."

"I've been thinking, since we are officially moved in together and are now talking marriage and baby, what would you think if I turned my house into a bed and breakfast? I've actually been tossing the idea around since I moved in with you."

I set my spoon down and focused on her. "I think that's a great idea. The downtown area of Oak Springs is starting to really grow, and Lucy mentioned a ton of people are asking about places to stay close to the river and the square."

Her expression was pure happiness. "Okay, so now I have another idea."

"Hit me with it," I said before taking a bite of salad.

"Now that we are trying for a baby…" Her cheeks flushed. "If we do have one, I don't want to work. I'd want to stay home with him or her."

"I'm totally fine with that."

She nodded. "Okay! I can help run the B and B and still be at home with our little one."

My heart felt like it was floating in my chest. *Our little one. Damn, I liked the sound of that.*

"And I was thinking after leaving Chicago, what if we asked my mom to move to Oak Springs and run the bed and breakfast full-time?"

"Corina, I think that's a great idea!"

She clapped her hands and did a little dance in her seat. "I do too! I mean, she loves Chicago, but I know she would love Oak Springs. My brother isn't planning on kids anytime soon, and if we told Mom we were going to have a baby and we had a job she'd be excited about, I kind of think she'd be game for it."

"I think she would love that. I mean, even if you got pregnant today, you'd still be finishing out the school year, right?"

"Yes, and we still have to make the changes to the house so that we could do the B and B. Get it all set up with the permits and all that fun stuff. It would be awhile before it's actually open and ready to take people in. That would be plenty of time for Mom to come down to Texas, check it out, and let us know if she wanted to do it or not. Otherwise, we can hire someone to help run it."

I couldn't help the goofy-ass smile on my face. "Holy shit. Are we really making all these grown-up decisions right now? Marriage. Baby. Job changes. New business. Who are we?"

Corina laughed. "I say we get daring and order a bottle of champagne and celebrate all our news!"

Holding up my hand, I motioned for the waiter. "We'll take a bottle of champagne."

"Yes, sir. We have a Dom Perignon that is a hundred and seventy-five dollars a bottle."

Before I had a chance to answer, I saw Kristi walk into the restaurant. I turned to the waiter. "May we have that delivered to our cabin? I think my fiancée and I would rather enjoy the view from our room while we celebrated."

"Of course, sir. Would you like me to send up anything else, as well?"

"Yes. A cheese and fruit platter would be nice. If you could put the rest of this on my bill, we're going to be leaving now."

Corina looked down at her soup then back at me with a confused look. I simply winked.

"Was your meal okay, Mr. Parker?"

"Oh yes, it was delicious. We've just decided we want a bit more privacy."

The kid smiled and nodded. "I'll have some soup delivered to your room, as well. Let me get the bill."

When he walked away, Corina gave me a questioning look. "Why are we leaving?"

"Good afternoon, Mitch and Corina," Kristi said. "How are you enjoying this weather?"

Corina snarled before plastering on a fake smile. "Hello there, Kristi. The weather is amazing. Magical, if you will."

Kristi let out a halfhearted chuckle. "If you say so. May I join you for lunch?"

The waiter had perfect timing. I quickly wrote out the tip and total and signed the bill. Standing, I reached for Corina's hand.

"I'm sorry, Kristi. We've decided to head back to the cabin. We have a bit of celebrating to do."

She lifted her brow as she looked between Corina and me. "Really? What type of celebrating?"

"The type that has Corina wearing my engagement ring on her finger. Now, if you'll excuse us, we were leaving."

I gently pulled Corina toward me and led her out of the dining room. I didn't need to look back to know that Kristi was staring at us with piercing eyes. I could practically feel darts in my back.

"Well, if that didn't leave her with a clear message, I don't know what will!" Corina said with a giggle.

I brought her to my side, and we walked toward our cabin. "Come on. I want to make love to my future wife."

"Sounds like an amazing idea to me!"

CHAPTER 31

Corina

"Aunt Corina! What are you dressing up as?" Chloe asked, her eyes wide with anticipation.

"I think a school teacher."

Chloe's smile faded. "You can't dress up as something you already are! That's cheating!"

Laughing, I bent down. "I'm going as a witch."

"Me too!" Chloe shouted.

Paxton told us Chloe had been secretly hoping we were all dressing like witches. "The Parker witches," she wanted to call us. Even though I wasn't an official Parker yet, Chloe had already deemed me so.

"You are?" I asked, pretending not to know.

Jumping, Chloe said, "Now we will have six witches at the party."

I frowned. "Six?"

Paxton sighed. "Oh, you haven't heard yet? Patches will be joining the birthday party dressed as a witch."

"Well, he's actually a warlock, Mommy. You know, 'cause he is a boy and all."

With a lift of her brow, Paxton replied, "That's right. How silly of me." When she looked at me and rolled her eyes, I couldn't help but giggle.

Chloe climbed onto the stool and rested her chin on her hands, watching me decorate pumpkin cookies. "You know, Aunt Corina, you're gonna have to paint your face green."

"Green!" I gasped. "Why?"

"Um, hello, you're a witch, and they have green faces."

"Are you painting your face green?" I asked.

Chloe laughed. "Well, no! I'm a witch princess, and they don't have green faces."

"Does Aunt Waylynn know about this?" I asked, peeking over to Paxton, who made a face that said Waylynn had no clue.

Chloe shrugged as if she hadn't a care in the world. "Don't know."

As if on cue, Waylynn came rushing into the kitchen, dressed in her Halloween costume. She looked more like an angel than a witch. Chloe gasped. Paxton whispered, "Oh hell."

I prepared for a six-year-old meltdown.

"Stop being so difficult!" Amelia said, pushing Waylynn's hand away.

"You're putting so much of it on my face! I look like a…"

"Witch?" I replied with a grin.

Waylynn shot me a dirty look. "You need to hush. You look cute in your little blonde ponytail and green face. Besides, you're engaged so it doesn't matter that you look hideous. I need every opportunity I get to find a man! I'm not going to find one with a green face!"

With a shocked expression, I replied, "Hey! I don't look hideous! You said I looked cute!"

Waylynn half shrugged. "Fine! Meli looks hideous. You look adorable. I need to look hot!"

Amelia gave Waylynn's hair a tug, causing her to cry out.

"I still can't believe you're engaged!" Amelia said, looking my way.

"It's been surreal. The trip up to Canada was amazing."

Waylynn wiggled her brows. "That's because y'all got snowed in. What wouldn't be crazy nice about being stuck in a beautiful cabin for a few days."

I chuckled. "That's true. We did make good use of the time."

Mitchell and I had decided not to share the fact that we were hoping for a baby. Until it happened, there was no use talking about it.

"Whatever happened with you and Jonathon? Y'all not getting it on anymore?" Amelia asked.

Letting out a gruff laugh, Waylynn rolled her eyes. "Please. It was one time. He's too young for me."

"He is not," I said.

Waylynn turned to me. "Corina, I'm going to be thirty-three soon. He's twenty-six."

"Almost twenty-seven!" Amelia added.

"That makes me feel *tons* better. Thanks, sis."

Gently hitting her leg, I said, "Oh, come on, Waylynn. That's only six years' difference. That's not a big deal."

I couldn't help but notice how sad Waylynn's eyes looked. Was it from not being with Jonathon—or was she just lonely? She'd moved into the other guest house on the ranch, but from what Melanie had told me, she stayed in her old room more than she did in her own house.

With a raised brow, I asked, "Was it only that one time y'all were together?"

When she didn't respond, I had my answer. "Waylynn Parker, are you still sneakin' 'round with that boy?" Amelia asked with a shocked tone and deep southern accent.

Waylynn grinned. "I told him it wasn't going to work. And yes, it was only that one time. Although, I wouldn't mind another round with him. Preferably in a bed and not up against a wall."

"Mmm... Still sounds hot, if you ask me," Amelia added.

"It was hot as hell! The boy gave me two orgasms that rocked my ever-loving socks off."

"Who gave you *two* orgasms?"

We all froze as Cord appeared in the doorway of Amelia's old bedroom, where we were getting ready for the party. It took us five seconds to start laughing hard. Cord was dressed in all black, with a giant piece of bacon that ran down his entire body. His face was framed by the end of the bacon. He looked adorable and ridiculous, all at the same time.

"What the hell, Cord? Bacon!" Waylynn cried out as she held her stomach laughing.

Cord looked down at his costume then back at Waylynn. "That's right. Chloe picked out the bacon costume for me because she said I loved bacon."

"You look ridiculous!" she added.

He walked into the room, and I had to cover my mouth to keep from laughing harder. "You ever wonder why she wanted you to be a witch?"

"Okay, now, wait," Amelia said. "You just insulted all three of us. If you haven't noticed we are all witches."

Cord smirked. "If the shoe fits." He glanced over to me. "Except for you, Corina. You're like the good witch from *The Wizard of Oz.*"

"Why thank you, Cord. I appreciate the love."

He shrugged. "Don't get used to it. The moment you become a Parker…all bets are off and you're open game."

My grin faded.

"Now, let's get back to what I overheard. Whose ass do I need to beat for having sex with you?"

Waylynn lost it laughing. "Right. Because I'm only thirty-two years old, jerk-face."

Cord attempted to sit on the bed but the bacon pushed into his chin.

"Besides, you don't see me trying to run after every girl you poke your dick into," Waylynn added.

"You'd be running all over Texas," Amelia added.

"Don't be jealous because I have a good sex life. I can't help it if I like sex. It's fun."

Amelia put more green make-up on Waylynn's face.

"You don't have any desire to settle down with someone, Cord?" I asked.

He looked my way, tilted his head like he was really giving it thought. "None at all. I like the way my life is. If I met the right woman, would I settle down? Yes. But I'm young, in good shape, and I like to fuuu…ahh… Hey, Chloe! I see you've got Patches."

All of us snapped our heads to find Chloe standing in the door-way, holding Patches the goat with a lead rope.

"Chloe Lynn Parker, you know you're not allowed to have Patches in the house!" Waylynn said in a firm voice.

"But I'm the party planner. Daddy said I could invite whomever I wanted."

"Not a goat, Chloe," Amelia added.

Chloe's eyes filled with tears. "I say Patches should be a part of the party."

Everyone looked at me. "Chloe, I'm sure your Grammy won't mind, as long as Patches stays outside, in case he has to go potty. We'll be outside mostly anyway, so Patches won't miss anything."

The wide smile on Chloe's face told me she was happy with this.

"You best get Patches out of the house before your mommy sees him, though," I said with a wink.

"Okay!" Chloe said as she pulled on Patches' lead.

Waylynn took a few steps back. "Do you see how the goat is looking at me? It's like he knows I don't like him."

Cord laughed. "You did try to convince Wade to slaughter the poor thing."

"Waylynn Parker!" Amelia gasped.

"I wasn't serious," Waylynn replied with a half shrug.

Cord lifted a brow and gave his sister a look that screamed he didn't believe her.

"Fine. Maybe I was a little serious."

"Hey, I came up to ask if you've talked to Jonathon the last couple of days?"

The three of us froze. Had Cord overheard our whole conversation? Was he fishing to get more information?

"Um, he stopped by the other day to check on the progress of the dance studio, but I didn't have a chance to talk to him. I was with the interior designer. Why?"

Cord shook his head. "I don't know. I'm just trying to figure out what's going on with him. He's been acting strange and hasn't been by the bar in weeks. I invited him to the party."

"The party?" Waylynn asked. "This party? As in the birthday party?"

"Ah, yeah. Why? Do you have a problem with that?"

Waylynn let out a fake laugh. "Why would I have a problem with that?"

With a shrug, Cord replied, "You seemed like you didn't want him here."

Waving Cord off, Waylynn smiled. "Nonsense. Amelia, we better get this make-up finished."

That was Cord's cue to leave. "I'll see y'all downstairs."

Sinking down into the chair, Waylynn stared at herself in the mirror. She looked adorable, even with the green make-up.

"Well, Jonathon will take one look at me and probably be glad we only screwed once."

Amelia and I looked at each other. Then I got an idea.

"Pigtails."

"Little girls," Amelia said with a laugh. "Your turn, Waylynn!"

"Um, what?"

I lightly pushed Amelia to the side. "No, we need to put Waylynn's hair in pigtails."

Waylynn stared at me. "Why in the hell would I put my hair in pigtails?"

Smiling, I pulled her hair down from her pony and started dividing it evenly on each side. "I had my hair in pigtails the other day, and when Mitchell got home from work something happened. He went all caveman and we…well…we had a bit of fun."

With a huge smile on her face, Waylynn playfully said, "Oh, my, *my*. To think I thought you were the innocent one."

"If you put your hair in pigtails, it will drive Jonathon insane. Y'all might even sneak away for a quickie!"

Amelia and Waylynn both looked at me with their mouths gaping.

"Who are you and what did you do with Corina Miller?" Amelia asked.

I giggled and pressed my lips together before saying, "What can I say? The Parker boys really are naughty cowboys."

All three of us started laughing. I curled Waylynn's pigtails a few times and then we were ready to go.

"I don't want to sleep with him again, y'all," Waylynn said as we headed downstairs. "It will never work between us."

"Sure, keep telling yourself that," Amelia replied.

When we walked outside, Amelia rushed over to Wade. "Excuse me, y'all. I need to dance with my hotter-than-hell husband."

I couldn't help but smile when I saw Wade two-stepping with Chloe across the makeshift dance floor.

My eyes scanned the area until I saw Mitchell. He was dressed as a scarecrow, Chloe's pick.

"Well, maybe I can at least find someone to dance with me," Waylynn said, adjusting her black dress. The moment I saw Jonathon walk up the driveway, my heart dropped for Waylynn. He had a girl on his arm.

"Why don't we head on over Paxton," I said, trying to guide Waylynn away.

Paxton was also dressed like a witch, but had gotten out of painting her face green by using Gage as an excuse.

Right as we walked up, Cord looked past us.

Crap. Crap. Crap.

"Hey, there's Jonathon. Jon! Hey, over here!"

Waylynn glanced over her shoulder, and it was hard not to notice her disappointment.

"He brought a date," she whispered.

Amelia pulled Waylynn into the seat next to her. I sat down, and Mitchell sat on the other side of me.

"Wipe that look off your face right now, Waylynn," Amelia said, pointing her finger at her sister.

Snapping out of it quickly, Waylynn smiled again. "Right. No big deal."

I reached for her hand and squeezed it. "Are you okay?" I asked in a hushed voice.

Nodding, Waylynn replied, "Yep. This is what I needed. A good kick in the ass to move on. So that's what I'm going to do."

She smiled, but it didn't reach her eyes. Mitchell leaned in closer to me and asked, "What's going on? Waylynn didn't seem too pleased to see Jonathon here."

I faced Mitchell and forced a grin. "I'll tell you later, but everything's okay."

He looked at me like he knew I wasn't telling him the truth.

Everyone said hello to Jonathan and his date, Bethany. Even Waylynn was pleasant—and putting on a total show. I couldn't help but notice how Jonathon kept stealing glances and peeks at Waylynn. There was no doubt in my mind; he liked Waylynn. A lot.

When Jonathon and Bethany sat down at the table, Waylynn jumped up and made her way across the room.

"What's going on with Waylynn and Jon? He can't keep his eyes off of my sister, and she can't stop looking back at him. I know you know. Spill it," Mitchell said.

Cheese and crackers.

I swallowed hard, trying to think of something to do or say that would alter the course of this conversation.

Leaning in, I placed my lips against Mitchell's ear.

"I want you. Now."

He drew back and smiled at me. "Oh yeah? You're gonna have to do better at convincing me to change the subject. And you're not getting me to leave yet another party."

My cheeks heated. Moving in closer so no one would hear us, I whispered, "I want you to fuck me. Now."

And like that, I'd worked my witchy magic, and Mitchell had forgotten all about Waylynn and Jonathon.

CHAPTER 32

Mitchell

I walked into the kitchen and smiled when I saw my brothers and Wade sitting there.

"You ready for this shit?" Trevor asked before pushing a forkful of eggs into his mouth.

Mom reached across the table and slapped Trevor on the side of the head. "Do not swear at my table, Trevor Parker."

"Yes, ma'am," he replied with a wide grin.

"How are you liking your new job, Mitch?" Cord asked, leaning back in his chair with a cup of coffee.

"I'm sore as shi…um…I'm sore as heck," I answered, peeking over to my grinning mother.

Trevor and Wade laughed.

"I forgot how much daily work goes into this place. I don't know how you did it before Wade," I said to Trevor.

"We made do with the other ranch hands and y'all when you could make it."

A large plate of pancakes sat in the middle of the table along with bacon. Damn, it smelled good, and my stomach let me know how hungry I was.

Mom clapped her hands and said, "Eat up, boys. You've got a lot of work to do today."

Steed walked into the kitchen with Chloe at his side.

"Good morning, uncles!" she shouted as she shot by us and made her way to Dad's office.

Trevor laughed. "I see where the uncles fall in the order of most-loved."

Mom laughed and added, "What about me? She ran right on by me."

Steed kissed Mom on the cheek. "She loves you all equally. It's just Dad has promised her she can drive one of the tractors today. Good Lord, that girl couldn't even go to sleep last night she was so excited."

Steed sat across from me.

"Eat up, Steed," Mom said.

"No thanks, Mom. Paxton made us a big breakfast this morning."

His eyes caught mine, and he smiled. He and Paxton were the only two who knew Corina and I were trying for a baby. "How's the planning coming?" he asked.

Everyone else probably thought he meant the wedding planning, but I knew what the bastard was asking.

"It's going great. Stayed up half the night working on it."

Steed laughed and shook his head as he said, "Damn."

Reaching for Steed's hat, my mother took it off and set it on the long buffet table. She did the same thing with mine when she walked by.

"You boys know better than to keep those hats on during breakfast."

"Yes, ma'am," we said together.

Our mom sat down and glanced around the table. Anytime she had all her boys there, she went in for the kill. We were all holding our breath, waiting to see who would be the first victim.

"Wade, how are things going with you and Amelia?"

The rest of my brothers and I breathed matching sighs of relief.

Poor Wade's head snapped up like he had been called to attention. "Things are going amazing, Mrs…"

She tilted her head and held up a finger.

"Melanie. Things are going great."

"Do y'all have the house where you want it yet? I haven't been there in a few weeks, I'd love to stop by."

Wade nodded. "Please do. I know Amelia would love that. Her office on the second floor is finished. The only things we really have left to do are the guest bedrooms and the kitchen."

Wade shifted over to me to throw the conversation. Bastard. He was a quick learner. "How about you, Mitchell? Y'all getting your place fixed up?"

I took a bite of toast and nodded. "Yeah, it's coming along. We didn't have much to do. A little bit of painting. Corina has been focusing on her old place, getting it ready to make into a bed and breakfast."

"I just love that idea!" Mom said. "Now, is her mother still coming down next week for Thanksgiving?"

"She sure is."

"Good! I can't wait to talk to her about the wedding."

I flashed my mother a smile. Before I focused back on my food, I caught Cord giving me a shit-eating grin.

"What?" I asked.

"Dude, I still can't believe you're getting married. I mean, Tripp I can see getting married 'cause the bastard is getting old and all."

"Hey!" Tripp said. "You do know I'm only four years older than you, Cord."

Cord ignored Tripp and kept talking. "But man, oh man, never imagined Mitchell would be settling down."

"He's found love," Trevor said with a laugh.

Steed grinned widely as he took a drink of coffee. "Y'all wait until it happens to you. You're gonna be knocked flat on your asses."

"Language, boys," Mom purred happily. She loved having us all together.

"I'm not afraid of love." Cord stated. "I mean, I don't want to walk around looking like a Smurf all the time."

My mother wore a confused expression. Leaning over, I whispered, "Let it go, Mom. Trust me."

She nodded.

"When love comes walking through my door I'll let it in. But it ain't happening anytime soon," Cord announced.

Trevor lifted his glass of orange juice. "I'm with Cord. This cowboy plans on living it up for as long as he can."

Mom cleared her throat. "And by living it up, what exactly do you mean, Trevor?"

His smile dropped. "Um. You know."

She folded her hands in her lap, and I tried like hell not to laugh. "No, I *don't* know. Why don't you fill your mama in on this plan. Seems to me like it's time you found yourself a nice girl to date."

Dropping his fork to his plate, he sat back. "I'm not going out with her."

"Why not? Trevor, she is a sweet girl!"

"Who are we talking about?" Tripp asked, looking between Mom and Trevor.

Trevor pointed to Mom, grimacing. "Our mother has been trying to fix me up with one of her friend's daughters. She went to some fancy school in Austin for high school, then went off to Boston for college and is now back in Oak Springs."

"Fresh meat," Cord mumbled under his breath. Trevor nodded.

"You boys know her," Mom said. "Scarlett Littlefield."

Cord sat up straight. "Scarlett Littlefield? I remember her. She was spit and fire. Didn't she set a trashcan ablaze behind the courthouse?"

"That was her?" Trevor asked with a chuckle. "Hell, I remember her now. She was always arguing that it's cruel to slaughter cows. Wasn't she a skinny, plain-looking girl?"

"Trevor Parker!" Mom gasped.

"What? She was, Mom! I'm just speaking the truth."

I finished off my pancakes and pushed the plate away. "Mom, you're wasting your time. Trevor doesn't know the meaning of *date*."

"That's right. Mom, I'm only twenty-four. You've got three older sons yet to settle down."

Her brow rose. "Mitchell is almost there. I have three left."

Tripp held up his hands. "Don't look at me, Mom. I've got a career to focus on, and the last thing I need is a woman to add drama to my life. No, thank you."

Mom stared at Tripp. She had that look in her eyes like she was up to something—sort of like when she knew Paxton was Chloe's teacher and kept it from Steed. This couldn't be a good thing.

Chloe came rushing into the kitchen. "I got a show goat! Granddaddy got me a show goat! I don't know what he's got to show...but Patches is gonna have another friend! His name is Lincoln!"

Steed's jaw fell, and he looked over at our dad who had walked into the kitchen behind a very excited Chloe. "Dad. You didn't."

Our father stood there with his chest puffed, looking as proud as could be. "I sure did. It will be good for her to raise him and learn the responsibility of taking care of him."

Mom shook her head. "John, you should have spoken to Steed and Paxton before you did this."

"Yeah...*Dad*. You really should have!" Steed added. "Besides, she helps Wade each morning and night to take care of Patches and the other goats. She's already learning."

Chloe walked around the table to give each of us a good morning kiss. Of course she lingered longest with Wade. When she got to me, she wrapped those little arms around my neck.

"Uncle Mitchell, can I come spend the night with you, Aunt Corina, and Milo?"

"Of course, you can, pumpkin. Anytime you want."

"Tomorrow night?" she asked, her little blue eyes looking hopeful.

"Tomorrow night, it is."

She did a hop and spin, and then turned to Tripp. "Uncle Tripp, guess what?"

"Chloe, honey, don't you need to help me with something?" my father quickly said.

Chloe faced him. "Nope." Focusing back on Tripp, she said, "My new goat is coming from—"

"Chloe!" my parents shouted, causing all of us to jump.

Spinning around, Chloe held her hand over her heart. "You scared me right out of my skin. I wasn't going to tell Uncle Tripp your secret."

Oh hell, here it is. The reason my mother has that look on her face.

My mother closed her eyes and sighed while my father shook his head in defeat.

"Secret?" Tripp asked.

Chloe turned on her heels. "Yep. I'm a good secret keeper. So, you won't be hearing from me that your old friend is the new vet."

Tripp's brows pulled tight. "My *old* friend?"

Leaning in close, Chloe whispered loudly, "I can't tell you Harley's name, 'cause that's the secret, and granddaddy said he needed to find a good way to tell ya about it."

"Oh hell," Cord and Trevor said at once.

Steed and I looked at each other and then back to Tripp. Tripp wore a carefully schooled face, but I knew the hurt beneath the surface. Swallowing hard, he cleared his throat. "Looks like my wish for a drama-free life isn't about to come true."

Harley Carbajal was back in town.

"You really think you should let him drive the tractor with the forks on it? I mean, look at how he's jamming it into the hay," I said as we watched Tripp drive around and pick up the hay bales and load them onto the trailer.

"Wade's got the dangerous job. He's on the trailer directing him," Trevor answered.

I wiped the sweat from my forehead. "I can't believe Harley's back in town."

"And is going to be the new vet. Talk about sticking a knife in Tripp's back."

"How do you think he's gonna take it when he sees her?"

Trevor shrugged. "Not good. Especially if she's married."

My chest ached for my brother. "Shit, I hope that isn't the case."

"You know she met some dick in college. That was one of the reasons she broke things off with Tripp. They could still be together."

Nodding, I put my cowboy hat back on my head. "He's gonna have to get used to the idea of her living here."

Trevor let out a gruff laugh. "Considering anytime she's come to town, he's left for one reason or another, he probably hasn't seen Harley in over five years…at least."

Steed pulled up in the John Deere tractor that had the cutter on it. Chloe had driven it for a bit before she got bored out of her mind. Dad had to take her back up to the house after about an hour.

Steed opened the door and started talking. "I need to fill the for-ty-six with fuel. We still have the north pasture of alfalfa to cut. You gonna follow behind me with the baler, Mitchell?"

"That should work. You think the dew is dried off?" I asked Trevor.

"Yeah, it's hot enough for it to be ready. You still want round bales on that, Mitch?"

I nodded. "Yeah, it's easier for the horses."

Shortly after I started working full time on the ranch, I stared to focus on getting a few good stallions and mares for breeding. I'd re-cently purchased a champion barrel racing horse named Firelight. I was hoping to breed more champions out of him. Chloe had already shown an interest in the horses, along with barrel and pole racing. I'd started working with her on Firelight, and I could tell she was hooked.

Steed looked past me. "Jesus, is Tripp trying to kill someone? He's whipping that tractor and hay all around."

Trevor and I glanced that way. "Yeah, I don't think he's taking the news about Harley so well," I said.

Slapping me on the back, Trevor said, "Let's get this taken care of then head to Cord's Place. I have a feeling Tripp is gonna need a hard, stiff drink."

A horn honked, drawing our attention to one of the ranch trucks as it pulled up. Amelia and Corina jumped out of it. Wade motioned for Tripp to take a break before he jumped off the trailer and made a beeline straight to our sister. He wrapped his arms around her and kissed her.

"At least we know he treats her good," Trevor said.

Steed replied, "Yeah, he's good people, that's for sure. I don't think I've ever seen Amelia so happy."

Giving me a slight push on the shoulder, Trevor laughed. "Or you, for that matter. Dude, you walk around with a fucking smile on your face all the time."

"I can honestly say I've never been so happy and content with my life."

"You miss being a Ranger?" Steed asked.

I shook my head. "Not at all. I thought I might, but I'm happy here."

Corina made her way over to us. Damn, she looked good in her jeans, boots, and a baseball cap. The white T-shirt she wore had a picture of Milo on it, and I couldn't help but laugh. She loved that damn cat.

"Hey, dove. What brings y'all here?"

She went up on her toes to kiss me gently on the lips. "I need to talk to you. It's kind of important, and I couldn't wait until you got home later." Glancing over my shoulder, she grinned. "Hey, guys. How's it going?"

"Good," both Steed and Trevor replied at once.

I was curious as hell as to why she made a trip out here to talk to me, but I refused to get my hopes up.

"We can take a walk, if you want."

She nodded.

I took her hand in mine, and we walked away from everyone. Corina had a hold on my hand like she was afraid I was going to take off running.

"What's going on?" I asked.

We kept walking, and she didn't say a word. When we got damn near all the way across the pasture, she stopped and faced me. Her eyes were dancing with happiness, and I dared to let myself think she might be pregnant.

"I couldn't wait to tell you. I was about to explode."

My eyes searched her face. "What is it?"

She gave me a smile so bright and brilliant there was no doubt in my mind what she wanted to say.

I took a few steps back. "Oh my God." With a wide grin, I asked, "Yeah?"

Corina nodded. "I'm pregnant."

I tossed my hat in the air. "Yee-haw!" I shouted before pulling her into my arms and spinning her around. Then I gently placed her back on the ground. Framing her face in my hands, I gazed into her beautiful blue eyes.

"You're pregnant? It happened so fast. I can't believe it."

"I know! I honestly thought it would take longer."

The news was settling in. "We're having a baby," I barely spoke.

Corina placed my hand on her stomach. "We're having a baby," she whispered.

I pressed my lips to hers and kissed her like I'd never kissed her before.

Just when I didn't think life could get any better, I'd been proven wrong again.

I was going to be a father.

CHAPTER 33

Corina

The smell of food was taking its toll on my uneasy stomach. I had to force myself to stay in the kitchen with everyone and help with the cooking.

"Are you okay?" Paxton asked. My eyes landed on Gage. She was holding him while giving him a bottle. My heart soared. On Monday we had a doctor's appointment to take a pregnancy test. Although we were already pretty sure we were pregnant—especially after Mitchell brought three more tests home just to make sure.

"Yep, just not feeling so well."

Paxton's eyes lit up, and I knew she knew. We had told Steed and Paxton we were trying for a baby.

"Melanie? Do you want to feed the little man?" Paxton asked her mother-in-law. It was a no brainer, Melanie wanted Gage in her arms twenty-four-seven.

"Yes! Give me him."

"I left a pie at the house. Corina and I are going to go get it."

Amelia glanced our way and gave us a questioning look. She'd helped Paxton carry in three pies so she knew Paxton wasn't telling the truth.

"I think I'll go with y'all," she said. Her eyes narrowed as if trying to read our reaction.

We both smiled. "Sure, if you want to," Paxton said in a calm, cool voice.

Waylynn was too lost in trying to decorate cookies with Chloe for her to notice we were leaving. They were having a decorating competition and both of them were bound and determined to win. Chloe was for sure a Parker woman, and took after Waylynn in more ways than one. The two of them were stubborn as mules and fiercely competitive.

Paxton laced her arm in mine. "Let's go. I'll drive. Chloe cat, I'll be back in a few, I'm running to the house."

Chloe acknowledged her mother with a simple, "'Kay."

As we walked toward Steed's truck, I knew Paxton was trying to keep her question in.

"You take shotgun, Corina," Amelia said.

After we got into the truck and started down the road toward Paxton and Steed's house, Amelia popped her head up into the front seat.

"You honestly think you can hide it from me? *Please.* I see the signs. You keep touching your stomach and then covering your mouth. You look like you want to throw up every time Mom asks you to smell or taste something. Your face is glowing like all get out, and my brother is walking around with a permanent smile on his face."

I turned in my seat to look at Amelia.

She wore a wide grin. "Girl, please, you're pregnant."

Paxton let out a scream. "Ahhh! Oh my gosh, Corina, are you?"

Letting out a chuckle, I replied, "I am."

The truck came to a halt and we all jumped out. Amelia and Paxton pulled me to them, and we stood there in a circle hugging each other. I was crying; they were crying, and then Amelia's perfume hit me like a brick wall.

"I'm going to throw up!"

Amelia pushed me away so fast I thought I was going to stumble onto my ass. "Don't! If you throw up, I'll throw up!" Amelia shouted.

All eyes were on her now.

Paxton's mouth dropped. "Amelia, are you pregnant, too?"

With a look of horror, Amelia gasped. "What? Hell no! My God, Paxton, bite your tongue! I just can't see anyone throw up. If I do, I'll throw up. I'm a sympathy puker, through and through."

My stomach was rolling with vengeance. I was going to get sick.

I spun around and started to gag. Then I heard Amelia gag, which made me gag even more.

"Oh God," Amelia moaned.

"Just get back in the truck, Amelia," Paxton urged.

There was no way I could hold it in. I lost my cookies.

"Don't! Amelia, no!" Paxton shouted.

Amelia threw up. And I threw up some more. It was like a contest to see who could make the other one throw up *by* throwing up!

"You threw up on me!" Paxton shouted. I turned around to see that Paxton's shirt was covered.

I clapped my hands over my mouth and started to laugh as Paxton stood there with a disgusted look on her face.

"Gross!" she shouted, pulling her arms through her shirt and carefully taking it off.

Amelia was leaning against the truck, trying to take deep breaths. "I need water."

Paxton walked to the back of the truck and reached into the cooler. Thankfully, Steed had brought drinks over for Thanksgiving and hadn't unloaded them yet. She handed Amelia a water and said, "Oh, for the love of all things good and holy, you're not even the pregnant one, Amelia!"

She grabbed the water and began swooshing it in her mouth. Paxton handed me a bottle, as well. I took small sips, not wanting to make my stomach angry again.

Amelia looked at each of us. "We're a team. You puke, I puke. Hoorah!"

"Is the morning sickness bad?" Paxton asked me.

"It's getting worse. And it's all day long. Every little thing makes me sick."

"I'm never getting pregnant," Amelia groaned as she climbed back into the truck.

Paxton laughed. "Let's get you to the house. You need a peppermint to calm your tummy." She looked down at her black bra. "And I need a new shirt."

By the time we got to the house, I'd told Amelia all about Mitchell saying he wanted a baby and what our plans were going to be. She couldn't have been happier.

"You know it's going to be hard to keep this from everyone. I figured it out pretty quickly, and I'm sure Aunt Vi is catching on. What about your mom? She's going to know the moment she sees you."

I laughed. "No way. I don't think my mom will know."

My phone beeped with a text from Mitchell.

Mitchell: *Your mom is here. She took an earlier flight to surprise you. Where are you?"*

My head snapped up. "My mom is here! She's early!"

Me: *With Paxton and Amelia at Paxton's place.*

Paxton's phone went off with a text message. She stared at it for a few seconds before laughing.

"What is it?" Amelia asked.

"It's from your mom, Amelia. She told me to give Corina some crackers and almonds if I have them. She also said to cut up lemons and have Corina smell them. Your mother is here, and if you don't get your morning sickness under control, she'll know the second she sees you."

My stomach dropped.

Melanie knew. Of course she did—she's carried quite a few children in her life.

"Mom is the coolest mother on Earth. I swear, I want to be her when I grow up," Amelia said with a laugh.

"Wait. Lemons?" I asked, snarling.

Paxton nodded. "Yep, if a smell is making you feel sick, something fresh like lemons or rosemary will help. Melanie was always shoving rosemary in my face when I was pregnant with Gage."

"Won't Lori know if she sees her daughter walking around with a lemon under her nose?" Amelia asked with a chuckle.

Paxton nodded. "Corina, if you want to keep this a secret, you're gonna have to hide it better."

I sighed. "I don't know what to do. Should we tell everyone? Don't they say you should wait? You know…just in case."

"Nonsense," Paxton said. "You can tell anyone anytime. You can't control fate by keeping something in, no matter how hard you want to believe you can."

This was why Paxton and I were best friends. She kept everything real, and I knew she was right.

Amelia let out a scream that made me and Paxton scream. "I have an idea! You have to call Mitchell though, and get his okay."

"What is it?" Paxton asked.

With a look that said she was up to no good, Amelia handed her phone to me. "Tell Mitchell we need him here. Now."

I had no idea what she was up to, but I did what she asked. She turned to Paxton and said, "And you might want to go put on a shirt, Paxton! I need Chloe's fabric paint and a white T-shirt!"

Paxton jumped up from next to me and ran into her bedroom. "Don't say anything else 'till I come back!"

Amelia sat down next to me and flashed me a grin. "This is going to be the most epic Thanksgiving ever!"

Mitchell and I stood on the front porch holding hands while staring at the front door. Paxton and Amelia had already gone back into the house.

"Are you sure we should do this?" I asked.

Mitchell lifted my chin. "I wanted to shout it from the highest mountain the other day when you told me. It's just family. We won't tell anyone else."

I nodded. "Who is going to be the first to notice?"

He shrugged. "I don't know. Mom already knows, so she won't say anything to ruin it. Maybe your mom?"

Chewing on my lip, I glanced at the shirt. "I can't believe Amelia was able to make this!"

Mitchell looked down and laughed. "She was always painting when she was little. It's that artistic side to her, I think. She got it from our grandmother. She loved painting and was good at it too."

Amelia had used fabric paint to make two little orange baby feet near the bottom of the shirt. Then above it, she wrote the words, "I am stuffed" in the same color.

Taking in a deep breath, I looked into Mitchell's eyes. "Can you believe how far we've come in just a few short months?"

He lifted his hand and placed it on the side of my face. I closed my eyes at the feel of his warmth on my skin. "I thank God every single day for you."

Our eyes met. "Back at ya."

He leaned down, brushed his lips over mine and whispered, "Marry me."

I giggled. "You already asked me that, and I believe I said yes."

His lips moved across my jaw to my neck. Each kiss was soft and sent tingles through my entire body.

"I want to marry you now."

My head dropped back, giving him access to my neck. "Right now?" I asked in a muffled voice.

"Tomorrow. Let's get married tomorrow."

Jerking my head up, I looked at him. "What?"

"Everyone we love is here. Well, I mean, your brother isn't which sucks, but everyone else is. Let's get the pastor, go down to the river, and get married."

My heart was racing. I'd marry Mitchell at the justice of the peace if he asked me to. I'd already begun dreading wedding plans. It seemed so silly to spend all that money when all I really wanted to do was become Mrs. Mitchell Parker. I didn't need all the bells and whistles like my brother did. He'd had a beautiful wedding, but I was like Pam. I wanted simple.

Mitchell's eyes searched mine. "Unless you want a big wedding. I don't want to take anything away from you, dove."

I wrapped my arms around his neck. I lifted up on my toes, and our lips met again.

Our kiss was soft and slow. I could feel his love pouring into my body. The way he drew me closer made my knees weak. I loved this man more than I could have ever imagined. And I loved this baby. I didn't care how or where we said our vows. All I knew was that I wanted to be Mitchell's wife and give him this baby.

He pulled his lips away, and rested his forehead against mine.

"Was that a yes?" he asked.

"That was a yes. Let's get married tomorrow."

Mitchell wrapped me in his arms and lifted me up, kissing me more passionately this time. When he set me down, we both seemed to be lost in each other.

"Let me call Pastor Burch. If he can do it, all we need is a time."

I nodded with excitement. The front door opened, and Amelia stepped out. "Are y'all going to come in or not?"

Spinning around, I said, "We are. We just need to call Pastor Burch to see if he can marry us tomorrow."

Amelia's mouth fell open. "Come again?"

Mitchell started talking on the phone and took a few steps away. I grabbed Amelia's hands. "Everyone is here, we don't need anything fancy, and I really want to be Mrs. Mitchell Parker."

She went to talk and nothing came out. Then she closed her eyes for a few seconds and popped them open. "I've got this. Miriam Meyer is a good friend of mine, and she owns Meyer's flowers. I can run down in the morning and buy some flowers and make you a bouquet."

"Can you make four more?"

She already knew what I was asking. "Yes! I'll keep it very simple."

"A dress?" I asked.

"I have an idea, if you're willing to wear a dress that's been worn before."

"Whose?"

"My mom's. She tried to give it away a few years ago, but I snuck it out of the pile. I wanted to make something for her with it, but if she sees you in it…"

Tears filled both of our eyes. "I'd be honored to wear you mom's dress. Will it fit?"

She nodded. "Oh yeah."

"This is crazy, isn't it?"

Amelia laughed. "Not to me! I did the same thing in New Orleans! At least this will be here on the ranch with our family. Our folks will be over the moon. They don't care how it's done, just knowing you and Mitchell are happy is all my folks care about, and I'm sure your mom is the same way."

I nodded, and this time tears slipped down my face. "Thank you, Amelia. I couldn't have done this without you."

She pulled me into her arms. "If you leave it up to me, I promise to give you the best last-minute, shotgun wedding ever!"

I held on to her tighter.

"Pastor Burch can do it," Mitchell said.

Stepping away from Amelia, I grinned. "What time?"

"He said he is open all day. His wife is going shopping for Black Friday."

I covered my mouth and laughed.

Amelia clapped her hands. She was in full-on planning mode. "Then it's set. Call him back and tell him we are doing a sunset wedding. He can meet us here at the house. You know that lookout by the cabin? I think it would make a beautiful place to get married."

Mitchell smiled. "You are brilliant, Amelia."

She grinned. "I know. The girls can get ready at the cabin. It's perfect. I've got so much to plan."

Turning on her heels, Amelia rushed into the house, leaving Mitchell and me standing there.

"Holy shit," Mitchell said. "We're not only having a baby, we're getting married tomorrow!"

I tried not to laugh, but I couldn't hold it in. "This is insane!"

Mitchell kissed me on the forehead. "That's what makes it so perfect. You ready to go in?"

"Yes, let's do this."

We both took deep breaths and started to walk into the house.

"I can't wait to see the look on everyone's faces when they find out," Mitchell said.

My chest fluttered with excitement. "You do know Amelia is about to tell everyone we're getting married tomorrow."

He laughed. "I have a feeling this is going to be the craziest twenty-four hours of our life!"

CHAPTER 34

Mitchell

It had been two hours since we walked into the house with Corina wearing the shirt. Her mother rushed over to her and wrapped her in arms. They talked for a few minutes in a corner and when I saw Lori start crying, I knew she had either noticed the shirt or Corina had told her. I couldn't pull my eyes off them. I'd never seen Corina so happy, and Lori was clearly over the moon.

Chloe instantly loved Lori and dragged her to the sofa to read a book together. I loved how Corina's mother seemed to fit right in with my family. It was a sign, for sure.

"Not one person has said a word about the shirt! My mom didn't even notice! I had to tell her," Corina whispered as we stood in the line to grab food. My parents had always done Thanksgiving like a buffet. The food was lined up, you got what you wanted, and everyone squeezed in around the dining room table. This year we had more people in the family and some had to sit in the kitchen.

"I know!" I said. "Mom saw it but hasn't mentioned anything, and I think Aunt Vi knows. She just wants Dad to figure it out on his own."

"The feet look like baby feet, so what the heck? I can't believe not even Chloe has said anything."

We laughed.

After everyone got their food, we made our way into the dining room. I had Corina sit next to Dad. The room was filled with conversations and laughter. Glancing around, I took it all in. My father, Steed, and Tripp were talking about politics and the city council. Amelia, Paxton, and Waylynn were talking about hanging lights in trees and getting enough chairs for everyone. Chloe was sitting next to Paxton, adding her two cents to the party planning. She had no clue what they were even talking about or what the party was for, but she insisted Patches had to be a part of it.

My mother was oblivious to their conversation, even though they were not in the least bit trying to be quiet. Mom, Lori, and Aunt Vi were talking about a tea party Aunt Vi was going to throw at the house she was renting from Wade and Amelia. She wanted to introduce Lori to some of Mom and Aunt Vi's friends. A sort of welcome to Oak Springs, since Lori had announced she would be moving to Texas soon. Of course, she didn't tell everyone the reason why she had made the decision.

Cord, Wade, and Trevor were all in the kitchen. I could hear them laughing and talking about heading to a rodeo in Uvalde in a few weeks. Cord was also trying to talk Wade into singing at his place this coming weekend.

I cleared my throat and turned to my father. "So Dad, I had an idea I wanted to run by you this week."

My father turned his attention to me. "Really? I'll be interested to hear it. And how do you like working full-time on the ranch now?"

"I love it."

"Do you miss your other job, son?"

"I really don't, Dad. I thought I might, but everything is working out like it should."

"Does anyone want any more tea?" Corina asked.

"I'll take some, but I can get it," Tripp said as he went to stand up.

Corina held up her hands to stop Tripp. "I need to stretch my legs. I don't mind getting it."

Corina made her way over to the buffet table. I was trying like hell not to smile because I knew exactly what she was doing.

She walked back over and stood right next to Dad as she reached for his glass and filled it up. Tripp looked down at her shirt and his fork froze. He quickly looked at me, and I nodded. He shook his head slowly and let out a slight chuckle.

"I can't believe it," he said with a smile.

My father looked at Tripp, confused, before turning his attention to Corina.

"Thank you, sweetheart." His eyes fell to the writing and baby feet. He stared at the shirt as Corina walked to the other side of him and poured Tripp a drink. My brother winked at her before she walked off.

My dad stood and followed Corina to the buffet table. Everyone stopped talking and watched him. I'm sure they were wondering what he was doing. Amelia jumped up and grabbed Wade, Trevor, and Cord from the kitchen and brought them into the dining room.

"Corina, sweetheart. Will you turn around?" my father asked her.

She slowly did. My eyes burned with tears as I watched her blink to hold back her own.

My father looked down at the shirt. It was almost like time stood still as he let the pieces fall together in his head. "Oh, baby girl, tell me this isn't a joke."

Her tears broke free. "It's not a joke," she said as her voice cracked.

"Why are Granddaddy and Aunt Corina crying?" Chloe asked.

I heard Paxton whisper something, and Chloe gasped.

Standing, I made my way over to them and stood next to Corina. I wrapped my arm around her waist and placed my other hand over her stomach. "We're having a baby. We just found out the other day."

Cheers erupted as my father wrapped Corina and me in his arms. "You've just made me the happiest man alive," he said. After a few moments of holding us, he turned to face everyone.

"Another grandbaby!" he called out.

Chloe stood on her chair, placed her hands together and looked up in prayer. "Please let it be a girl, God!"

Another round of laughter hit the room as Steed picked up his daughter and hugged her. Everyone made their way over to us. Hugs, kisses, handshakes, and congratulations were given.

Amelia hit the side of her wine glass to get everyone's attention. "There is more news! Because no one in this family likes to keep with tradition, we have another little announcement from Mitchell and Corina. Hold onto your socks, y'all…this is gonna be good."

All eyes were back on us now. I cleared my throat as I pulled Corina closer.

"Corina and I are getting married tomorrow at sunset at the lookout by the cabin."

"That's what you girls were talking about!" my mother said pointing to them. "My goodness, this is exciting! Another wedding!"

Chloe fist-pumped and started running around the room. "Lincoln and Patches can be the flower goats!"

All eyes fell on Chloe, then me and Corina.

With a chuckle, Corina threw up her hands. "Why not! Sounds like a plan to me!"

The rest of dinner, everyone talked about the baby and how in the world they had missed the shirt for so long. Then it was time for wedding talk and my mother, Lori, and Aunt Vi started figuring out food and a tent for the reception. My father barked orders for what time we needed to be up at the lookout to start decorations. It was chaos.

I faced Corina and shook my head. "Are you ready for all of this insanity?"

Placing her hand in mine, she replied, "I've never been more ready."

"You don't want to run off tonight to Vegas and get married to avoid all this craziness?"

Corina looked past me at the people we loved. She shook her head and laughed. "I love the crazy. I love the chaos." Her eyes met mine. "I love you."

I stared into those beautiful blue eyes of hers. Never in my wildest dreams would I have dared to believe I could be this happy. And so very much in love.

Amelia had me, Wade, and Steed putting lights up in all the trees. Waylynn had gotten lanterns, and Trevor was hanging them in the tree that hung over the place where the ceremony was going to be held. Small tea candles gave off the perfect glow.

Trevor and Cord came up with the idea to use the hay bales for places to sit. Since it was just family and a few close friends who could make it at the last minute, we didn't need a whole lot of seating.

Dad was helping one of his closest friends he had known since college put up the reception tent. We were keeping it simple. A grill had been brought over from the guest house, and the menu was hotdogs and hamburgers. Lucy offered to make up a batch of her homemade potato salad and her macaroni salad because she knew Corina loved it. Mrs. Johnson was making a few of her famous, award-winning, blueberry lemon lavender pies. They were Corina's favorite, and she had asked for those instead of a cake.

The guest list had been pretty much kept to family, with a few exceptions. Robert and Mary were there with their newborn son, Jimmy. Lucy, Sheriff Miller, and Mrs. Johnson were also invited.

"I think we've got enough bales out," Cord called up to me in the tree. "You need any help with the lights?"

"We've about got them all up. Maybe check with Dad to see if they need anything. If not, we should head back to the house to get ready."

Cord gave me a thumbs up.

I put the last set of lights up and climbed out of the tree. It was going to look beautiful.

After climbing down, I looked around. "Wow, I can't believe we pulled this off."

Tripp hit me on the back. "That's what happens when you have a big family who comes together to make it happen."

I nodded, the lump in my throat keeping me from speaking.

Tripp continued, "I have to say, I'm impressed, little brother. You seem pretty calm in light of the fact that you're getting married in a few hours."

Wade chuckled. "You nervous at all?"

"A little," I said. Truth was, my stomach was in knots. "Were you nervous, Wade?"

"Hell yeah. Not because I didn't want to marry Amelia. It was a different type of nerves. I can't explain it."

I nodded. "I get you. That's how I feel. I'm ready to marry her, but at the same time, I'm nervous as hell."

"The pre-wedding nerves. Boys, each of you will experience it." We turned to see our dad walking up.

"You were nervous before you married Mom?" Trevor asked.

Dad laughed. "I was so nervous I couldn't eat. I just knew she was going to come to her senses and realize she was making a mistake by marrying me."

We each chuckled.

My father placed his hand on my shoulder. "I'm proud of you, Mitchell. You followed your heart and that's all I've ever wanted for my kids. Your happiness." He looked around at his sons and Wade. "I'm proud of each and every one of y'all."

The moment was getting heavy, and I knew my father was fighting to hold back tears.

Wade cleared his throat. "If you don't want to be late for your wedding, we better get out of here and head back to the house."

Everyone agreed and we started making our way to the trucks. I slipped in with Tripp, and we set off toward my parents' place. It was the first time I'd had a chance to be alone with him since he found out Harley was back in town.

"You doing okay?" I asked.

He gripped the steering wheel harder. "I'm fine."

"Liar. If you grip the wheel any harder, you're going to pull it out of the dash."

Tripp sighed heavily and pushed his hand through his hair. "I can't believe she's back. Why now? Why, after all these years, does she decide she wants to live in Oak Springs? It wasn't good enough when I asked her to come back. I don't fucking get it."

"Are we sure she's back for good?" I asked.

He looked at me and then back to the road. "I did some digging around. Well, actually, I had Karen do some digging around to get information."

"You made your secretary do your dirty work?"

"Hey! I pay her well. Besides, she is one of the biggest gossips I know. The woman knows everything that happens in this town. I'm surprised she didn't know Corina was pregnant. Kudos to your future wife for keeping her business on the down low."

I laughed. "Okay, well, what did Karen find out?"

"Doc Harris asked Harley to take over his practice a few months ago. I guess the few times she's been in town she's helped him out, and he was really impressed."

"And she agreed? I mean, she hated Oak Springs. Couldn't wait to get out of here."

Tripp shrugged. "I guess. Dad said when he saw her at the vet, she told him she would be coming back to town a few times a month and would be here permanently by Christmas. Doc wants to retire and travel with his wife while they can still get around good."

"Wow. And she never called to tell you?"

He let out a gruff laugh. "Why the fuck would she call me? She made her stance on us known a long time ago when she left me for the fucker she met in college. For all I know, they're still together. I don't ask her parents when I see them. Mom said from what she can gather from Harley's folks, Harley still isn't married. I don't know for sure, though."

"I'm surprised Mom hasn't done more poking around."

"Yeah, unless she knows and isn't saying."

"That's possible. I guess you'll be finding out soon enough."

"I guess," Tripp said. He hit my shoulder. "Enough of my drama, dude. You're getting married."

I smiled. "I'm getting married."

The closer we got to my folks' place, the more my stomach became a jumbled-up mess.

If anyone had told me a year ago I'd be getting married, I would have arrested their ass and let them sit in jail for a night. But now? Now I couldn't wait to make Corina my wife. I couldn't wait to hold her in my arms each night and wake up next to her. The idea that she was carrying my baby made me realize that this was the only thing I wanted. A life with Corina and our baby.

Tripp pulled up and parked behind Steed's truck. He turned off the engine and looked at me. "You ready to do this?"

With a wide grin, I replied, "Never been more ready."

CHAPTER 35

Corina

Standing in front of the mirror, I stared at myself in the wedding dress that once belonged to Mitchell's mom, Melanie.

"Oh my gosh, you look stunning," Waylynn said as she buttoned up the last button.

"Why would she ever get rid of this dress?" I asked.

Amelia sighed. "That's why I kept it. It was too beautiful to give away."

My eyes met Waylynn's. "Are you sure you don't want to save this and wear it?"

A sadness swept over her face, but she quickly replaced it with a grin. "If I ever get married again I want a sexy-as-hell dress that will make my future husband want to…you know what…in his pants."

We peeked at Chloe. She was attempting to put a bow in Gage's peach fuzz. Poor little thing. She wanted a baby sister desperately.

I focused back on my reflection in the mirror.

This was happening. I was getting married. And, boy, did I look the part. Amelia had put my hair up and pulled pieces down to frame my face. She had nearly burned my cheek trying to curl my hair.

The dress was stunning—silver lace over an ivory tulle. The A-line flowed down to a tight bodice and finally to the tulle skirt. It was light as air as it flowed with each movement I made. The sweetheart neckline was covered in lace and crystal beadwork—and made my breasts look amazing, if I did say so myself. The lace straps gave the whole gown an organic feel.

Why would Melanie want to give this dress away?

"I can't believe how well this dress fits you," Waylynn said as she placed a pair of white ballet shoes in front of me.

"It fits me like a glove," I said softly.

"Thank God! And so do my shoes. I think these will be perfect!"

I lifted the dress up and slipped on the shoes. Paxton walked up to me and studied me intently before pushing sprigs of baby's breath into my hair.

"There, that is the exact touch we needed. Chloe, what do you think?" Paxton asked her daughter.

Lifting her gaze, Chloe stood. She sucked in a breath and covered her mouth.

"Well?" I asked as I spun around in the dress.

Dropping her hand, Chloe said, "Oh no, your dress isn't white!"

I glanced down and laughed. "It's like an off-white."

"They should call it a dirty white," Chloe added.

"Chloe Parker!" Paxton said, her hands on her hips.

Her little face fell, and she stared at the ground. "I still think you look like a princess."

I chuckled and Paxton shook her head. "I'm sorry, Corina. It's a stunning gown. She doesn't understand."

Waving it off, I walked to Chloe and bent down. The dress puffed out around me, and Chloe's eyes lit up.

She ran her finger over the straps. "It's so pretty!"

"It is pretty, and it's supposed to be this color. You don't always have to wear white. Some brides wear pink!"

Chloe gasped. "Pink! I'm wearing pink when I get married."

"Mom's coming!" Amelia cried out. "Paxton, get Corina in the bedroom!"

I took Chloe's hand and we quickly went into the bedroom. She was giggling like this was the funniest thing ever, hiding us from Melanie.

"Gage!" Paxton said.

"I've got him," Waylynn said, scooping Gage out of his carrier.

Paxton kept the door open a bit so that we could hear them talking.

When the door opened, I put my finger to my lips to tell Chloe to be quiet.

"Girls, did you know Lincoln and Patches are tied up outside and they have ribbons and little Smurfs around their necks? Not to mention, Patches is eating the basket of flower petals."

Amelia cleared her throat, and I could guess she was pointing to the bedroom to alert her mom Chloe was in there.

Chloe whispered, "Oh no!"

"That's okay, Chloe cat, I have more!" Paxton said with a wink.

"Chloe's got the goats all ready for the wedding, and I didn't bother to question Cord as to why he was tying on Smurfs," Waylynn said.

Melanie sighed. "Oh, good. Good. I see they're still in the ceremony then."

Amelia let out a chuckle. "Yes, indeed."

"Is Corina in the bedroom with Paxton and Chloe?"

"Mom, why don't you sit down here?"

"Nonsense, I don't need to sit down. Waylynn, let me hold Gage."

"Um, no, you can't."

I covered my mouth to keep from laughing. I could only imagine Melanie's face when Waylynn told her no.

"What do you mean I can't? I want to hold my grandson."

"Well, I'm holding him right now, and I just got him. Stop being a baby hog, Mom!"

"I am not a baby hog! He's my grandson, Waylynn."

"Well, he's my nephew, so take that!"

"Listen, Mom, we sort of have a surprise for you, and you can't be holding Gage when you see it. You might drop him."

"Drop him? Amelia, I will have you know I raised seven of you kids and never did I *drop* one of you!"

"Never? Are you *sure?* Because sometimes I have to question Cord's mental state," Waylynn said.

"Yes, I am sure! Then again, maybe I dropped you two. What is going on?"

Amelia called out, "Come out now, y'all!"

Chloe threw open the door and rushed out. "Grammy! We have your dirty dress!"

I closed my eyes and tried not to laugh.

Paxton groaned, "Lord, that girl…and Steed wants another!"

"My dress is dirty?" Melanie asked. I followed Paxton out of the room. Melanie had her back to me, thanks to Chloe running in front of her and keeping her put while she tried to figure out where her dress was dirty.

"Mom?" Paxton said softly. Melanie turned around and went to talk, but saw me standing there in her wedding gown. Tears filled her eyes while her gaze traveled up and down the dress.

"How? Where did you…? Oh my! You look so…beautiful!"

"Mom, don't cry. You'll make Corina cry and then I'll have to do her make-up again!" Amelia said, hugging her mother tightly.

Melanie's hands came up to her mouth, and she stared at me.

Waylnn stood next to her mother. "Amelia kept your dress and was going to make something out of it."

"But when Mitchell and Corina decided to get married at the last second, I knew she had to wear your wedding dress."

Tears streamed down Melanie's face, and she turned to sit on the sofa. Paxton sat down next to her.

"Please don't cry, Melanie," I said, barely above a whisper.

She wiped her tears away and looked at me. "You look beautiful. The dress looks like it was meant for you!"

I tried to laugh, but a sob came out instead.

"Dab! Don't wipe!" Amelia cried out.

I dapped at the corners of my eyes. "You don't mind me wearing it?"

Melanie walked over to me, taking my hands in hers. "Mind? I'm honored. And when Mitchell sees you in this dress, I hope he does what his father did!"

"What did Daddy do?" Waylynn asked, handing Gage back to Paxton.

Amelia handed everyone a tissue.

"Oh, your father has always been so sweet and romantic. The moment he saw me walking down the aisle, he started to cry. I don't know how I held it together when I saw those tears rolling down his cheeks. My father had to hold me up because he thought I was going to fall right there on the spot when I first saw John."

We all sighed.

I took Melanie's hands in mine. "I pray that Mitchell and I will be as blessed with our marriage as you and John have been. You're both such amazing examples of true love and I...I..."

Melanie tilted her head as she reached up and dabbed away my tears. "I don't remember what I was going to say!" I blurted out.

Drawing me into her arms, Melanie held me. "It's the baby. Just blame the baby!"

I laughed and held her tighter. The knock on the door made us both take a step back. Steed walked in and stopped when he saw me.

"Mitchell is going to faint."

John walked in behind Mitchell, and he paused the second he saw me. His eyes darted over to Melanie and back to me.

"Mel, your wedding dress."

"Wait, this is your wedding dress, Mom?" Steed asked.

"Yes! Amelia kept it and look how it fits Corina like it was made for her."

John stood in front of me and took my hands in his. Lifting my right hand, he kissed the back of it. "Once upon a time, a beautiful young girl wore this dress. I was mesmerized by her when she walked down that aisle. It felt like a dream and I prayed she didn't take one look at me and run, thinking she'd made a mistake."

"Never," Melanie whispered, and my chest felt light.

John took another look at me in the dress and then caught my gaze. "I dare say, you are just as beautiful as my beloved bride, and my poor son has no idea what is about to happen to him."

I let out another stupid giggle-sob.

"It's time we find out," Steed announced. "Chloe, you get Patches and Lincoln ready?"

"Yes! Mommy, the petals!"

Paxton walked over to the table and grabbed a bag. "Got them!"

Amelia clapped her hands. "Okay, people, this is it! It's show time! Mom, pull yourself together!"

"I am together, I'll have you know," Melanie said as she shot Amelia a dirty look. John and I both laughed.

"Waylynn, flowers! We need the flowers stat!" Amelia called out.

Waylynn shot Amelia a look as she started gathering the bouquets. "Jesus, when did the wedding planner from hell show up?"

Amelia pushed Waylynn lightly, "Shut up, we need the flowers! Paxton! Here is your bouquet."

Paxton moved a sleeping Gage as she took the flowers. Then Waylynn handed me mine. They were stunning. A little bit larger than the ones the girls were carrying. Pink and white roses.

Everyone started to head out of the cabin, but John and I stayed back.

"I have something to give you," he said.

My heart dropped when he handed me a small Bible. "It was my mother's. You're wearing her engagement ring."

I gasped. "Oh, John."

"Melanie carried it at our wedding, and I know it blessed our marriage, just like it will yours and Mitchell's." Tears filled my eyes again. "Don't cry. The girls will be mad if I make those beautiful blue eyes bloodshot."

I kissed him on the side of the cheek. "Thank you for the Bible. And thank you for walking me down the aisle."

Now it was his turn to have watery eyes. "It is my honor, Corina."

Paxton peeked back in. "I'm about to walk! Get ready!"

Taking in a deep breath, I nodded. We would step outside onto the cabin porch and make our way down the steps. Once we rounded the corner, I would have a clear shot of the lookout and Mitchell.

Each step seemed to go in slow motion as John and I made our way out of the cabin. My heart hammered in my chest.

"Slow down there, darlin'. He's not going anywhere."

I chuckled and squeezed his arm. "I didn't realize I was walking fast."

"Speed walking is more like it!"

Another laugh and we turned the corner. The only person I saw was Mitchell and what he did next knocked the wind right out of me.

He dropped down, covered his mouth, and started to cry.

I sucked in a breath and kept my eyes on him as John guided me to the love of my life. Mitchell stood back up and gave me a beautiful, brilliant smile as I made my way closer to him.

John lifted my hand toward Mitchell's. "She's a treasure, son. Honor her always."

Wiping his tears away, Mitchell replied, "Yes, sir. I will."

As I stepped next to Mitchell, we turned to face each other. He hadn't let go of my hand, and I didn't want him to. I was completely lost to him. His touch was the only thing keeping me grounded. Keeping my knees from going out from under me.

The pastor started talking, but I didn't hear a word he said. In that moment, it was only Mitchell and me. And our baby. I didn't even flinch when Patches briefly got away from Chloe and took off running before Wade whistled and got the goat back. Nothing else in the world mattered except for Mitchell. The man I had given my heart to over a year ago. Since the first moment he kissed me, I had known this man would forever be the one to hold my heart in his hands. He had showed me a life I'd never dreamed imaginable.

Before I knew it, we were exchanging rings. I was getting ready for the kiss when Pastor Burch threw me a surprise.

"Corina, Mitchell would like to say something before I pronounce you husband and wife."

I looked at the pastor and then back to Mitchell. "O-okay," I whispered shakily.

Mitchell held onto my hands, rubbing his thumbs over my skin. "The first moment I knew I loved you, it scared me to death, and I ran from you. I wasn't ready. Then when my heart finally let that love in, I felt like a new man and I ran to you, but you weren't ready to forgive me."

My chin trembled as I listened to him talk.

"Then it happened. Our love was too strong for us not to come together. Each day I woke up with you in my life, and I told myself I couldn't possibly be so happy. So in love. And each night when I laid down next to you, I knew I had been wrong because there was always something else that made me love you more. Because I fall more in love with you and grow happier with each second of the day, Corina."

He squeezed my hands and rubbed his thumbs across them, sending my stomach into a fluttering frenzy.

"I can't believe the way I feel about you, Corina. You're my life. My future. My everything. Thank you for loving me and for making me the man I am today."

Tears fell from my eyes, and I didn't even care. I'd never in my life felt so loved and so complete as I did in this moment.

"I love…you…so much!"

Mitchell cupped my face within his hands and turned to Pastor Burch. "Can I kiss her now?"

Everyone laughed.

"We have one thing left to do. I now pronounce you husband and wife. You may kiss your bride."

Mitchell's lips pressed against mine. He dropped his hands from my face and wrapped them around my body, pulling me to him while I did the same. He lifted me up and kissed me deeper as our family cheered.

When he slowly set me down, he pulled back slightly and looked into my eyes. In a voice barely above a whisper, he asked, "So, Mrs. Parker. What position are you thinking we start our marriage off with? The seated wheelbarrow?"

Laughing, I dug my teeth into my lip and felt my lower stomach pull with desire.

"Why, Mr. Parker, what makes you think we'll only be trying one? It's our wedding day and I'm feeling rather adventurous."

His full-blown dimpled smile nearly brought me to my knees.

Chloe let out a scream as Lincoln and Patches ran right by us, causing Mitchell and me to jump out of the way.

"Oh my God! He's going for the food!" Waylynn screamed as everyone started running after the goats.

Mitchell wrapped his arms around me and dipped me back. With a light brush of his lips against mine, he looked into my eyes. "Let the adventure begin."

THE END

...for now.

Enjoy a Sneak Peek from

Love Again

Waylynn

I stepped into my office and tossed the paint samples onto my desk. Lauren was going to be the damn death of me. Who in the hell knew there were so many shades of green?

I moaned and dropped my head back. At least in here I could lose my shit if I needed to. The windows in my office were now covered up with brown paper, giving me a sense of privacy. Once the studio was finished and we were open, I'd have a view of the main dance floor from my office. I would also have shades to pull down.

Turing, I faced the window that looked out back to the small courtyard. I smiled, thinking about how fun it would be to take the little ones outside and practice our stretches.

"Waylynn?"

His voice sent tingles through my entire body. Taking in a deep breath, I turned around and faced Jonathon.

"Hey," I simply said, leaning against the windowsill.

He stepped inside my office. "I need to talk to you."

I was never one to be nervous or scared around men, but being in the same room with Jonathon Turner scared the living daylights out of me and I wasn't used to that. It also pissed me off, knowing how much this man held a power over me.

"About?" I asked.

He shut the door and stood there, his cowboy hat in his hand. I tried not to let my eyes scan his perfect body. He was toned beyond belief. Those three miles a day of running kept the man in shape. Not to mention the nightly trips to the gym I knew he took.

"I can't stop thinking about you."

My breath stalled in my throat.

"I've already told you, Jon, this can't work."

He took a few steps closer to me and I stayed as still as I could. My fingers itched to touch him.

"Then why did you seem pissed off that I brought a date to Steed and Mitchell's birthday party?"

"I wasn't upset," I lied.

Jonathon took two long strides and stood in my space. His large, fit body inches from mine. I had to force myself to breathe.

"Can you honestly look me in the eyes and tell me you don't feel anything for me?"

Lifting my chin, I kept my face neutral. "I'm too old for you."

He laughed. "Fuck that, Waylynn. You're scared and you're using it as an excuse. Look at me and tell me you didn't feel anything when we were together."

My chest rose and fell with each labored breath. Goosebumps broke out across my body as I thought about that afternoon a few months back. My eyes closed as I remembered Jonathon moving deliciously fast and hard as he fucked me on the desk and then against the wall in my dance studio. It was raw. Passionate. Spontaneous, and hot as hell. And, yes…I had felt something. I felt something every time the man was near me. A feeling I'd never experienced with any other man, but I couldn't admit that to him.

I smiled. "I felt two amazing orgasms."

He leaned in closer, the smell of his cologne tangling with my libido.

Shit. I needed him to step back before I lost control and begged him to take me right then and there.

He reached up and twirled a piece of my hair between his fingers. "I know that wasn't all you felt. I see it in your eyes."

I turned my head. "I'm six years older than you, Jon. I want things you can't possibly give me."

He huffed. "How do you know I don't want the same things?"

With a harsh laugh, I looked back into his eyes. "I want to get married, and I want kids. At least three. Can you honestly look me in the eyes and say you want that, too?"

"Yes!" he said, cupping my face in his strong hands. "Waylynn, I'm not twenty fucking years old, I'm almost twenty-seven and I want those things too. I'm not saying let's run off and get married tomorrow, but why won't you even give us a chance? I don't care that you're older than me."

My heart was racing. "You want kids? What, like when you're thirty-five, or something?"

He closed his eyes and slowly shook his head before opening them and pinning me with his intense stare. "You can't push me away with that, because I can honestly tell you if it were up to me, I'd already be settled with a wife and kids. But no one has made me want to even think it's a possibility...until you."

My body trembled. "It...it could never work."

"Why? And stop saying because you're older than me."

"It just wouldn't."

He pressed his body into mine, causing a rush of lust to race through my veins. His lips were inches from mine. The wall I had built was beginning to crumble piece by piece. I needed to be stronger.

When his lips brushed across mine, I gasped.

His hand moved up my dress, slowly pulling it up as he pushed his hard-on into me. I gripped onto his strong arms to keep my legs from going out under me.

Damn it. What is this man doing to me?

"Please don't push me away. Waylynn, I want you in more ways than just fucking you against a wall. Please give me a chance to show you that we can make this work."

Electricity ripped through my body. I was about to break—give in to what I knew my heart truly wanted.

Maybe we could be together one more time and that would satisfy the itch I had for Jonathon Turner. His fingers brushed across my panties and I squeezed his arms.

One. More. Time.

No. This feeling was more than an itch. It was an aching desire to have more from this man. So. Much. More.

My mouth opened to tell him to take me, when the perfect moment came to an immediate halt with a knock on my office door.

I pushed Jonathon away and dragged in a deep breath as I fixed my dress.

Jonathon walked around to the other side of my desk, his hat positioned in front of his jeans to hide the bulge in his pants.

"Come...come in."

Shit. My voice was shaky.

The door open and Cord walked into my office. He smiled when he saw me, which made my heart drop. I was still leaning against the windowsill, trying like hell to act like I wasn't turned on or that my panties weren't soaking wet.

"What's up, big sis? I saw your car parked out front and thought maybe you'd like to go to lunch?"

My eyes darted over to Jonathon.

Cord turned to see Jonathon. "Hey! I was hoping I'd see you here. Was I interrupting anything?"

"No," I said.

"Yes," Jonathon said.

Cord bounced his gaze between the two of us.

Jonathon grinned. "I mean, no, it's fine. I needed to find out if Waylynn had picked out which flooring she wanted."

My head was spinning. I thought I had already told him.

"Birch is fine," I softly said. Jonathon nodded.

"Listen, I know this is last minute, but a few of us are heading to Vegas tonight for the weekend. I'm taking a few days off from the bar. We're each renting our own room just in case there hook-up potential in the making." Cord wiggled his brows while I looked away and I rolled my eyes.

Jonathon looked at me. "I can't, I've got to handle installing the light fixtures in the ballet room."

Our eyes met, and I knew what he was doing.

"You can't take the weekend off, dude? I mean, it's Vegas. Flights are wide open so getting a ticket won't be a problem."

Jonathon continued to stare at me. I regretted my next set of words before they even came out of my mouth.

"It's fine, the lights can wait and Cord's right. It's the weekend."

Jonathon narrowed his eyes at me.

Cord clapped his hands. "Awesome. Then you're free to go. What do you say?"

The look in Jonathon's eyes about killed me. He looked so hurt and it gutted me that I was the person who'd made him feel that way.

Placing his hat back on his head, Jonathon faced Cord. He plastered on a fake smile and nodded. "Yeah, sounds like a plan. I could use a little bit of fun, it's been awhile since I've had any. Count me in."

My heart dropped to my stomach and I had to grip the windowsill to keep myself upright. It took everything out of me not to show any physical reaction to Jonathon's words. They hurt me more than he could ever know.

Making his way toward the door, Jonathon cleared his throat. "I've got to run if I'm heading out with y'all."

Cord gave him a light slap on the back as he walked by. "You won't regret it." He leaned in more and said, "I promise."

Before leaving my office, Jonathon looked back at me, tipped his hat and said, "Waylynn." It was meant to sound like a goodbye, but I knew what he was doing. He was giving me one more chance to stop him.

My heart was fighting with my head. I swallowed hard, trying to convince myself I was about to do the right thing by letting him go. "Enjoy Vegas, Jonathon," I replied, trying to keep my voice even.

I thought I was pulling it off until his next set of words fell like a knife straight into my chest.

"I will." Jonathon looked at Cord and said, "Maybe I'll even get lucky this weekend. Hell, maybe I'll even find myself a girlfriend, someone to marry and have three kids with."

Cord laughed and said, "Jesus dude, we're going to Vegas, not church. Hey, let me walk you out, I'll fill you in a bit more on the plans."

Glancing over his shoulder at me, Cord called out, "Be right back, Waylynn."

Look for LOVE AGAIN coming April 2018

Contains Spoilers

Vince Gill – "Trying To Get Over You"
Beginning of Tempting Love

Vince Gill- "I Can't Do This"
Mitchell and Corina in Cord's Office

Carly Pearce – "I Dare Ya"
Corina and Mitchell at the land he bought

George Straight – "Carried Away"
Mitchell cooking dinner for Corina

Brett Young – "In Case You Didn't Know"
Mitchell telling Corina he was crazy about her before the street dance

The Chainsmokers and Coldplay – "Something Just Like This"
Mitchell and Corina in Canada

Lifehouse – "You and Me"
Mitchell asking Corina to marry him

Miranda Lambert – "Pushin' Time"
Mitchell telling Corina he wants to start a family

Love and Theft – "Love Wins"
The entire Parker family getting ready for the wedding

"Taylor Swift – "This Love"
The whole book! This songs reminds me of Mitchell and Corina's love story!

Brad Paisley – "Then"
Mitchell and Corina's wedding

THANK YOU

As always, thank you to Darrin and Lauren. I couldn't do this without y'all! Thank you for all of your patience with me with each book I write. I know I keep saying I'll be ahead soon and I promise I will be!

Lauren – I can't believe you are a senior this year. When I was writing *Wanted* you were having a birthday party and I think it was sixth grade! Time is going by way too fast. I love you to the moon and back!

Darrin – Don't stop giving me endless things to write about…I seriously need to just tie a recorder around your neck. Seriously though, thank you for supporting me with this crazy dream called writing. It takes a lot of my time away from you, but we somehow manage to make it all work! I love you more!

Danielle Sanchez – Thank you for everything you do for me! I couldn't do this without you!

Kristin Mayer – Where to start? First off…I CANNOT believe you've never seen *Will & Grace* or *Seinfeld*…or *FRIENDS*! How are we BFF's? We need a marathon weekend for each one. Okay I got off the point of this thank you…thank you for always being there when I need someone to help me through a scene…or a synopsis, or a word that makes me sound smarticles (yes I know that isn't a word…I like it) or just brainstorming in general. Thank you for being an amazing friend in general. You make me laugh. You support me in everything and are there when I just need to talk. I love you, Special K. I'm so glad to have you in my life, even if you don't know what "JUST JACK" means. **rolls eyes**.

To Kelly's Krew – Y'all…where do I EVEN begin. This is the best reading group on the planet! Yes…the planet! Thank you so much for being such amazing people. Your love and support for each other is something I love to see each time I'm in the group. I'm blessed to have each and every single one of you in my life. Even you lurkers…oh yeah…I know you're there!!! Love y'all to the moon and back!

Wranglers – Without y'all release day wouldn't be the same. THANK YOU for everything you do for me. Each of you go above and beyond and I am in awe of your support. You'll never truly know how much I appreciate each of you. Love y'all to the moon and back!

The readers. The best for last right? Totally! If it wasn't for you, I wouldn't be typing up these thank yous! So thank you so very much for your support. Each story I sit down to write is a part of me. In every single book there is something…whether it be big or small…that is a part of my life. Every story comes from a place in me that longs to keep filling pages with the movies I see in my head. For you to invest in that is something I don't think I will ever get used to. It means a great deal to me so thank you doesn't even really seem like enough. I hope that you are enjoying the Cowboys and Angels series. I am totally and utterly in love with the Parker family and the deeper I get into this family the harder it will be to walk away. But we still have a few books left!!!

So with that said…happy reading y'all.

Love you to the moon and back!